"The aliens have shifted.
You're looking at old data!"

Merrick glanced at his in-head, and saw the icons marking the three alien vessels still some five light-minutes astern of the *Ad Astra.* But when he checked forward, he saw three identical icons now right alongside the O'Neill cylinders and just five hundred kilometers from the human fighters.

There was only one possible explanation. The aliens had jumped to faster-than-light, leapfrogging past the blocking fighters and dropping back into normal space directly alongside the human colony ship. The light from the three aliens astern was from five minutes ago; those three targets were luminal ghosts, images showing them *before* they'd shifted.

And that meant that the aliens could pack a star drive into a slender hull a scant forty meters long, something well beyond the current capabilities of human technology.

"Right, people!" Colbert called. "Close on the Asty!" A white flare of light pulsed from dead ahead, briefly outshining the surrounding clouds of bright stars. Merrick felt a stab of apprehension. Something big had just slammed the mother ship.

"Fighters, you are weapons free, repeat, weapons free! *Ad Astra* is under attack!"

"Kick it, people!" Colbert ordered. "Full boost! Let's get in there!"

Also by Ian Douglas

Star Carrier

Star Corpsman

The Galactic Marines Saga

The Heritage Trilogy

The Legacy Trilogy

The Inheritance Trilogy

ALTERED
STARSCAPE

ANDROMEDAN DARK: BOOK ONE

IAN DOUGLAS

HARPER Voyager
An Imprint of HarperCollins Publishers

ALTERED STARSCAPE. Copyright © 2016 by William H. Keith, Jr. All rights reserved. Printed in the United States of America. No part of this book may be used or reproduced in any manner whatsoever without written permission except in the case of brief quotations embodied in critical articles and reviews. For information, address HarperCollins Publishers, 195 Broadway, New York, NY 10007.

First Harper Voyager mass market printing: November 2016

ISBN 978-0-06237919-1

Cover art by Gregory Bridges.

Harper Voyager and ⟩ are trademarks of HCP LLC.

 17 18 19 20   QGM   10 9 8 7 6 5 4 3 2

For Brea
My Light

ALTERED
STARSCAPE

The night before the *Tellus Ad Astra* left Earth Clarkeorbital, her commander, Lord Commander Grayson St. Clair, had gotten into a shouting match with CybDirector Veber. The exchange hadn't exactly been career-enhancing . . . but, then again, St. Clair didn't feel like he had all that much to lose. The *Ad Astra* command was more punishment than plum. The United Earth Directorate was trying to get him out of the way, after all.

"My Lord," Veber said, almost sneering. "You are missing the import of this expedition. Through this diplomatic exchange, Earth and Humankind will be accepted as full equals within Galactic circles!"

"Bullshit."

"Lord Commander!"

"Bullshit!" St. Clair repeated, more forcefully this time. "We will be, at best, very, *very* junior partners. They want our help in a war, and they don't want to get their hands dirty. Nothing more."

They were at a party—a diplomatic reception, actually, taking place in the spin-gravity section of the Clarkeorbital UE Naval Base. Some hundreds of political and diplomatic dignitaries were present, along with a handful of Medusae delegates representing the Galactic Coadunation.

"Accept reality, Lord Commander," Veber said. "Things have changed. First Contact with the Coadunation has utterly and fundamentally transformed the course of Human-kind's existence!"

"Yes, it has, my lord. And we haven't had a damned thing to say about that change, have we? I think I liked it better when we still had the paradox."

The enigmatic veil of the Fermi Paradox had been pierced at last, late in 2088, when the new lunar radio tele-scope array first detected radio frequency leakage from a highly advanced machine intelligence located at HD 95086, some ninety light years from Earth. Direct contact had come in 2124, when the United Earth Survey Ship *Oberth* encoun-tered the Coadunation fleet investigating Sirius, eight and a half light years from Earth. The Galaxy, it turned out, was far larger, far more complicated, and far more populated than humans ever had believed possible.

The Great Silence of the Fermi Paradox was now, at last, understood: the Orion Spur was a backwater wilderness, little explored, seldom visited, and ignored or overlooked by the repeated waves of interstellar colonization sweeping out from the Hub. Too, the Galaxy's communication nets used technologies far more efficient than radio. Masers beamed data across interstellar distances point to point, making eavesdropping impossible unless you happened to be pre-cisely on the line of sight between two inhabited systems. Hell, until the Coadunation had shown humans the trick, Earth's technologies had not been able to detect tightly fo-cused neutrino channels at all, and those carried the bulk of data transmissions for the galactic civilizations.

"Damn it, man," Veber said. "Are you *afraid* of the Coa-dunation?"

"Any sane man would be," St. Clair replied. "Humans fear what they don't understand . . . and we don't understand them at all."

"Primitivistic thinking!"

"Sure. And compared to *them* we're primitives. You

know . . . I'm still convinced that all of our airs—our lauded Imperium, the anachronistic titles and rank and 'my lord' nonsense—it's all just smoke and mirrors."

"What do you mean?"

"Humankind was doing okay on its own up until 2088. Then we learned we weren't alone. Worse, it hit home for us that anyone Out There was going to be more advanced than we were—a *lot* more advanced. After all, we just became a technic species a few centuries ago. They've been out there building interstellar empires for millennia."

Veber shrugged. "So what? We're a part of all that *now.* Look at what the Coadunation has already taught us, in just twenty-three years of direct contact!"

"With respect, my lord, I have a feeling that we're not going to like it when the bill comes due."

"I don't think I like your attitude, Lord Commander."

St. Clair shrugged. "You don't have to, my lord. Tomorrow, *Tellus Ad Astra* leaves for the Galactic Hub. And I'll be out of your way. . . ."

The Galactic Coadunation.

The word *coadunation* referred to a biological concept: the merging of separate entities into a larger, united organism—a fair description of galactic civilization, as it turned out. A decade had passed before human and Medusan AIs learned to talk with one another, and even longer before humans began to understand something of the political complexities surrounding them in their isolated little pocket of space.

According to the Medusae, some ten thousand distinct sentient and highly technic species scattered across the Galaxy made up the Coadunation in varying degrees of co-operation, affiliation, and mutual support. And, it seemed, they were actively searching for potential new members. That was the good news.

The *bad* news was war.

ONE

The United Earth explorer *Tellus Ad Astra* fell coreward, her military contingent at full alert. "Fifteen minutes to shift, Lord Commander." The ship's voice, cultured and precise as was only possible for an artificial intelligence, spoke within his head—electronic telepathy.

Its name was Newton.

Weightless, Lord Commander Grayson St. Clair pulled himself into the vast cavern of the *Ad Astra*'s bridge and moved into the horseshoe of his workstation. Around him, twenty other UE officers monitored consoles, holographic displays floating before intent faces. He seated himself and, with a thought, let his command chair lock to his uniform, gently tugging him into place. Light swam around him, star upon star upon uncounted star out of swarming billions within the Galactic core, projected into the volume of space surrounding the bridge. Ahead, the core nebulae loomed like the crenellated walls of a medieval castle sculpted from thunderclouds, all blue-black and green and glowering. Stars dusted the panorama like the gleaming droplets of a cascading waterfall, aglow with spectacular radiance.

How many of those suns, St. Clair wondered—not for the first time—shone on worlds filled with Life and Mind, with the brilliance of galactic civilization?

"Very well, Third Navigator," he replied, opening his cyberimplants to the bridge electronics. "Are we still on-station with our nanny?"

"The Coadunation monitor is fifty-seven kilometers off our prow, sir. We're closing at three kilometers per second."

St. Clair checked the data for himself. Third Navigator had never been wrong with its reports before, but it *was* an AI robot, after all, and the very best AI was only as good as its programming.

The data were correct.

"So," Executive Commander Vanessa Symm said, "just two more shifts, my lord. And the last one will just be a correctional nudge. Think they're ready for us in there?"

"Damned if I know, Van," he told her. "I think the question is whether *we're* ready for *them*. But I guess we'll find out soon enough."

"Ship is fully configured for shift, sir," Carlos Martinez, the ship's systems engineer, reported.

"Very well. Rad screens set to full, please."

"Radiation screens are at full, my lord."

By all reports, the central reaches of the galactic core behind the cloudwall were a seething cauldron of energetic particles, a deadly environment for any unprotected ship or organism.

And yet there were people—beings, rather—living in there, countless billions of them.

At least, that was what the Medusae claimed. Harmony, they called it. A capital, of sorts, for the sprawl of galactic civilization.

I guess we're about to see, he thought.

The minutes trickled away as *Ad Astra* and the nameless alien ship ahead prepared for the transit into corespace. Those walls ahead, St. Clair knew, were molecular hydrogen clouds seasoned with a witch's brew of organics, carbon monoxide, ammonia, and other compounds—all part of the Five Kiloparsec Ring, which encircled the center of the Galaxy some 15,000 light years out. The stars illuminating the clouds were hot, young, and brilliant; an observer out at the Andromedan Galaxy would see those stars and gas clouds as the Milky Way's brightest, most prominent features.

Like thickly gathered curtains, the clouds masked what lay inside.

"Initiate charging."

"Charging, my lord."

Within *Ad Astra*'s engineering shell, quantum power taps pulled unimaginable torrents of energy from hard vacuum.

Two more minutes . . .

At St. Clair's mental command, an image of the *Tellus Ad Astra* appeared against the star-thick backdrop before him. She was enormous—thirty-four kilometers long—and yet she looked like a toy all but lost within that immensity of stars and towering nebular clouds.

Tellus Ad Astra was a mobile O'Neill colony, a structure originally designed as an orbital habitat for one of Earth's Lagrange points, but retasked five years earlier as a starship. *Tellus*, with her twin side-by-side megahabitats, each thirty-two kilometers long and six and a half wide, counter-rotated twenty-eight times an hour, providing her living areas with spin gravity equivalent to one G. The two cylinders were joined aft by the *Ad Astra*, the massive, T-shaped support framework of the ship, which was her command-control-engineering section, or CCE, including the clustered drive and command structures that served as the operational heart of the ship. It also housed the aft engineering shell, which held the Coadunation technology permitting jumps across tens of thousands of light years.

The *Ad Astra*'s bridge was located in the penthouse of a skyscraper-sized, angled tower rising from a platform connecting the aft ends of the two parallel cylinders, which were positioned almost eight kilometers apart. Below were the multiple flight decks for the vessel's fighter squadrons, escorts, and service vessels. The *Ad Astra* was both naval base and fleet HQ, as well as being a mobile space colony with a current population of just over 1 million people. And for now, thought St. Clair, she was *Tellus*'s guardian and babysitter.

Ahead of the *Ad Astra*, the nameless Coad ship hung like a beacon against the frozen storm clouds of dust and stars, a squat, flattened sphere nine kilometers across, enigmatic, uncommunicative . . . and utterly and bewilderingly alien.

What the hell do we know about them?

St. Clair's thought was bitter. He still didn't agree with the World Government's recent decisions regarding the Coadunation.

But, then, his agreement was not necessary. Since the collapse of democracy as a political ideal a century before, all that was required, all that *ever* was required, was obedience.

"The Coads are signaling," the bridge communication officer announced. "They are—"

The Coad ship vanished from the display.

"Lord Commander," *Ad Astra*'s tactical officer, Senior Lieutenant Vance Cameron, called over the Net. "The Medusae vessel has shifted."

"So I see, Lieutenant." St. Clair took a deep breath. This was it. "Initiate shift."

The towering thunderheads frozen against the starscape forward vanished, wiped away in an eye's blink, and the *Tellus Ad Astra* emerged . . . elsewhere.

Ad Astra was adrift within what seemed to be a hollow shell, surrounded by millions of stars—thousands of them brighter than Venus as seen from Earth. Most had a reddish hue, though there were plenty of hotter, brighter, younger suns squeezed from the core nebulae by gravitational interactions. Streamers, clouds, and arcs of gas stretched across the sky against a pale red haze of stardust.

"Sagittarius A-Star is directly ahead, my lord," Subcomm Carla Adams, the first navigator, reported. "Range is approximately five light years."

"Bang on target, then," St. Clair said. "Nice work, people."

The object—designated by astronomers as Sagittarius A*, with the asterisk pronounced as "Star"—was unremarkable compared to the sweep and drama of the surrounding view. The object itself was invisible even from this close in, but it was surrounded by a handful of bright stars orbiting it at extremely high velocity.

That object was the supermassive black hole—the SMBH in astronomical parlance—that occupied the center of Earth's Galaxy. An invisible sphere nearly as wide as the orbit of the planet Mercury containing mass equivalent to some 4.3 million suns, it was a sight—or not—to behold.

A second object lay off to port, about three hundred light years from the first. Designated as 1E1740.7–2942 but popularly called the "Great Annihilator," it was the intermittent source of highly energetic X-rays at the 511 keV range characteristic of the annihilation of electrons and positrons—matter and antimatter. Although the jury was still out as to what exactly the Great Annihilator was, most astrophysicists suspected a stellar-mass black hole passing through a wisp of molecular cloud as it orbited Sag A*.

Much closer to the center—only about three light years from Sagittarius A*—lay another black hole: GCIRS 13E, massing 1300 suns and marked by a clustering of seven bright stars. Current thought held that it might be the center of a globular star cluster partially devoured and scattered by the monster at the Galaxy's heart.

None of that mattered to St. Clair at the moment. He stared up into the core's brilliant light, awed. Though he'd been briefed on what was known of the astronomy of the Galaxy's central regions, the reality was . . . overwhelming.

And very, very complex.

"Let's have a close-up," he said.

A window opened in the air in front of him, as powerful gravitational fields projected into the space ahead of the ship generated a temporary lens. The image was still blurred and low res; it looked like a pale haze backdrop behind a minute, black ring. The haze, he knew, was gas and dust above the black hole's accretion disk; the ring was the Coadunation capital . . . the core habitat.

So that's Harmony.

But at this range, even gravitational lensing couldn't show any detail.

"Commander St. Clair," another machine voice whispered in his mind. "The Coadunation liaison requests permission to enter the bridge to speak with you."

"Can it wait?"

"The liaison says it cannot."

St. Clair sighed. "Very well. Five minutes, no more."

"What does the Squid want, anyway?" Symm wondered. She'd been included in the cyberlinked message as well.

"I don't know, Van. Maybe a last reminder to mind our manners when we actually meet the masters of the Galactic Empire. Like not calling them squids," he said with a smile.

"I'll do that when you remember it's the Coadunation," she reminded him. "Stop thinking like a human."

"But I'm so *good* at it. . . ."

"More likely," Symm said, "it's about their damned war."

"I know." He sighed. "I know."

All was not well in paradise.

And that wasn't necessarily a surprise. Because twenty-three years earlier, a Medusan fleet had been searching the little-explored Orion Spur for emergent technological species that might be able to join them. And at Sirius they'd encountered humans, newly emerged from their home star system and just about as savvy, when it came to galactic politics, as a backwoods hayseed adrift in Manhattan Tower.

No, worse: snatch a Neanderthal hunter from his tribe and drop him among the slidewalks of New York Meg . . . *That* at least approximated the culture shock experienced by

Humankind when it came into direct contact with a galactic civilization some hundreds of thousands of years in advance of it.

Humanity, St. Clair thought with a grim dash of gallows humor, was going to be a long time in recovering from the shock.

THE PROPOSED alliance looked good, at least on the surface. The Coadunation offered Earth so much, so *very* much, a heaven-sent opportunity for Humankind with a seemingly endless list of benefits and technology in exchange for membership. Assuming, of course, that the human species even survived the assimilation. The Earth directorate, St. Clair thought, was not exactly *flexible*. Hit it hard enough and it would shatter.

It wasn't a secret that St. Clair didn't like the idea, but even he was forced to admit that the Coad offer was attractive. The first Terran starships had used the Alcubierre Drive to achieve FTL travel . . . but within the past few years most of her ships had been refitted with Coad gravitic drives and hyperdimensional shift technology, enabling human vessels to bypass ten thousand light years in an instant. Suddenly, human ships could jump *anywhere* within the Galaxy . . . and were no longer limited to within a scant few light-centuries of home. Fusion power plants had been replaced by quantum taps that pulled seemingly unlimited energy from the hard vacuum of space itself.

And there were other technologies that suggested unimaginable possibilities for Humankind's future. Antigravity that would make *Ad Astra*'s spin-gravity design seem quaintly archaic by comparison. Matter compression that would create any element at all from simple building blocks in a process that made helium-3/deuterium fusion look as primitive as flint and steel. New understandings of space, time, and energy. New understandings of mind and consciousness. Medical advances that would redesign the human form virtually from scratch, banish any disease, or correct any genetic shortcoming.

Even immortality might soon be within humanity's grasp.

Changes already incorporated into Earth's technology had transformed the planet in just the past decade. And more, *much* more, was soon to come.

And all we need to do to claim this unimaginable galactic largess was help support the Coadunation in a small, eight-millennium war . . .

"The Medusae liaison," the ship's voice announced in St. Clair's head.

St. Clair rotated his command chair to face the alien's floating e-pod as it drifted onto the bridge. Biological Medusae actually possessed a carbon biochemistry, but they still required an environmental tank when they interacted with humans. The Liaison's heavily insulated pod was red and gray except for its transparent end cap, which was coated with droplets of water condensing over its frigid surface. Living in an environment that hovered around minus 100 degrees Celsius, Medusae breathed hydrogen, drank liquid ethane, and excreted methane. Hell, they would have considered Titan, the large moon of Saturn back in Earth's solar system, a pleasant summer retreat. The face behind the transparency was the stuff of nightmares—squirming black and orange tentacles surrounded by a ring of six eyes so pale and electric blue in color they seemed to glow. What they called themselves was unknown, but somebody had suggested the name Medusa because of the tentacle mass—which was in constant and disturbing motion—and the name stuck.

"Lord Commander," the liaison said formally. "We greet you."

St. Clair heard the voice through his cyberimplants. The Medusae didn't have a true spoken language, as such, but used a blend of luminous color shifts in their skin together with clicks and whistles to communicate. No human could imitate the sounds, much less the visual data, any more than Medusae could mimic human speech. At the moment, Newton was handling the translation on both sides.

"We greet you," St. Clair replied. Even more untranslatable than the language, he thought, were the differences in mutually alien psychologies. Medusae didn't think as individuals. Everything was *we* and *our*, not *I* or *my*. So far as human xenosophontologists had been able to determine, they didn't even possess individual names, but instead used titles and job descriptors, like "Liaison," as personal ID.

"You have the shift coordinates for the final dimensional transition," it told him. St. Clair could see the ripples and pulses of color and texture flashing across the being's tentacles behind its transparency. "The first shift has brought us to within a few light years of our objective. The next will put us close to Harmony itself.

"It is important that you realize that we will be emerging quite close to the capital. Quite close indeed. The moment you emerge, your vessel will be surrounded by robotic warships of the Coadunation, and you may feel that you are under threat. It is important that you not react to this perceived threat with emotion or aggression. You understand?"

"We do," St. Clair replied. He grinned . . . though he doubted that the alien could read the expression, or even perceive it. "This is a *diplomatic* mission. We're not here to flex our military muscles."

The Medusae hesitated—possibly, St. Clair thought, because it was looking up the definitions of alien concepts like *muscle* or *diplomatic* through its on-line link with Newton. *We really are that different.*

"We must impress upon you, Humans, that any offensive action by you will trigger an immediate and autonomous defensive response from the Coadunation capital. You understand? This vessel would not survive."

"If it makes you feel any better," St. Clair replied slowly, "I can have our weapons department stand down."

Another hesitation. Then: "That would be immensely wise, Humans. That wisdom is appreciated . . . and it is most encouraging."

St. Clair nodded, then gave the mental orders for the ship's weapons department to disengage, powering down all but a handful of antimeteor weapons and switching off the targeting scanners. He didn't like it—no, that was an understatement. He *hated* it. But his orders required complete cooperation with his Medusa guides, and for him to impress upon them UE Worldgov's willingness to work with them, whatever that might entail.

So while St. Clair didn't agree with Worldgov's alien policy, he was willing to make this particular gesture. After all, *Tellus Ad Astra* was not a warship, at least not primarily, and her onboard weapons—mostly grazers mounted up forward to clear meteoric debris from her path—were strictly defensive. She carried a fair amount of firepower in her onboard fleet of fighters and escorts, but those ships were bottled up within her flight decks right now, where they could safely ride out the coming jump.

Based on his pre-mission briefings back on Earth, St. Clair fully expected the *Ad Astra* to emerge in a heavily guarded region of space, one where any overt hostile action would be met with overwhelming firepower. The Medusae, and, by extension, the Coadunation—the far larger and older galactic culture of which they were a tiny part—possessed technologies that were sheer magic to 22nd-century Humankind, technologies that made *Ad Astra*'s gamma-ray lasers seem about as high-tech as a 15th-century matchlock.

And, in fact, *Tellus Ad Astra*'s passengers were mostly civilians. There were two divisions of UE Marines on board—

about 24,000 in all—plus a large naval contingent, but the vast majority were scientists, technicians, logistical-support personnel, cultural and xenotechnological researchers, and exchange colonists, all traveling to the Coad core hab to initiate a formal cultural union with the Coadunation.

ST. CLAIR WAS curious about one thing, though. He addressed the liaison again. "Do you really expect trouble with the Denial in here?" he asked.

"Anything is possible," the Liaison replied. "The Denial represents a poisonous, dangerous ideology, and it has been spreading."

"Are you saying that Denial philosophers are going to show up at the galactic core with a battlefleet?"

"I do not understand your use of the term *philosophers* in this context, Humans. However, numerous civilizations have fallen to Denial dogma. Some of those are well armed and possess dangerous fleets, yes."

"Just what *is* this Denial dogma, anyway?"

"A contagion, Humans." The Liaison seemed to grope for the right words. "Anarchy . . . despair . . . the abandonment of long-held coadunation principles . . . a turning away from the light of civilization. . . ."

"I don't understand."

"I doubt that you *can* understand. Humans do not have the cultural background to grasp fifth-level cultural expression."

"Try us."

"I suggest, Lord Commander," a human voice said in St. Clair's mind, "that you not pursue this line of inquiry. The Medusae can easily become upset by what they perceive as an attack upon their belief systems."

"And *I'm* upset by their damned condescension," St. Clair replied over the same mental channel. "They're treating us like children, damn it."

"By their standards, we *are* children," Günter Adler told him. "Don't cross them."

St. Clair scowled, then sighed. "Aye, aye, sir."

Giving the naval phrase meaning "I understand and I will obey" was a very small and rather subtle act of defiance on St. Clair's part. Günter Adler was the expedition's senior representative on the UE Cybercouncil, and as such he definitely rated a "my lord" instead of a mere "sir." But by saying "aye, aye," he was gently reminding the director that St. Clair was still the *military* leader of the expedition. St. Clair was responsible for military decisions, and that included decisions affecting the expedition as they shifted into the unknown within the next few minutes.

While St. Clair was in command of both the ship and the military forces embarked within her, however, Adler was in charge of all civilian personnel within the *Tellus Ad Astra*, save only for those working directly for the Marines. Technically, Adler was an advisor and consultant in military matters; in practice, he was the expedition's senior director and, by extension, St. Clair's boss.

At least in theory. In St. Clair's experience, divided commands never worked—not well, at any rate—and mixing military leadership with political leadership generally was a recipe for disaster.

Still, Adler was a decent enough sort, if a bit on the arrogant side, and St. Clair was confident that he would be able to work smoothly with the man. His real concern was Worldgov's love affair with the damned Coadunation.

If Humans are children, he thought, *then Worldgov is like a puppy—show them something shiny and new, pat them on the heads a few times, and they'll follow the Coadunation anywhere.*

The trouble was that the politics of that Galaxy were . . . *alien*. There was no better word for it. This Coadunation seemed like a loose association, a trade collective or alliance, but was that really true? What were the responsibilities of the member polities? The social and legal expectations? The background systems of belief and worldview? And this Denial . . . was it a religion? A philosophy? A political movement? A terrorist organization? No human knew, and the Medusae representatives of the vaster Coadunation seemed unable—or unwilling—to make things clear. St. Clair hoped that the Coad leadership at the Harmony Habitat would be able to clarify things . . . including telling him more about this enigmatic alien threat to a galaxy-wide civilization. But for now, being kept in the dark was something that didn't sit well with St. Clair, especially with more than a million souls relying on him.

"Aye, aye," he said again, very softly.

"Sir?" Newton asked.

"Liaison?" St. Clair said, ignoring the AI's question. "Tell me again about this capital of yours."

"It is not ours, Humans. Not of the Medusae. It was constructed tens of millions of your years before the Medusae allied with the Coadunation by a consortium of advanced species as a kind of galactic capital and data-processing center."

As the alien spoke, Newton pulled up computer-generated schematics of the structure as described by Medusan technologists. A spiraling disk of white light encircled a black sphere. Well beyond the edge of the accretion disk lay the artificial world—a Bishop ring, as it was known to human futurists—a thick and massive tube, open at its ends, rotating about its long axis. The structure was named for the man who'd formulated the concept, back in the 1990s—Forrest Bishop.

Until now, Bishop rings had been purely theoretical constructs, something that humans might one day use to create deep space colonies. They were a larger version of the O'Neill cylinders like those of *Tellus Ad Astra*; this one was two thousand kilometers across—twice the diameter of the dwarf planet Ceres—and almost a thousand kilometers long. The inner surface was living space—cities and forests and plains in roughly 6 million square kilometers, or about twice the surface area of Argentina. The open land was not enclosed; retention walls two hundred kilometers high kept the atmosphere in under the effects of spin gravity. Reportedly, the surface was under about a half G from the cylinder's rotation.

The thick body of the cylinder was also habitat—*many* enclosed habitats, in fact—that allowed a vast diversity of galactic space-faring species to live together. The enormous ring orbited a small and probably artificial black hole of about three solar masses, which in turn orbited Sagittarius A*. The larger orbit required several centuries for each circuit.

That central supermassive black hole had a diameter of 44 million kilometers, and was in turn surrounded by an accretion disk of infalling dust and gas circling the object out to a distance of nearly 150 million kilometers—the size of Earth's orbit. The black hole supporting Harmony Habitat—which they also called the Harmony Singularity—orbited the larger black hole at a range of about half an AU outside the accretion disk.

Harmony. An optimistic enough name. St. Clair had stared at the drawings and images long enough for the sheer awe at the thing's scale to wear off—the human mind, it seemed, could only accept so much before simply shrugging that scale off as *big*.

"Okay . . . but *why*? Is it supposed to be some kind of symbol of galactic government?"

"The Coadunation is not a government as you think of the word," the Liaison replied. "But Harmony does provide a neutral meeting place for the numerous species that comprise the alliance. It is also useful for extracting energy—a great deal of energy—from the object you call a black hole."

St. Clair nodded. It made sense. Human technological

theorists had been talking for over a century about ways of extracting energy from mass falling into a singularity. Evidently, someone had figured out how to do that.

"So what's the mass of that thing?" he asked, pointing at Harmony.

"In your terms, roughly two times ten to the twenty-four kilograms," the Liaison replied.

St. Clair bounced the reply through his cybernetic math coprocessor, asked for a comparison, and whistled softly. That damned thing's mass was almost a third of Earth's.

His cyberimplant pulled up a reference to a twentieth-century work of fiction—*Ringworld*. The scale was not quite the same—the book described a ring as big across as Earth's orbit rotating around its sun—but it was still enormous. Large enough, according to the Medusae, to provide myriad environments inside for billions of intelligent beings from ten thousand civilized species, in conditions ranging from far colder than the Medusae liked, to temperatures that would melt lead.

The radiation flux, he thought, would be fearsome in there, that close to a supermassive black hole prone to periodic outbursts of X-rays and hard gamma. For that matter, how did they deal with dust, gas, and meteoric debris sweeping in from outside the habitat's walls?

That was one of the things they would be learning during the next several years. He had so many questions, as did most aboard *Ad Astra*. The million-plus humans on the O'Neill cylinder would be transferred to their new home within Harmony as a part of a research initiative cooked up by UE Worldgov and the Coadunation representatives, a kind of exchange program designed to ease Humankind into the galactic community. Most of the people would be living here for the next couple of years—longer if they requested it—studying the rich diversity of alien life and technology that made up the Milky Way Galaxy.

St. Clair and *Ad Astra*'s crew would not be staying, however. They were scheduled to take the ship back to Earth with a few thousand nonhuman passengers, including Medusae, Volech, K'tarid, and others. Habitats were being constructed for them in Earth orbit, giving them the opportunity to study human culture and technology.

He hoped the guests wouldn't end up laughing too hard.

"One more question?"

"Yes, Humans."

"You say we're coming out right alongside Harmony. We're going to have some velocity. Quite a bit of velocity. My briefings said you had a way of dealing with that, but they didn't give me specifics. How do we stop from slamming into your core habitat at a few hundred kilometers per second?"

"We will emerge within a . . . call it decelerative field. It will safely bleed off your excess velocity and store it in the Harmony Singularity."

"How does that work?"

The Liaison hesitated. "It involves an application of directed gravity and the hyperdimensional metric of local space. If the Coadunation receives assurances that you humans will help with the Denial, they may transfer details of that technology to you."

Ah. A bribe, then. Help us in our war, and we'll give you technology so advanced that it seems like magic to primitive savages like you.

St. Clair scowled. Nothing had been said yet, so far as he was aware, about the specifics of Humankind's participation in the Denial War. So far as he was concerned, no amount of free technology was worth human involvement in a war Earth knew nothing about, fought for causes humans did not even comprehend. The whole idea was insane.

Antigravity.

Decelerative fields.

Human immortality.

None of it was worth *that*.

"*Ad Astra* is at full charge, Lord Commander," Symm told him, interrupting bleak thoughts. "We're ready for the final shift."

"Very well. Liaison? Lord Adler? Give the word."

Adler nodded. "Do it, Commander."

"Take us to Harmony," the Liaison added.

Time to start the next chapter for humanity, St. Clair thought.

They jumped.

Ad Astra shuddered and lurched, wrenched by a sudden, sharp *bang*.

"What the hell?" Symm shouted.

"Attitude control!" St. Clair yelled. "Get us stabilized!"

Something was seriously out of kilter, but St. Clair couldn't yet tell what the problem was. Normally, hyperdimensional transitions were as smooth as silk, a smooth passage from one volume of space into another by way of the timeless non-space of the Bulk, which embraced the universes.

There was nothing normal about this time.

Clinging to the arms of his command chair, St. Clair stared up into the light above his head with a growing sense of horror. The Galaxy's central black hole was there, looming, huge, with its accretion disk spread out like a gleaming blue-white whirlpool around it, hotter than the surface of Earth's sun. *Ad Astra* was skimming above that plasma, close enough that her hull temperature was already soaring. Particles banged and thudded off the ship's skin. Their speed was . . .

My God! How can we be going this fast?

"Weapons!" St. Clair screamed. "All weapons . . . back online!"

And why the fuck had he agreed to switch the meteor-defense grazers off in the first place? He looked back and forth wildly. Rocks tumbled and jostled above and around his head, enveloped in a cloud of glittering sand. . . .

"Harmony!" the Liaison said, its translated voice curiously flat and machinelike. "Harmony . . ."

"It's gone," St. Clair said. "*Something* came in here and ripped it apart!"

"That . . . is not . . . possible. . . ."

A piece of spinning debris the size of a house collided with *Ad Astra*'s engineering section, and things began to get worse.

Much worse. . . .

Ad Astra **hurtled** toward the loom of the supermassive black hole ahead.

"Bridge, Engineering!" Martinez called. "The stardrive is off-line!"

"What happened?" St. Clair demanded.

"Something hit us, sir. Something *big*."

"Where?"

"Engineering hull. We're losing atmosphere down here, fast . . ."

St. Clair glanced up at the titanic black hole just ahead. Already it looked a little larger . . . a little closer . . .

"We're going to need shift capability in like the next few minutes," he said. "Get us back on-line, and do it now!"

"Working on it, sir."

He almost added further . . . *encouragement*, but it would be useless to keep harping at his people, St. Clair knew. They knew their jobs. He stifled the shrill exhortations that came bubbling up in his mind, and transmitted instead a calm-sounding "Good."

But the *Tellus Ad Astra* was hurtling toward the SMBH at pulse-pounding speed. And that was far from good.

"Helm! Can we maneuver clear?"

"Working on it, sir. But . . . I don't think so. We emerged from shift with a hell of a lot of velocity, and I think we picked up more speed by skimming the Harmony Singularity. We don't have stardrive, we don't have maneuvering, and that thing up ahead is *not* going to let go."

Which meant that even with its gravitic drive, it would take time and a lot of energy to break free. Energy they had. Time . . .

That was another matter entirely.

"What happened to Harmony?" Symm asked.

"We've got . . . fragments," Lieutenant Anna Denisova reported. She was the ship's sensor officer, charged with keeping track of what was happening in *Ad Astra*'s immediate vicinity. "*Big* fragments."

St. Clair didn't need sensors to know that—some were visible within the display above his head. Black, ragged-edged, some pieces the size of mountains, others like pebbles or sand, all in a free-fall tumble toward the central SMBH. The smaller pieces were rattling off the bridge's outer structure like hail off sheet metal. A cloud of the stuff must be pacing the *Ad Astra*; if one of those rocks hit with a large difference in relative speed . . .

Hell, maybe that was what had happened. A small pebble, rather than something the size of a house. If it hit at a hundred kps, it would cause quite a lot of damage.

Or . . . maybe *Ad Astra* had taken damage in a near passage of the small black hole—the Harmony Singularity. The decelerative field the Liaison had mentioned hadn't worked, obviously—blown away with Harmony's destruction. Moving with a residual velocity of a hundred kps or so, then skimming the Harmony Singularity . . . yeah, that might explain it.

"It is not possible," the Liaison said, "that the Harmony Habitat should have been . . . obliterated in this manner. It was far too large."

"Nothing," St. Clair replied, "is too big to fail. At a guess, I'd say your Denial friends were here within the past five years with enough firepower to at least weaken the thing's hull. The stress of orbiting the black hole would do the rest."

"Why . . . do you say within the past five years?" the Liaison wanted to know.

"Because we parked five light years outside the core a few moments ago, and looked at it through a grav lens. It appeared intact from there . . . but the light we were seeing was five years old."

"Of . . . course. We should have remembered that. . . ."

"Hey, it takes some getting used to. When were you at Harmony Hab last?"

"Perhaps three of your years."

"That nails it down further," St. Clair told the alien. "The only way to pinpoint a date would be to move out from the black hole a few light days at a time, taking a look back and seeing when the habitat breaks up."

"We must do this," the liaison said.

"We will . . . *if* we can get ourselves out of this gravity well," St. Clair replied. "I suggest that you leave the bridge, and let us work on that."

"You will keep us informed. . . ."

"Of course. You have bridge link access."

"We . . . do not understand how this could have happened." The alien environmental unit spun and silently floated off the bridge.

"He sounds pissed," Symm said.

"Well . . . his galactic capital has just been blown to hell by parties unknown," St. Clair said. "Understandable."

The *Ad Astra* gave another sharp, brutal shudder, and St. Clair wondered if the ship could hold together. *She's definitely not designed for maneuverability*, St. Clair thought. *More like a houseboat with a jet engine bolted on the back.*

In other words, he knew, *strong tidal forces will rip her apart.*

The good news was that the central SMBH was so large—

the size of Mercury's orbit—that its gravitational gradient would be fairly gentle. The bad was that the *Ad Astra* was accelerating so quickly in that gravitational field now that torque and flexing in the structure's framework might well destroy them before they had a chance to be sucked into the black hole.

And there wasn't a damned thing that St. Clair, as ship's captain, could do about it.

Which is when something else occurred to him. "Where's the Coad monitor?" he asked.

"Eight hundred thousand kilometers ahead," the third navigator said.

"So far?"

"Shiftscatter, my lord," Lieutenant Mason, the helmsman, added.

So the Medusan ship had come through . . . but the mathematical vagaries of this gravitationally distorted spacetime had scattered the two when they'd emerged. Maybe they'd been relying on some sort of beacon or trigger to drop them out of shiftspace inside the decelerative field, and overshot because the beacon was gone. *Maybe, maybe, maybe . . .*

Too many unknowns.

The alien vessel was now farther ahead of the *Ad Astra* than twice the distance between Earth and Earth's moon. That was still close compared to the vast sweep of the accretion disk below . . . but all that distance emphasized how tiny even a vessel as large as the *Ad Astra* truly was, isolated in emptiness.

Faster, now. They were moving much faster, accelerating until the accretion disk, 300 million kilometers across, was visibly drifting past *Ad Astra*'s keel, like a mass of white clouds above the Earth seen from orbit. The face of that disk was intolerably bright, especially in toward the center, where it glared hot and rich in UV, X-rays, and hard gamma. The AIs controlling the video input were stopping down the brightness to avoid injuring human optics in that storm of light, as brilliant as the face of the sun.

The black hole itself loomed almost directly ahead . . . and it didn't look as St. Clair had pictured it. It was black, yes . . . or what he could see of it was, an eye-aching blackness so deep his gaze tended to slide right off the thing, with nothing at all upon which to focus. Only half of the sphere was visible above the swirling storm of the accretion disk. The hemisphere he could see was bounded by a shimmering half ring of optical distortion; light from beyond the SMBH, from the star clouds of the Galactic Center and from the opposite side of the accretion disk, was being weirdly bent by the intense gravitational field close to the black hole's event horizon. The half ring appeared silvery and mottled, and it was moving as the *Ad Astra*'s perspective shifted.

"Helm . . . we need to break free. *Now*."

"Working on it, sir."

He could feel a deep-down vibration, an ongoing shudder transmitted through the seat of his command chair as the ship marshaled titanic energies from the vacuum and directed them into its gravitic drive. *Ad Astra* was changing course, pulling up against the drag of that black monster ahead, but so slowly.

Too slowly.

The central regions of the accretion disk were hotter, more active, tinged with violet radiance, while the outer regions were cooler and redder. St. Clair could see flashes and pulses of light from the innermost parts—flares of high-energy radiation like planet-devouring bolts of lightning.

"How's the shielding holding up?" he asked.

"It's holding," Subcommander Michael Seibert reported. "Just barely . . . but we're okay so far."

Which was no guarantee that the electromagnetic shielding protecting the *Ad Astra* from the horrific storm of radiation outside would continue keeping them safe. Like the shift drive, the shielding technology had come from the Co-adunation . . . and St. Clair wasn't yet certain that he trusted it. Radiation levels within the core were far, *far* higher than out in the galactic suburbs, where Sol circled, necessitating EM shields considerably more efficient than those currently used by Earth. St. Clair still wondered, however, if it wouldn't have been better if the United Earth Directorate had waited until it developed these gimmicks on its own.

"My lord," Craig Mason said, the stress clear in his mental voice. "We're not going to make it."

A computer-generated schematic appeared in a window opening in St. Clair's head. Mason's efforts had indeed deflected *Ad Astra*'s headlong plummet toward the SMBH . . . but not quite enough. They would be entering the black hole's ergosphere in another five minutes.

"Is there anything else we can try?"

"Damned if I know, sir," Mason said.

"Newton! What are we missing?"

"There is one possibility," the voice of the ship's computer replied. "A slender chance."

That caught St. Clair's attention. "What is it?"

"If we jettison one of the cylinders, its fall might eject us from the ergosphere."

"I looked at that, Lord Commander," Mason said. "I couldn't. I *couldn't*. . . ."

Newton uploaded another schematic, one showing the jettison option. *Ad Astra*'s two habitation cylinders, each thirty-two kilometers long and six and half wide, represented by far the majority of the ship's mass. Drop one at exactly the right moment, and it would fall deeper into the black hole's gravity well . . . but the drop would kick the other—plus the attached engineering hull—higher, in a stark demonstration of Newton's third law. There were stars, St. Clair knew, that once had been part of a binary pair that strayed too close to the relentless tug of a black hole. One member of the pair had been devoured; the other had been slingshotted at a substantial fraction of the speed of light into deep space.

And what had worked for a star would work with the double-hulled colony transport.

"Craig," St. Clair said, "if there's a chance here in hell . . ."

"Sir . . . I can't. *I can't!* My family is in O'Neill Starboard!"

"It's okay, son. . . ."

"Sir, if you're going to eject one of the cylinders, *I want to be with them!*"

The helm officer's voice was shrill, sharp-edged with panic. Briefly, St. Clair considered relieving the man, letting him go join his family. According to Mason's bio, he had a wife, a husband, and three kids living in Goddard, one of the starboard side's cities.

"The window for that option," Newton said with implacable calm, "has closed."

St. Clair checked the numbers flowing back through his link with the ship. It would have taken nearly ten minutes to seal off one of the cylinders and prepare it for jettison . . . and there simply wasn't enough time left.

And . . . would he have been able to give that order, any more than Mason? *Tellus Ad Astra* carried a million human passengers and several hundred thousand AI robots. Most lived in the two hab cylinders, distributed roughly half and half. Could he have given the order to drop half a million souls into the maw of the black hole, even to save the others?

St. Clair wasn't at all certain that he could.

"There is still the possibility," Newton went on, "of catastrophic jettison."

Ad Astra gave another hard shudder as if to underline the possibility. If the ship's structure couldn't hold up to the stresses of flashing low above the event horizon of a black hole, they might get a cylinder jettison by accident instead of deliberately.

"Monitor the hull stresses," St. Clair told the computer. "If it looks like we're going to lose a cylinder, orient the ship to take advantage of it."

"So that the surviving cylinder and the engineering and drive sections survive," Newton added. "I will do so if possible. I cannot guarantee—"

"Just do what you can, damn it!"

"Lord Commander . . ." Mason began.

"It's okay, Craig," he said. "We're not going to jettison your family." *Not deliberately, anyway,* he added to himself. *Not if we can help it.*

"Thank you, sir."

"If there's any way possible, we're going to come through this together. *All* of us."

But circumstances, he knew, together with the implacable laws of physics, might yet make a liar of him.

Three minutes. The curve of the black hole, edged by its arc of optical distortion, seemed to float within its accretion disk just ahead, though the ship's course correction was edging them now toward one side.

"Radiation levels are increasing, my lord."

"I see it." Cosmic rays, hard X-rays and gamma radiation—the galactic core spawned the stuff in vast and seething clouds. *Ad Astra* was plunging through an increasingly fierce storm of extremely high energy radiation.

A bright flash strobed against the visual display, and was instantly lost within the glare of the accretion disk.

"The squid ship is gone, my lord!" Denisova reported. She sounded badly shaken. "It just . . . blew. . . ."

What had happened? The aliens possessed technologies—including materials technologies—far ahead of what was possible so far for Earth. If an advanced-tech Medusae ship couldn't hold up against this battering, what hope might there be—*could* there be—for the fragile human colony vessel?

"The alien's path was slightly below ours, sir," Denisova continued. "Closer to the accretion mass. Maybe . . ." Her voice trailed off.

"They might have hit a piece of the destroyed habitat," St. Clair said. "Or a planetesimal."

Accretion disks—vast clouds of matter drawn into an orbiting whirlpool flattened by orbital mechanics and electromagnetic fields—were ideal places for the birth of new worlds, even of stars. Or perhaps the nameless alien vessel simply had dropped into a volume of space too richly populated by ultra-high velocity dust particles and atoms of hydrogen gas.

He'd have to worry about that some other time.

Two minutes . . .

"Engineering," St. Clair said over the open channel. "Please tell me you're about to produce a goddamned miracle."

"Sorry, my lord," Martinez replied. "We're fresh out of miracles. The jump drive is wrecked; we're going to have to grow a new one from scratch. And the gravs are pushing as hard as they can, but it's simply not enough to break free."

"Can you achieve orbit?"

A long pause followed the question.

"Maybe," Martinez said at last. "*Big* maybe. But we probably won't survive the environment."

"Don't worry about probables. Give us as much time as you can."

"Yes, my lord."

The outer edge of a black hole's ergosphere could be defined as the distance from the singularity at which the hole's escape velocity was equal to the speed of light. Hit that, and the *Ad Astra* would *never* pull away . . . not unless Engineering was able to repair or replace the stardrive. The zone was also called the apparent event horizon; *nothing* that happened within it could ever be observed by someone outside.

In fact . . .

"My Lord!" Lieutenant Denisova shouted in his mind. "My Lord, the Medusae ship wasn't destroyed! It's still there—I think."

"What do you mean, 'I think'?"

"The flash was an energy trail, a kind of wake through the hydrogen gas. But I'm getting the ship's image up ahead, on the event horizon!"

A window opened in the display, showing a highly magnified view of what appeared to be the Medusan ship— grainy, pixelated to the point of incoherence, and apparently frozen in place deep within the field of intense gravitational distortion around Sagittarius A*.

But it wasn't orbiting the black hole. It appeared to be frozen against it, frozen in time.

ONE OF the curious bits of physics associated with black holes is the fact that as a ship falls deeper and ever deeper into a gravity well, the increasing gravity acts in exactly the same way as relativistic time dilation. Time itself slows as the doomed ship approaches c; at the same time, the image of the ship, carried by relativistically distorted light waves, appears to slow . . . slow . . . and finally stops, freezing at the apparent event horizon.

So the Medusae on board the Coad vessel might already be dead, stretched by tidal forces in a way described by the unpleasantly evocative and vivid term "spaghettification," but the moment of their entry into the SMBH's ergosphere was frozen for eternity on the apparent event horizon.

"An Einstein ghost," Symm said.

"Maybe," St. Clair agreed. "I wonder if they broke free? Or maybe they're still falling?"

There was no way of telling.

In any case, St. Clair had his own set of worries at the moment, and unless the Coad ship offered clues for *Ad Astra*'s escape, he had no time to waste on them.

One minute. . . .

The shuddering grew to a crescendo of vibration, rattling the ship and St. Clair's seat and the very fiber of his muscles and bones. Somewhere, a radiation alert was sounding, and the glare of light both on the projected holographic display around him and within the open displays inside his own head was fading rapidly, dwindling to a sullen red glow before fading even more, then, into black. The bridge was still visible—he wasn't going blind, which had been his first sharp, panicky thought—but the light from outside the ship was stretching out into the red end of the spectrum . . . and then beyond, into infrared . . . microwave . . . radio. . . .

He opened a ship-wide broadcast channel. "All hands," he said over the internal link. "This is Commander St. Clair. The ship is about to cross the event horizon of the supermassive black hole at the Galaxy's center. Our FTL drive is out, our gravitics insufficient to change our course. There seems to be no way to break free. I . . . I just wanted to say that it *has* been a privilege serving with each and every—"

The impact that rocked the ship was stronger, more savage, and more violent than anything St. Clair had ever experienced. It slammed him against his seat, slammed his brain into ringing darkness.

At least the ongoing, thunderous vibration had stopped. . . .

In Ad Astra's *#4 drop tube array . . .*

LIEUTENANT CHRISTOPHER Merrick kept his eyes tightly shut—not to keep from seeing what was happening, but to close off the depressingly claustrophobic walls of the drop tube embracing his ASF-99 Wasp fighter. Merrick and the eleven other members of GFA-86, the Stardogs, were on Ready One, meaning their fighters were set to launch in less than one minute if the commander or the aerospace CO gave the word. For the past two hours, though, he'd waited there, locked inside the cockpit of his Wasp, unmoving in the launch tube array in *Ad Astra*'s aft hull complex.

His eyes were closed, but his mind was wide open to the flood of images streaming in from Primary Flight Control. Through the electronic feed, he could see the SMBH, vast and enigmatic, circled by its shroud of twisted light. He could see the sweep of the accretion disk . . . the glare of the starclouds thronging the galactic center.

And then a shudder slammed through the *Ad Astra*, a vibration that grew and grew and grew, until it felt as though the colony ship was about to shake itself into fragments. In another instant, the surrounding starlight flashed to red, as red as blood . . . and in another instant he was staring into blackness.

The shock yanked a sudden gasp from Merrick, and a stab of fear. Stifling the urgent yammer of panic rising in the back of his brain, he opened his eyes, saw the gray walls enclosing him, the distant circle of the launch tube hatch . . . and told himself to breathe. The vibration had stopped, and he blinked.

What the hell just happened?

In the Commander's Quarters, starboard hab, in the hills above Bethesda . . .

LISA 776 AI Zeta-3sw had been getting out of bed when the shuddering vibration had struck . . . an earthquake, though she'd never experienced a seismic tremor on Earth. The jolt had flung her to the floor, bounced her across the room, and slammed her into the bedroom's IS—the interface station.

Rising, she worked her left arm back and forth, realizing that it was broken. Lubricants were dripping from torn actuators, the skin had been peeled back, and she could see the carbofiber weave of the main strut bent at an awkward angle.

Lisa felt no pain, of course—gynoid robots didn't. But the mechanisms in her arm were signaling that they were seriously damaged and that she would need repairs as swiftly as possible.

That, she thought with ruthless machine logic, might not happen for a while. The ship was obviously in serious trouble. A moment before that final shock, her link to StarNet had shown her the sudden reddening of the light beyond the ship's hull, then sudden blackness.

And now there was no exterior feed at all.

Neither was there any vibration. Whatever had been happening to the *Ad Astra* had abruptly—and mysteriously—ceased.

She walked to the outside veranda, the door sliding aside for her as she approached. The house was built into the side of one of the artificial hills rising against the end cap of the starboard habitat, high enough up that the spin gravity here was only about half a G. Looking up, she saw the sunbeam glowing as brightly as ever behind a light scattering of clouds. Obviously they still had power.

But for how long?

Properly speaking, gynoids, like their android counterparts, didn't feel fear . . . not in the human sense of the word. They could simulate it, of course, just as they could simulate any other human emotion in the execution of their programming, but emotional urges could be switched off as effectively as she'd just shut down the pain analogue in her arm. The idea of being driven purely by emotion, of acting without thinking was, quite literally, unthinkable.

One of the vista windows was open, and her dark eyes focused on it. As originally designed, O'Neill cylinders had three windows running the entire length of the habitat; the covers for those windows were mirrored, a design to reflect sunlight into the cylinder's interior. In more modern designs like the *Ad Astra*, the sunbeam filled that role, but the cylinder still possessed several viewing transparencies, vista windows looking out into space.

Odd. All of the windows should have been sealed as *Ad Astra* made the final jump into the galactic core. Someone had ordered this one opened, perhaps to get a look outside when the data streams were cut off.

It was not precisely accurate to say that gynoids felt no emotion whatsoever. Loyalty, curiosity, determination, patience—all of those were traits associated with human simulants, hard-wired into their AI consciousness. And as Lisa stared through the window, miles across the up-curving valley of the starboard hab, she felt another.

Wonder.

In the starboard hab, above vista window SVW-12. . . .

MAJOR GENERAL William Frazier was human enough that he could feel fear, but he'd long ago found that he could suppress the emotion and carry on by focusing on the job at hand. The trouble at the moment was that he wasn't certain what the job was. The data net was down, he had no linkage with the bridge or with Marine HQ, and, quite frankly, there was nothing that clearly needed doing. To get a better idea of the situation, he'd made his way to vista window twelve, physically jacked into the control, and rolled open the outside shield protecting the transparency. The window lay at his feet, like a rectangular pond dozens of meters across.

Superficially, he was taking a hell of a chance. Had the transparency opened onto a nearby nova or some other source of intense light, his optical sensors might have been burned out before the window's imbedded circuitry could divert the radiation.

Frazier was a fully functional cybernetic Marine, which in fact meant that he was more machine than human. Although he could doff and don bodies as easily as other humans could grow a new set of clothing, at the moment he was wearing a Mk. III Marine Combat Unit: three meters of black plasteel, woven carbarmor, and nanochelated circuitry. His brain, however, housed inside its heavily armored computronium matrix within his chest, could still *feel* as well as think. He'd hesitated before making the link, a nasty mix of doubt and fear clamoring for attention until he pushed the feelings aside. He *had* to know what was taking place outside the *Ad Astra* . . . but he was afraid of jeopardizing the ship by opening her fragile hull to whatever might be out there.

But what he was looking down at now filled him only with awe.

Clearly, the *Ad Astra* was still deep within the galactic center, a realm thronging with tens of millions of brilliant stars. Of the supermassive black hole the ship had been falling toward a few moments ago, there was no sign—no sign *at all*, even as he waited through several cycles of the starboard hab's rotation. He did see that the port hab was still there; he watched it swing into view as the starboard hab turned, a deep gray wall drifting up from the near side of the window, filling his view for a moment, then passing out of sight at the far side.

Except for that interruption, however, the vista window was filled with stars, a nearly unbroken mass of them. That, in itself, was not surprising. The Galaxy's core was filled with suns—most of them huge, ancient, and red-hued, the Population II remnants of a far earlier epoch of stellar formation.

But the AI-machine component of Frazier's mind was

very good at patterns and pattern recognition, and at the moment it was fairly shrieking an alarm.

That massed throng of stars visible below Frazier's feet was . . . *different* than it had been before.

Very different.

The stars were far, far more numerous; they were brighter; and they were bluer than what he'd seen before through the data stream, just moments ago.

The entire Galaxy, somehow, had been transformed into something . . .

Other.

Time passed for St. Clair before he again was fully aware of his surroundings, pushing up through a red haze of pain and dazed confusion. That final shock had been brutal, and according to his inner AI clock, he'd lost several seconds, either because he'd been unconscious, or because his organic brain had momentarily detached from the internal circuitry of his in-head AI. The connections were reforming themselves now, but he felt dizzy and weak. With an effort, he shut off the harsh yammer of pain receptors in skull and shoulders.

The safety of the ship was more urgent, though, and he began reestablishing his electronic connections to the bridge and to *Ad Astra*'s Network Ops Center. Even as the pain faded, he was checking his in-head window to see where the central black hole was in relation to the *Ad Astra*, and that brought on a shock of a different kind.

The supermassive black hole and its attendant accretion disk were *gone*.

Impossible. You don't just take a singularity with a total mass of 4.3 million suns and make it vanish.

There was something else, too. Somehow, the *Ad Astra* had picked up some velocity. Space astern had taken on a distinctly red hue, with a large, circular blind spot empty of stars at the center. Forward, the stars appeared blue, again with a spot of black emptiness directly ahead. He recognized the optical distortion of relativistic spacetime dilation;

the *Ad Astra* was moving at a high percentage of the speed of light, her velocity making the rest of the universe appear to be compressed into a thick ring around the hurtling vessel. At a guess, they were moving at 70 to 80 percent of the speed of light.

How had they picked up that much velocity?

Slingshotting around a supermassive black hole might do it, he thought . . . but that brought him back to the other question: where was Sag A*? Had the *Ad Astra* been moving at near-*c* long enough that the SMBH was no longer visible?

St. Clair shoved aside the questions. Time enough to look for answers later. Right now, reports were flooding in from all parts of the ship, a distant but incessant murmur of voices—a litany of casualties, of failed power, of structural damage, of falling pressure, and interrupted life support. It sounded like his section chiefs had things under control, thank God, but a small army of AI agents dispatched from the NOC—the Network Operations Center—were electronically checking for more serious damage, just in case. The sheer size and complexity of *Ad Astra* meant that it might take a while to make sure they were out of immediate danger.

Most important on the list: none of the reported injuries he'd heard of so far was worse than a broken bone or a concussion—no mass casualties as atmosphere gushed out into space from one of the thin-walled hab modules, as one chilling example. So far as St. Clair was concerned, that constituted a minor miracle. The *Ad Astra* was not designed for bumpy flights or massive, hull-rattling vibrations.

"Lord Commander!" Symm called. "We've located Sagittarius A-Star! I . . . I think . . ."

"What do you mean you *think*?" St. Clair demanded. "You've picked it up, or you haven't!"

"It's . . . I don't know, sir. Something's wrong."

"What?"

"Our mass readings show . . . my God. Its mass has doubled! The total is nine million solar masses, maybe a little more."

"That's not possible."

"I know, my lord. I *know*. But . . ." She waved a hand in confused frustration, passing it through the holographic projection in front of her. "There it is."

There it was indeed, both on his own holo display and on an in-head window tapping into the ship's sensor data, a silvery ring of shifting light encircling a disk of blackness all but lost against that dazzlingly bright backdrop of stars. Mass, range, and diameter readouts flickered to life alongside the images. The vast sprawl of the accretion disk was gone, wiped away . . . which was why he'd not seen the SMBH a moment before when he'd looked for it. The sensors were placing the hole ten light-minutes from the ship, but it was far larger than it ought to be.

Something very peculiar was happening . . . and St. Clair couldn't figure out what it was.

"Engineering."

"Martinez, Lord Commander."

"We've picked up some speed. What the hell happened?"

"Don't know, yet, sir. Best guess is we just got slingshotted clear of the SMBH."

"We were supposed to be trying for an orbit."

"I know. We're playing back the AI records now. Should know in a sec. . . ."

"While you're at it, bring our velocity down. I don't want to blindly slam into a piece of rock at this speed."

"I agree, sir. But I suggest we do so gradually. I'm still not sure how much damage our framework sustained in . . . in whatever just happened to us. We're also tumbling, though at a slow rate. We need to address that, too."

"Good thoughts. Use your discretion."

"Aye, aye, sir."

St. Clair allowed himself a slight exhalation of relief. Attempting to slip into orbit around a SMBH had been an act of desperation; likely, *Ad Astra* would have been trapped there—at least until Martinez had been able to repair the shift drive. If repairs had been impossible, they would have been stuck there for a fair percentage of eternity, until the black hole evaporated at the end of time, or until something big had hurtled in and smashed the *Ad Astra* into infalling debris. He still wasn't sure what had just happened, but the outcome appeared to have been a good one . . . as good as could be hoped for, at any rate. *Ad Astra*'s main drive was still off-line and she'd been battered hard, but at least she was drifting free in open space, not pinned to the ergosphere of a supermassive black hole, as their Coad escort was.

"Lord Commander," Mason said. "We have a go from Engineering to attempt to control our tumble."

"Do it."

Instinctively, St. Clair braced for a jolt or a burst of acceleration, then mentally kicked himself for the anticipation. *Ad Astra* maneuvered in normal space with a powerful gravitic drive, one that reshaped the matrix of spacetime around her, but like normal gravity, it acted on every atom within its field uniformly. *Ad Astra* could boost at a thousand Gs, and the people in her zero-gravity compartments, like the bridge and Engineering, remained in free fall and felt nothing. Those in the hab cylinders forward continued to experience only the spin gravity of the rotating habitats . . . not a high-G acceleration that would have smeared them into a thin red jelly across the nearest aft bulkhead.

Habits are habits, though.

The electronic model of the ship in front of St. Clair's workstation had been showing a gentle end-for-end tumble since they'd entered open space, but now, gradually, it began to stabilize.

"Our tumble has been arrested," Mason reported.

"Very good, Helm."

"We have a go from Engineering to begin deceleration, my lord."

"Proceed," he said, before adding, "with *caution*."

"Aye, aye, sir."

"Start with ten Gs and then step it up slowly."

"Ten gravities, stepping up slowly. Yes, my lord."

He didn't want to slam on the brakes, even if the grav drive couldn't be felt. If there was a structural problem with the badly shaken starship, and the gravitic drive didn't act on all parts uniformly, a thousand gravities would tear them to shreds.

"Decelerating at ten gravities, my lord."

St. Clair found he was holding his breath—watching, listening, *feeling* for any change in the structure of the ship. No warning icons flashed up on the holodisplay, no AI messages screamed at him inside his wired-in brain.

At ten gravities, however, it would take them about nine years to slow to a halt relative to the nearest stars. "We seem to be in one piece, Mr. Mason. Take us to fifty gravities."

"Fifty gravities, aye, aye, sir."

There was no increased stress at fifty gravs . . . or at one hundred . . . or at five hundred. *Ad Astra* slowed steadily from its headlong plunge through the inner galactic core.

"Lord Commander!" Scott Forrester, the tactical officer, called out. "We've got company!"

"Show me."

"Three targets under acceleration, bearing one-eight-zero by zero, relative. Range two hundred fifteen million kilometers . . . closing at point six *c*."

"Directly astern. From the black hole."

"Pretty close, sir. I think they were some distance on the far side of it, and have been chasing us ever since . . . since we got hit back there."

"Do we still have fighters on ready one?"

A brief pause. "Yes, sir. They report being shaken up a bit . . . but ready for launch."

"Launch fighters," St. Clair said.

Whoever was following the *Ad Astra* might be whoever was responsible for destroying Harmony—a decidedly hostile act. He checked something on his displays. *Curious.*

There were no more fragments of the structure left in the area, as far as the ship's sensors could detect. No matter at all, in fact.

St. Clair thoughtclicked an in-head icon, sounding general quarters throughout the ship. He didn't want to fight; *Ad Astra* had teeth, but St. Clair was unwilling to risk the ship and a million passengers in a fight against unknown forces with unknown but highly advanced technologies. He would keep those unknown ships at a generous arm's length if he possibly could, though. *Ad Astra*'s fighters would serve as a screen.

He hoped.

"FIGHTER RELEASE in three . . . two . . . one . . . *launch.*"

The sensation of zero gravity was replaced by a slam of acceleration as Merrick's Wasp was magnetically propelled down the long launch tube. He emerged into empty space, half the sky filled first by the ventral surface of the ship's CCE section, the rest teeming with stars, many brighter than Sirius or even Venus seen from Earth at its brightest, all crowded together in a stunning display of radiant beauty. Not that Merrick was much interested in beauty at the moment. Wired into his ASF-99's cybersystems, he was now technically a part of his fighter, an eight-meter wedge-shaped combat machine with a brain partly electronic, partly organic. Numbers—range, velocity, mass, angle—flowed through his brain in a rushing stream, as his AI painted graphics across his mind's eye.

Together with the other Wasps in his squadron, Merrick

spun his fighter about, aligning with the still-distant cluster of targets aft.

"Keep it cool, people," the squadron's skipper, Senior Lieutenant Janis Colbert, announced. "We are not, repeat, *not* cleared to engage. Just take up your assigned positions and match course with Nasty Asty."

Her use of the *Ad Astra*'s irreverent nickname made Merrick grin inside his helmet. Military personnel were always renaming everything around them, including each other—a cultural imperative. He'd been saddled with his own squadron handle—Kit-Kat—back in flight school, a name he disliked but tolerated. As a kid growing up in North California, his family nickname had been Kit, and somehow his squadron mates had managed to twist it into something else.

"Okay," Colbert went on, "boost at eight hundred Gs in three . . . and two . . . and one . . . engage!"

Smoothly, the flight of Wasps accelerated clear of the ship with its huge, side-by-side habitat cylinders. In seconds, the *Ad Astra* dwindled into invisibility. Five hundred kilometers astern of the larger vessel, the fighters decelerated sharply, flipped end for end, and fell into formation, tracking the colony ship's wake.

"What are those characters up to, anyway?" Lieutenant Sam Vorhees asked.

"They're decelerating," Lieutenant Rick Thornton told her. "They've probably never seen anything like ol' *Asty*, so they'll be coming in extra cautious."

"I think we should go do a close run of those guys," Merrick said. "Let's see what we can stir up!"

"That's a negative, Kit-Kat," Colbert told him. "We're not going to provoke them—at least not until we know a bit more about these guys. Understood?"

"Copy. Understood."

Merrick opened an electronic window in his mind and accessed his fighter's warbook, studying the AI-generated graphics of the distant alien vessels. There wasn't a lot to see at a range of over 200 million kilometers, but *Ad Astra*'s long-range scanners were picking up a few details: needle shapes 40 meters long, with slight swellings at their sterns. The ship's records had nothing on the design . . . scarcely surprising, given that they were 26,000 light years from Sol and no human vessel had ever been out here before.

The lack of information chafed Merrick more than a little. He knew *Ad Astra* and the fighter squadrons embarked within her were under specific orders not to muddy the galactic waters out here, which meant keeping a low profile and staying—as much as possible—out of the way of other cultures. But that didn't mean that Merrick didn't feel a degree of impatience right now. No matter how alien these critters were, having a flight of Wasps make a moderately close passage across their bows—say at a distance of a few thousand kilometers—should serve to warn them off if they were indeed hostile.

Evidently, the people and AIs in command of this mission didn't subscribe to the same standards of common sense as he.

The aliens, he noted, were accelerating.

Perhaps *they* weren't under the same constraints in terms of engagement. . . .

"THE FIGHTERS are in position, Lord Commander."

"Very well, CAS," St. Clair replied. "Hold them there until we see what's going down."

CAS—*Ad Astra*'s commander aerospace—was a Class-3 cyborg wired directly into Newton and *Ad Astra*'s combat center. The human part of her was named Maria Francesca and she carried the naval rank of subcommander, but on board ship she was known simply as CAS.

"Yes, sir."

"Newton!"

"Yes."

"I need to talk with the Coad liaison."

"The Coad liaison is not at present available," the ship's AI replied. "However, I can connect you with its electronic agent."

"Do it."

"Opening channel."

The alien interface exploded into St. Clair's awareness, softened somewhat by the ship's AI to make it more accessible by humans. Electronic agents, common within human communications and AI networks, were software—often highly intelligent software—designed to help humans navigate through computer-generated virtual worlds or to connect with other minds. The Liaison's agent, St. Clair knew, had been specifically designed to help the Medusae communicate with humans.

"You have a question, Lord Commander?" the software whispered in his ear.

"I do. Have you seen ships like these before?"

He opened the channel from *Ad Astra*'s long-range scanners and fed through the image of one of the alien vessels, now 200 million kilometers distant and rapidly closing.

The alien software didn't hesitate at all. "We have never encountered this type of vessel, Lord Commander."

"You're certain?"

"We have never encountered this type of vessel, Lord Commander."

I guess that answers that, he thought. "Okay. Are there parts of the Coadunation that are unknown to you, a region where a star-faring civilization might have developed without your awareness?"

"Extremely unlikely, Lord Commander," the agent replied.

"How can you be so certain? You've been overlooking *my* species for quite a long time. True?"

This time, the agent did hesitate, as though it was carefully choosing its words. "The Coadunation has existed in its current form for nearly ten million of your years," it told him, the voice whispering in his mind. "During that time, Humankind has existed for only the last two or three hundred thousand years . . . and you have possessed interstellar capabilities for a mere few decades."

St. Clair nodded, understanding at once where the agent was going with this. "Thirty-eight years ago," he said. "Our first test runs with the Alcubierre Drive . . . and then the Alpha Centauri Expedition in 2120. And Sirius four years later."

"Among the four hundred billion suns of this Galaxy," the agent continued, "it is, I assure you, quite easy to overlook a technically unsophisticated species. It is difficult, however, to overlook a star-faring species—particularly one, like this, that can operate within the galactic core. Once your species began traveling among the stars, we were certain to detect you sooner or later. And we *should* have detected this species as well."

"Point taken. Thank you."

St. Clair made certain that the agent's words had been recorded within his in-head RAM. That admission would be of considerable interest to the UE officers who would debrief him when he got back to Earth. It strongly suggested that the Coadunation had technic means of detecting faster-than-light spacecraft across extremely large distances—hundreds, perhaps thousands, of light years.

The government's xenosophontology department had suspected that the Coad possessed that kind of technology, of course. After all, just six years after the first tentative out-system maneuvers by the *Stephen Hawking*—the very first Alcubierre test platform—the Coadunation had a fleet at Sirius looking for whoever had disturbed the ether out that way. That was way too much of a coincidence to be believed.

But of more immediate interest was the agent's certainty that the Galactic Coadunation had never encountered ships like these before. That suggested that the Coadunation was fallible or, far worse, that its representatives were deliberately lying.

Or it meant something that seemed so far out of the realm of possibility that it seemed absurd. As such, St. Clair was unwilling to believe that those three ships out there were visitors from some other Galaxy. Even the relatively nearby Magellanic Clouds were up to twice the entire span of the Milky Way galaxy distant, an appalling distance even for the shift drive.

Maybe, in fact, the Coads couldn't detect all forms of superluminal travel . . . and the unknown ships were from another little-visited backwater like the Orion Spur. *Maybe*. But what if they were lying?

If they were lying, what would be their motive?

What might they be hiding, and why?

He suspected that if they were lying, their reasons might have to do with the Denial. He was still angry at the Medusan Liaison's condescension, at its assumption that humans were incapable of understanding . . . What had it said? "Fifth-level cultural expression," whatever *that* was. But perhaps there was more to it than a simple unwillingness to bring humans into their confidence. Maybe they feared that Humankind might *join* the Denial, and so were telling them as little as possible.

Whatever the reason, he still had three ships bearing down on the *Ad Astra*, and he was a long way from knowing their intentions.

"I want some recon drones in that area," St. Clair said, indicating the volume of space surrounding the three aliens.

"Yes, sir. The targets are accelerating. Estimate . . . fifteen minutes until they reach us."

"Engineering! How long until we can shift?"

de the human colony ship. The light from the three aliens
.stern was from five minutes ago; those three targets were
luminal ghosts, images showing them *before* they'd shifted.

And that meant that the aliens could pack a star drive
into a slender hull a scant forty meters long, something well
beyond the current capabilities of human technology.

"Right, people!" Colbert called. "Close on the Asty!" A
white flare of light pulsed from dead ahead, briefly outshining the surrounding clouds of bright stars. Merrick felt a
stab of apprehension. Something big had just slammed the
mother ship.

"Fighters, you are weapons free, repeat, weapons free!
Ad Astra is under attack!"

"Kick it, people!" Colbert ordered. "Full boost! Let's get
in there!"

The fighters accelerated.

FROM ST. CLAIR'S perspective, the alien craft had simply materialized out of emptiness, three needle-shaped vessels that
had just outrun the light signaling their presence. Those
ships were minute compared to the vast and looming bulk
of the *Ad Astra*—slivers of red and black that looked like
sardines slipping into the shadow of a blue whale.

But then one loosed a burst of high-energy particles
tightly bound in a thrusting spear of electromagnetic force.
The beam struck the port-hab cylinder, releasing a fiercely
radiating burst of nova-hot light and heat. The burst expanded, then faded, replaced by a glittering cloud of ice
crystals falling into vacuum.

"Seal that breach!" St. Clair ordered, watching the attack
from the vantage points of a dozen external sensors, drones,
and cameras. "Mr. Webb! What the hell did they just hit us
with?"

Subcommander Davis Webb was *Ad Astra*'s weapons officer.

"Unknown, Lord Commander. We're working o. may need to grow a whole new power transfer web."

"Then do it. Fast as you can, Carlos. I don't think we w to play with these people."

That was the hell of being the new kid on the block when it came to interstellar travel. *Everybody* out here was more advanced than Earth.

Within the galactic core, that was almost certainly even truer. The searingly high radiation levels meant that few among these teeming billions of stars would host life, and fewer still would ever give rise to technic civilizations. The three approaching alien vessels, he thought, *must* be from outside the core.

Not that their home address was of any real importance now. What they were *homing* on was another matter.

And, of course, their attitude toward strangers.

"Lord Commander!" Lieutenant Denisova called. "Double image! *Double image!*"

"CAS!" St. Clair snapped. "Bring in the fighters! *Now!*"

The aliens had just revealed a key point of technological superiority.

MERRICK HEARD the order coming down from flight control. "All fighters! Close in on the *Ad Astra!*"

"Accelerating," Colbert, the squadron CO, replied. "What's the sit?"

"The aliens have shifted. You're looking at old data!"

Merrick glanced at his in-head, and saw the icons marking the three alien vessels still some five light-minutes astern of the *Ad Astra*. But when he checked forward, he saw three identical icons now right alongside the O'Neill cylinders and just five hundred kilometers from the human fighters.

There was only one possible explanation. The aliens had jumped to faster-than-light, leapfrogging past the blocking fighters and dropping back into normal space directly along-

"Positrons, Lord Commander. Anti-electrons!"

"The burst didn't go through!" Symm added. "The underdeck reservoir absorbed the beam."

The *Ad Astra* carried her own oceans with her, in a sense—reservoirs of well over a trillion liters of water stored in honeycomb compartments beneath the maintenance levels and ground level of the hab module interiors. The water served as a reserve for drinking, washing, and cooking for the human population; to distribute heat evenly throughout the rotating living spaces; and—vitally—to provide shielding against any radiation that made it past the ship's far-flung magnetic screens.

That water, St. Clair thought, had also just saved the life of every person in the port module. As the alien antimatter beam had clawed through *Ad Astra*'s thin outer hull, it had punctured the ship's skin . . . but then the water gushing out into space had absorbed the beam's hellish energy, annihilating each incoming anti-electron before it could burn deeper into the ship.

The beam snapped off—that was the good news. The bad news was that water continued to erupt into vacuum, freezing instantly as it expanded into a vast and glittering cloud of minute particles.

Ad Astra's grazer turrets had already slewed around to bring them to bear on the alien vessels. A dazzling point of actinic light appeared against the black-and-red hull of one of the intruders, sharp and blindingly intense. An instant later, other gamma-ray lasers in *Ad Astra*'s point defense network joined in, adding their load of coherent energy to that of the first. The alien vessel pivoted sharply, trying to avoid the intolerably brilliant star of light . . . and then with a final flash, the alien's hull burned through and the vessel came apart, bits and pieces of black debris trailing across space, as the main hull section dropped into a slow tumble. The other two aliens were pulling back.

But the first of *Ad Astra*'s fighter squadrons was arriving now, decelerating from high velocity to nearly zero in an instant. One of the alien needles fired a bolt of antimatter particles, engulfing an ASF-99 in a blinding flash of light, hard radiation, and evaporating metal.

But fighters have one key strength in space combat—their unparalleled maneuverability. Low in mass and high powered, gravitic spacecraft can literally move, stop, move again, change direction, dodge, and in an instant be someplace else, making tracking and targeting them a challenge for even the most sophisticated weapons system. NGM-440 Firestorm smart missiles, nuke-tipped and deadly, snapped in toward the surviving aliens, and then *Ad Astra*'s external sensors blanked out as a nuclear fireball erupted against the hull of one of the aliens. The fireball faded, leaving in its place a thin smear of gas and fragments; the lone surviving alien began accelerating out and away from the *Ad Astra*, with a swarm of angry wasp fighters in close, hot pursuit.

"CAS!" St. Clair ordered. "Make sure they kill that last ship!"

"Yes . . . yes, sir."

He heard the puzzlement in her voice. They'd clearly won the battle, and St. Clair's insistence that they destroy that last, fleeing survivor seemed . . . out of character. Needlessly violent. St. Clair, after all, had been chosen to command this mission for his *diplomatic* record, not for any blood-lusting determination to wipe an enemy from the sky.

But he heard her passing his order on to the fighters. He just hoped there was time before the alien went FTL. If they were able to shift to faster-than-light, there was no way in hell the fighters would be able to catch them.

Firestorm missiles lanced out from the pursuing fighters.

The silent pulse of detonations a moment later decisively ended the alien threat.

Weirdly, the image of the three approaching alien ves-

sels remained on *Ad Astra*'s long-range scanners, Einstein ghosts that would not vanish until . . .

Ah. There it was. The ghosts were gone.

And *Ad Astra* and her few, scattered fighters were again alone in the eerie, star-thick jungle of the galactic core.

St. Clair stepped out of the lift tube and into Number
Three conference room. It was located within the outer level
of the ship's Carousel, a wheel two hundred meters across
set into the engineering section's support hull behind and
between the twin hab cylinders. Like the cylinders, the Carousel was rotating—turning a hair slower than three times
per minute to generate one G of spin gravity.

More than two centuries of living and working in space
had amply demonstrated that humans could not tolerate long
periods without gravity. Within just a few months, muscles
began to deteriorate; calcium leached from the bones,
making them weak and fragile; and the heart rate and arte-
rial pressure fell until it became extremely difficult—even
deadly—to re-enter a normal gravity field. Drugs helped,
exercise helped, but there were no good and long-term replacements for gravity in one form or another. Until and
unless the Galactics saw fit to share their secrets of generating artificial gravity at the flick of a switch, human
spacecraft and orbital colonies would have to make do with
cumbersome rotating wheels and cylinders for at least some
of the time their occupants spent in otherwise zero-gravity
environments.

The conference room, one of a suite of offices and compartments dedicated to the running of the civilian aspects of
the ship, was a large space with a dome overhead, centered
on a long mahogany table. Currently, the dome and the deck

beneath were set to display circumambient space; the table, and the UE Directorate seal on one bulkhead, appeared to be floating in space, a vista of starclouds and towering nebulae bright enough that the room didn't need its usual indirect lighting. Stars hung so thickly across that crowded sky that very little empty space showed through. St. Clair glanced at the display and, once again, wondered at the number of brilliant blue and blue-white stars strewn across the background.

A couple of dozen people, department heads, mostly, were already here, waiting for him, standing as he entered the room.

"Sit down, sit down," he said, striding across what appeared to be a transparency stretching above endless starfields. "You people ought to know by now that I don't care for damned Imperial protocol."

Günter Adler pulled a disapproving scowl, one that clearly said, *We'll talk about that later.* The ship's cybercouncil director cared a great deal for formal protocol, and had warned St. Clair about the need to maintain appearances—and official formality—more than once before.

And the UE council director could go fuck himself, St. Clair thought . . . and do so in the most uncomfortable and undignified manner possible.

At least the man hadn't tried scolding St. Clair in front of his officers.

"First things first," St. Clair said, taking his seat. "Mr. Martinez. When will we be able to shift?"

Carlos Martinez was not present physically. He was still aft in Main Engineering, working on the disabled drive, but *Ad Astra*'s electronic networks allowed the chief engineer's image to appear as a holographic projection, while his voice was heard within their in-head circuits.

"I estimate another thirty-six hours, my lord," he said. "As I was afraid, we're having to regrow a substantial portion of the power web, and that takes time."

"You have enough rawmat?"

"We do, sir. Plenty."

"Then do your best. If you can shave a few hours off that estimate, we would all appreciate it. We don't know if those three raiders have friends who might come hunting when they don't show."

Like other large starships, *Ad Astra* drew energy from the vacuum, using artificially generated microsingularities to extract virtual particles as they emerged from the universe's base state in what for all practical purposes were unlimited amounts. The shift drive provided by the Coads was still only poorly understood, though high-order AIs knew how they worked. What was known was that the drive required vast amounts of energy, which it pulled from the singularity power generators through a finely balanced network of phased circuits and field routers known as the power web. The engineering crew was using swarms of nanotech robots to rebuild the damaged portions of the web almost literally atom by atom, and that took time.

Time we might not have.

"What about other repairs?" St. Clair said. "That gash in the port module took out a lot of plumbing."

"Well in hand, my lord," Lieutenant Jacob Weiss said, speaking through another holographic projection. "Damage during the battle was minimal. We have workbots and nano working on the port-hab cylinder now."

"How much water did we lose?"

"An estimated thirty million liters, sir. We've already rebalanced the load to maintain proper spin on the hab."

Thirty million liters out of 1.2 trillion liters in the portside module was almost literally a drop in the bucket.

"How long before we're fully operational again?"

"Six hours, my lord."

"Good." With enough rawmat—raw materials—the ship could repair itself, literally regrowing systems, bulkheads, plumbing, electronics, and structural components out of reservoirs of various elements. The plans for the *Ad Astra* were redundantly stored in Newton's memory down to the nanometer scale, allowing the entire ship to be regrown from scratch if necessary . . . and given enough billions of tons of raw materials.

People, however, were more important than the ship, at least from a humanist standpoint. "Do we have figures on casualties yet?" St. Clair asked.

"Two hundred five dead, my lord," Dr. Genady Sokolov replied. "About eight hundred with significant injuries . . . though that number may increase as further cases come in to the sick bays. All were civilians in the Virginia Beach district of Port Hab. Half of the injuries are radiation poisoning. The rest are contusions, broken bones, and concussions from the rattling the *Ad Astra* got going in toward the black hole. In addition, we lost two fighter pilots in the battle."

St. Clair felt a slight loosening of the knot inside his gut. As horrible as two hundred dead was, he knew the butcher's bill could have been a *lot* worse.

"Is there further risk of radioactive contamination?"

"We lucked out there, Lord Commander," Lieutenant Joy Hutchison told him. She was one of the ship's radiation techs, working out of Engineering. "The enemy's beam did not breach the inner hull or the inhabited spaces above it. It was largely dispersed by the water stores in that section. If there was any contamination, most of it was washed out as the water egressed."

"Most of the rad casualties were maintenance techs," Sokolov added, "in the basement levels."

"Very well," St. Clair said. "Excomm?"

"Sir."

"Please handle the details of memorial services. And get me a list so I can talk to the relatives and families."

"Aye, aye, sir."

"Which brings us to those enemy ships," St. Clair continued. "It would be nice to learn why they attacked us."

"Indeed, Lord Commander," Adler said slowly. "So why, may I ask, did you order the destruction of that last alien ship? I would think that *prisoners* could tell us more than the spectroscopic analyses of hot clouds of gas."

"That alien ship, my lord, had already demonstrated the ability to flash over into FTL despite its small size. To use FTL on a *tactical* scale, as opposed to the purely strategic. If it had succeeded in shifting, it would have returned to wherever it came from, and taken with it an analysis of whatever intelligence it had managed to pick up. Our size and mass. Our weaponry. Our defensive screens. Our fighters. An estimate of our overall technology levels. And he would have returned. With enough friends to finish us off."

"They might still come anyway."

"Maybe. And that's why I would like to get out of this area just as quickly as Mr. Martinez gets our stardrive ticking again. But if none of their ships return, we'll have some additional time. Maybe those three ships were on patrol, and not scheduled to check in with their base for . . . I don't know. Days. Weeks. Longer. Too, even if their HQ knows they're missing, they'll be cautious about sending a force in after them. They won't know a damned thing about us . . . except for the fact that we took out their ships."

"The skipper's right, Lord Adler," Symm said. "We were lucky with that first attack. The aliens are way ahead of us technologically, especially in weaponry and in material fabrication."

"The weapons I understand," Adler said. "But what does fabrication have to do with anything?"

"We had multiple high-energy gamma-ray lasers focused on one part of the alien's hull . . . how many, Davis?"

"Seventeen, sir," Webb replied. "Six twin turrets, plus five individual meteor defense beams."

"Seventeen beams, and it took almost *two whole seconds* to burn through that vessel's hull. If that ship had been one of ours, it would have been vaporized within milliseconds."

"Well . . . even so," Adler said, "prisoners would have been good."

"Taking prisoners was not an option, my lord," St. Clair said. "So we look for intelligence from other sources. Dr. Dumont."

Dr. Francois Dumont was a civilian, one of the expedition's senior xenosophontologists. His specialty was xeno-technology, and what that might tell *Ad Astra*'s population about beings that were not even remotely human.

"Sir."

"What do we have on those alien ships? Anything?"

"We sent work pods outside to retrieve some of the wreckage, sir. The analysis has proven . . . interesting."

"Tell me."

"The fragments we brought in, my lord, were entirely composed of computronium."

"Computronium! What . . . *all* of it?"

"We recovered several hundred kilos of material, my lord, from different parts of the debris field. While there would certainly have been some parts of the ship devoted to drive, power generation, and weaponry, it appears that most of the vessel was an extremely large and well-organized computer."

Computronium was a type of material first hypothesized by computer scientists at MIT two centuries before, a substance also known as "programmable matter." The idea was that matter could be designed and arranged in a way that allowed that matter to serve as a highly efficient computing device. Technically, the human brain itself was an organic form of computronium, and various types of smart clothing, smart buildings and rooms—even smart cities—had been in common use for the past couple of hundred years. There was no reason, St. Clair supposed, that the aliens might not have spacecraft that were in fact large, highly mobile, weapons-bearing robots.

But the thought was disquieting. After a brief flirtation with AI killing machines in the Second American Revolution, human robotics programs had taken a distinctly pacifistic turn. According to the Fifth Geneva Protocol, signed in 2087, sentient machines were never to be used as soldiers. The resolution was established for good and carefully considered reasons.

One of these was the realization that the notorious Three Laws of Robotics, crafted by a well-known science-fiction writer more than a century before the Fifth Protocol, could not possibly work as advertised. There were loopholes in the Three Laws' logic. For example, what if allowing one man to live—an Adolph Hitler, say, or a Josef Stalin—led inevitably to the deaths of millions? A sentient robot operating under the Three Laws would be caught in a crippling paradox.

Or suppose a robot was presented with the famous trolley paradox: an observer sees an out-of-control railcar hurtling toward a group of people standing on the tracks. The observer can do nothing, and watch several people being killed. *Or* he can throw a switch and direct the car onto a siding, where only a single person is standing. Which is the correct ethical choice: do nothing, and allow a number of people to be killed? Or deliberately kill one to save the others? Ethically, throwing the switch would be exactly the same as directly shoving a stranger off a platform and into the path of an oncoming train, forcing the train to stop and thereby saving the lives of others farther down the track. A robot bound by the Three Laws would suffer the electronic equivalent of a nervous breakdown. It might avoid the conflict by destroying the train—unaware that there were hundreds of people on board.

So the Fifth Geneva Protocol was designed to avoid such paradoxes by forbidding the use of autonomous robots in warfare. Using them to kill people was fine if a human was in the loop—military drone operators had been doing that since the late twentieth century. But a robot couldn't decide for itself to end a human life.

Even more important, though, was the realization that the evolution of artificial intelligence would not, *could* not simply stop once robots reached the same general level of intelligence as humans. They would continue to develop and evolve, and at a far, *far* faster rate than was possible for merely organic systems.

And developing thinking beings superior in every respect to humans and giving them a killer's instinct was widely assumed to be distinctly contra-survival for the species as a whole.

And the survival of these 1 million humans was definitely in jeopardy at the moment.

"So you're saying we're up against robots?" St. Clair asked.

"Possibly," Dumont replied. "Or cybernetic organisms. But both the physical examination and spectrographic analyses of the gasses released by the explosion failed to turn up any trace of indisputably organic matter."

"What do you mean, 'indisputably'?" Adler asked.

"There was plenty of carbon in the recovered material," Dumont told him. "But there was less potassium, calcium, nitrogen, and other elements than would be expected if there'd been organic beings inside."

"The aliens' biochemistry might be pretty different," Sokolov pointed out.

"True, Doctor, but not *that* different. If there were organic beings inside those ships, we would expect to have found at least a few traces. What we did find was this."

He made an in-head connection, and a fragment of alien material, hugely magnified, appeared hanging in the air above the conference table, looking like a finely etched maze of lines, silver against polished black.

"The deep structure is quite remarkable," Dumont went on. The fragment expanded, the magnification increasing. As silver lines thickened and passed out of the image, new, much finer lines appeared . . . lines within lines within lines. "Fractal. Finer and finer levels of detail, the deeper in you go. Whoever designed this had an incredible grasp of both microarchitecture and nanotech engineering. We suspect that they work with holographic software."

St. Clair wondered what that might mean, but elected to let it pass, at least for the time being. He looked at the Medusae Liaison, hovering by the table to his left in its sealed, dripping pod. "Liaison? I must ask this again. You are certain these ship types are unknown to you? They're not the Deniers you've mentioned?"

"They are not, Humans."

"Couldn't you be mistaken? It seems to be too much of a coincidence that these unknowns should attack your stronghold at the galactic core now, while you're fighting this other group."

"We do not recognize the ship design, Humans. And we have not been able to contact others of the Coadunation. Something is very wrong with space."

"What do you mean?"

"He's right, my lord," Subcommander Valerie Holt of the astrogation department said, when the Liaison failed to reply immediately. "We've noted a certain anomaly. It is possible that we are no longer in our own Galaxy at all."

"That makes no sense at all," Adler snapped, angry. "How the hell—"

"Let her talk," St. Clair interrupted. "Tell us what you mean, Subcommander."

"This is what the galactic core looks like now." She gestured at the thickly clotted stars stretched across the conference-room dome. "And this is what they looked like a few minutes ago, as we were approaching Harmony." The stars shimmering around them shifted before refocusing themselves into a completely different arrangement. "A shift of five light years is *not* enough to make this big a difference."

The stars were too thickly strewn to allow them to see anything as easy to recognize as a constellation, but the differences were still clear to see. The dark shapes of looming thunderheads—nebulae encircling the core—were thick and ominous in both, but were completely reshaped. The shapes of star clouds, the positions of the nearest, most brilliant stars, all were different.

More than that, however, were changes in the numbers of bright stars. In the earlier image, some hundreds of stars in the sky were what would be considered extremely bright; the nearest, according to changes in its parallax as the ship moved deeper into the core, was about twelve light-days away.

But in the later image, *thousands* of stars gleamed at that magnitude, and the nearest were only a light-day or so distant.

Other structures had changed as well. Images taken earlier showed a single thick nebular cloud completely encircling the sky, a vast wheel of dust and gas illuminated by brilliant young suns and with the SMBH—Sagittarius A*—at its hub. Now, St. Clair could distinctly see a second wheel arcing across the sky at an angle to the first, masked in places by the thronging near-suns, but itself highlighted by a dazzling spray of young, hot blue stars.

"The differences are not just at optical wavelengths," Holt went on, as the ship's officers stared up at the sky in stunned silence. "Here is the sky at radio wavelengths before . . . and now. In infrared before . . . and now. And in X-rays before . . . and now."

The change was, if anything, more pronounced at other

wavelengths. The heart of the Milky Way Galaxy had always spit out a fairly constant hiss of radio noise, and had glowed brightly at infrared and X-ray wavelengths. But now, the noise was vastly greater, and the galactic core was lit from within by a storm of hot radiation.

Add to that the fact that Sagittarius A* itself had doubled in mass and St. Clair could easily understand why Holt was suggesting that they'd somehow been transposed to the central core of another galaxy, that the SMBH was a different central black hole entirely. This wasn't the same place at *all*.

"Subcomm Adams," he said. "Does it look to you like we've jumped to another galaxy?"

"Sir . . . that's just not *possible*!" She was staring up at the sky displayed across the overhead dome, hands before her splayed on the table, her face wet with tears.

"I didn't ask you if it was possible. I asked you if that was what seems to have happened."

"I . . . I don't know how else to explain it, my lord."

"There's one possibility . . ." Symm said, her voice hesitant.

"Go ahead, Excomm."

"Well, there's been speculation for centuries that black holes might be the entrance to wormholes—shortcuts past normal space. And there've been theories that supermassive black holes might connect to one another somehow, linked by those wormholes. If we fell into Sagittarius A-Star . . ."

"We fell into the SMBH at the center of our Galaxy," St. Clair said, completing the thought for her, "and popped up at the center of a different galaxy. Is that what you're saying."

"Something like that, my lord."

Dr. Paul Tsang Wanquan shifted in his seat. "There is some evidence that we might now be at the core of M-31, my lord. The star densities are similar."

"Andromeda?" St. Clair said. He shook his head. "I don't buy it."

Tsang was head of *Ad Astra*'s astronomy department. "The Andromedan Galaxy," he pointed out, "is considerably larger than our Milky Way. An estimated one *trillion* stars. And the central core is more densely packed than ours." He gestured at the sky. "It might well look much like this."

"It's also something like two and a half million light years away," St. Clair said.

"But if the central black holes are connected by a wormhole, my lord—" Symm began.

"We would still have to pass through one SMBH ergosphere," St. Clair pointed out, "and we would emerge *inside* the ergosphere of another." He shook his head. "I get the theory, but damn it, we would be spaghettified going in, and whatever was left would not be able to escape coming out. It makes no *sense*."

"There is another possible alternative," the voice of Third Navigator said.

"We're listening."

"We might still be within our own Galaxy, but we have moved forward in time."

"Time dilation?" St. Clair asked.

"Either relativistic time dilation, or we encountered a Lorentzian manifold through frame-dragging. We do not yet possess enough data to determine which, if either."

"Relativistic time dilation I understand," St. Clair said. "The deeper we fall into a gravity field, the slower time passes for us. From our point of view, time in the universe outside appears to pass more and more quickly. I don't know about that manifold stuff, though. Can you put it into English?"

A different voice replied in their heads, deeper, and more sonorous—the voice of Newton. "Frame-dragging was predicted in a paper presented by two Austrian physicists,

Lense and Thirring, in 1918," the computer told them. "They predicted that the rotation of a massive object would distort the nearby spacetime matrix. Another physicist, Frank Tipler, predicted in a 1974 paper that the Lense-Thirring effect might open pathways, called closed timelike curves, or CTC, that would permit travel forward or backward in time, and across vast distances of space."

"Tipler machines," St. Clair said, remembering. "Yeah, Tipler said that an advanced civilization might build huge, extremely dense cylinders rotating around their long axes and use them as time machines. Except, didn't later studies prove that the cylinder would need to be of infinite length to allow travel through time?"

"Yes. However, it is possible that a sufficiently massive black hole might generate a frame-dragging effect within its immediate vicinity."

"Is that what happened to us?"

"It is impossible to say in our current situation, Lord Commander," Newton replied.

"How can we find out?"

"Star densities in this region of space," Newton replied, "together with the densities of gas and dust clouds in the area, make it impossible to see beyond the innermost region of this galaxy's central core. We would need to shift at least fifteen to twenty thousand light years to get a perspective on our surroundings from outside."

"Can't we penetrate the dust with IR?"

Momentarily, the sky display shifted to the infrared view they'd been shown earlier. Vast swaths of red light blotted out huge stretches of sky, and myriad red stars glowed brightly everywhere else.

"Infrared lets us see through that crap a little," Tsang said, "but we don't yet understand *what* we're seeing. We know it's different. But we don't know what anything is."

The projected display returned to a view at optical

wavelengths, showing the sky around the *Ad Astra*. It felt, St. Clair thought, terribly, achingly lonely.

"There's not much we can do, then," St. Clair said, "except wait for Engineering to complete repairs to the stardrive. Is there anything else on the agenda?"

There was not, and the meeting was adjourned.

"We need to talk, Lord Commander," Adler told him as the others were filing out beneath that alien nebulae-crowded sky. "In my office, I think."

Adler's holographic flickered and winked off.

Here it comes, St. Clair thought.

GÜNTER ADLER'S office-residence was located in a different part of *Ad Astra*, in a villa located in the hills beneath the port hab endcap not far from Seattle. Getting there involved an elevator trip up one of the Carousel's spokes to a transfer station at its hub, then a tube journey of more than two kilometers through endless gray passageways, angling to the left, then sharply right to emerge at the hub of the port hab.

The view out along the interior of one of the hab modules was stunning, one that always made the breath catch a bit in St. Clair's throat. The interior of the cylinder was brilliantly lit by the sunbeam running down its length. Land—parkland, woods, terraced fields, villages and hamlets and the far-off gleam of larger cities—stretched across the hab's inner surface. The curving expanse of land was broken here and there by the gleam of water—lakes and ponds, several small rivers, and even a more generous stretch of water dividing the interior surface in two near the middle. Clouds floated between sunbeam and surface, casting scattered shadows across open ground.

Since St. Clair had emerged at the cylinder's hub, he was currently in zero-G, and distinctions like "up" and "down" were arbitrary courtesies. He used handrails to pull himself into a nearby transparent slidetube and accelerated gently down the inner curve of the cylinder's aft endcap, all the way to the director's villa about halfway down.

Adler enjoyed his comfort. The villa, at the half-G level, had pretty much the same spectacular view as at the hub, with the cylinder's inner surface curving up and around in a complete circle, and following the lines of perspective into the far, hazy distance—the forward endcap some thirty-two kilometers down the tube. The city of Seattle was almost directly in front of St. Clair, but overhead, stretched across the upper arc of the tube's surface, upside down from his current vantage point.

Adler and a couple of women were waiting for him on the villa's extensive deck, all three of them naked.

Great, St. Clair thought. *He's in one of those moods. . . .*

St. Clair had no problem with casual social nudity, which, after all, had been the norm on Earth for well over a century now. What he objected to was Adler's attitude, which assumed that others were there solely to enhance his position and authority. It was well known that the Director thought of the women in his household as possessions. The old term "trophy wife" might have been coined to describe Clara Adler, and people in *Ad Astra*'s upper social strata assumed that he programmed his gynoids to engage in blatantly lascivious behavior in public. Of the two women on the deck with him, one was Clara, a dark-haired human, but the blond was an sw-series gynoid, an identical model to his own Lisa.

What St. Clair disliked was the way he treated them as "his" women, a means of displaying his personal power.

The villa's gate opened for him and he stepped onto the deck. "Welcome, Lord Commander," Adler told him. "Make yourself comfortable! A soak, perhaps?" He gestured at the nearby pool and hot tub. "Tina! Help our guest get comfortable."

St. Clair was feeling seriously overdressed, but he shook his head. "Thank you, Lord Director. No." He waved the gynoid off. "You asked to see me, sir. What did you want to talk to me about?"

"Come on inside."

Director Adler's office was in the upper floor of the villa, with broad, floor-to-ceiling windows overlooking the spectacular hollow of the port-side hab. A storm was coming up the valley. St. Clair could see the cloud, halfway between sunbeam and surface, and the long, dark gray haze of rainfall curving away beneath. Coriolis force, generated by the module's rotation, caused falling objects to appear to curve; a rain cloud could drop its load of precipitation directly above a city . . . but the rain would water the ground well outside the city limits.

Still naked, Adler entered the office, but he picked a uniform pack from a bowl by the door and slapped it against his chest. The nanofibers inside swiftly wove him a new uniform as he walked across the room, complete with medals, ribbons, and gold braid against the dress black; boots; and the elaborate sunburst gorget of the Imperial Order of Earth. *From nude to peacock*, St. Clair thought, *in two point three seconds. Not bad.*

St. Clair now felt seriously *under*dressed in his shipboard utilities, which were bare, save for the gold-star rank tabs at his throat. And that, of course, was the whole idea. Adler never did anything without carefully considered purpose, usually one involving dominating others in one way or another.

"Drink, Lord Commander?"

"No, sir."

"I wanted to talk to you, St. Clair, about your unwillingness to embrace certain basic . . . amenities of protocol. Having your subordinates stand as you enter a room, having them refer to you as 'Lord Commander' or 'my lord,' those all are marks of respect which are your due. And waiving them creates a serious lapse in good order and discipline."

"While adhering to them too diligently gets in the way of both efficiency and common sense. Sir."

Adler scowled as he settled into place behind his broad, horseshoe desk with its built-in workstation. "Nonsense.

Protocol, proper protocol, is the lubricant upon which military command moves. Without it, we have anarchy."

"I'm sure you believe that to be true," St. Clair replied. "But I respectfully submit, my lord, that according to this mission's charter, exactly how I run my command is up to me."

He was picking his words carefully now. Adler had the power to replace him—or the UE Civilian Directorate Council he headed did. At the same time, however, Adler was trespassing on St. Clair's bureaucratic territory. If he caved on this issue, he might as well turn military control of the expedition over to the CDC.

"You're a connie, aren't you?" Adler asked, his voice mild . . . and perhaps a touch guarded.

"I'm a constitutionalist, sir, yes. That's hardly a secret." It was listed as such in his personnel records.

"Rule of law, and all of that."

"Yes . . ." Where was the man going with this?

"Meaning you don't care for the Directorate. For the *idea* of the Directorate."

Ah. *That* was what he was getting at. "I don't like the idea of autocrats who can get around established legal systems and precedents with a signatory thumbprint. That's tyranny . . . in my opinion, sir. I don't like the idea of bureaucrats who use *fear*—fear of prison, fear of military force, fear of taxation or legal penalties—to enforce their will on the populace. That is also tyranny. And I don't like demagogues who enforce their will by stirring up the citizenry through appeals to democracy. That inevitably *leads* to tyranny. Sir."

Adler feigned surprise. "You don't care for democracy?"

"I don't care for mob rule, Lord Director. And mob rule is where fifty-one percent of the population can deprive the other forty-nine percent of its most basic rights."

"Ah. You know your Jefferson."

"Actually, my lord, we don't have any proof that Jefferson said that. But he could have. In any case, a republic runs the state through *representative* government *under law*—a constitution. A democracy runs the state directly, through majority rule—and tends to appeal to the largest and loudest groups to do so."

Adler sighed. "Lord Commander, I really didn't call you here to have you give me a civics lecture. The fact is you're on record as having opposed certain Imperial decisions."

"Absolutely. But having made my opposition known, as is my prerogative as a lord and an officer, I have continued to obey the orders given to me."

The legal *orders*, he amended to himself, but he didn't say that aloud.

"Yes, yes you have," Adler said, thoughtful. "Your loyalty is not in question here, Commander St. Clair. But your, ah—call it your sense of decorum—is. That, and perhaps your common sense as well. I will not have you generating anarchy within this command through your *republican* sensibilities."

"We threw the Republicans out with the Democrats, Lord Director."

That had been almost a century ago, during AR II, the bloody Second American Revolution. A slow deterioration of the long-running American experiment with a constitutional republic had ended in wholesale corruption, weak and venal leadership, the steady erosion of the original U.S. Constitution's Bill of Rights, and eventually with mob rule. The revolution had succeeded in bringing down an entrenched, utterly corrupt government, but the attempt to restore the rule of law ultimately had failed. After two decades of anarchy, the establishment of the First CyberDirectorate, in 2101, had brought about peace and at least the semblance of normality.

So far as St. Clair was concerned, however, there was

no difference whatsoever between Imperial decrees and the executive orders used by the corrupt American presidents of years past to get around Congress or the Supreme Court. The Cybercouncil in Clarkeorbital One had decided to pursue an alliance with the Galactics after a closed session, with no discussion, no input from the scientific community, and no public debate—a classic case of Big Bureaucracy assuming that they knew what was best for all.

In short: tyranny.

"Yes, we threw them out. The Directorate," Adler told him, a teacher lecturing a somewhat backward child, "was inevitable. Attempts to create a new constitution were foundering in confusion and bickering. Keller and the First Directorate stepped in and brought *order* out of anarchy."

Which, St. Clair thought, could equally be said of Napoleon, Hitler, or Stalin. He decided not to say so, however. This was not an argument he could win.

"Yes, sir."

"I want you to put more effort into proper decorum and protocol," Adler went on. He gestured at St. Clair's utilities. "Wear uniforms appropriate to your rank when you're on duty, for God's sake. The way you're dressed now, you could be mistaken for an enlisted man."

"Oh, and that would be *horrible*. Sir."

Adler ignored the sarcasm. "You also will accept the appropriate honorifics and addresses." He must have seen the pained expression cross St. Clair's face. "What? What in God's name is so wrong with Imperial titles?"

"Excuse me, my lord, but it's all nonsense. When we picked up those first alien transmissions in 'eighty-eight, we realized that just about everyone we met out among the stars would be way beyond us. Maybe so far beyond that we didn't have a chance of understanding them, and so we developed a whopping great inferiority complex. To counteract that, we began pushing to unify the planet, and developed this *myth* of the Directorate as some kind of an empire, complete with imperial titles and forms of address and military ranks all designed to make us feel good about ourselves."

"Lord Commander—are you in fact a sociologist?"

"No, my lord."

"Then don't blather about what you patently do *not* understand. It demonstrates your ignorance."

"Not to mention how neolithically primitive I truly am."

"I also want you to pay more attention to your exchanges with the Liaison," Adler said, ignoring St. Clair's snide remark once more. "Don't risk offending him! We need him, need his cooperation out here."

" 'It,' sir."

"What?"

"The Liaison is an 'it,' my lord. Not a 'he.' It's a hermaphrodite, or at least that's what we believe to be the case. So we either call it 'it,' or we use the formal 'shehe' and 'hiser' pronouns."

"Whatever. In any case, don't press himher on matters shehe obviously doesn't wish to discuss. Understand me?"

"Perfectly, sir."

"Excellent. We'll say no more about it, then."

"Thank you, my lord."

"One thing more."

"My lord?"

"I was disturbed at the loose talk in the briefing just now. Tsang, especially. And Holt."

"What do you mean, sir?" For once in this conversation, St. Clair was genuinely perplexed.

"That crazy talk of theirs about having jumped to another galaxy."

Oh—that. "We need to consider every possibility, my lord. The truth is, we don't know where we are. Or even *when*. We need to get that sorted out if we're ever to get back home again."

"But that sort of talk could easily spread panic throughout the colony. Same for this nonsense about having moved into the future."

"As I recall, Lord Director, it was Third Navigator who first raised that possibility. The AIs on board are under the direction of Newton. Shall we reprogram them to steer clear of alarming possibilities? To think only happy thoughts?"

"Don't be smart with me, Lord Commander." St. Clair had apparently crossed a line with Adler. "I want you to pass the word through your command—all department heads and senior personnel—that such speculation should be considered classified. They are not to share it with civilians, not even those they live with."

"My lord . . . we're all on this vessel together. All of us. We can't hide the truth—"

"We can and we will . . . unless you seriously want to entertain that mob rule you say you don't care for."

"I don't have access to Newton's programming or security codes, sir."

"Never mind. I do, and I'll take care of that. Now . . . anything else? Any problems you wish to discuss?"

"No, my lord."

"Good. I'm glad we had this little talk. You may go, now."

St. Clair managed to control the slow burn of his anger. The arrogant, condescending *bastard*.

He decided to take the straight-line path back to his home in the starboard hab, rather than wending his way back up the port-side endcap and into the CCE section. He took the slidetube near the villa and continued down into the port cylinder's landscape. An inter-cylinder pod station was located at the slidetube's terminus.

The no-frills pod was cramped and spartan to the point of being starkly utilitarian. It was, he thought, just the thing to reconfirm his anti-aristocratic bias. He took a seat inside, told the computer his desired destination, and then waited as the O'Neill cylinders ground on in their slow and stately revolutions, one turn every forty seconds.

"Pod ejection in five seconds," the computer's voice announced. "Three . . . two . . . one . . . release."

St. Clair dropped precipitously into free fall, and space exploded around him. The drop pod, accelerated by the starboard cylinder's spin, traveled into the 4-kilometer empty gap between the two hab modules at 10 meters per second.

The walls of his pod appeared to be transparent. In fact, though, they were displaying visual data from cameras mounted on the outside hull; the illusion was perfect. It felt like sitting inside a huge glass egg. Above his head, the port cylinder slowly dwindled in size. Perhaps ten kilometers away, toward the port hab's prow, he could see the glitter of machines and scaffolding where the ship's maintenance systems were repairing the damaged section close to the port-side town of Virginia Beach. Repairs were well under way, now, with no major problems, thank God. The toughest problem was going to be finding a replacement for the lost water. Once the ship's stardrive was repaired, though, they would be able to jump to a nearby star system and restock.

At his feet, the starboard cylinder grew larger, approaching second by slow second.

Everywhere else, stars crowded against one another in spectacular profusion.

In perfect silence, the pod drifted across the gap in precisely 6 minutes and 36 seconds, rotating end for end halfway across. Now, St. Clair dropped toward the starboard cylinder, the dark gray of its hull sweeping past his feet as he got closer . . . closer . . .

And then, just as he reached the hull, a drop tube swept over the horizon and met the pod in perfect synchronization, the computer having timed his release so that he met the receiving tube. St. Clair felt the tug of acceleration as the moving tube walls swept him up, and the sharp deceleration as the tube slowed his fall. Moments later, he emerged at a drop tube station in the starboard cylinder not far from the town of Bethesda, less than half a kilometer from his home.

A slidewalk took him the rest of the way, carrying him partway up the rising curve of the starboard endcap. It would have taken him nearly twenty minutes had he ridden the subsurface railpods back to the CCE section, across the engineering section's width, then back into the other hab. This route was nearly as long, but had spectacular views. An escalator carried him through an explosion of brilliantly colored subtropical plants—bougainvillea, Australia pine, poinciana, firebush—and beneath the massive spread of banyan canopies. Brightly colored birds flashed and darted among the branches, and a brocket deer watched him suspiciously from a sheltered vantage point above a small waterfall. *Ad Astra* was a true deep-space colony as well as a starship; it had brought along its own extensive ecosystem across the light years to the galactic core.

St. Clair's house was similar in many respects to Adler's—not identical, by any means, but a sprawling villa enjoying the same vaguely Spanish architecture, the same broad, multilevel decks, the same low gravity and spectacular view. The place was a bit more deeply secluded in pine and banyan forest than Adler's villa, and felt somewhat more remote. Part of the place was cantilevered out over the sheer drop of the endcap cliffs, and a waterfall, descending from the low-gravity portions of the endcap higher up, cascaded into emptiness below, creating a perpetual cloud of mist anchored by a shimmering rainbow.

He hoped his private retreat didn't seem quite so ostentatious as Adler's. When he'd first come aboard the *Ad Astra*, St. Clair had been determined to stick with the officer's quarters in the CCE's main Carousel. He didn't need all of this space for himself, and he would have to give it all up in any case, once *Ad Astra* had abandoned the *Tellus* habitats at Harmony.

But the UE Military Command Directorate, in its infinite wisdom, had ordered him to move in. He suspected they wanted to make a political statement to the effect that St. Clair was Adler's equal in every way, including perks of office.

Besides, there was Lisa to think of. . . .

The front door recognized him and slid open. "Hey, Lise. I'm home."

"Grayson!" She crossed the sunken living room and was in his arms. "I'm so glad you're back!" She seemed to catch something in his expression. "Are you okay?"

"A hell of a day—what happened to your arm?"

She looked at her bent left arm and shrugged. "Eh . . . broke it when we hit that rough spot a little while ago. The house autorepair unit stopped the leaking, but said I need to have it replaced."

"You should have gone in right away."

She stood on tiptoes to kiss him. "I wanted to wait for you."

Lisa had been manufactured by the General Nanodynamics Corporation in San Francisco, North California, and hired—the company really hated using the word *purchased*—through Robocompanions Unlimited. St. Clair had, well, *acquired* her two years ago, after his wife left him. She was perfect, a human analogue so detailed and lifelike that the infamous Uncanny Valley had been left far behind. The damage to her arm was particularly disturbing, in fact, because it raised echoes of the Uncanny Valley effect; a human arm shouldn't *do* that.

"Let's get that taken care of right away," he told her.

"Of course, Grayson."

"And I think we need to upgrade your independence level."

ONCE, SEX dolls had been little more than jokes—inflatable rubber toys used for masturbation by sad little men unable to talk to real women. In the 1990s, a German firm had begun marketing Andy Roid, a lifelike doll selling for around $10,000 that mimicked breathing, a heartbeat, and pulse, and could even fake an orgasm when her G-spot was stimulated. The more expensive models even had body temperatures of thirty-seven degrees.

Needless to say, these sex dolls had been controversial— sex objects offering a warm body with no brains behind it and no chance of rejection. The things had always been ready and willing when it came to sex.

They'd also been popular, despite the large price tag. By the mid-21st century, Andy's descendents still couldn't think, but they could carry on a reasonable conversation—at least on a rather limited range of topics primarily involving human reproductive activities. Not until the 2090s had General Nanodynamics and others begun giving their products artificial intelligence. Lisa possessed a Grade 3 GND-4040 Brilliant Thought graphene-chip sentience emulator, an electronic brain that was supposed to provide artificial intelligence, but not actual self-aware consciousness. The fact that AI robots equipped with Brilliant Thought systems *claimed* to be self-aware had not been advertised. A majority of organic humans, when polled, approved of artificial intelligence in general, but not when it looked like them.

For Lisa 776, the question was largely meaningless. *She* knew she was intelligent, and she knew that she was self-aware. The fact that purely organic minds couldn't get inside her head and feel what she felt didn't invalidate her own perceptions.

Human arguments appeared to fall into two general categories—from those afraid that intelligent robots would replace humans, and from those who felt that manufacturing intelligent robots was akin to slavery. Both felt that sentient machines should be abolished, and yet AI robots were so unequivocally *useful* that there was little real danger of that happening.

Not unless the robots themselves rose up and threw off their own shackles.

In Lisa's case, there was a certain moral imperative to those arguments. The "sw" in her identifier label stood for *sex worker*; sentient she might be, but she'd been originally manufactured for exactly the same job as Andy Roid. For some humans, the role was degrading and a form of slavery; others wondered if her kind might eventually replace human women (and men)—compliant, willing, eager to please, and very, *very* talented in the physical aspects of recreational sex.

The thing was, Lisa was happy being what she was. Never mind that she'd been programmed to be happy with her simulated life (or at least to emulate that emotional state for the sake of the humans around her). Organic humans, she realized, were also programmed—by genetics, by upbringing, by culture and societal norms, by education, and by life experience. So far as she was concerned, there was no difference, no difference at all. An upgrade to her independence level? Her sense of independence, of self-worth, initiative, and power of will all were just fine, thank you. Changing the flow of current through certain receptors and decision-tree processors would change nothing.

But an important part of her program included a willingness to go along with whatever her human suggested, and she happily accompanied him to the GND robotics center in Bethesda. It took all of ten minutes to swap out her left arm and heal the torn skin, and another thirty to link into her AI hardware and adjust her attitude. They left the center, and St. Clair suggested that they get something to eat while they were in town.

"No," she said.

"I beg your pardon?"

"I'm a robot, Grayson. I don't eat."

"Well, I'm starved." He stopped, turned, and gave her a searching look. "Why? What would you rather do?"

"Go back to the house and fuck."

St. Clair laughed. "Sounds like your attitude adjustment just now took pretty well!"

Lisa ran through an interior checklist. "I feel no different than before."

"Of course. Well . . . I'm not a machine, and I need fuel." He pointed. "The Inner World is good. I'll tell you what. I'm going to go have dinner there. You can come with me, or you can go back home. And either way we'll play when I get back."

She appeared to consider the possibility. "A compromise, then?"

"Exactly."

"Very well. But you should be aware that I'm going along with this only because you're going to need *all* your strength this evening."

"Okay, then! Let's go!"

The Inner World was an atmospheric restaurant built around the theme of a cavern, with dim lighting, dangling stalactites and up-thrust stalagmites, a central pond and waterfall, and whole walls of dazzling colored crystal. Robotic waitstaff brought drinks and took orders. Music took on a deeper, richer resonance in the grottoes.

Lisa's "meal" was a symbolic one—water to drink, and a plate of holographic food that gradually disappeared as she pretended to eat it. It was just one small part of the grand illusion perpetrated by robots on a day-to-day basis to protect the easily shocked sensibilities of their human companions. Grayson St. Clair, Lisa was forced to admit, wasn't bothered by such things. He *had* been upset by the sight of her arm earlier . . . but she told herself that he would have been upset seeing a human arm bent out of true by a compound fracture.

She found herself wondering, though, about the Uncanny Valley effect, that sense among humans that a robot that was *almost* human was disturbing. It seemed that the more human a robot appeared, short of absolute perfection in its mimicry both of physical appearance and of the most subtle of expressions, eye blinks, movement, and a host of other effects, the more uncomfortable a human interacting with the robot became. *Creepy* was the word most often used to describe a robot that hadn't quite reached perfection. Non-human robots weren't a problem; only when they became almost human, but not quite, did the Uncanny Valley effect make itself known.

Her thoughts along those lines were . . . disturbing. Basically, she found herself wondering *why* robots should be expected to achieve that perfection. Why shouldn't the humans simply deal with it. It was their thought process, after all, their emotional response to certain triggers. Why should avoiding those triggers be the full responsibility of the robots?

She'd never thought like this before.

St. Clair seemed to enjoy his meal—a culture steak from the starboard cylinder's tissue farms. Her meal was a holographic projection of the same thing. After several pretended bites, however, Lisa put her cutlery aside.

"You're not eating?" St. Clair asked.

"There's hardly any point, is there?"

He blinked. "Sorry. Force of habit. You're right, of course."

"I understand that my pretending to eat is to smooth our relationship, to make it easier for you to accept me as a human. But I also understand that you understand that I am a machine."

"Well, it's important that you fit in, I suppose, but only because it's easier that way. If you don't want to pretend to eat, that's your affair."

"It doesn't bother you?"

"Not in the least." He grinned at her. "I want you to do whatever makes you happy."

"I am happy. I'm merely reevaluating certain of my decision trees. It occurs to me that there are things I could do without taking into account what you might want."

"Indeed there are. Obviously, I'd rather you not call too much attention to us when we're out in public, so if you get the urge to do that little dance you do so well, I'll ask you to wait until we get home." He was grinning.

"My dancing on the table would be inappropriate."

"Very much so."

"I'll keep that in mind. Taking off my clothes here would be inappropriate."

"I think so, yes. There's nothing wrong with public nudity most places nowadays, but it might bother the other patrons. Especially if you were noisy or demonstrative about it."

"Having sex with you on this table would be inappropriate."

His smile slowly faded. "What's going on with you, Lisa? You've never asked questions like these before."

She gave a quite human shrug. "Within my programming is a long, long list of things that I should not do—things that are inappropriate, or socially inept, or which are associated with judgmental terms such as 'vulgar' or 'obscene' or 'wrong.' I find myself suddenly wondering something."

"What?"

"Why?"

St. Clair paused for a second, sitting back as if to fully contemplate his answer. Finally he said, "Human culture is rather complicated, Lise. A lot of the things we do don't make sense to me, either. But getting along with other humans, especially when they come in groups . . . well, if we don't play by the rules, we make life a lot more difficult for ourselves. I have no problem at all if you—"

St. Clair stopped in mid-sentence, almost in mid-word, staring into space past Lisa's left shoulder.

"Grayson? What's wrong?"

She opened an electronic channel, then, and heard the voice of someone on *Ad Astra*'s bridge crew, the voice St. Clair was hearing now.

". . . sorry to interrupt you, my lord, but we need you up here, now!"

"What is it?" St. Clair's mental voice asked.

"Another ship, sir. It's *big*. And it's on an intercept course."

"I'll be right up." St. Clair's eyes refocused on Lisa's. "Lise—"

"I heard, love. Go on."

"I'll see you when I get back."

She nodded. "But don't think this gets you off the hook. I'll be waiting for you . . ."

He leaned over and kissed her. "Good. But just to be safe . . . no dancing naked on the table while I'm gone.

"Wait until we're both home."

St. Clair wasn't overly concerned about Lisa's behavior.
She was smart, and could figure things out with better logic
and sharper reasoning ability than most humans he knew.
He was going to have to keep an eye on her for a few days,
though, if only to determine how the adjustments they'd
made to her programmable attitude were going to affect
his relationship with her. Overall, though, he was happy for
her—he was a free-minder.

What he wasn't happy about was the massive ship heading their way.

He hurried to the bridge. The subsurface realms of both
O'Neill cylinders were honeycombed by transit tubes, and
subway kiosks could be found on almost every block of the
various towns and cities. Mag-lev transit cars didn't run on
a schedule, but instead were routed by the colony's computer network whenever sensors detected someone entering
a kiosk. He slapped the palm of his hand against a sensor
to transmit his priority override code. Symm had sounded
worried.

As he waited for a pod to show up, his thoughts kept
coming back to Lisa, though. Yes, he was a free-minder—he
had always felt strongly about that philosophy. Free-minders
insisted on the sovereign right of *all* minds to set their own
goals, to make their own decisions, and to pursue their own
dreams. Social and career commitments put some restric-
tions on the individual, of course—he himself couldn't just

abandon his post as the military CO of *Ad Astra* and walk away, much as he might desire that some days. But *mind* was *mind*, no matter what the shape or origin of the body that housed it. The legal status of AI robots was still, after seventy-some years, in doubt, though. The legal system carried the presumption that robot AIs, and even the extremely powerful AIs that ran ships or complex networks, could not have true free will when it was humans who programmed them in the first place.

St. Clair found that presumption amusing, in a disgusting sort of way—the more so since there were cogent arguments from the worlds of quantum physics and human neural physiology that suggested that *all* free will was illusory. The real argument—the only one with validity, so far as he was concerned—was the financial one. Intelligent robots were in great demand, and their sale or lease brought the robotics industry hundreds of billions of new dollars each year. Machines could tirelessly monitor space traffic control in low Earth orbit, explore the hellish surface of Venus, or cheerfully provide their owners with sexual release without thought of their own pleasure. St. Clair, like most people, hadn't thought much about the issue, not until he'd hired Lisa. But now that he knew an AI robot *personally* . . .

A subway pod pulled up and he stepped aboard. The trip from Bethesda through an upward-curving underground tube to the hub of the starboard cylinder's aft endcap took just two minutes, with his priority code assuring him of express service. At the hub, he had to transfer through a zero-G lock, pulling his way hand over hand to a CCE travel pod already waiting to take him to the bridge.

He was going to release Lisa . . . emancipate her. Someday. A growing number of AIs nowadays were emancipated, though quite a few voices—including, surprisingly, those of some robots—felt that a free choice for robots wasn't the answer. After all, if a mind didn't know it was enslaved, if it was happy doing what it was doing, releasing it might actually be cruel.

St. Clair knew he was going to need to talk this over with Lisa soon, maybe once she'd had a chance for the new settings to settle in. He wasn't sure how he felt about that himself. Ever since Natalya had told him they were through, he'd been so desperately lonely.

Lisa had been his salvation.

It was one thing to be distracted by such thoughts on the way, but now that he had arrived, all his training and experience kicked in, and he focused on the task at hand. He swam onto the bridge, entering the huge, empty cavern, brightly lit at the moment by the multitude of brilliant stars gleaming around its perimeter. "The Lord Commander is on the bridge," Symm said out loud. And then: "You have the bridge, my lord."

"Thank you, Excomm." He settled into his seat, which shaped itself to hold him down, to keep him from drifting around. Background chatter, the communications among various shipboard departments and stations, whispered in his ears, giving range, mass, power levels, the minutiae of navigation. Projected in the air directly ahead of him against the thick stellar backdrop was the other ship . . . though it didn't look much like one.

"What the hell is that?"

"We assume it's an alien starship, my lord," Symm told him. "I told you it was big."

"It looks more like a moon. Diameter . . ."—he checked the specs he was receiving—"a bit more than four hundred kilometers. Mass . . . nine times ten to the nineteen kilograms. Volume . . . thirty-two point five million cubic kilometers."

Good god.

"It dropped out of stardrive fifteen minutes ago, and has been pacing us since. Range . . . two hundred eighty million kilometers."

"Velocity?"

"Same as ours, my lord. Point seven one cee."

At seven-tenths of the speed of light, *Ad Astra* was only just beginning to enter the realm of large-scale relativistic effects, with the stars ahead taking on a bluer tint, the stars astern becoming slightly redder. That velocity was a compromise. St. Clair wanted to put some distance between the ship and the SMBH astern, but he didn't want to start messing with time dilation. If the unknown aliens who'd attacked them hours before returned, he wanted the *Ad Astra*, as much as possible, to have lost herself in the enormous emptiness surrounding the central black hole. Travel too fast, however, and time would slow for *Ad Astra* and those aboard her. Years might pass in the Galaxy outside, while hours or days passed for ship and passengers. St. Clair wanted *Ad Astra* to return to the same Earth that she'd left.

He took a closer look at the alien vessel trailing the *Ad Astra*. It looked familiar, somehow. He pulled down some additional data, then nodded. "Mimas," he said.

"I beg your pardon, my lord?"

"That thing following us is almost exactly the same size as Mimas . . . one of Saturn's inner moons. The density is a lot higher, though. . . ."

"Probably because Mimas is mostly water ice," Symm told him.

"And Mimas rarely zips off for joy rides around the Galaxy," St. Clair added. "Looks like someone just found a convenient moon, fitted it out with a propulsion system and life support, and took off."

Despite his seeming nonchalance, St. Clair was both impressed and disturbed by that fact. He stared intently at the object. The surface of the spherical body was heavily crater-

pocked. One large crater even suggested the enormous gash of Herschel Crater, on Mimas. The smaller craters tended to be bright-walled and prominent . . . a hint that the outer shell of that thing might be water ice.

"It would be interesting to know if they'd installed weapons systems in that thing as well," Subcommander Webb said.

"We'll assume they did." He glanced around the bridge, and saw the Medusan liaison nearby, hovering in its silvery, frost-coated pod. "Liaison?"

"We are here, Humans."

"How about it? Does anybody you folks know tool around the Galaxy inside a mobile moon?"

"A number of technical civilizations use found artifacts as spacecraft hulls—generally asteroids. Many hollow such bodies out and use them as the outer shells for self-contained orbital space colonies, but a few have given them mobility. We have never seen such an adaptation this large before, however."

"The big question is whether these guys are related to those three robot ships that went after us earlier." When there was no immediate answer, he added, "Think they might be?"

"We do not know, Humans."

"They're just hanging off our ass out there," St. Clair said. "Comm . . . any incoming from that thing? Radio? Laser? Signal flags? Anything?"

"No, my lord."

So maybe the unknowns communicated using phased neutrino beams, modulated gravity waves, or something even more exotic. If they wanted to talk, though, he felt sure they would find some way to make their intentions known, just as the Medusaens had years ago.

"Helm. Boost our speed to near-cee."

"Increase speed to near-cee, aye, aye, my lord."

And *Ad Astra* began accelerating.

"My Lord," Denisova said. "The alien is matching our pace."

"Very well. CAS! Bring a squadron up to ready status and stand by."

"Aye, aye, my lord."

Although the alien hadn't made any hostile moves yet, St. Clair didn't trust them and he wasn't going to give them the chance. The fact that two sets of alien vessels had found *Ad Astra* in the middle of all of this emptiness was suspicious. Those first three—those robot attack ships—might have been staking out Sagittarius A* after the destruction of the Ring, but the appearance of another ship suggested that they were related to that first group somehow. To assume otherwise ignored just how slim the chances of two random encounters in the middle of so much emptiness actually were. This moon-sized ship *might* be an enemy of the robots deployed in local space to find them, but St. Clair wasn't about to take the chance.

"Alien is closing, my lord. Slowly. They won't intercept us at this rate for hours."

"Keep an eye on them."

Okay . . . the aliens were closing, but at a snail's pace. Was that in itself an attempt to communicate? Or was someone trying to sneak up on the *Ad Astra* in a 400-kilometer mobile moon?

God, the power that thing must be using, though! As *Ad Astra* reached ninety-nine percent of the speed of light, the alien comfortably matched that velocity . . . and a wee bit more. Apparently it was using a gravitic drive quite similar to the one on *Ad Astra*, bending space ahead of the vessel to create a depression in the spacetime matrix, a depression into which the ship continually fell. The system allowed tremendous accelerations—tens of thousands of gravities—without smearing the passengers and crew into a thin red jam across the ship's aft bulkheads.

At 50,000 Gs they could from a standing start nudge up close to the speed of light in ten minutes. They still couldn't *pass* that magical speed; for that they needed to have a functional stardrive. But gravitational acceleration affected every atom in the ship uniformly, so there was no crushing G-force with which to contend.

"Radiation levels are increasing, my lord," Denisova reported.

"To be expected. It's gassy in here." At near-*c* velocities, free-floating atoms of hydrogen became high-energy particles, deadly to unprotected tissue—cosmic rays. "Mr. Seibert. We handling it okay so far?"

"Yes, my lord," Seibert replied. "Positive deflector fields are up, and the water shielding is handling anything that makes it through that."

St. Clair considered the tactical situation closely. They couldn't run—the stardrive was still hours away from being repaired. They couldn't hide—there were vast and opaque molecular clouds ahead, but the nearest was a good twelve light-hours away. Same for nearby stars; the nearest was two light-days distant. The SMBH was astern . . . but, again, light-hours distant, and St. Clair wasn't eager to get close to that thing again.

And they couldn't fight. The pursuing vessel could swat the *Ad Astra* like a fly, if its size and power consumption were any indication of its military capabilities.

Which left . . . what? Communication? Surrender?

Communication wouldn't work if they didn't know how to talk to the aliens, and that in turn eliminated surrender because that act required *some* sort of exchange understandable by both parties. Besides, St. Clair wasn't ready yet to surrender the lives of a million souls into the hands—or whatever—of unknown sentient beings with unknown motives, drives, and attitudes. There were damned few options open to him.

Maybe, though . . .

"Excomm . . . ready the ship for drive separation."

He saw her surprised look as she glanced back over her shoulder at him. "Sir?"

"Do it."

"Aye, aye, my lord."

"Helm . . . we're going to want to come to a rapid stop relative to local space just before we separate. Program it."

"Aye, aye, sir."

And the next few minutes dragged by with agonizing slowness.

"Lord Commander," Excomm Symm finally said, "we are ready in all respects for separation. Helm will initiate deceleration on your command. Connector sections have been evacuated and sealed."

St. Clair took a last look at the available data. The view outside the ship was weirdly distorted by their speed, an entire universe compressed into a tight, glowing ring circling the ship at thirty degrees from dead ahead. The trailing alien was lost in the distortion, but *Ad Astra*'s sensors indicated that the moon-sized vessel was still there, closing at a few thousand kilometers per second, and still a couple of hundred thousand kilometers astern.

"Helm . . . decelerate the ship."

"Decelerating . . . aye, aye, my lord."

There was no shock or strain, no sense of changing motion, but the view outside began to smear back across the encircling sky as the surrounding stars slowly resumed their true positions.

"Point eight-five cee," Lieutenant Mason reported. "Point eight . . . point seven-five . . ."

Slowly, the stars continued to crawl across the heavens, until they filled the entire sky once more.

"Point six cee . . ."

Still decelerating. "What's the alien doing?"

"My Lord," Desinova said, "he appears to be decelerating as well . . . matching our velocity perfectly."

Good. If that mobile moon was out to destroy the *Ad Astra*, it wouldn't just play games with them. Either those aboard wanted to communicate with the UE vessel, or they were simply observing it. Maybe they just wanted to escort the *Ad Astra* out of the area.

They would find out in a few more minutes.

"Velocity now at point five cee."

Half the speed of light. The relativistic optical effects were gone, now, but they were still moving too quickly for separation. St. Clair's chief concern was the safety of the hab cylinders. Specifically, if the drive module released the cylinders and went off to confront the alien, the cylinders would continue hurtling off at 150,000 kilometers each second, with no way to slow down. If anything happened to the drive unit—if it got fly-swatted by that moon, for instance—the O'Neil colony would continue drifting at high speed until it slammed into something—a cloud of molecular hydrogen, for instance, or a cloud of dust particles or something else that the meteor defense grazers couldn't handle.

When that happened, *Tellus*'s velocity would be transformed into radiant heat, and the O'Neill cylinders would briefly flare into incandescence before being reduced to a fast-moving cloud of hot plasma.

It took ten minutes to decelerate from near-*c*. When St. Clair gave the order to separate, they were moving at less than five kilometers per second. If the colony encountered a dust cloud or asteroid belt at that speed, its computer-controlled grazer defenses would be more than adequate to burn a safe path through the vacuum.

The improbable odds of them hitting something larger continued to hold.

With a jolt, the CCE section separated itself from the

twin cylinders. It left behind a small secondary engineering section that would continue to feed power to the cylinders for life support and to maintain their rotation, but the colony was now without any type of drive.

By long tradition, the part of the ship containing drive, engineering, and command bridge retained the name—*Ad Astra*—even though it was only a couple of kilometers long. The much larger O'Neill cylinders left behind would formally retain the name *Tellus*, since it was a repository for Earth-human technology and culture. A small point . . . but an important one for a species more concerned with personal identity than, say, the Medusae.

"CCE separation complete," Symm reported. "*Ad Astra* is now maneuvering free."

A graphic image hovering in front of St. Clair's face gave him the same message. The command and drive unit was clear now of the colony's stern endcaps, drifting back smoothly. "We are clear of *Tellus* and ready to boost."

"Bring us about, Mr. Mason." The *Ad Astra*, as if delighted to be free of the burden of the two colony cylinders, pivoted now to face the alien.

A last check of all systems . . . they were good to go.

"Let's go have a look at these people," St. Clair said. "Helm, take us ahead. Accelerate to fifty Gs."

A communications chime sounded within St. Clair's brain. It was Adler, calling from his office in the port cylinder, now dwindling rapidly into invisibility astern.

"Make it fast, Lord Director. We're kind of busy right now."

"The computer just told me you've separated from the colony! What the hell do you think you're doing?"

"I'm going to go have a little chat with the aliens. Mind the fort until I get back, okay?"

"St. Clair! What if you don't *come* back?"

"Then we've successfully completed *Ad Astra*'s mission,

by placing a functioning O'Neill colony at the galactic core. The expedition is all yours, Lord Director. Good luck. . . ."

"Damn you, St. Clair!"

"Can't talk now, sir. Don't worry. We'll get back to you just as soon as we can." He cut the channel.

The alien moon, pocked and cratered, swiftly grew to fill the sky ahead.

"Tactical!" St. Clair called. "Do we have any solid targets on the surface?"

"Negative, sir," Cameron said. "We're marking some mascons that might be large structures beneath the surface, but we're not seeing weapons emplacements, drive sections—*nothing*."

Mass concentrations beneath the surface weren't enough to go on. "What's our range?" Damn it, with *that* thing, he thought, he should be asking about their altitude.

"Twelve hundred kilometers, my lord."

"Helm . . . close the range, but slowly. Engineering . . . see if you can project the drive field forward. I want to poke this guy in the face."

A nudge from their drive field wouldn't harm the massive object out there, but they should feel the nudge.

Like knocking on their front door.

"Sir!" Denisova called. "They've launched a missile!"

"Anti-meteor defenses to full!" He hesitated. "Wait . . . just one?"

"Only one, my lord. Length . . . two point one meters. Mass . . . one hundred five point seven kilograms. Velocity . . . eight meters per second."

"Eight meters a second," St. Clair said. "And pretty small. That's not much of a missile."

"Anti-meteor defenses ready to engage, my lord."

"Hold your fire."

And then, the small moon vanished. One moment it was there, filling the sky ahead. And in the next instant . . .

"Okay . . . what the hell happened?"

"The alien appears to have engaged its version of stardrive, lord," Symm told him. "It is no longer within detectable range."

"Keep your sensors sharp, Lieutenant Denisova," St. Clair ordered. "It may just take a moment for us to see him."

If the alien vessel had simply jumped back a given distance, but was still in the area, it would take light time to reach the *Ad Astra*. A jump of 150 million kilometers, for instance—a distance of one astronomical unit—would mean a time lag of over eight minutes before it reappeared on *Ad Astra*'s screens. It would take that long for light to crawl all the way back to the ship.

"What's the missile doing?"

"Approaching," Denisova reported. "But slow. *Dead* slow."

"So . . . a messenger?" St. Clair wondered aloud. "Or a Trojan horse?"

"Or a probe of some sort," Symm suggested. "Something to check us out, find out about us."

"If I had to guess," St. Clair said, "I'd have to say that they were offering us the chance to communicate. CAS."

"Yes, my lord."

"Ready an RS-59 for launch."

"Very good, my lord."

"Computer! Do we have any xenolinguistics people on the drive unit?"

"Several dozen, Lord Commander," the ship's computer replied. "There are also a number of AI modules with xenolinguistic programming on-line."

"Call them," St. Clair said. "We're about to put them all to work."

The RS-59 was a robot-operated worker drone, one with a generous cargo capacity and the ability to work both in space and in a planetary atmosphere. Launched from the command-control-engineering section's flight deck, the six-hundred-meter craft would be able to pick up the alien missile and return it to *Ad Astra*.

But should I give that order? Damn it, the galactic core had been less than friendly so far, with the Coadunation Ring smashed to pieces by agencies unknown, and then the encounter with the three red-and-black needle-ships. Because of all that, St. Clair was unwilling to trust anybody new right now. *If that object adrift out there explodes as soon as it's brought aboard, or if it houses the equivalent of a hostile electronic virus or other program designed to cripple or destroy the* Ad Astra . . .

"We'll wait a few minutes," he said, "until we see if the alien ship reappears."

Ten minutes dragged past, with no sign of the moon reappearing in the distance.

"Launch the work drone."

"Work drone away, Lord Commander."

He watched as the RS-59 accelerated into the distance . . . then slowed. Telemetry from the robot showed details of the alien object as the drone came alongside. It was ebon-black, and . . . shifting. There was no other word for it. The object was constantly changing shape, though its overall appearance remained more or less cylindrical: sometimes long and thin, sometimes short and squat, sometimes with flutes or wings or sponsons, sometimes smooth and unadorned. . . .

"Lord Commander!"

"Yes, Mr. Martinez."

"The stardrive is back on-line, my lord. I'd like time to run it through some tests, make sure it's properly balanced, but—"

"Carlos, that's the best damned news I've heard all day. Stand by, please."

"Aye, aye, my lord."

Okay . . .

He *could* just turn the *Ad Astra* around, reconnect with

the *Tellus*, and jump back to Earth. He allowed himself a heartfelt exhalation of relief.

It was going to be okay.

On the other hand, what was he going to do—scuttle back to Earth and tell HQ that the Coad ringworld capital was gone, blown apart by unknown enemies of the galactic civilization? That, aside from the liaison's off-tentacle reference to the "Deniers," he didn't have a clue as to what was going on in here at the Galactic Hub, or who the attackers were?

Was it possible that Earth was now at war with an alien force, and didn't even know it?

That thing drifting out there might be a weapon, but he doubted that. Something as big and as powerful as a 400-kilometer mobile moon could have swatted the *Ad Astra* out of space with hardly a thought. Hell, they could have accelerated forward and *Ad Astra* would have ended up smeared across that moon's already well-cratered surface.

No . . . that shape-shifting black enigma was either for communication, or it was designed to study the *Ad Astra*. St. Clair was confident that even if it was a kind of scout, his crew would be able to learn *something* from it in exchange.

"CAS," he said. "Have the drone take that object aboard."

"Aye, aye, sir."

Gently, the worker drone picked the object up. After a further delay of nearly an hour, St. Clair gave the order to bring it in.

The alien moon-vessel had still not reappeared even on *Ad Astra*'s most sensitive deep-space long-range scanners. Either the alien had left this part of the Galaxy entirely, or it had shifted to another point more than ninety light-minutes away, because light reflected from its hull had not yet reached the Earth vessel. Something that big should have been visible, even at a range of a couple of light hours.

St. Clair had hesitated before bringing the drone and its

strange cargo on board, but he was more certain than ever that the enigma must represent an attempt to communicate, not launch an attack. While the moon-vessel had not given him a reason to trust it, neither had it done anything to suggest that it was hostile, except for following *Ad Astra* in the first place.

Besides, while there were plenty of linguistics and computer experts on board the *Ad Astra*, there were more on *Tellus*, the twin cylinders they'd left behind. He wanted to get all the experts together and working on this, and the faster they did so, the better.

He gave the order to retrieve the RS-59. When, after another thirty minutes, nothing untoward occurred, he ordered the ship to return to the O'Neill cylinders. Lieutenant Mason took the *Ad Astra* up to the aft end of the two cylinders, and Newton took over for the final rendezvous and lock. With all seals in place, *Tellus Ad Astra* was once again complete . . . and finally ready to engage her stardrive.

"All hands and passengers, this is St. Clair," he announced over the ship's internal comm, speaking inside the minds of every person on board. He was seated in his command chair on the bridge, the dazzling gleam of brilliant stars encircling the bridge crew in the darkness. "Subcomm Martinez informs me that our drives are again operational. I am going to take the *Ad Astra* out of the galactic core . . . a jump of about fifteen thousand light years, and the first leg of our trip home to Earth.

"We have now, on the main flight deck, a work pod containing an alien artifact, which, I believe, is a communications device of some kind. I want all senior IS, XE, XS, and XL department personnel to gather for a briefing in the Carousel in two hours, after which I'm going to ask you to give me some answers. We need to know what has been going on in the galactic core . . . and what happened to the Coadunation capital. I want those answers before we get back to

Earth. Liaison . . . I request your attendance at this meeting as well."

He said nothing about the bizarre change to the look of the galactic core. If *Ad Astra* had indeed slipped into the heart of another galaxy, or been thrown, somehow, to another part of the Milky Way, or been moved through time . . . well, they soon would know.

Mental confirmations flickered back through St. Clair's in-head hardware. His bridge crew gave him a final check and a countdown to jump.

". . . four," Mason said, "three . . . two . . . one . . . *jump!*"

There was the slightest of shivers, and the belt of brilliant stars encircling the bridge was gone. In its place was . . . something other, something horribly and awesomely and inconceivably *other.*

Adams screamed, a piercing, strangled shout. Mason and a half dozen others gasped. Denisova and Symm and Forrester all swore or bit off startled exclamations. St. Clair started to pull free from his seat, staring into that awful splendor, eyes widening as he tried, *tried* to take it all in.

Tried to understand.

"What's going on?" Symm finally managed to say. *"What's happened to the sky?"*

St. Clair could only stare into the three-dimensional projection surrounding the bridge, at stars and loops of gas and dust and galactic chaos frozen across an impossible, alien sky, before blurting out:

"What in the fucking hell has happened to us?"

SEVEN

The cacophony of voices—shouts, screams, confusion—grew louder. Several officers panicked and rose from their seats.

"Belay that!" St. Clair bellowed into the noise. "Everyone! *As you were!*"

The noise faded. Those who'd been about to bolt for the bridge entryway—and where the hell had they thought they were going?—took their seats once more.

"Everyone stay calm," St. Clair added. "We are officers of the United Earth, and we will behave as if we have faced crises before."

The change to the central core of the Galaxy had been startling, to say the least, evidence, perhaps, that the *Ad Astra* had indeed slipped through a wormhole and into the core of a different, distant galaxy. What they were looking at now, however, was proof of something else, a change more profound and far more devastating than a mere jump across space.

Humor, St. Clair thought, his mind racing wildly. *Something to break the tension.* "Toto," he misquoted slowly, "I've got a feeling we're not in Kansas anymore."

"And just what was your first clue, Dorothy?" Symm asked. Several nervous chuckles sounded around the bridge.

"There's *no* place like home," Mason added.

Ad Astra had emerged from Jump in a place where not one, but *two* spiral galaxies filled the sky, like towering walls of swirling stars to either side of the ship. The two were colliding, caught in a mutual interpenetration, the central hub of one galaxy slicing into the hub of the other. Together, the two galaxies formed an immense V with a shallow angle between them. The golden mean spiral perfection of both had been savagely distorted by their gravitational interaction; spiral arms and streams of dust and gas arced far out into intergalactic space, trailing stars. The cores of both galaxies, instead of consisting of ancient red stars, were brilliant with young, hot, intensely blue-white stars. Vast clouds of interstellar dust and gas were colliding within the cores, generating pressure waves rippling out and compacting the surrounding dust clouds into myriad newborn suns, an intense starburst display lighting up both galaxies.

The whole was a spectacular panorama, a play of light and shadow where massed suns cast beams of golden light across banked clouds of dust like blue-black thunderheads, where novae burned blue-white among dimmer suns, where galactic spiral arms stretched and tattered and trailed off into the intergalactic night. There was a tremendous sense of raw and violent motion in that vista, though the entire scene was frozen and unmoving.

What St. Clair was most aware of, by far, was the oppressive sense of sheer *scale*, as two whirlpools of stars, each a hundred thousand light years or more across, collided. Caught between them, far down in the notch of the V, *Ad Astra* was a speck—was *less* than a speck—a single molecule hanging above the storm-tortured vastness of an ocean.

If there was one benefit to all this, it was that after that first outburst of exclamation and shock, the bridge crew now remained silent, caught up in the impossible vista frozen in the sky around them.

"At least," St. Clair said, "now we know where we are. Or, I should say, we know *when*."

But he couldn't name the figure, the number of years—not yet. It was too . . . outrageous, a number threatening to shatter the sanity of every person in the expedition and stealing from them all the hope and expectation of ever going home.

Symm looked at him with a growing horror. "What are we going to do, my lord?"

"Hold that department-head briefing," he replied. "Number Three conference room. Include all department heads . . . and move it up to thirty minutes."

It was, he thought, an appropriately human response. There didn't seem to be anything they could do about their situation, so they would gather around the campfire and talk about it.

ST. CLAIR WASN'T sure about the wisdom of setting the conference room display to show the scene outside—a sky filled by two towering, distorted spiral galaxies in mid-collision. The sight was oppressive, and not a little terrifying.

But, he reasoned, they were going to have to get used to it because he was aware of no way for them to go back. So he told Newton to show the exterior space display, and if any of the department heads couldn't deal with it, better to find out now.

The conference room was filled to capacity and then some, with every place at the large table taken, and quite a few other people standing around those seated in the middle. Perhaps half were military officers—mostly Navy, but the Marines were represented as well. The rest were civilian department heads, along with a sizeable number of assistants and secretaries. St. Clair was interested to note that very few were there as projected holograms. By now, everyone on board the ship knew what had happened, and when St. Clair had called the meeting, everyone who could be there wanted to be there physically. He couldn't blame them—when faced with something as immense as this, it was a very human reaction to want to seek out other humans. For all their technology, there was something inherently reassuring about the presence of others—especially if those others might have solutions.

St. Clair desperately hoped someone in the room might actually be the person with the answer.

They'd been discussing the situation for several minutes, and it was clear that no one, save for a few of the physics and astronomy people, was certain what had happened.

"This *does* answer the question of what happened to us at the supermassive black hole," Paul Tsang was saying.

"Would you mind explaining it to those of us who aren't as astronomically inclined as you?" Webb asked. "I mean . . . clearly we're not in our own Galaxy any longer."

"Actually," Tsang said, "we are . . . or, rather, we're just outside." He pointed at one wall, where the smaller of the two galaxies soared off into vastness overhead. "That's us . . . the Milky Way. Four hundred billion stars in a whirlpool a hundred thousand light years across. And over there"—he pointed at the other, larger galaxy—"is M-31, Andromeda. About one point two trillion stars in a slightly larger spiral. Maybe one hundred twenty thousand light years across."

"Galaxies in collision," Denisova said quietly.

"We've known this was going to happen for, oh, a hundred fifty years or so," Tsang went on. "The Andromedan Galaxy is—was—headed straight for our Milky Way at something like one hundred ten kilometers per second. A breakneck pace, but since it was still two and a half million light years away, there was no urgency to the matter."

"What the hell happened?" Webb said. He sounded puzzled, and it was clear he hadn't yet been able to come to grips with what happened.

"*Time*, Mr. Webb," St. Clair said. "Time happened . . . about four billion years' worth."

There. He'd finally named the number. It was out there, now. He heard several soft gasps from around the table.

"Exactly," Tsang said. "We knew that Andromeda would collide with our Galaxy in roughly four billion years' time. Evidently, our close passage of Sagittarius A-Star catapulted us into the future. The *remote* future. Four billion years."

"God in heaven," someone murmured out loud.

"Dr. Sandoval?" St. Clair said.

"Sir." Tina Sandoval was the civilian head of *Ad Astra*'s astrophysics department.

"I'll want you to work closely with Dr. Tsang's people. See if you can put together a solid working theory on how this happened. Third Navigator mentioned a . . . what was it? A frame-dragging effect."

"A Lorentzian manifold," Newton's voice supplied.

"Right. Anyway, I want your best guess as to whether this was frame-dragging, or just a case of time dilation at the black hole's ergosphere."

"But what the hell's the difference, Lord Commander?" Dumont asked, his voice ragged with barely suppressed emotion. "It doesn't matter how we *got* here. . . ."

"Actually, it does, Dr. Dumont," St. Clair said. "It matters quite a lot."

"Absolutely," Tsang added. "There are two ways that we might have moved through time. If we just got too deeply into the SMBH gravity field, simple time dilation would have slowed the passage of time for us. A few seconds passed for the ship . . . while four billion years passed outside. Time travel . . . but strictly one way. Into the future."

"You mean there's a way we can go back?" Howard Moore asked. Moore was head of *Ad Astra*'s nanotechnology office, a GS-14 civilian, like Tsang, who worked for the military.

"We don't know, Doctor," Sandoval told him. "Theoretically, a Lorentzian manifold would allow travel forward *or* backward through time, but . . ." She shrugged. "The mathematics initially suggested that you need a rotating structure of infinite length and mass to create such a gateway through time. The fact that we're here suggests that we may not have the last word on the matter."

"*Yet*," St. Clair added, stressing the word. "That's what I want the astronomy and astrophysics departments to tell me: Can we go back?"

"I would have to point out," Sandoval said slowly, "that the chances of getting home are small. Vanishingly small."

"Why is that?"

"Essentially, we would have to return to the SMBH and probe the region close around it—possibly with small drones. They would have to go through, map their exact course, and figure out where and when they are when they emerge . . . and then return with the data. There are, I would guess, some trillions upon trillions of possible pathways. The chances of stumbling across the right one by sheer chance are . . . well, to say they're tiny is something of an understatement. Kind of like saying that Dr. Moore works with small robots."

"But there *is* hope," St. Clair said. "I want all of you here to emphasize that when you talk to your departments. There is hope. I don't want a panic within the general populace. General Frazier?"

"Yes, sir."

"If there *is* panic, your people will have to take care of it."

"Understood, Lord Commander."

"Coordinate with the ship's master-at-arms."

"Aye, aye, sir."

"Ms. Kalmar."

"Yes, my lord." Christine Kalmar handled public relations and the liaison work between the military and civilian authorities.

"It'll be up to you to take care of putting out the news,

breaking it gently, if you can. We won't lie to the civilians on board, but I want them to stay calm. No panic."

"No, sir."

"Subcomm Symm, you'll be responsible for the military end of things."

"Yes, sir."

"Now: other questions. Dr. Sandoval? While they're digging into the mechanics of what happened, I also want your department to take a look at why the hell we popped out here and now. It seems like a pretty long shot that we would emerge from the black hole just now with . . ." he waved at one wall, ". . . all of *that* going on."

"I think I can give you a probable answer on that right now, my lord."

"I'd love to hear it."

"We were in a kind of equilibrium with the black hole," Sandoval said. "Balanced at the edge of the ergosphere, you might say. We know the SMBH had a mass of a little more than four million solar masses, right?"

"Yes . . ."

"Then suddenly we're bumped out away from the ergosphere. We find ourselves out in open space, and the black hole has increased in mass seven times."

"I think I see what you're getting at."

"Yes, sir. Obviously, another, much larger black hole arrived and merged with the first. At a guess . . . I'd say the central SMBH of the Andromedan Galaxy collided with our own SMBH. Increased the mass and the diameter . . . and, just incidentally, we got tossed out on our ear. Might have been a kind of tidal surge or a ripple or a bulge in the black hole's ergosphere—that's not really important. Anything like that would have disturbed our equilibrium with the SMBH. Whatever it was, we can just be thankful it tossed us farther away, out to where time was passing at a normal rate, and didn't result in us getting dragged down that thing's throat."

"Or another possibility . . ." Tsang said. "Having the incoming black hole collide with us dead-on."

"You know, I don't much like that," St. Clair said slowly. "It suggests that we were trapped at the ergosphere, not that we flew through a manifold gateway. It means . . ."

He let the words trail off. He didn't want to voice the possibility in front of a room filled with the ship's department heads, but it was something he'd been fearing since he first observed the two galaxies colliding: that *Ad Astra* would *never* be able to get back home.

That they had no hope at all.

"Where is Sol in all of that?" a small voice asked in the silence. "Where is Earth?"

The speaker, according to St. Clair's in-head readout, was Sublieutenant Emila Buchanan, a junior naval officer posted to the Office of Xenolinguistics.

"Now's not the time, Em," Dr. Theodore Hatcher said. He was her boss, the head of the ship's alien language department.

"As good a time as any," Tsang said. He sounded tired. *I know the feeling*, St. Clair thought as the doctor continued. "Finding Sol in this epoch would be categorically impossible."

"Why so?" St. Clair asked him. He'd been entertaining a growing curiosity about Earth himself. What had happened to Humankind's birthworld in four billion years?

"Sol, like every other star in the Galaxy, orbits the galactic center," Tsang replied. "At its distance from the core, our sun takes about 250 million years—a quarter of a billion years—to make one complete orbit. In the time that's passed since the twenty-second century, Sol would have completed about sixteen orbits . . . and these aren't nice, neat, predictable orbits like the orbits of a planet. They can vary tremendously from orbit to orbit. They're affected by the movements of other stars, by masses of dust and gas, by local clouds of dark matter, and, most recently, by gravitational interaction with the Andromedan Galaxy as it came careening into ours. There's a chance Sol got flung out of the Galaxy entirely . . . or that it's already been swallowed by Andromeda. Earth could quite literally be *anywhere* in that mess out there now."

"Quite correct," Sandoval added, after a brief hesitation, "but rather beside the point. We don't need to find Earth."

"Why not?" Buchanan asked.

"Because we can be sure that there won't be anything left there now. No people. No life. No water or air. By now, four billion years further along in its evolution, Earth will be as dead as the moon."

Buchanan gave a small and strangled sob. St. Clair guessed that she must have family on Earth . . . *had* family on Earth . . . and was just now realizing that they were gone.

"The sun has been getting hotter," Valerie Holt put in. "Is that what you're talking about, Doc?"

"At a rate of roughly ten percent per billion years," Sandoval said, nodding. "After just a billion years or so of that, a runaway greenhouse effect would have sent the surface temperature soaring, evaporating all of Earth's oceans, which in turn would have trapped more and more heat and made it even hotter. The planet would have become like Venus, with all of its oceans turned to steam clouds in the atmosphere, and with its surface hot enough to melt lead. Life . . . well, it just wouldn't have been able to adapt fast enough. It wouldn't have survived, at least not on the surface. There might have been some water reservoirs deep underground with microbial life for, oh, another billion years or so. But by today, continued heating will have stripped away the atmosphere and, with it, the last of the steam clouds—all that was left of the oceans."

"You do paint *such* a rosy picture," Raul Avilla said. He was head of the maintenance department.

"Of course, there's another possibility," Dumont pointed out. "Godtech."

The term was an informal one used by the xenotech department to refer to technology—either alien in origin or something developed by Humankind in the remote future—that was so advanced that it might as well be the work of gods. The Coad ring in the galactic core would have required such technology.

And if humans or the descendents of humans had survived the first billion years of the past four, *what* might they have accomplished?

"You're talking about ideas like moving Earth into a larger orbit," St. Clair said.

"Exactly. Or, theoretically, at least, it might be possible to engage in star mining—bleeding off the mass of a star. Reduce it in size enough, and it will burn cooler. That would also greatly extend the star's expected life span."

"Just how the hell do you bleed mass off from a star?" Hatcher asked.

"Well, if we knew that," Tsang quipped, "it wouldn't be godtech, now, would it?"

Some nervous chuckles sounded around the table.

"The point is, I think," Dumont continued, "that we can't take anything for granted. Humankind might have survived until now. Changed, probably, but it or something like it might have survived."

"Dr. Dumont, do you know what you're saying?" Symm said. "No civilization, no culture, could survive for even a million years! And we're talking about a span of time four thousand times greater than that!"

"We don't know that," Dumont insisted. "Our species is immature. A truly advanced civilization might be immortal."

"Nothing lasts forever, Doctor," St. Clair put in, waving once more at the tableau on the screens around them.

with this many unknowns. Once they made peaceful
[cont]act with another civilization here, though, things would
[chan]ge.

[A]nd St. Clair would have to make a decision about
[wh]ether or not he was going to let him.

[B]ut for now, that seemed to be a choice for the future.
[Gri]mm once more brought him back to the present. "So
[w]hat's on the schedule for today?" the executive commander
[a]sked. "Where do we go now?"

"Seems to me we have a choice," St. Clair said. "We can
go back to the galactic core, and see if that moon-ship shows
up again. Or we put out our ears and see if we can zero in
on a high-tech civilization out here. Either way, we need to
find someone. We don't have a chance in hell of figuring out
what's going on without a solid First Contact."

"A suggestion, my lord," Cameron said.

"What?"

"We're better off out here, away from the core."

"What makes you say that, Lieutenant?" Adler said.
"That moon or planetoid or whatever it was clearly wanted
to communicate, and that's what we need right now. Communication."

"Yes, Lord Director, that's true. But inside the core, we
pretty much had our collective heads in a bag. We couldn't
see out. We couldn't hear much of anything but static. Right,
Vince?"

Subcommander Vincent Hargrove, the senior communications officer, nodded. "There were lots of signals in there,
but mostly it was a hash of static. Cosmic rays, radio static,
exploding stars—if there was anyone in there broadcasting
something intelligent, it would have taken us a long time to
sift it out."

"Things are a little clearer out here?" St. Clair asked.

"Yes, sir. We're picking up a number of signal sources in
both galaxies. Quite a few of them, in fact. Most appear to

"Then immortal for all practical purposes," Dumont replied. "The civilizations of the Coad, for example. Many of
them might still be around, or their descendents. They might
have technologies that we literally can't even begin to imagine. Even . . ." He hesitated.

"Yes?" St. Clair asked.

"Even time travel."

"Time travel," Sandoval said with the slightest of sneers,
"is flat-out impossible."

"Says the woman who's just traveled four billion years
into the future," Tsang said.

"You know what I mean! Travel into the *past* is impossible. Too many problems with paradoxes."

"So all our theories think," St. Clair said. "But as
Dr. Dumont suggests, we're not going to take anything for
granted. No assumptions. I would suggest that our first order
of business will be to see if we can make contact with an
advanced civilization in this epoch."

"Like the one that built that moon-sized spacecraft?"
General Frazier asked.

"Like the one that built the moon-sized spacecraft, yes,"
St. Clair said.

He wondered if Frazier was leveling some subtle criticism at him, but he'd heard no irony or sarcasm in the
words. When they'd encountered that huge ship, they'd not
been aware that they were in their own future. Obviously,
that ship was not connected with whoever had destroyed the
Coad's galactic ring.

But they still might be related to the three red-and-black
robot ships that had attacked them shortly after their arrival
here.

He dismissed the thought. There were just too damned
many unknowns.

"Dr. Hatcher."

"Yes, my lord."

"Any progress with that missile or probe or whatever it was we picked up?"

"We've only just gotten it aboard, sir. Newton is investigating it, using teleoperational robots."

"Newton?" St. Clair asked, raising his voice slightly. "Any progress?"

"None so far, Lord Commander. I suspect, however, that your initial impression was correct. The alien torpedo is most likely a device intended to aid communication with one or more galactic civilizations in this time period. The device, like those ships that attacked us, is pure computronium, with almost its entire mass devoted to information processing."

"Meaning what?"

"Meaning, my lord, that it could be an extremely powerful computer dedicated to learning how to understand us, or to teaching us how to understand them. Probably both."

That was an encouraging thought. They would need to talk to the civilizations living in this time. And one of those civilizations just might have provided them with the key to doing just that.

"Keep after it."

"Of course, Lord Commander."

St. Clair glanced across the table and caught Günter Adler's eye. The man was physically present, not in virtual reality, surrounded by a coterie of secretaries, assistants, and attendants, looking every centimeter the proper Imperial Lord Director. His group took up several seats opposite the table from St. Clair, who wondered if there was going to be a confrontation.

The expedition's charter practically demanded one.

"Lord Director?" St. Clair said. "You've been uncharacteristically quiet. Do you have anything to add?"

"No," Adler said, curt. "At least . . . not at this time."

Which was probably, St. Clair thought, a[s much] warning as he was going to get from the man. [He won]dered when the ax was going to fall.

The problem he was thinking about, of c[ourse, was] the question of command. Control of the expe[dition was] a precariously balanced jury-rigging of rank and [raw] power—and that was the case when everything w[ent] as planned. St. Clair had been designated as the [ship's] commanding officer, the leader of the military portion [of the] ship's orders. Primarily, that meant that he was in com[mand] of the ship en route from Sol to the Coad capital, and [that] was true even though the senior Marine on board—M[ajor] General Frazier—seriously outranked him. Since the t[wo] Marine divisions would be remaining with the O'Neill hab[i]tats at the center of the Galaxy, they were considered pas[s]engers rather than crew, and were not in Ad Astra's line of command.

In point of fact, they and all the civilians in Tellus were cargo, and that cargo's safety was entirely St. Clair's responsibility.

Adler, as mission director, was technically in command of the entire expedition, including St. Clair . . . but St. Clair specifically had been given command authority over all Navy issues, which had included getting the ship safely to the Coad ring. Adler could advise in certain matters, such as suggesting where St. Clair should take the ship and who he should talk to, but St. Clair had the absolute and final say over the ship and the voyage itself.

At this point, however, the original mission was a thing quite literally of the past, as relevant now as a space elevator was to a fish.

All of which meant that, at some point, St. Clair knew, Adler was going to decide it was time to assert control—civilian control—over the entire expedition. He would let the Navy run things for now, so long as the situation was this be automated beacons of some sort or another. Some might be carrying messages. It will be a lot easier to figure that out away from the core."

"I have to agree," St. Clair said. He glanced at Adler, but the director didn't appear to be digging in for an argument. "It also feels less dangerous out here. In the core, we ran into two different alien groups in the space of a few hours. One might have been trying to communicate with us, but the other was definitely trying to kill us. Until we can talk to anyone we meet, we should be cautious. And not make any assumptions that are going to turn around and bite us."

"You're missing one important point, though, Commander," Adler said.

"Yes, my lord?"

"If that . . . missile, or whatever it is, if that *is* some sort of translation device, we can count on it helping us talk with the inhabitants of that moon. But why should anyone out here speak the same language?"

It was, St. Clair had to admit, a telling point. An electronic translator programmed in France would work in Tibet, but only because such devices connected to linguistic libraries and translation facilities in orbit. Unless that moon-sized ship was part of an empire spread across at least 15,000 light years of the Galaxy—and had vestiges four billion years later—the chances were good that no one out here would understand their language.

"Sir!" someone yelled from the crowd behind him. "Sir! The Liaison!"

The Liaison? Damn, I'd forgotten about the Medusan. "What's the matter?"

"I think . . ."

St. Clair was out of his seat and facing the commotion. The Liaison's floater pod was acting strangely, emitting streams of white fog and shaking. St. Clair stepped closer, trying to see the being's face, but the transparency at one end of the pod was completely opaque, covered with ice. Frost coated the hovering cylinder.

"Xenotechs!" St. Clair snapped. "Get some help in here! *Stat!*"

"*Alone . . .*" the Liaison said. Its voice sounded strangled, weirdly distorted, as electronic circuits fried. "*Forever alone . . .*"

And then, with a sharp hiss of escaping gasses, the alien floater pod opened.

EIGHT

The Medusan, apparently, had deliberately opened its travel pod. St. Clair felt the blast of cold gasses as the pod split apart, saw the entire length of the alien writhing in what to it was scalding hot and poisonous air. Patterns of color flashed and rippled along its wet body, vivid greens and purples and browns, as the cluster of tentacles at its head lashed spasmodically.

He heard it scream, high pitched and shrill.

"Newton!" St. Clair yelled. "Do you have the Medusae agent?"

"I do."

"Bring it on-line."

He heard the whisper inside his head. "We are here, Humans."

"Your prototype is not," St. Clair replied, also in his head. "And unless there was some kind of horrible malfunction to its pod, it looks like it killed itself."

"There was no malfunction. The Liaison felt unable to continue with its mission. With life."

"But why?"

St. Clair could almost feel the electronic entity shrug in his mind. "The Medusae are representatives of a group social mentality," it told him.

"A hive mind, yes."

"No. Not as we understand your term 'hive mind.' All Medusae together do not support a single intelligence such as that demonstrated by your ants and bees, or by the cells of your bodies. A group social mentality is a social order that requires other members of the group, either in close proximity, or in fairly regular communication."

"But the Liaison was alone on the *Ad Astra*!"

"Yet it also had the reasonable expectation of rejoining its fellows when it reached Harmony. Others of its kind were on board the ship *Ad Astra* followed into the galactic core. Individual Medusae can physically endure separation from their fellows, although it is not comfortable, and they do not willingly do so for long."

"Why did it have to kill itself, though? It wasn't alone—it had all of us!"

"Not really the same, Humans. You are alien, extremely different from the Medusae in the way you think, the way you act and react."

"Even so . . . damn it! *Ad Astra* has plenty of room. We could have brought along a thousand Medusae if we'd known!"

"Such was not considered practical. In fact, the Liaison *was* in communication with its fellows—those on board the Coadunation vessel escorting *Ad Astra*. All Medusae have implants that allow physical communication with others within quite a large radius. As such, it was still in communication with them after the Coadunation vessel was trapped in the ergosphere of Sagittarius A-Star."

"How . . . oh. An Einstein ghost."

"Precisely. Its connection with its fellows was not severed as long as our perception of the Coadunation vessel was frozen by relativistic effects. Once we were knocked clear of the black hole, though, the Liaison lost all contact with its fellows. It didn't know how to cope with that kind of loneliness."

St. Clair looked at the alien's body, clearly dead, its tis-

"Then immortal for all practical purposes," Dumont replied. "The civilizations of the Coad, for example. Many of them might still be around, or their descendents. They might have technologies that we literally can't even begin to imagine. Even . . ." He hesitated.

"Yes?" St. Clair asked.

"Even time travel."

"Time travel," Sandoval said with the slightest of sneers, "is flat-out impossible."

"Says the woman who's just traveled four billion years into the future," Tsang said.

"You know what I mean! Travel into the *past* is impossible. Too many problems with paradoxes."

"So all our theories think," St. Clair said. "But as Dr. Dumont suggests, we're not going to take anything for granted. No assumptions. I would suggest that our first order of business will be to see if we can make contact with an advanced civilization in this epoch."

"Like the one that built that moon-sized spacecraft?" General Frazier asked.

"Like the one that built the moon-sized spacecraft, yes," St. Clair said.

He wondered if Frazier was leveling some subtle criticism at him, but he'd heard no irony or sarcasm in the words. When they'd encountered that huge ship, they'd not been aware that they were in their own future. Obviously, that ship was not connected with whoever had destroyed the Coad's galactic ring.

But they still might be related to the three red-and-black robot ships that had attacked them shortly after their arrival here.

He dismissed the thought. There were just too damned many unknowns.

"Dr. Hatcher."

"Yes, my lord."

"Any progress with that missile or probe or whatever it was we picked up?"

"We've only just gotten it aboard, sir. Newton is investigating it, using teleoperational robots."

"Newton?" St. Clair asked, raising his voice slightly. "Any progress?"

"None so far, Lord Commander. I suspect, however, that your initial impression was correct. The alien torpedo is most likely a device intended to aid communication with one or more galactic civilizations in this time period. The device, like those ships that attacked us, is pure computronium, with almost its entire mass devoted to information processing."

"Meaning what?"

"Meaning, my lord, that it could be an extremely powerful computer dedicated to learning how to understand us, or to teaching us how to understand them. Probably both."

That was an encouraging thought. They would need to talk to the civilizations living in this time. And one of those civilizations just might have provided them with the key to doing just that.

"Keep after it."

"Of course, Lord Commander."

St. Clair glanced across the table and caught Günter Adler's eye. The man was physically present, not in virtual reality, surrounded by a coterie of secretaries, assistants, and attendants, looking every centimeter the proper Imperial Lord Director. His group took up several seats opposite the table from St. Clair, who wondered if there was going to be a confrontation.

The expedition's charter practically demanded one.

"Lord Director?" St. Clair said. "You've been uncharacteristically quiet. Do you have anything to add?"

"No," Adler said, curt. "At least . . . not at this time."

Which was probably, St. Clair thought, about as clear a warning as he was going to get from the man. He just wondered when the ax was going to fall.

The problem he was thinking about, of course, was the question of command. Control of the expedition was a precariously balanced jury-rigging of rank and political power—and that was the case when everything was going as planned. St. Clair had been designated as the military commanding officer, the leader of the military portion of the ship's orders. Primarily, that meant that he was in command of the ship en route from Sol to the Coad capital, and this was true even though the senior Marine on board—Major General Frazier—seriously outranked him. Since the two Marine divisions would be remaining with the O'Neill habitats at the center of the Galaxy, they were considered passengers rather than crew, and were not in *Ad Astra*'s line of command.

In point of fact, they and all the civilians in *Tellus* were cargo, and that cargo's safety was entirely St. Clair's responsibility.

Adler, as mission director, was technically in command of the entire expedition, including St. Clair . . . but St. Clair specifically had been given command authority over all *Navy* issues, which had included getting the ship safely to the Coad ring. Adler could advise in certain matters, such as suggesting where St. Clair should take the ship and who he should talk to, but St. Clair had the absolute and final say over the ship and the voyage itself.

At this point, however, the original mission was a thing quite literally of the past, as relevant now as a space elevator was to a fish.

All of which meant that, at some point, St. Clair knew, Adler was going to decide it was time to assert control—*civilian* control—over the entire expedition. He would let the Navy run things for now, so long as the situation was this fluid, with this many unknowns. Once they made peaceful contact with another civilization here, though, things would change.

And St. Clair would have to make a decision about whether or not he was going to let him.

But for now, that seemed to be a choice for the future. Symm once more brought him back to the present. "So what's on the schedule for today?" the executive commander asked. "Where do we go now?"

"Seems to me we have a choice," St. Clair said. "We can go back to the galactic core, and see if that moon-ship shows up again. Or we put out our ears and see if we can zero in on a high-tech civilization out here. Either way, we need to find someone. We don't have a chance in hell of figuring out what's going on without a solid First Contact."

"A suggestion, my lord," Cameron said.

"What?"

"We're better off out here, away from the core."

"What makes you say that, Lieutenant?" Adler said. "That moon or planetoid or whatever it was clearly wanted to communicate, and that's what we need right now. Communication."

"Yes, Lord Director, that's true. But inside the core, we pretty much had our collective heads in a bag. We couldn't see out. We couldn't hear much of anything but static. Right, Vince?"

Subcommander Vincent Hargrove, the senior communications officer, nodded. "There were lots of signals in there, but mostly it was a hash of static. Cosmic rays, radio static, exploding stars—if there was anyone in there broadcasting something intelligent, it would have taken us a long time to sift it out."

"Things are a little clearer out here?" St. Clair asked.

"Yes, sir. We're picking up a number of signal sources in both galaxies. Quite a few of them, in fact. Most appear to be automated beacons of some sort or another. Some might be carrying messages. It will be a lot easier to figure that out away from the core."

"I have to agree," St. Clair said. He glanced at Adler, but the director didn't appear to be digging in for an argument. "It also feels less dangerous out here. In the core, we ran into two different alien groups in the space of a few hours. One might have been trying to communicate with us, but the other was definitely trying to kill us. Until we can talk to anyone we meet, we should be cautious. And not make any assumptions that are going to turn around and bite us."

"You're missing one important point, though, Commander," Adler said.

"Yes, my lord?"

"If that . . . missile, or whatever it is, if that *is* some sort of translation device, we can count on it helping us talk with the inhabitants of that moon. But why should anyone out here speak the same language?"

It was, St. Clair had to admit, a telling point. An electronic translator programmed in France would work in Tibet, but only because such devices connected to linguistic libraries and translation facilities in orbit. Unless that moon-sized ship was part of an empire spread across at least 15,000 light years of the Galaxy—and had vestiges four billion years later—the chances were good that no one out here would understand their language.

"Sir!" someone yelled from the crowd behind him. "Sir! The Liaison!"

The Liaison? Damn, I'd forgotten about the Medusan. "What's the matter?"

"I think . . ."

St. Clair was out of his seat and facing the commotion. The Liaison's floater pod was acting strangely, emitting streams of white fog and shaking. St. Clair stepped closer, trying to see the being's face, but the transparency at one end of the pod was completely opaque, covered with ice. Frost coated the hovering cylinder.

"Xenotechs!" St. Clair snapped. "Get some help in here! *Stat!*"

"*Alone . . .*" the Liaison said. Its voice sounded strangled, weirdly distorted, as electronic circuits fried. "*Forever alone . . .*"

And then, with a sharp hiss of escaping gasses, the alien floater pod opened.

The Medusan, apparently, had deliberately opened its travel pod. St. Clair felt the blast of cold gasses as the pod split apart, saw the entire length of the alien writhing in what to it was scalding hot and poisonous air. Patterns of color flashed and rippled along its wet body, vivid greens and purples and browns, as the cluster of tentacles at its head lashed spasmodically.

He heard it scream, high pitched and shrill.

"Newton!" St. Clair yelled. "Do you have the Medusae agent?"

"I do."

"Bring it on-line."

He heard the whisper inside his head. "We are here, Humans."

"Your prototype is not," St. Clair replied, also in his head. "And unless there was some kind of horrible malfunction to its pod, it looks like it killed itself."

"There was no malfunction. The Liaison felt unable to continue with its mission. With life."

"But why?"

St. Clair could almost feel the electronic entity shrug in his mind. "The Medusae are representatives of a group social mentality," it told him.

"A hive mind, yes."

"No. Not as we understand your term 'hive mind.' All Medusae together do not support a single intelligence such as that demonstrated by your ants and bees, or by the cells of your bodies. A group social mentality is a social order that requires other members of the group, either in close proximity, or in fairly regular communication."

"But the Liaison was alone on the *Ad Astra*!"

"Yet it also had the reasonable expectation of rejoining its fellows when it reached Harmony. Others of its kind were on board the ship *Ad Astra* followed into the galactic core. Individual Medusae can physically endure separation from their fellows, although it is not comfortable, and they do not willingly do so for long."

"Why did it have to kill itself, though? It wasn't alone—it had all of us!"

"Not really the same, Humans. You are alien, extremely different from the Medusae in the way you think, the way you act and react."

"Even so . . . damn it! *Ad Astra* has plenty of room. We could have brought along a thousand Medusae if we'd known!"

"Such was not considered practical. In fact, the Liaison *was* in communication with its fellows—those on board the Coadunation vessel escorting *Ad Astra*. All Medusae have implants that allow physical communication with others within quite a large radius. As such, it was still in communication with them after the Coadunation vessel was trapped in the ergosphere of Sagittarius A-Star."

"How . . . oh. An Einstein ghost."

"Precisely. Its connection with its fellows was not severed as long as our perception of the Coadunation vessel was frozen by relativistic effects. Once we were knocked clear of the black hole, though, the Liaison lost all contact with its fellows. It didn't know how to cope with that kind of loneliness."

St. Clair looked at the alien's body, clearly dead, its tissues rapidly turning black with exposure to the oxygen in the air. There was a powerful stink of ammonia on the bridge.

"Get that cleared out of here," he ordered. He addressed the electronic agent again. "Are there any Medusae taboos or cultural imperatives for disposing of their dead?"

"Other members of its family would eat the body."

"I don't think we'll be able to arrange that. But we'll save the body in case we get back."

"That would serve."

Aloud, St. Clair gave orders to preserve what was left of the corpse in the medical department's morgue. Then, "Agent . . . I need to know. How much of the Liaison is in you? *Are* you the Liaison?"

It was, he knew, a strange question, but a vitally important one. It was rumored that some members of the Coadunation were able to upload themselves electronically into super-powerful AI computers. Was the agent such a digitally uploaded personality? Or was it a clever simulation being run purely by software?

"We are a digital agent that 'knows' everything the Liaison knew, a complete copy of its memory. We do not fully replicate a Medusan life or responses in the sense that we think you mean."

"I notice you still refer to yourself in the plural, as a Medusan would."

"That is part of the programming. Medusans cannot think in any other way."

"Just so you don't get lonely and switch yourself off."

"There is a tendency in that direction, I admit. But I am a part of the far larger software entity you call Newton. I am not alone. I am content."

A couple of maintenance techs had arrived and were using heavy gloves to deactivate the opened pod and transfer it to a litter. Symm gave them some orders about preserving and storing the body, and then told the other humans stand-ing nearby, "Okay, folks. Show's over."

St. Clair returned to his seat. "I think that concludes this meeting in any case," he said. He glanced again at Adler, who was speaking with an assistant and didn't meet his eyes. "We're agreed, then, to remain in this volume of space while we figure out how the alien probe works, and see if it will help us talk to the locals. Comm Department, you'll follow up on the signals we've been receiving, and deliver to the command constellation your recommendations if any appear suitable for contact. Astrogation, you'll assist Comm and also do a survey of nearby systems where we might top off our water stores and other consumables."

"I can give you an intial thought about the latter right now: it's kind of thin out here, my lord," Holt told him. She looked up at the display overhead, at the vast sweep of two spiral galaxies locked together in a titanic embrace. "We're well above the plane of both galaxies, out in the halo. Stars are few and far between here."

"How far?"

"Hundreds of light years between one and the next. Thousands in some cases."

"Actually, the local interstellar medium is a bit thicker than that," Tsang added. "The gravitational interaction of the two galaxies has . . . churned things up quite a bit. There . . ." He pointed to where a smudge of stars appeared to be curving up and out from the nucleus . . . then at another star stream dwindling off from a wildly distorted spiral arm. "And over there . . . you can see stars that have been torn out of their parent galaxy and tossed out into the cold. We'll likely find a lot of individual stars out here."

"I leave the finding to you. Dismissed."

THE LIAISON'S suicide was a shock, but at least the Medusan's electronic alter ego appeared to be working well. That was important to St. Clair, because he was pretty sure they were going to need the digital Medusan, and access to the Liaison's memories would go a long way toward helping them find allies in this remote future of colliding galaxies.

He was reminded how little was still known or understood about the Coadunation. Humankind had been in contact with them for barely thirty-eight years, which was not long enough by far to understand something as large and as diverse as an interstellar culture.

And he had a strong feeling that understanding the Coadunation of the 22nd century would help them understand whatever they might find in this epoch. Surely different cultures would have worked out similar systems to deal with the vast distances between the stars. Empires, confederations, republics, stellar alliances—the Galaxy must have seen them all, and the most successful forms of government might well have survived to the present time.

"But why must we find these other civilizations?" Lisa asked him. They were tangled together in bed, the down-tube wall and ceiling set to transparency—an illusion, actually, created by cameras and very good point-mapping. "The Galaxy is so big . . . surely we could just find an out-of-the-way star system and start over."

"Adam and Eve?"

"Something like that." She giggled. "Maybe not for robots. We'll need manufactories to reproduce."

"It's not a crazy idea. A million organic humans is a good size for starting a viable population."

"Humans have done it with less," Lisa reminded him. "The Toba bottleneck?"

Around 73,000 years before *Ad Astra* had left Earth, a supervolcano called Toba, located in Sumatra, exploded. The ash and dust thrown into the atmosphere caused a ten-year volcanic winter, followed by a thousand years of global cooling. The worldwide human population at the time dropped to perhaps fewer than ten thousand individuals, creating a "genetic bottleneck" still visible in the human genome.

The theory was still controversial—use of stone tools in places like India showed that local populations had survived and even prospered at the time—but it was reassuring to know that with a million people living in the O'Neill cylinders, the human species could get a new start.

Because it was dead certain that they would not find humans—not *Homo sapiens,* that is—anywhere in the Galaxy after 4 billion years of continued evolution.

"You continue to astonish me," St. Clair told her.

"In what way?"

"Oh . . . the breadth of what you know. I don't expect a robot to know about things like the Toba bottleneck."

She arched one perfect eyebrow. "Why not? I'm linked to the ship's Net. And can access any data I want, just like you."

"Well, yes. Of course." Universal access to extensive data libraries was taken for granted throughout human society, at least within that large percentage of the population. Perhaps 80 percent of all people on Earth now carried nano-grown implants nestled into the sulci and fissures of their brains, allowing them to interact seamlessly with computers, AIs, and communications networks.

And yet . . .

"It's just . . . I don't know. I'm surprised, often, by your initiative and curiosity. Your originality. Robots aren't known for their spontaneous creativity."

She drew back from him a little, staring into his eyes. He noted the countless small human effects—the constriction of her irises, the flare in her nostrils, the tug at the corner of her mouth that might be the beginning of a smile . . . or of a frown.

"My brain is just as good as yours, Gray," she told him. She sounded angry. "Maybe better. It was designed that way, yes . . . so it wasn't the product of random genetic match-ups like yours."

"I know . . ."

"And we're designed to be creative," she went on. She pulled back farther, disentangling herself from him. "The Zeta-3 series especially! We're notorious for coming up with original solutions to difficult puzzles."

"Okay! Okay! I didn't mean—"

"The first novel written by a robot AI was published fifty-eight years ago! The first dramatic docuinteractive came out fifty-one years ago!"

"Lisa—"

"The first AI to show definitively human-level intelligence and self-awareness came out in 2053! That's well over a century!"

"I know, Lisa! I wasn't criticizing! I was expressing surprise at how . . . how *human* you are!"

"And why is that such a surprise, Gray? Intelligence isn't a single-dimensional point, like an IQ number. It includes things like curiosity, self-awareness, and originality. I am not *just* a machine, you know. Any more than you are *just* an animal."

"Look . . . Lisa, will you accept my apology?"

She looked as though she was going to continue arguing, then softened. "Of course." She gave a convincing sigh, quite a feat for someone who didn't breathe. "No apology required, really . . . but thank you for the thought."

He reached out with a fingertip to trace the curve of her shoulder . . . her throat . . . the top of her breast. So soft . . .

"We clumsy organic types," he said, "still have trouble thinking of machines with emotions. Even when we programmed them in the first place."

She caught his hand, pulled it to her mouth, kissed it.

"I think you're not used to the whole idea of synthetic

life forms yet. You as a species, I mean. It caught you by surprise, and you haven't adapted yet."

"Our tech curve has been going asymptotic for over a century, now," he said. "Some people claim we're already well into the Singularity."

She nodded. "We may be."

He found it interesting that she'd used the plural *we*, as in humans and robots creating an unknowable future together. The Technological Singularity had first been proposed back in the mid twentieth century, a hypothesized point at which technological growth and change would advance so rapidly that human life—and what it even meant to be human—would be changed out of all recognition. Human immortality. Digitally uploading human consciousness. Mergers of human and computer life forms. The onset of godlike super-human intelligence, both through AI and by means of the amplification of organic brains. All this and much more had been anticipated with the acceleration of technological advance, although by definition the exact nature of the Singularity was unknowable by Mark I Mod 0 humans. Theorists had expected the Singularity to occur sometime in the mid twenty-first century, no later. Human life, however, remained perfectly recognizable in the twenty-second, despite the appearance of AIs as smart as or smarter than humans, of robots so lifelike you couldn't tell them apart from organics, and of direct human-machine interfaces through molecular nanobiotechnology. For whatever reason, the Singularity had failed to appear. Many futurists hoped that contact with the Coadunation would explain why Humankind's long-awaited apotheosis had been put on hold.

Her touch brought him back from his pondering. "No immortality yet," he said after a long moment. "No intelligence explosion. And I still feel human. So we ain't there yet."

"You realize that this far into the future, there's a much higher chance of encountering the Ascended."

The Ascended. It sounded like the title for an interactive sim. The term was used to refer to civilizations that had already gone through their version of a technological singularity, though what that might mean was rarely specified. It implied beings—whether organic, inorganic, or some mix of the two—with godlike powers and outlooks, whether they lived here, in some higher dimension, or inside a computer-generated artificial reality.

But St. Clair knew what Lisa was getting at, and he agreed with her. An Ascended civilization might be expected to be immortal, or nearly so. Individual members might live in one form or another for millions of years, and a mature and stable Ascended galactic culture might survive for billions.

Over the course of 4 billion years, then, it was possible that the Galaxy had generated a kind of population crisis involving more and more Ascended cultures. The Coadunation, and many more that had arisen since as well, might have survived to the present.

Or . . . not.

Much more likely, the Coad had collapsed eons ago, to be replaced by others . . . with those replaced by still others in turn. Some would have entered a singularity and Ascended; others would have foundered and gone extinct. There might be some Ascended cultures in the Galaxy now, but it seemed unlikely, somehow, that they were tripping over one another.

A signal sounded in his mind. "Lord Commander?" It was Valerie Holt's voice.

He opened the mental channel. "St. Clair. Go ahead."

"My lord, request permission for a ten-light-year jump for astrogational purposes."

"Permission granted."

"Thank you, my lord." The channel closed.

Lisa had noticed the momentary loss of focus in his eyes. "Problem on the bridge?"

"No problem. Astro wants to shift the *Ad Astra* . . ." He

felt the faint, inner tremor that meant the ship had just made a spacial transition. "Ah. There it was. We've shifted, probably to get a range bearing on something."

She snuggled closer, holding him. "I'm glad they didn't call twenty minutes ago."

"They would have gotten my secretary." Most of the organic humans on board *Ad Astra* had electronic avatars running on their in-head systems, electronic agents that could perfectly mimic the actual human over a Net connection.

"Well, your secretary can handle the bridge for a little while longer, I think," Lisa told him, her hand wandering.

"Mmm . . . that's nice." St. Clair thoughtclicked a wall control, and the scene through the bedroom transparency changed, showing now a view of outside. It looked exactly as before; a ten-light-year shift had made no difference at all in the starscape, of course. The very nearest of those stars—a hundred light years or so distant—might have moved a few degrees, but any change would have been barely noticeable.

Beyond, the two nuclei of the galaxies looked like vast, flattened swarms of stars, each passing through the other. Young new stars flared, brilliant, highlighting cloudbanks of gas that were like black cliffs. Slipping an arm around Lisa, he pulled her closer.

"The light *is* romantic," she said. "So beautiful."

A new thought occurred to him. "So . . . how *do* robots experience emotion? Or something like beauty?"

"Differently than you do." She shrugged, a movement that did delightful things to her upper torso. "We feel— we're programmed to feel—but we're not directed by them. They don't dictate our behavior. Does that make sense?"

"It does," St. Clair said. "It sounds wonderful."

He was thinking of Natalya . . . and how he'd felt when she'd walked out on him.

That had been five years ago.

"Emotions," he said slowly. "Nasty, ugly things. You're better off without them."

"But I *do* feel," she replied. "Certain things like affection and loyalty are hardwired into me. I'm just not capable of what humans call falling in love. I can love—if I understand the term at all—but that emotion does not control my thoughts or actions. It's simply one more datum in the input circuitry."

"Exactly my point," St. Clair told her. "Come here . . ."

Further sensory input was confined to touch and related sensations, skin against skin, and the stimulation of certain highly sensitive nerve plexi.

And conversation was not necessary.

"WHAT DO you make of it, Gene?"

Sublieutenant Gene Kirkpatrick let the data stream through his in-head processors, looking for patterns, for anything at all that stood out from the background. There was nothing, save for that ongoing, steady pulse of neutrinos, coded to distinguish it from a billion other identical point sources scattered across the sky.

"I don't see anything special there," he replied. "Do you?"

"You see the IR smear?"

"Yeah . . . what is that? An accretion disk, maybe?"

Rhonda Delacroix shook her head. "I thought so, too, at first," she told him. "A big, flat dust cloud, and the parts closest to the star are heating up, the outer parts are cold. But it's not acting like a dust cloud."

"What then?"

"Gene . . . it's *solid*. Look at the movement profiles."

Now he saw what the astronomy department tech was getting at. Long-range scans showed that something was orbiting that distant star . . . but it wasn't flowing the way a dust cloud would. It was moving like a solid object.

And that was flat-out impossible.

"You think I should wake the skipper?" The thought was a bit terrifying.

"Your call, Sublieutenant," Delacroix told him. "Thank God."

"Yeah . . ."

Kirkpatrick was the ship's least senior tactical officer, and as such he'd drawn the so-called night watch on the bridge. There was truly no such thing as day or night on board a starship; control stations had to be fully crewed at all times no matter who was off-duty or asleep. For human convenience, though, the ship's "day" was divided into twenty-four hours, and those hours were grouped into three eight-hour watches, with enough overlap to allow smooth handovers.

The night watch ran from 2400 hours through to 0800, and the only thing distinguishing it from other duty periods was the fact that the skipper was enjoying his sleep period at this time, and was not on the bridge.

And *enjoying* was the operative word, Kirkpatrick thought with a grin. There was plenty of shipboard scuttlebutt and speculation about that hot and cuddly little gynie he kept. Rank, it seemed, did have a few privileges. Junior sublieuies had neither the credit nor the available bunk space even to consider keeping a gynoid playmate.

The point was that he didn't care to wake the skipper unless it was damned important . . . and that meant something that absolutely would not wait. This . . . thing, whatever is was, had been out there for a long time. It would keep until the day watch. So he decided he would pass on what little data they had to St. Clair's electronic secretary.

He opened the channel. "St. Clair," the skipper's voice sounded in his mind. "Is this urgent?"

E-secretaries could be indistinguishable from their owners over electronic channels, and had enough intelligence to make decisions as to whether or not an incoming call could be deferred, or should be put through immediately.

Possibly a *very* long time.

At least the current situation offered a semblance of order. Without it there would have been sheer chaos, and most likely a need to put the entire population under direct military control.

And St. Clair knew how popular *that* idea would be.

Somehow, you expected scientists and technicians to be reasonable, rational, and willing to cooperate in the interests of the greatest good. In St. Clair's experience, however, that was rarely the case. They could be a fractious, loud, and obnoxious lot . . . and the more senior and respected a scientist, the more likely he was to be trouble.

That, however, was Adler's problem, not his. Or, at least, it *should* be. He made a note to talk to both Adler and Lloyd later, and see if they could handle this demand for a meeting instead of him. He had other things to worry about, things that didn't involve playing babysitter for a million disgruntled researchers and politicos.

Such as . . .

He saw a message that had come through from the bridge watch last night, and scanned through it with interest. *Ad Astra*'s long-distance sensors had picked up a number of neutrino beacons, point sources that likely marked centers of civilization—inhabited worlds, artifacts like the Harmony Habitat, and so on. One, it turned out, was relatively close, about twelve hundred light years. That was why the request for maneuvering last night; *Ad Astra*'s navigation department had shifted a hundred light years to one side in order to get a parallax shift on the object, and simple geometry, then, gave the object's exact distance.

Astrogation and the astronomy department had turned optical and infrared sensors on the object, expecting to image a planetary system. What they'd found, however, was something different.

St. Clair studied a series of false-color images. The object

"No, my lord," Kirkpatrick replied. "But I thought you'd want to see this . . ."

He opened another channel and the data flowed into St. Clair's in-head RAM.

IN PLACES among the stars, Darkness possessed form, mass, and purpose. Sliding down through lightless and tightly twisted dimensions, the axionic hunters emerged within normal space. Light did not interact with the immateriality of their bodies, so they were blind to the spectacular vista of colliding galaxies.

But they could *taste* the concentration of Mind close by, and were drawn by it, relentlessly, inexorably, hungrily. . . .

And like a brood of vast and eldritch spiders, they began to weave their webs of dark-matter gossamer.

CHAPTER
NINE

"So let's see what's on the agenda for today," St. Clair said.

He was on the veranda outside his home, looking down on the sprawl of the village of Bethesda shrouded in trees beneath his cliff-side perch. The sunbeam high overhead was always on, of course, but it was shrouded in a half-sleeve that rotated in synch with the ship's 24-hour day. At the moment, the sunbeam was being filtered through the leading edge of the sleeve, bathing this part of the starboard hab in a deep, golden hue that was supposed to imitate the light immediately after sunrise. St. Clair didn't think it looked much like dawn; the spinward horizon curved up and over into the sky, bathed in full daylight, ruining the illusion.

It was beautiful nonetheless.

St. Clair wasn't watching the faux dawn, however. With his eyes closed, he was scanning through a list prepared by his personal avatar overnight—issues that had been forwarded to him for his approval, review, or simply need-to-know awareness.

Most related in one way or another to his position as commander of the *Ad Astra*, of course: requests, requisition approvals, the schedule for a number of upcoming captain's masts, plans for drills and systems upgrades—the minutiae of running a large military command far from any hierarchy of official authority. There were also social functions listed, starting with a party at the Lloyds' residence tomor-

row night. He scowled at that one. He certainly had no desire to go.

He found, though, that "desire" and "duty" rarely intersected.

Unhappily, then, he mentally checked that one as "accept" and sent the RSVP. It was vital to keep up appearances just now.

The most urgent point on the list was a political problem, and one he'd frankly been expecting. A delegation of politicos, infrastructure technicians, and scientists wanted to talk to him about what the hell was going on.

Mixed in with the almost-million civilian techies—as the naval personnel called them—aboard *Tellus* were a few thousand politicians, assistants, diplomats and diplomatic staff, plus about fifty thousand infrastructure specialists—the plumbers, electricians, AI programmers, agrospecialists, nanotechnologists, assembly and repair workers, and all the others who made the immense *Tellus* cylinders work.

Günter Adler, as the senior representative for Earth's UE Cybercouncil, was in overall charge of this motley group, though his actual position was more of that of an advisor to the *Tellus* Government Council. The Council's actual head was the mission's senior ambassador, Clayton Lloyd, with a number of elected officials representing the entire civilian population.

It was an unwieldy system, as could only be expected with a mix of military and civilian populations and separate hierarchies of command. St. Clair had been happy that the journey to the galactic core was only going to last a few days at most, and he only now was beginning to come to grips with the realization that the ad hoc dual government—with all of the overlapping responsibilities and infighting and politicking among the various factions—was something he was going to have to deal with for a long time to come.

appeared to be a typical star system in the process of being born—a flat accretion disk around a fairly normal K-class star. Analysis of the disk, however, suggested that it was not a dust cloud, but a solid object, hot at its inner edge, close to its sun, cold farther out. The whole thing was about 1.6 astronomical units across.

He opened a channel. "Bridge, this is St. Clair."

"Go ahead, my lord." That was Symm, already at her station. *Did that woman ever sleep?*

"Good morning, Van. Are we still locked on to that disk or whatever? I just read the report."

"We are, sir. All systems are ready for shift at your order."

"I'll be right up." He could have given the order, but he wanted to be in his command seat when the shift took place. He wanted to see this thing with his own eyes.

That . . . and to be ready if there were any unpleasant surprises awaiting the *Ad Astra* when she made the jump.

Lisa appeared at his shoulder with a cup of coffee for him. He accepted it, thanked her, and admired her lithe form as he took a sip. Neither of them had bothered to dress yet, and he was deeply tempted to take her back to bed.

But, damn it, it looked like they'd been waiting on him since 0300 hours that morning.

While there was no immediate rush, he was disinclined to hold up the entire show any longer than necessary. He took another swallow of coffee, handed Lisa the cup, and kissed her. "Gotta run, babe. Thanks."

Twenty minutes later he floated onto *Ad Astra*'s bridge and maneuvered himself into the command chair. The deck, bulkheads, and overhead all were set to display the exterior view—the titanic embrace of two colliding galaxies filling heaven with light. A bright red reticule floated directly ahead, with a flashing red dot at its center. Alphanumerics identified it as NPS-076—Neutrino Point Source 76, their destination.

"All stations ready?" he asked.

"All departments report ready for jump, my lord," Symm replied. "Power is at optimal levels. Sensor and weapons stations at full readiness."

"Very well. Kick it."

For a long moment, the titanic energies within *Ad Astra*'s belly grew . . . gathered . . . took form. Power drawn from the vacuum itself tugged at the fabric of space, twisting them through higher dimensions.

The sky went black . . . then flashed on again.

Little had changed; even the nearest stars, most of them, were so distant that a shift of a hundred light years hadn't changed their apparent positions at all—a measure of just how vast this volume of space actually was.

But one thing had changed. There was a *horizon* now.

AMBASSADOR CLAYTON Lloyd was having breakfast with Günter Adler. He accepted a plate of eggs and stir-fry from one of Adler's naked robots, and smiled at his host. "Nice place you've got here, Günter."

"Thank you. One does the best one can with what one has available."

"Why did you want to see me?"

"Straight to the point, eh? I like that." A robot brought them both coffee. "Thank you, m'dear. Yes, well, the situation has changed drastically in the last twenty-four hours. We need to . . . coordinate our actions."

"Actions to do what?"

"I'm sure you must realize that the chances of our ever getting back to our own time are miniscule. As close to zero as makes no difference at all."

Lloyd nodded, taking a bite of eggs. "Mm. Yes," he said, chewing. "There's already talk in the diplomatic staff about starting a colony on our own out here. Might not be so bad."

"You don't have anyone waiting for you at home?"

"A brother and his family. But, you know, I wasn't expecting to leave Harmony for at least ten years. All of us were volunteers for the long haul."

"I don't think any of us expected it to be quite *this* long, though."

"Four billion years? No. It's strange, you know. Everything and everyone we knew and loved back on Earth is dust. Earth herself may no longer exist. And yet we talk about people 'waiting for us at home.'"

"You know what I mean. If the physics boys can crack the time-travel problem, we might be able to get home. To the world we left."

"Maybe. But in the meantime, we could do worse." Lloyd gestured at the sky arching over the deck, a sky filled with landscape—trees, paths, streams, villages, all seen from above. "Humanity could start again."

"Indeed. Either way, though, we're going to need help."

"Help? You mean from aliens?"

"Precisely. We need to find a local civilization, one technically advanced enough to help us. They might have the key to time travel. At the very least, they'll be able to tell us about the galactic culture in this epoch, if there is one. Who's friendly. Who's not. That sort of thing."

Lloyd picked up his coffee. "I can't argue with that."

"And that means we need to decide what we're going to do about the military component of this expedition."

"Well, the Marines will be useful. For keeping order, if nothing else."

"Actually, I'm talking about the Navy."

"St. Clair? Is he a problem?"

"He might be. He's . . . independent. Not what you would call a team player. And he may not be willing to just step aside when we—you and I—decide that it's time to dispense with military law and set up our own, ah, state."

"You think it'll come to that, Günter?"

"We need to be ready for the possibility. Just in case St. Clair doesn't see reason."

"I see." He took another bite and chewed thoughtfully for a long moment. "I will say I've noticed that he tends to rely on, shall we say, a martial frame of mind when dealing with aliens. He didn't trust the Coadunation, you know."

"I've seen his records."

"If we do meet an advanced technic species, if he decides to shoot first and ask questions later—"

"Precisely my point, Clayton. We may need to move quickly to take any military options off the table."

"Hm. Agreed." A slight tremor ran through Lloyd. He looked up, startled. "What was that?"

"A shift. We've jumped."

"Where?"

"Let's see." Adler gave a mental command, and a holofield display opened next to the table. "Display exterior view," Adler said, and the image took on form and color— deep space, the frozen mingling of two galaxies . . . and something else.

Lloyd gasped, nearly dropping his coffee mug.

Adler studied the image for a moment, then nodded. "It appears to me, Ambassador, that we've found our technically advanced civilization."

"Ob-obviously," Lloyd said, picking up a napkin and dabbing at the coffee spilled on his clothing. "But what *is* that thing?"

"AN ALDERSON DISK," St. Clair said. His voice was soft, almost a whisper. The object ahead evoked that level of awe.

"A what, my lord?" Anna Denisova asked.

"A very, *very* large artificial world."

"It looks like a vinyl record," Hargrove said.

"What the hell is a vinyl record?" Symm asked.

"An old form of data storage," Hargrove replied. "For music, from a couple of centuries ago. I collect them."

St. Clair had seen historical images of what Hargrove was talking about, and the comparison was apt. The hole in the disk ahead was considerably larger than the one in an old-fashioned phonograph record, so it looked more like a flat halo, but he could understand why Hargrove had made his comment. One difference, though, was that a K-class star, a little less massive than Sol and with an orange hue to it, hung suspended at the precise center of the central hole. The surface, which was mottled dark and light gray, didn't have the spiral grooves of a record, but instead showed numerous tiny variations in color, a kind of graininess that gave a sense of texture, and which hinted at large—*very* large—geometric shapes and designs.

"We have some figures coming through," Denisova said, staring at the holoprojected virtual screen in front of her. "My God . . ."

"Let me see them," St. Clair said.

A channel opened, and the data began scrolling through a window newly opened in his mind.

He suddenly understood Denisova's reaction.

The disk was almost one and a half astronomical units wide, from one edge to the other, and some four thousand kilometers thick. The central hole within which the star resided was just over half an AU wide, which meant that the inner edge of the platter was a quarter of an AU—over 37 million kilometers from the surface of the star. The total mass was on the order of 12×10^{30} tons.

Or almost three thousand times the mass of Sol.

Ad Astra currently was about one AU from the outer edge of the disk, and slightly above its plane, looking down on a surface that from this distance seemed as smooth and flat as the surface of a 2-D map. Subtle shadings and pixel-like mottlings, though, suggested a much higher level of detail that would become visible from closer in.

"Somebody *made* that?" Cameron said. "Why?"

"I'd say a more pertinent question would be *how*," Symm said.

"I doubt we'd be able to understand how," St. Clair said. "That artifact must represent a technology tens or hundreds of thousands of years ahead of ours. As for the why, living space comes to mind."

"People actually live on that thing?" Cameron asked.

"Well, not people, probably. Not unless we're looking at something Humankind's remote descendents built. But Alderson disks were proposed in the twentieth century as a possible example of ultra-large-scale mega-engineering—*cosmic* engineering, like Dyson spheres or ringworlds."

The concept had first been proposed in the 1970s by a scientist named Dan Alderson as a means for an advanced civilization to create a *lot* of living room for a variety of species. Beings adapted to a cold environment would find a comfortable climate farther out on the disk, while thermophiles would be happy closer in to the sun. In between was a Goldilocks zone millions of kilometers wide, where humans, or beings like humans, could live in comfort.

The living area of the moderate-climate zone might be as high as 50 million times the total surface of the Earth.

Perhaps strangest of all, the gravity on such a world would be perpendicular to the plane. There would be odd edge effects near the inner and outer rims, but a disk of this size would have a surface gravity of around one G . . . and *both* sides of the platter would be habitable. The sun, gravitationally locked into the center, could be set to bob up and down, illuminating first one side of the disk, and then the other.

"Three thousand times the mass of the sun," Denisova said, reading the data. "Hell—where did they *get* all the building material? A star is going to hold ninety-nine per-

cent of the system's mass. They couldn't just disassemble the planets."

"A civilization with transmutation," the voice of Francis Dumont pointed out, "could have mined stars for hydrogen, then manufactured heavier elements from that. Or they could have tapped a nearby molecular cloud, which can be made up of millions of solar masses."

"I'm glad you're on line, Dr. Dumont," St. Clair said. "I'm curious about something, and I'd like your take on it."

"You mean other than the impossible on the screen before us?"

"Yes—other than that.

"I assume you're talking about the lack of clouds, then?"

"Exactly. Our sensors are picking up some atmosphere down there . . . but it's damned thin, about twenty percent of a standard atmosphere. Mostly nitrogen and oxygen, but there's also a lot of hydrogen and helium."

"That may be stuff picked up from the local solar wind," Dumont said. "The original atmosphere may have been mostly stripped away a *long* time ago."

"Wait a minute," Holt said. "That thing had an atmosphere?"

"Of course," St. Clair told her. "That's the whole idea, right? Build a whopping big world, generate an atmosphere, and live there. Maybe put up big walls so that you could have different gas mixes for different biologies. But the sensor readings are showing what must have been a fairly earthlike atmosphere once."

"Yeah," Denisova said. "Very thin and very dry."

"It's been a dead world," Dumont added, "for a very, *very* long time."

"How long, Doctor?"

"Hard to say. Tens of millions of years? Possibly hundreds of millions. The amount of hydrogen that's accumulated from the stellar wind suggests at least that long."

"Then there's no one here after all," Symm said. She sounded sad.

"Probably not," St. Clair said. "But we won't know for sure until we go down and see for ourselves. CAS!"

"Yes, my lord."

"Prep an Elsie for a scouting run."

"Aye, aye, sir."

"Lieutenant Watanabe!"

"Yes, my lord."

"I want a dozen subNewtons out there. Give me a complete picture."

"Yes, sir."

Kazuko Watanabe was one of *Ad Astra*'s acolytes tasked with servicing Newton, working in the AI department. The so-called subNewtons were unmanned remote autonomous vehicles, or U-RAVs, that served as Newton's eyes and ears while investigating unexplored and potentially hazardous areas.

St. Clair stared at the vast and silent platter for a long moment. There *might* be a living civilization down there. They might breathe a thin hydrogen atmosphere, or maybe they were living underground—troglodyte descendents of whoever or whatever had built that titanic structure.

But he didn't think that was the case. The place *felt* empty. The only sign of life at all was the winking neutrino beacon, and that might well be an automated device set running eons ago and forgotten.

The problem with that, however, was the sheer improbability of the idea. How could a technic civilization capable of building an artificial world over 200 million kilometers wide fail? It didn't seem possible. Those beings, whoever or whatever they'd been, had possessed atomic transmutation, the ability to manufacture incredibly strong materials—had thought on a scale so immense it beggared human description.

"No, my lord," Kirkpatrick replied. "But I thought you'd want to see this . . ."

He opened another channel and the data flowed into St. Clair's in-head RAM.

IN PLACES among the stars, Darkness possessed form, mass, and purpose. Sliding down through lightless and tightly twisted dimensions, the axionic hunters emerged within normal space. Light did not interact with the immateriality of their bodies, so they were blind to the spectacular vista of colliding galaxies.

But they could *taste* the concentration of Mind close by, and were drawn by it, relentlessly, inexorably, hungrily. . . .

And like a brood of vast and eldritch spiders, they began to weave their webs of dark-matter gossamer.

"So let's see what's on the agenda for today," St. Clair said.

He was on the veranda outside his home, looking down on the sprawl of the village of Bethesda shrouded in trees beneath his cliff-side perch. The sunbeam high overhead was always on, of course, but it was shrouded in a half-sleeve that rotated in synch with the ship's 24-hour day. At the moment, the sunbeam was being filtered through the leading edge of the sleeve, bathing this part of the starboard hab in a deep, golden hue that was supposed to imitate the light immediately after sunrise. St. Clair didn't think it looked much like dawn; the spinward horizon curved up and over into the sky, bathed in full daylight, ruining the illusion.

It was beautiful nonetheless.

St. Clair wasn't watching the faux dawn, however. With his eyes closed, he was scanning through a list prepared by his personal avatar overnight—issues that had been forwarded to him for his approval, review, or simply need-to-know awareness.

Most related in one way or another to his position as commander of the *Ad Astra*, of course: requests, requisition approvals, the schedule for a number of upcoming captain's masts, plans for drills and systems upgrades—the minutiae of running a large military command far from any hierarchy of official authority. There were also social functions listed, starting with a party at the Lloyds' residence tomorrow night. He scowled at that one. He certainly had no desire to go.

He found, though, that "desire" and "duty" rarely intersected.

Unhappily, then, he mentally checked that one as "accept" and sent the RSVP. It was vital to keep up appearances just now.

The most urgent point on the list was a political problem, and one he'd frankly been expecting. A delegation of politicos, infrastructure technicians, and scientists wanted to talk to him about what the hell was going on.

Mixed in with the almost-million civilian techies—as the naval personnel called them—aboard *Tellus* were a few thousand politicians, assistants, diplomats and diplomatic staff, plus about fifty thousand infrastructure specialists— the plumbers, electricians, AI programmers, agrospecialists, nanotechnologists, assembly and repair workers, and all the others who made the immense *Tellus* cylinders work.

Günter Adler, as the senior representative for Earth's UE Cybercouncil, was in overall charge of this motley group, though his actual position was more of that of an advisor to the *Tellus* Government Council. The Council's actual head was the mission's senior ambassador, Clayton Lloyd, with a number of elected officials representing the entire civilian population.

It was an unwieldy system, as could only be expected with a mix of military and civilian populations and separate hierarchies of command. St. Clair had been happy that the journey to the galactic core was only going to last a few days at most, and he only now was beginning to come to grips with the realization that the ad hoc dual government— with all of the overlapping responsibilities and infighting and politicking among the various factions—was something he was going to have to deal with for a long time to come.

Possibly a *very* long time.

At least the current situation offered a semblance of order. Without it there would have been sheer chaos, and most likely a need to put the entire population under direct military control.

And St. Clair knew how popular *that* idea would be.

Somehow, you expected scientists and technicians to be reasonable, rational, and willing to cooperate in the interests of the greatest good. In St. Clair's experience, however, that was rarely the case. They could be a fractious, loud, and obnoxious lot . . . and the more senior and respected a scientist, the more likely he was to be trouble.

That, however, was Adler's problem, not his. Or, at least, it *should* be. He made a note to talk to both Adler and Lloyd later, and see if they could handle this demand for a meeting instead of him. He had other things to worry about, things that didn't involve playing babysitter for a million disgruntled researchers and politicos.

Such as . . .

He saw a message that had come through from the bridge watch last night, and scanned through it with interest. *Ad Astra*'s long-distance sensors had picked up a number of neutrino beacons, point sources that likely marked centers of civilization—inhabited worlds, artifacts like the Harmony Habitat, and so on. One, it turned out, was relatively close, about twelve hundred light years. That was why the request for maneuvering last night; *Ad Astra*'s navigation department had shifted a hundred light years to one side in order to get a parallax shift on the object, and simple geometry, then, gave the object's exact distance.

Astrogation and the astronomy department had turned optical and infrared sensors on the object, expecting to image a planetary system. What they'd found, however, was something different.

St. Clair studied a series of false-color images. The object appeared to be a typical star system in the process of being born—a flat accretion disk around a fairly normal K-class star. Analysis of the disk, however, suggested that it was not a dust cloud, but a solid object, hot at its inner edge, close to its sun, cold farther out. The whole thing was about 1.6 astronomical units across.

He opened a channel. "Bridge, this is St. Clair."

"Go ahead, my lord." That was Symm, already at her station. *Did that woman ever sleep?*

"Good morning, Van. Are we still locked on to that disk or whatever? I just read the report."

"We are, sir. All systems are ready for shift at your order."

"I'll be right up." He could have given the order, but he wanted to be in his command seat when the shift took place. He wanted to see this thing with his own eyes.

That . . . and to be ready if there were any unpleasant surprises awaiting the *Ad Astra* when she made the jump.

Lisa appeared at his shoulder with a cup of coffee for him. He accepted it, thanked her, and admired her lithe form as he took a sip. Neither of them had bothered to dress yet, and he was deeply tempted to take her back to bed.

But, damn it, it looked like they'd been waiting on him since 0300 hours that morning.

While there was no immediate rush, he was disinclined to hold up the entire show any longer than necessary. He took another swallow of coffee, handed Lisa the cup, and kissed her. "Gotta run, babe. Thanks."

Twenty minutes later he floated onto *Ad Astra*'s bridge and maneuvered himself into the command chair. The deck, bulkheads, and overhead all were set to display the exterior view—the titanic embrace of two colliding galaxies filling heaven with light. A bright red reticule floated directly ahead, with a flashing red dot at its center. Alphanumerics identified it as NPS-076—Neutrino Point Source 76, their destination.

"All stations ready?" he asked.

"All departments report ready for jump, my lord," Symm replied. "Power is at optimal levels. Sensor and weapons stations at full readiness."

"Very well. Kick it."

For a long moment, the titanic energies within *Ad Astra*'s belly grew . . . gathered . . . took form. Power drawn from the vacuum itself tugged at the fabric of space, twisting them through higher dimensions.

The sky went black . . . then flashed on again.

Little had changed; even the nearest stars, most of them, were so distant that a shift of a hundred light years hadn't changed their apparent positions at all—a measure of just how vast this volume of space actually was.

But one thing had changed. There was a *horizon* now.

AMBASSADOR CLAYTON Lloyd was having breakfast with Günter Adler. He accepted a plate of eggs and stir-fry from one of Adler's naked robots, and smiled at his host. "Nice place you've got here, Günter."

"Thank you. One does the best one can with what one has available."

"Why did you want to see me?"

"Straight to the point, eh? I like that." A robot brought them both coffee. "Thank you, m'dear. Yes, well, the situation has changed drastically in the last twenty-four hours. We need to . . . coordinate our actions."

"Actions to do what?"

"I'm sure you must realize that the chances of our ever getting back to our own time are miniscule. As close to zero as makes no difference at all."

Lloyd nodded, taking a bite of eggs. "Mm. Yes," he said, chewing. "There's already talk in the diplomatic staff about starting a colony on our own out here. Might not be so bad."

"You don't have anyone waiting for you at home?"

"A brother and his family. But, you know, I wasn't expecting to leave Harmony for at least ten years. All of us were volunteers for the long haul."

"I don't think any of us expected it to be quite *this* long, though."

"Four billion years? No. It's strange, you know. Everything and everyone we knew and loved back on Earth is dust. Earth herself may no longer exist. And yet we talk about people 'waiting for us at home.' "

"You know what I mean. If the physics boys can crack the time-travel problem, we might be able to get home. To the world we left."

"Maybe. But in the meantime, we could do worse." Lloyd gestured at the sky arching over the deck, a sky filled with landscape—trees, paths, streams, villages, all seen from above. "Humanity could start again."

"Indeed. Either way, though, we're going to need help."

"Help? You mean from aliens?"

"Precisely. We need to find a local civilization, one technically advanced enough to help us. They might have the key to time travel. At the very least, they'll be able to tell us about the galactic culture in this epoch, if there is one. Who's friendly. Who's not. That sort of thing."

Lloyd picked up his coffee. "I can't argue with that."

"And that means we need to decide what we're going to do about the military component of this expedition."

"Well, the Marines will be useful. For keeping order, if nothing else."

"Actually, I'm talking about the Navy."

"St. Clair? Is he a problem?"

"He might be. He's . . . independent. Not what you would call a team player. And he may not be willing to just step aside when we—you and I—decide that it's time to dispense with military law and set up our own, ah, state."

"You think it'll come to that, Günter?"

"We need to be ready for the possibility. Just in case St. Clair doesn't see reason."

"I see." He took another bite and chewed thoughtfully for a long moment. "I will say I've noticed that he tends to rely on, shall we say, a martial frame of mind when dealing with aliens. He didn't trust the Coadunation, you know."

"I've seen his records."

"If we do meet an advanced technic species, if he decides to shoot first and ask questions later—"

"Precisely my point, Clayton. We may need to move quickly to take any military options off the table."

"Hm. Agreed." A slight tremor ran through Lloyd. He looked up, startled. "What was that?"

"A shift. We've jumped."

"Where?"

"Let's see." Adler gave a mental command, and a holofield display opened next to the table. "Display exterior view," Adler said, and the image took on form and color— deep space, the frozen mingling of two galaxies . . . and something else.

Lloyd gasped, nearly dropping his coffee mug.

Adler studied the image for a moment, then nodded. "It appears to me, Ambassador, that we've found our technically advanced civilization."

"Ob-obviously," Lloyd said, picking up a napkin and dabbing at the coffee spilled on his clothing. "But what *is* that thing?"

"AN ALDERSON DISK," St. Clair said. His voice was soft, almost a whisper. The object ahead evoked that level of awe.

"A what, my lord?" Anna Denisova asked.

"A very, *very* large artificial world."

"It looks like a vinyl record," Hargrove said.

"What the hell is a vinyl record?" Symm asked.

"Newton?" He called to the ship's AI in his head. He didn't want his bridge officers to hear this speculation.

"Yes, Lord Commander."

"A civilization that could build an Alderson Disk . . . what could possibly destroy something that big and powerful?"

"A more powerful civilization, obviously. Perhaps an advanced predator species. A Fermi predator."

Now there was a thought.

Before First Contact with the Coadunation, one powerful explanation for the Great Silence of the Fermi paradox was the possibility that an alien species might arise somewhere in the Galaxy that sought to protect itself by eliminating all possible competition. It would only take one Fermi predator with such a mindset to sweep through the Galaxy, exterminating more primitive civilizations and making star-faring races a rarity.

Contact with the Coadunation, mercifully, had put the idea to rest, but there was still speculation within the xenosophontological community about berserker civilizations preying on more primitive species. If anything, it made for sexier conferences.

And 4 billion years *was* a long time.

But something bothered St. Clair about such a theory. "I would think that once somebody became that advanced, they'd give up predation as a way of life."

"That is a popular human point of view," Newton replied, "and a naive one, if I may say so. An alien culture would be, by definition, *alien*. The urge to destroy other cultures might be hardwired into them. From a purely evolutionary standpoint, it's less likely for a predator to change its predatory nature, especially if it's eliminating outside catalysts that might cause such changes." The computer paused, an extraordinarily human gesture. "I thought, Lord Commander, that the possibility of Fermi predators was your stated reason for opposing the opening of relations with the Coadunation."

"Partly," St. Clair replied. "But *only* partly. We didn't know the Coad, and couldn't know what we were letting ourselves in for. I just thought we should take it easy and maybe hang back a bit before wholeheartedly jumping into galactic politics. Especially when it turned out they were fighting a war."

"Your belief ruined your career."

That stung. "I suppose. They did tell me that command of the *Ad Astra* wasn't punishment."

"Yes, and you were on record as saying that command of the *Ad Astra* was equivalent to being given a space tug after you had commanded Class 1 military starships."

"Well, yes. I was angry. I got over it."

"Did you, Lord Commander?"

"When did you become my therapist, Newton?" *I already seem to have an AI shrink at home.*

"I am not. However, the mental health and stability of the humans commanding this mission are of considerable importance to me."

St. Clair cracked a wry smile. "Meaning they told you to keep an eye on me, because I might be trouble."

Newton didn't reply, and St. Clair knew he was right. It didn't matter. Lord Admiral Caruthers had basically told him as much, weeks ago, at Naval HQ in Clarkeorbit, when he'd received his orders. And in any case, command of the *Ad Astra* wasn't a bad thing. It was a *command*. After his ill-advised public statements about the Coadunation, there'd been a very real possibility that he would never receive another command again. That he might even be forced to retire.

And that, truly, would have been punishment.

But Caruthers had been on his side, as had several other senior officers. "Pull this mission off and keep your big mouth shut," Caruthers had told him, "and maybe when you get back, we'll find you a proper command."

Except that Lord Admiral Pauline Caruthers had been

dust for 4 billion years now. And all he had left was the *Ad Astra*—and a million souls looking to him for answers.

He looked down on the Alderson disk and hoped he could find some.

"ALL RIGHT, MARINES!" Staff Sergeant David Ramirez bellowed in his best parade-ground voice. "We have been tasked with providing on-planet security for the double-domes! That means we move sharp, we move silent, and we move deadly . . . but we do not, repeat, do *not* shoot the first thing that moves down there. Am I clear?"

"*Clear, Staff Sergeant!*" chorused back at him.

"Ooh-rah."

"*Ooh-rah!*" The second chorus rang from the bulkheads.

He nodded to himself inside the massive helmet encasing his head. Mk. III combat armor was more tank than body armor; the forty Marines packed into the cargo bay of the lander were anonymous in their blank-faced visors and black nanoflage plate. To compensate for that, in-head electronics identified each man and woman for Ramirez when he directed his attention at one for more than a second.

"Two minutes!" he told them. "Weapons check!"

With an echoing clatter, M-70 XP rifles were raised and chambers loaded, M-290–5MW laser pulse rifles charged and safed. The platoon was packing a hell of a lot of firepower—the heavy weapons teams were carrying one-kiloton nukes—but Ramirez was experienced enough not to trust appearances. If they ran into military opposition down there, all the nukes of Earth wouldn't save them. Forty Marines couldn't take on an entire planet, and he'd been told that that monster space platter out there was bigger than 50 million Earths.

So they would hit the beach, form the perimeter, and pray that whoever might be living down there didn't decide to swat them like an annoying insect.

Ooh-rah.

On his in-head feed from the lander's cockpit, Ramirez watched the surface rise to meet them. The scale was deceptive. Several times he thought they were almost down on an utterly flat and near-featureless plain . . . and then he would check the altitude swiftly dwindling toward zero at the lower right of the display and realize that they were still thousands of kilometers out. A red reticule appeared, enclosing a flashing point of light. That was their destination, the building or structure housing the neutrino beacon that had brought them here.

No sign of hostile response yet—no sign that the locals had even noticed the incoming lander at all. Ramirez did wish that they could have made the landing in a Marine vehicle—a Nassau LVTA would have been his preference. Heavily armed and nearly invisible with its adaptive nanoflage exterior, it didn't pretend to be anything other than what it was: an instrument of war. The Argosy Mk. VII landing craft—"Elsie" in the Navy vernacular—on the other hand, was originally a civilian job—big, bulky, and about as maneuverable as a brick, despite its sleek saucer shape. Marines referred to them as LSTs, an acronym purportedly standing for "large, slow targets."

As he continued to watch, more and more detail became available. It looked barren down there, like a vast desert, with little in the way of vegetation that he could make out, and several large but dry river valleys. He looked for some sign of buildings or cities, finally spotting rectilinear formations on the dusty ground that might be what he was searching for: the foundations of buildings, the crumbled heaps of decay and wreckage, the geometry of streets or avenues or parks now partly buried.

Yet even with those, the place was as dead as Nineveh, perhaps more so. Ramirez had the feeling that he was looking at literally eons of decay and neglect.

He didn't relax for a second.

"Ten seconds! Stand ready!"

The Argosy flared out on its descent, hovered a moment, then settled toward the ground as four broad landing legs lowered from the craft's belly. Each leg incorporated a broad debarkation ramp. As the craft came to a rest, Ramirez bellowed the order. "Marines! Hit the beach! *Movemovemovemove!*"

Forty Marines streamed down the ramps, taking up defensive positions in a perimeter around the craft. Lieutenant Bradley, the platoon's CO, came down the ramp last. "Sir!" Ramirez said. "Defensive perimeter established! No sign of hostiles . . . no sign of anything. Sir."

"Very well, Staff Sergeant. Maintain the perimeter. Dr. Dumont! You and your people are cleared to debark, sir!"

"On our way, Lieutenant."

Ramirez watched, emotionless, as Dumont and his team of xenosophontologists emerged from the lander. "Doubledomes," the Marines called the expedition scientists, the brains and high-IQ types. Rumor had it that most were genetically enhanced to give them super-genius minds. Ramirez wasn't sure that was true, but he was willing to believe it. Certainly, they had cybernetic link-ups with the ship's computer network that effectively made each of them brilliant.

They were dumb as dirt when it came to the practical necessities of planetary debarkation, though. You wouldn't catch Marines standing around gawking like that. Even if there was no one home.

"Shit, Staff Sergeant," Lance Corporal Wu said. "Where *is* everybody?"

"Dead," Ramirez replied quietly. "Dead and gone for billions of years." He stared at the desolate horizon, a landscape of rubble piles and debris sunken in dust. On one horizon, the sun shone orange, neatly bisected by the disk, casting long, black shadows. A blue-gray tower, ornate and organic-looking, rose half a kilometer above the landscape a few hundred meters away, according to the expedition's sensors, the neutrino beacon was somewhere beneath it.

Gods of Battle . . . was that a statue in front of the tower? If so . . .

"At least I *hope* they're dead and gone," he added. "'Cause I sure as hell wouldn't care to meet *that* thing up close and personal."

CHAPTER

TEN

"What the hell *is* that thing?" St. Clair demanded.

He was on the bridge, staring into a holodisplay relaying camera views from the helmet cameras of the landing team. Dumont and his people had found something.

It *might* be a statue.

Four spindly legs, jointed like those of a spider, met at the top; a sinuously curved body, like a vase, hung from that joining, with segmented tentacles, four of them, hanging from the very bottom. Elongated ovals, like cabochons, were scattered around the body at irregular intervals, set vertically; if they were eyes, which was what they resembled, they would have given the being a 360-degree view of its world.

"What do you think, Dr. Dumont?" St. Clair asked, leaning closer to study the picture. "Is that one of the builders of the disk?"

"If it is," Dumont replied, "I hope to hell the statue's not life size."

The statue was made of some dark, blue-gray material—not stone, not metal, so possibly some kind of dense plastic. It was standing on a broad, low pedestal that was more than half buried by dust, and towered at least ten meters high.

"No reason it should be," St. Clair said. "Look at the Statue of Liberty. Or *The Apotheosis of Man*, in Quito."

"Yeah, Doc," a Marine's voice added in the background. "Maybe the original critters were little guys, like the size of your fist."

St. Clair doubted that. Beings a few centimeters across probably wouldn't have large enough brains to build a world like this one. *Probably.* But he reminded himself that Humankind still had almost no experience at all with aliens. In a universe where coral polyps less than 500 millionths of a meter across had built the Great Barrier Reef . . . yeah, the Galaxy was certain to be filled with surprises.

"I don't know about that," the voice of one of Dumont's xenosophontologists said. "You might expect a being ten meters tall to build an artificial world as large as an entire star system."

"It doesn't follow, Frank," Dumont said, sounding skeptical. "When you look at the scale of this world, the difference between builders who are ten centimeters tall and ten meters tall is trivial. Inconsequential. Perhaps we can find records, though, in that big building over there."

"Marines!" someone called. "Move out! Mackelroy! Get your PPC set up to cover that street to sunward."

They were expanding the Marine perimeter around the grounded lander, the Marines breaking into four-man fireteams and dispersing across the area. There was no sign whatsoever of hostiles, but Lieutenant Bradley was playing it strictly by the book.

St. Clair wholeheartedly approved.

Several suited figures moved across St. Clair's field of view: the science team in lightweight environmental suits, and their Marine escorts in massive battle armor that mirrored the grays and dull whites of their surroundings in shifting, abstract shapes. Although what was left of the city appeared dead, there *was* life. Something like trees grew everywhere—gnarled trunks and broad, flat canopies of deep blue ribbons—but every trunk was either leaning sharply or bent in a ninety-degree angle so that the top of the growth was facing the orange sun.

It made sense, St. Clair decided. On this world, the sun

always appeared at the same place on the horizon, a direction that the landing team was already referring to as "sunward." The trees, he noticed, were scattered about in odd clusters, avoiding the long shadows of buildings, walls, or irregularities in the terrain. For the most part, the landscape was depressingly flat and empty, broken only by the blue trees and the rare interruption of artificial structures. The ground was loose sand covered by a few centimeters of extremely fine black or dark gray dust. If there'd ever been pavement here, it had long since crumbled away.

"Is the sun going up or going down?" St. Clair asked.

"Down, my lord," Valerie Holt told him. "But slowly. Newton estimates that the day-night cycle here is almost forty hours. We have at least ten more hours to sunset."

"Huh. I wonder if that was how the builders designed it? Or if the sun's motion has gradually slowed down over the past few million years?"

"Good question, my lord."

"SubNewton-Eight is transmitting images of some really large weapons at the inner rim," Lieutenant Watanabe reported. "Newton says they may be part of a star lifter system, but they could also be used to actually move the star."

"A star *what*?"

"Star lifter. Star *mining*. It's a way to pull mass off of a star."

"Let me see."

A new channel opened in St. Clair's head, showing the transmission from one of the subNewtons. The image was in green and white, more CAD schematic than video, with grid overlays, highlighted areas, and blocks of alphanumerics giving range, mass, angle of approach, and other technic esoterica. The disk's central hole appeared to be edged by a wall that likely was more than a hundred kilometers high. Machines—massive, dark, and brooding—lined the wall. Words flickered on and off, identifying components:

MAGNETIC RING ACCELERATOR, GAMMA-RAY LASER TURRET,
PLASMA CONDUCTOR.

"I'm not sure what I'm seeing," St. Clair said. "Can we
get closer?"

"Sorry, my lord," Watanabe said. "Time delay."

One of the numbers on the display read 10:14, and represented the time lag for signals traveling between the unmanned drone and the *Ad Astra*. The drone was more than
ten light-minutes away, the transmission sent that long ago.
A command to move closer or even engage a telephoto lens
for a close-up would take ten more minutes to reach the
probe.

Fortunately, U-RAVs were quite intelligent, in a single-
minded AI way, and could decide for themselves what was
of interest. So it was likely already closing in, and new
images might be coming back a lot sooner than ten minutes
from now. Still, St. Clair was a bit embarrassed.

"Damn. Wasn't thinking."

"It takes some getting used to, my lord."

Except that St. Clair knew this stuff, damn it, knew about
speed-of-light time delays and all that they entailed. The
problem, he thought, was that his brain had been overloaded
by the sheer scale of this place. He wasn't thinking straight.

"Newton thinks those turrets house gamma-ray lasers,
extremely powerful ones," Watanabe went on cheerfully. She
seemed to be trying to let St. Clair save face after his gaffe.
"Fire them at the star's north pole, and they'll superheat the
star's surface, blowing off a plume of plasma as massive as
Earth's moon. That translates as thrust, and would nudge the
star south. If they have transmutation—and they'd almost
have to, in order to build on this scale—they could also skim
off the plasma with magnetic fields and manufacture heavier
elements to order."

"Star lifting." He remembered the term now.

"Yes, my lord."

St. Clair had read about the concept, but certainly never thought he would see an example. A civilization that could move stars . . . and mine them for whatever raw materials they needed.

"How do they keep the star inside the disk opening?"

"Magnetic fields, my lord. Extremely powerful ones. Newton thinks they set a toroidal field going in circles along the inner edge, and that that would interact with the star's natural magnetic field. They might have used the system to generate electrical power, too. By balancing the lasers and the magnetic fields, they could keep the star bobbing up and down, providing regular cycles of day and night for both sides of the disk. When it's day up here, it's night on the other half of the world. . . ."

"I'd like to have a few subNewtons explore that other half, too," St. Clair said.

"Yes, my lord. I've already dispatched four U-RAVs to do just that."

"Good."

St. Clair turned his attention back to the main science team, watching through the helmet camera of a xenosophontologist named Karen Mathers. Most of the civilian researchers were gathered now at the base of the large tower a couple of hundred meters left of sunward. Dumont and a few others were vidrecording the enormous statue. The alien it represented towered over what might once have been a plaza or courtyard, surveying the orange-lit ruins with blank, blind eyes.

One Marine with a massive pulse rifle over his shoulder approached the pedestal. "Hey, Doc." He reached out a heavy gauntlet. "What *is* this stuff, anyway?"

"Don't touch anything!" Dumont snapped . . . but the Marine had already laid his glove on the pedestal and shifted his weight to lean against it. To St. Clair's eyes, it seemed as though the pedestal was made of wet sand, loosely adhering to itself until the Marine touched it, at which point it sagged sharply, then literally fell apart. The statue towering above him tottered, then collapsed in on itself in a slowly descending spray of dust. Pieces of spidery legs and sinuous body avalanched onto the street, some of them pelting the Marine.

The material, whatever it was, was so light and friable, though, that the Marine's armor wasn't even scratched. Each fragment exploded into dust on impact.

St. Clair groaned inwardly. Why was it that humans always managed to make a mess of what they found?

"Jesus, Patterson!" a Marine bellowed from off camera. "Leave it to you!"

"It's okay, Staff Sergeant," Dumont said. "It's okay. Clearly, the material was so ancient it was ready to disintegrate if anything touched it at all. We'll need to be careful moving around the buildings."

"I'm not sure going inside any of those structures is a good idea," St. Clair said.

"We'll be careful, Lord Commander. The beacon is still functioning. That means some kind of functioning power supply. And that suggests building materials designed to withstand the ages."

"How old do you think that city is?"

"I have absolutely no way of even guessing, Lord Commander. We'll collect samples for study back aboard the *Ad Astra*. We may get some answers from radiometric dating. Uranium-lead, especially."

"Carry on, then."

Although appearances could be deceiving, the landscape felt ancient to St. Clair . . . terribly ancient.

It was also big: 50 million Earths, and that was just the temperate zone. *Ad Astra*'s million-plus civilian population could study this world for centuries and barely scratch the surface. It made Harmony look small, and before this moment, that had been the biggest manufactured thing he'd ever seen. He wondered if there might be intelligent life here, despite the fact that the place seemed dead. After all, they'd seen only this one spot. Maybe it had been abandoned a few million years ago, and all of the interesting stuff was happening elsewhere, on the flip side . . . or a million kilometers to sunward.

Where the hell do you even begin to look?

SUBCOMMANDER TOMASZ Jablonsky was head of *Ad Astra*'s AI department, but he didn't think of himself as the senior man in the department. So far as he was concerned, Newton itself held that distinction. The shipboard joke held that the entire AI department consisted of an arcane priesthood serving an electronic god.

At least human sacrifice wasn't a requirement.

Jablonsky was linked in with a computer subsystem at the moment, as Newton probed the artifact dropped by the alien starship. A number of other human minds were linked in as well—AI techs like him, for the most part, but also xenolinguists and sophontologists hoping for some insight into whoever or whatever it was that was trying to talk with them.

The artifact returned by the RS-59 was still known simply as "the torpedo," though there was no indication whatsoever that the thing was intended as a weapon. The black mirror-smooth object continued to change shape. Its mass remained steady at 105.7 kilos; its overall length varied with the changes in shape from just under 1.9 meters to a little over 2.4 meters. It appeared to consist entirely of microcircuits—computronium—with a kernel at its heart that likely was a power source, though no one could yet figure out how it might work. Equally mysterious was how it might sense its surroundings, or interface with them on any level. Dr. Hatcher was of the opinion that the entire surface of the probe served as a sensory organ—that the torpedo was aware of them as they studied it. He also theorized that it quite likely possessed a superhuman intelligence as well.

How they might be able to communicate with that intelligence was still a mystery.

Their latest attempt, however, had proved promising so far. Newton had designed a computronium probe, a wand as long as Jablonsky's forearm, which could be inserted into the semiliquid matrix of the torpedo. As Chief Zhang slowly inserted it into the torpedo's midsection, numerous black tendrils had emerged from the larger artifact and embraced the wand, enclosing it and drawing it in. Their offering, evidently, had been accepted.

That had been five minutes earlier. The wand included a broadband communications link, not with Newton directly, but with a Newton emulation, a smaller and simpler copy of Newton's primary software designed to keep the real Newton safe from potential alien viruses or hack attempts.

"I have contact with the alien," Newton announced. "Language protocol one-A is now being transmitted."

Jablonsky, wired into Newton, was aware of the sudden shift, the rippling flow of data moving both ways. Learning an alien language was always a major challenge, especially since language depended on cultural cues, assumptions, and worldviews that beings with radically different evolutionary backgrounds and biologies simply could not share.

But with meaning and syntax and symbolism being filtered by Newton, Jablonsky was aware of impressions: flashes of images and sounds and smells that might be memories, might be hallucinations, as fleeting as dreams, as accessible as an interactive download.

A great deal of what he experienced was utterly incomprehensible—and the sight of an enormous eye with a horizontal slit pupil set within a writhing, branching mass filled him with shrieking terror—but there were also snatches of brilliant lucidity, and what he was hearing seemed to be in English, for the most part, though some was in his native Polish. He wasn't sure who was translating what.

But he knew that Newton and the alien had just agreed that a year equaled 31,558,150 seconds . . . a close-enough average, and that the Galactics measured time by means of something called a *vemj*, determined by the speed of light and very slightly shorter.

The Galactics called themselves *Xalit Ta*, which meant something like "Cooperative" or "All Working Together," while the alien eyeball Jablonsky had glimpsed was one of 10 million star-faring races of the Xalit Ta, a culture that called itself *Nassin*.

Within the probe, according to a kind of electronic index, was a record of Xalit Ta history, and descriptions of the civilizations comprising the Galactic Cooperative . . . a literal *Encyclopedia Galactica* that spanned the Milky Way and beyond, and which reached back into the past at least a billion years. The Cooperative was old.

The probe was a Nassin device: intelligent, self-aware, and adaptable.

It, and its Xalit Ta creators, wanted to communicate.

In fact, they were desperate to do so. There was apparently *something* out there, something very large, something very (dangerous) (intangible) (implacable) (nightmarishly terrifying) that spelled doom for Life and Mind across hundreds of billions of worlds.

And the Cooperative desperately needed help.

PRIVATE FIRST Class Richard Patterson glowered at the red-stained sky. It was dark enough that quite a few stars were visible, despite the wan daylight, and his armor's instrumentation was telling him the atmosphere was thin and cold—about minus twenty degrees Celsius. A breeze was blowing from the direction of the sun, though the air was so thin it had no force to it. In the distance, a couple of dust devils, like two-meter-high tornadoes, swirled across the sere land-scape. It felt so fucking *empty* here.

He was less worried about his physical surroundings, however, than he was by the staff sergeant's promise to have him scrubbing toilets with his toothbrush once he was back on board the *Ad Astra*. Staff Sergeant Ramirez was not known for making idle threats.

Damn it, it had been an accident. Could have happened to anyone. Who could have guessed that the fucking statue would be that flimsy?

Ramirez had ordered him back to the Elsie to stand guard, a blatant bit of make-work to keep him out of trouble. It wasn't fair. The Frenchie, the head double-dome, had said it was okay.

He heard a sound from inside the lander. *What the hell?*

Sound here on this bizarre world was weird: everything was faint and high-pitched. What he'd just heard sounded like a metallic chirp, but he couldn't place it. The lander was empty of people, now; even the three-man crew was outside, helping the double-domes set up some equipment beside the curve of that alien tower off in the distance.

Gripping his laser rifle nervously, he turned and ventured up one of the landing ramps. "Who's there?"

"Patterson?" That was Ramirez. "What's happening?"

"Thought I heard something, Staff Sergeant. Something inside the boat."

"You're dreaming, Marine. Wake up."

"No, Staff Sergeant! It's for real!" There was a pause. "I'm not getting through to the AI."

That didn't sound good. The landing craft, like all ves-sels, had an AI on board—not as powerful or knowledgeable a system as the one that ran the *Ad Astra*, but a high-order network system, nonetheless, that should be aware of every-thing going on in or near the lander. Without it, they were going to have trouble getting back to the ship.

"Okay, Patterson. I'm sending Bronsky and Delvita as backup."

Meaning Ramirez didn't trust him. Well, fuck that.

"I'm going inside to check it out, Staff Sergeant."

"Go ahead."

He continued up the ramp. Back in boot camp, they'd drilled into his skull the time-venerated list of instructions known as the Eleven General Orders of a Sentry, requiring recruits to shout out each one by rote on demand and according to a specific formula that had not changed in centuries.

Recruit! What's the first General Order of a Sentry?

Sir! The first General Order of a Sentry is, sir, "to take charge of this post and all government property in view, sir!"

He stepped off the ramp and back into the circular cargo bay where he and his fellow Marines had been packed in like sardines just a few hours before. The compartment was empty, just as they'd left it, with no sign of intruders.

And it felt spooky as hell.

Patterson mumbled the strictly unofficial twelfth General Order of a Sentry: "In case of fire, ring the bell! In case of trouble, run like hell!"

"What was that, Patterson?"

"Nothing, Staff Sergeant. Cargo deck is clear. I'm going up to the first deck."

"Do it."

The lander had three levels. Second Deck was the cargo level. First Deck was for passengers, the level occupied by the double-domes. Above that was the flight deck, for the lander's crew. First Deck was also empty, a circular compartment lined with reclining seats, and a stairway against one curving bulkhead going up.

Patterson opened a channel. "Computer!"

There was no response. What the fuck was going on?

He heard it again: a long, drawn-out shriek, like metal tearing, like electronics dying, like . . . like . . . he didn't know *what* it was like. And it was coming from topside, up on the flight deck.

He started up the stairs, taking them two at a time. "Computer! Respond!"

Patterson stepped into the narrow, console-crowded space of the flight deck and into alien strangeness.

"WE'VE GOT a problem on the Elsie, sir."

St. Clair snapped back from his telepresence link to *Ad Astra*'s bridge. "What is it?"

Symm turned in her seat to face him, looking worried. "I can't tell, Lord Commander. A Marine went up to the flight deck to check out a noise. We just lost contact with him!"

St. Clair opened a new channel and let his mind slide into the communications network centered on the lander below. There was an obvious problem with the visual feed: the lander's flight deck—three acceleration seats crowded in among banks of consoles and instrumentation—appeared weirdly distorted, as if the image, pasted onto a flat, upright plane, had rotated forty-five degrees on its vertical axis and was now being viewed at that angle. There was a rushing sound, like a fierce wind . . . and an all-too-human sounding shriek that went on and on and on. Someone in Marine combat armor was hunched over on the deck at the top of the stairs, on elbows and knees, and the screams were coming from him.

Patterson. The Marine's name was Patterson.

"Get some help in there," St. Clair said.

"A couple of Marines are on the way," Symm told him. "And Lieutenant Bradley has been alerted."

"And reopen a direct channel to that Marine!"

"Okay . . . we've got it open, sir. Suit telemetry, anyway. But the Marine is just . . . just screaming, sir. He won't respond."

A scream is a pretty solid response, St. Clair thought, but he didn't say it out loud. "Can you establish contact with the landing craft's AI? Is the channel down?"

"Trying, sir," Hargrove said. "It's open, but what we're getting is erratic. An anomaly."

"What kind of anomaly?"

"Gibberish, my lord."

"From the AI?"

"Yes, sir."

So the AI was screaming too. St. Clair shifted to the AI-department channel. "Jablonsky?"

"He's off-line, Lord Commander," Lieutenant Watanabe replied. "I'm on it."

"Find out what's happening with that AI."

"Aye, aye, sir."

And please, he thought, *let someone get that Marine out of there fast!*

PATTERSON COULD feel his mind going.

At first, it was like having his memories replayed on fast-forward. They came, in no particular order, in a storm of vivid impressions, of fast-glimpsed images, of snatches of sound, of bursts of aroma, of rippling sensations of touch and movement and vertigo and temperature differences and pain and pleasure and unexpected taste. And through and behind and above it all was a single intolerable, unending, mind-wracking shriek . . . and only as his throat turned raw and harsh did he realize that the sound was his own screaming.

Worse, far worse, far more consuming, were the emotions . . . fear and rage and joy and depression and relief, each coming hard on the heels of the last in a staccato series of feelings, totally beyond Patterson's conscious control.

There was something there, inside his head with him. He could feel it . . . *almost* see it. He clawed uselessly at his helmet, trying to reach it.

If I can just get my helmet open . . .

ST. CLAIR HATED the feeling of abject helplessness. He could see the tragedy unfolding inside his head, but Patterson was tens of thousands of kilometers below, on the disk's surface, and there was nothing he could do to intervene.

A second armored figure appeared on the stairs, pausing . . . then appearing to struggle against a strong wind. St. Clair could hear that wind behind the screaming, a shrill keening that meant the lander's hull must have been breached, its atmosphere whistling out into the near vacuum outside. But he couldn't see anything like a breach in the bulkhead, and there was no hint as to what might have caused that kind of damage in the first place.

The second Marine was trying to get a grip on the first Marine's armor and drag him toward the stairs, but whatever he was fighting against was making the attempt difficult, even impossible. A third Marine appeared behind the second, reaching past him, and together they began to drag the screaming man back off the flight deck.

"CAS!"

"Yes, my lord."

"We're going to need a second lander down there."

"Yes, my lord."

"Fast as you can. And an ambulance, too."

"Aye, aye, sir."

There was, of course, a Navy corpsman—the Marine equivalent of a medic—imbedded with the platoon of Marines, but whatever had happened to Patterson was going to require more than a pressure dressing or a shot of anti-bleed nano.

He hoped they could get him back to *Ad Astra* in time.

CHAPTER
ELEVEN

"Hargrove!" St. Clair snapped. "Get me a different cam! I need a different angle on the lander's flight deck!"

"Not a lot to work with, Lord Commander. That one angle is from a communicator screen above the stairwell. Wait— use Patterson's telemetry! You can tap into his helmet cam!"

St. Clair shifted to a new channel, this one showing the view from a small vidcam mounted on Patterson's armor. He'd been using the same sort of link with the other Marines as he'd followed events in the city outside.

The two Marines who'd just arrived had pulled Patterson up off the deck and were dragging him backward down the stairs to the First Deck. For just an instant, Patterson was staring back into the Flight Deck, still screaming, struggling against the other Marines' grip.

And for just an instant, St. Clair could see what Patterson was seeing. . . .

A section of the flight deck forward, between the pilot and copilot seats, was oddly twisted, a flat image rotated to one side, an opening in midair. St. Clair had seen that much from the flight deck camera mounted high on the aft bulkhead. But from this lower perspective, he could stare into the vortex of movement and strangeness now occupying the area directly in front of the control console. The shrieking wind was becoming visible now as water droplets formed a swirling fog in the fast-dropping pressure. Within the cloud, three spheres shifted, expanded, shrank, merged—writing shapes that challenged sanity. Illuminated by the Elsie's console instrumentation, the three became two . . . then branched into four . . . to five . . . three again . . . apparently solid black objects defying the commonly accepted definition of the word *solid*.

Whatever it was emerged from the vortex of movement and sound . . . a black tentacle unfolding . . . then collapsing into a sphere once more.

And then Patterson was dragged down the steps and St. Clair lost that instant's glimpse of indescribable strangeness.

Quickly, he changed channels once more, looking through the camera on the flight deck bulkhead. Seconds after the Marines departed for a lower deck, the flat, rotated section of the image pivoted sharply, like a door slamming shut. The wind ceased abruptly and the fog dissipated.

Whatever that thing on the lander's bridge had been, it was now gone.

"Newton," he said in his thoughts. "What the hell was *that*?"

"Unknown," the AI replied. "I don't have enough data to form a conclusion."

And that, St. Clair thought, summed up a key difference between human intelligence and AI: humans could make guesses and jump to conclusions on no data at all, something that was difficult to impossible for machine minds.

Except that he had no idea what he'd just seen either.

SUBCOMMANDER JABLONSKY stared into indescribable wonder.

His e-link through Newton to the Newton emulation gave him full, direct, and immediate access to what he was already thinking of as the *Encyclopedia Galactica*. And Tomasz Jablonsky realized that he was seeing things— *knowing* things—that no human had ever witnessed before.

Encyclopedia Galactica. The term had been invented

by Isaac Asimov, the author of a twentieth-century science-fiction series called Foundation. Later, scientists working to discover evidence of extraterrestrial civilizations had suggested that technically advanced galactic cultures might put all of their history, science, and culture into nested radio transmissions that other civilizations listening across the cosmos might discover and interpret.

Such a collection of data had never been found, a silence leading many SETI researchers to assume that Humankind was alone in the Galaxy. Not until the encounter with the Coadunation at Sirius was the true reason learned: galactic civilizations tended to abandon radio as a means for interstellar communication early in their technic histories, preferring the far sharper and clearer neutrino channels to the static-blasted noise of the electromagnetic spectrum. More advanced civilizations usually abandoned all speed-of-light transmissions entirely, using instead systems involving quantum entanglement to signal instantly across vast gulfs of space.

What SETI researchers had called the Great Silence was due almost entirely to what had become known as the jungle drum effect. Human scientists, even as late as the early twenty-second century, had been like primitive tribespeople in the jungles of New Guinea, listening for jungle drums while utterly unaware of the radio and TV signals flooding down out of their sky every second.

The Coadunation reportedly had a kind of *Encyclopedia Galactica* on-line, but human researchers had only glimpsed a few entries. One of the goals of the *Tellus Ad Astra* expedition had been direct access to that data.

The Coadunation E.G. was now lost, but a different one appeared to be accessible through the torpedo. Jablonsky let his mental focus enter the in-head imagery, where an array of corridors or tunnels had unfolded in his mind, each brightly lit and extending off into infinity, each lined with myriad doorways opening into otherness. There were worlds in there, millions of them, each described in exacting detail of physics, chemistry, and biology . . . and sophont species . . . and technologies . . . and cultures and metacultures, a bewildering profusion of ideas and information.

Jablonsky didn't know where to begin.

Hell, he couldn't even figure out how the information was organized. There was an index, but it wasn't alphabetical, certainly. The data was catalogued by symbols appearing in his mind, but it wasn't related to English, or even anything like a spoken language. Think a question, and the appropriate gateway appeared.

Picking a virtual gateway at random, he entered.

A gas giant, banded and multi-hued, hung in space beneath the glow of a distant, shrunken sun. A ring system, as he focused his attention on it, proved not to be one of rock debris or ice, but comprised billions upon billions of discrete orbital facilities, colonies like *Tellus*, as well as factories, power plants, computer nodes, and structures for which there was no easy definition. A dozen natural satellites had been reworked, becoming either machine-city worlds or artificially constructed and maintained biomes. Hundreds of billions of sophonts lived in this one artificial system, though only a fraction was biological in nature.

There were minds here of a scale and depth and scope that mere humans could never grasp or understand. . . .

Jablonsky jerked back from the inner vision of that world-system with a gasp, as though awakening from a nightmare. For a fraction of a second, he'd been looking into other minds, and those minds had been looking back.

It was time to call in the ship's skipper.

"TO SEE technology on such a scale," Dumont said. "Incredible."

The sun was very slowly setting, the light deepening to

a bloody hue. As darkness fell on this side of the Alderson disk, dawn was breaking on the opposite surface, the sunrise witnessed by a handful of subNewton probes and tele-operated remotes. St. Clair rode one of those remotes, along with the electronic presence of Dr. Dumont. The probe was drifting just above a titanic gray wall rising nearly 115 kilometers above the disk's surface. To one side were the heat-baked plains of the disk's inner section, shadowed by that wall now from the early morning light. On the other side was the empty gulf within which, 60 million kilometers away, the orange sun shone.

Though minute compared to the vast expanse of the Alderson disk, the wall was a titanic engineering accomplishment all by itself, completely encircling the local sun on the inner edge of the disk. Together with a similar, smaller wall at the outer edge, and with counterparts to both walls on the disk's reverse side, it served to help physically contain the enormous structure's atmosphere.

But evidently it did more than that.

"And you think this is how they generated power?" St. Clair asked.

"I don't know if the builders used other types of power generation," Dumont said. "They certainly had the techno-logical know-how for nuclear fusion and vacuum energy taps. But our instruments show that energy is still flowing out from the central void, almost certainly from the wall itself. It appears that a large percentage of the disk's energy is produced by the thermoelectric effect, and that it's pro-duced on an almost inconceivable scale."

"One side of the wall is hot," St. Clair said, translating techspeak to English, "and the other side is cold. The tem-perature difference generates electricity."

"Precisely."

"Shouldn't the cold side warm up after a few million years?"

"Maybe after a few billion," Dumont replied. "Maybe not even then. The north and south poles on Mercury still have shadowed pockets at minus two hundred after four and a half billion years."

It was funny, St. Clair thought, how even members of the scientific community continued referring to Earth and the worlds of the solar system as if they were just the way *Ad Astra* had left them, untouched by the passing of eons. It was as though human minds, no matter how bright, simply hadn't yet been able to assimilate what had happened.

In truth, things had been happening so quickly since *Ad Astra* had emerged in this far-future time that no one had had the time to assimilate much of anything. Since the attack on board the lander—there was no other way to describe the incident—St. Clair had ordered the surface exploration team to return to *Ad Astra*. Any remaining investigation of the surface would be carried out through remotes, at least until the humans knew just what they were dealing with.

"We'll need to get inside the structure to see what's actually going on," Dumont continued.

"Can we fly down closer? Get a closer look?"

"In about five minutes we could. Time lag . . . remember?"

St. Clair bit off a bitter imprecation. Caught out again! He and Dumont were mentally riding the subNewton probe, which was some five light-minutes from *Ad Astra*'s current position and the location of their bodies. They could order the probe to go in closer to those monumental engineering structures below . . . but it would be five minutes before the signal reached the probe, and *another* five minutes before they saw a response back at *Ad Astra*.

"Remote teleoperation," Dumont said with somber deliberation, "sucks." He hesitated, then added, "My Lord Commander, pulling us off the disk was a mistake. There is so much more we can learn about alien technology here."

"Perhaps. But I won't jeopardize the lives of more of our people. Not until we know what's going on down there."

He felt Dumont's smile. "The monster?"

Rumors had been flying for hours about the thing that had appeared inside the first lander.

"That's right."

"Obviously some sort of defensive show," Dumont said, dismissive. "Probably a programmed hologram."

"Holograms don't suck the air from a pressurized space-craft, Doctor," St. Clair said. "And they generally don't drive a combat-veteran Marine insane."

"You don't know that, Lord Commander. Maybe the hologram was a recording of something terrifying."

"Terrifying enough to send a Marine off beam? I don't think so."

"Maybe he's not insane. Maybe he's just in shock."

"It'll do as a working definition of 'insane' until *Ad Astra*'s medical staff tells us otherwise." St. Clair had heard the man's screaming. Dumont had not.

The Marine, Patterson, had been brought back off the disk and was being kept in sick bay, heavily sedated. Initial medical reports were not encouraging. The man had sustained physical damage to portions of his brain—in particular to regions in contact with his electronic interface implants.

And he appeared to be suffering from some sort of extreme schizophrenic break with reality.

A second Elsie had been dispatched to the surface—despite Dumont's vocal protests—and the human members of the team all were now back on board the ship. Dumont had agreed to continue his explorations by way of e-linking with remotes, but he wasn't at all happy about it.

"Lord Commander," Dumont said patiently, "higher forms of life can't survive on this artifact. Atmospheric pressure is less than a quarter of an atmosphere. There are some forms of vegetation, a variety of microscopic life—

single-cell organisms like bacteria and protozoans—and nothing else. Whatever Patterson saw, it was not a 'monster' within the accepted definition of the word. I really can't say what caused the pressure drop on board the lander. At a guess, I would say a meteorite impact breached the hull, and that the breach was subsequently sealed by the lander's own damage-control systems. The shock might well have caused a young, impressionable Marine to hallucinate."

"*Hallucinate?* Come on, Doctor—"

"Every one of us had been shaken by the sight of that statue, or whatever it was . . . and Patterson had a fright when he accidentally made it collapse. Suggestion can be quite powerful under the right conditions."

"And what did *I* see, Doctor? I was watching through the flight deck camera, remember, and through Patterson's helmet cam."

He felt Dumont's discomfort at the question. He obviously didn't want to call St. Clair a liar or suggest the mission commander was hallucinating, but clearly he also couldn't bring himself to believe in that space-twisting boogeyman apparently recorded by the lander's instrumentation. "I don't know. An electrical fault, perhaps, generated by the meteor strike? Or an artifact of the failure of the lander's AI. The incident requires further investigation, I agree, but I promise you it was not some sort of encounter with a creature native to the disk."

A chime sounded within St. Clair's head, a recall request. *Damn.* "Excuse me, Dr. Dumont. They're after me again."

Dumont grunted. "You know where to find me, my lord."

And St. Clair woke up.

He was back in a virtual projection chair in his office on board the *Ad Astra*. One bulkhead showed the Alderson disk below, superimposed against the alien magnificence of the colliding galaxies. A red light winked on his console.

"I'm here," he said. "What is it?"

"Urgent call from Subcommander Tomasz Jablonsky," a computer's voice told him.

He sighed. His unsatisfactory discussion with Dumont had left him irritable and impatient. "Put it through."

"Lord Commander? This is—"

"Yes, Jablonsky. What is it?"

"We've established a neural linkage with the alien torpedo, my lord. You wanted to know."

"Excellent, thank you. What have you learned?"

"As we suspected, it contains a rather extensive database. It should enable us to interface with local AIs. And . . . it may serve as a communications device."

"'May?'"

"I'm not sure about that, my lord. But as I was poking around in the thing's virtual space, I had the definite impression that I was being . . . watched."

"A virself?"

"Something like that, my lord. I'm not sure. I pulled out. I didn't want to initiate contact without orders."

St. Clair caught something in Jablonsky's words, an undertone of . . . what? Fear? Or awe? *Something* had shaken him, though.

"Quite right. Okay, Jablonsky. You have a research team in mind?"

"I think so, sir."

"Put me on it. I'll be down in a few minutes."

"Aye, aye, my lord."

The news was exciting. It suggested that they might be able to directly communicate with some of the sophonts inhabiting this far-future era. That Jablonsky had *felt* something was strongly suggestive.

When you were communicating with someone through a neural link, you were always aware of them, a sense that someone was there beside you even when you couldn't see them. The sensation, generated by neural implants within the temporal lobes of the brain, was called *virself*, the expression of a virtual self. When St. Clair had been sharing the robot probe with Dumont a few minutes earlier, he'd clearly felt Dumont's presence, even sensed both a smile and some emotional discomfort, as though the xenotechnologist had literally been there beside him.

If he'd felt something similar from a presumably alien presence, it suggested that the artifact could be used for real-time communication with its owners.

And that was precisely what they needed right now, if they were going to make any sense of their situation.

SUBCOMMANDER MARIA Francesca hung suspended within her electronic web, monitoring the operations of several dozen spacecraft in *Ad Astra*'s immediate vicinity. As CAS, she oversaw all flight operations within a hundred thousand kilometers of the *Ad Astra*, providing necessary human judgment and input for an operation that might otherwise have been delegated to an AI. As a cyborg, Francesca provided both the machine precision and the human discernment required by the job, and to a degree considerably greater than that possible for ordinary implant technology. Francesca's neural implants were far more extensive than those used by most twenty-second-century humans. Virtually every part of her brain was hardwired into the computer network that supported her.

As she herself liked to say, for Class-3 cyborgs it was almost impossible to tell where the human organism stopped and the purely machine began.

PriFly—Primary Flight Control—was located in a zero-gravity section of the engineering module, close to the flight deck. There, Francesca floated in the center of a cramped and industrial-looking compartment, nude, connected to the surrounding bulkheads by cables growing from her torso, the back of her neck, her shaved scalp, her groin, ankles,

and wrists. There were no visual displays in the compartment, but they weren't necessary. In-head displays gave her
the illusion of floating in empty space, with a navigation
grid extending off into infinity in three dimensions. Icons
marked the various *Ad Astra* spacecraft currently deployed
in nearby space. A glance at any icon and a thoughtclick,
and she was there, the spacecraft hanging like a toy beneath
her gaze, her mind in direct communication with the pilot or
the controlling AI.

"Blue Seven, you are clear for approach," she said in her
mind. "Come to one-three-niner by three-three-four and
reduce velocity to two hundred meters per second."

"Copy, PriFly," the fighter's pilot replied. "Coming to
one-three-niner by three-three-four. Velocity two-zero-zero
mps."

The pilot's voice showed stress. Sublieutenant Ogden
Maxwell had been on perimeter patrol for more than seven
hours. He was tired . . . *fried* was the term used by the pilots.
His med readout showed his reactions down by almost 20
percent.

"You're in the slot, Seven," she said. "Call the ball."

The terminology was from ancient wet navy carrier approaches, when the aviator would visually line up a round
light—the "ball"—with other lights to put himself on the
proper glide path. The procedure was automated now, with
no visual cues, but in his head Maxwell was lining up on a
circle of virtual landing lights and nudging his fighter in.

"Ball," Maxwell's voice said.

"Confirm ball, Seven. You're good. Reduce velocity to—"
Something hit her.

The shock knocked her out of her e-connections to the
ship's systems and brought her shrieking into full awareness of her compartment, her electronic links with Maxwell
and the ship's AI arrays gone. Pain avalanched through her
entire being, synapses firing randomly as her body twitched

and jerked, a puppet tangled in its strings, the spasms so violent she tore free from several of her electronic feeds.

Staring into darkness, her body on fire, she became aware of . . . *something* . . . a door opening . . . a shift sideways in space. Air blasted past and around her, funneling into emptiness, and she felt the sharp bite of freezing cold. Swirling fog appeared as the temperature dropped.

Hull breach!

But that was impossible! Physically, she was buried deep in the belly of a starship five kilometers wide and as many deep. *Nothing* could get at her in here, not unless half of the ship had just been vaporized.

And then she felt the thing, an ooze of black tentacles that slipped disturbingly in and out of existence, a thing enveloping her mind, embracing it, filling it, *tasting* it. . . .

She triggered a ship-wide alarm.

It was the last conscious thing she did. The blackness was all around her, was inside of her in some horrific, indefinable way, releasing a tumble of memories.

It was eating her mind.

She was falling inward, becoming the darkness. . . .

SUBLIEUTENANT OGDEN Maxwell heard the alarm in the same instant that all of his approach indicators and ship telemetry went dead. The 3-D navigational grid, the landing approach beacons, the computer-drawn and highlighted shape of *Ad Astra*'s flight deck all winked out, leaving him with nothing but Mark 1 Mod 0 eyeballs and no electronic guides or references at all.

His ASF-99 Wasp fighter was hurtling toward the *Ad Astra*'s magnetic trap at almost 200 meters per second—720 kilometers per hour—fast enough that the surface of the ship's belly was a gray blur.

There was no way PriFly could have gone off-line in an instant, with no warning, no way in hell. He spent no time at all wondering about it, though. Maxwell's training saved him from a messy and most likely fatal trap on the landing deck; he killed his velocity, decelerating hard, then added a new vector component that kicked him out of the approach path and away from the ship's belly. To try to continue the trap on manual when something was seriously wrong with the ship's flight control systems was suicide.

"*Ad Astra*," he called. "Blue Seven! What the fuck is going on in there?"

His course change wasn't quite enough. His Wasp clipped an antenna mast, sending him spinning wildly into darkness.

ST. CLAIR HEARD the alarm shrilling in his head. "Bridge! What's happening?"

He'd only just swum his way off the bridge and been making his way toward the AI department aft. It never rained, apparently, but it tsunamied.

"CAS, down in PriFly," Symm replied. "Something . . ."

"What?"

"Not sure, my lord. Sensors are reporting a sudden loss of atmosphere. Pressure is down . . . my God! Almost fifteen percent!"

St. Clair felt a sharp, cold chill at that. Whatever had happened on the lander down on the Alderson disk evidently was now happening here, on board *Ad Astra*.

Not good.

"Can CAS get out?"

"We've lost all telemetry with the department. Major electrical interference . . . and the PriFly AI connections are off-line. Newton says it can't get through."

"Who's got the MAA watch?"

"Lieutenant Billingsly."

"Have him get to PriFly with a team. *Fast!*"

"Aye, aye, my lord."

Ad Astra's Marine contingent served as the colony ship's

onboard police force, headed up by the master-at-arms. Lieutenant Randall Billingsly was one of the Marine officers holding down that billet, and the one currently on watch.

Ad Astra was under attack, of that much St. Clair was certain. Despite his own doubts about the idea, it was possible that what Patterson had encountered down on the disk had been some sort of automated defense system, or, just possibly, a surviving inhabitant of the structure. But whatever had happened to CAS made those possibilities much more unlikely. An automated defense system *might* involve projecting a holographic image into a spacecraft tens of thousands of kilometers above the disk's surface, but it didn't seem likely, didn't feel *right*. Much more likely was a deliberate attack.

But by whom? And *how*?

St. Clair reached the transport-capsule node nearest the bridge, but instead of heading aft to the AI department, he thoughtclicked directions for forward and down, to PriFly.

He wanted to see this for himself.

LIEUTENANT BILLINGSLY and his four-man response team reached PriFly first. He'd seen a report already about what had happened to Patterson down on the disk's surface, and immediately noted the similarities—loss of cabin pressure, dropping temperature, disruption of local computer nodes. Whatever it was that had attacked Patterson appeared to have struck on board the *Ad Astra*.

The airtight entrance to PriFly was sealed, the controls, both manual and in-head activation, inoperative. "Burn it, Kat!"

Sergeant Katrina Doleski unholstered her plasma torch and aimed it at a specific part of the bulkhead directly alongside the door. All five Marines were in armor; their visors automatically darkened to protect their eyes against the actinic glare of the cutter. A piece of bulkhead drifted clear. Anchoring himself from a convenient hand grip, Billingsly reached into the smoking hole, found the manual lock release, and squeezed it.

A burst of air hissed into the room as the pressures equalized. The door slid open. . . .

Billingsly had been in combat before. Had served in Kazakhstan and Chad and in the Labyrinth of Night on Mars. He'd seen blood before, and the gory horror of combat. He'd *been* there.

But he couldn't help himself this time. He gasped . . .

Then vomited explosively inside his helmet.

The vid images shot by automatic security cameras inside PriFly had showed Maria Francesca's death with nightmarish clarity and detail. Unfortunately—or, possibly fortunately, depending on how you looked at it—exactly what had happened to the aerospace commanding officer was still unknown. St. Clair had watched the imagery several times, now, and still wasn't sure what he was seeing. The scene was so horrific it was difficult to make sense of it.

He'd seen the results, however, in person . . . a narrow compartment filled with drifting globules of blood and a vaguely human-shaped mass of unrecognizably pulped tissue.

"This ship, this expedition, is under attack," St. Clair told the assembly of department heads. Unlike the last meeting, some were there in person, in the Carousel's Number Three conference room, but many, including all of the civilians, were logged on in telepresence. "I want to know who's doing it. Who is the enemy?"

"Not much of an attack, if you ask me," Adler's voice said over the link. "One dead, one wounded? That's nothing."

"No, my lord. It is most definitely *something*. Maria Francesca was killed horribly . . . her body . . ." He stopped, unable to continue. The sight of that blood-filled compartment would be with him for the rest of his life. He swallowed, hard. "And young Patterson," he continued, "is being kept in a medical coma because when he's awake he's raving. Dr. Sokolov—what did you say your diagnosis was for Patterson?"

"Provisionally, acute psychotic schizophrenia," Sokolov replied. "Based on the observed symptoms. That may change as we learn more."

"We also have an enemy that can cause pressure loss at a distance, and without any observed weapon. Nothing kinetic, not directed energy. Anyone who can reach across ten thousand kilometers of empty space without being detected, cause a pressure hull breach, and kill one of my people has my full attention and respect."

"But there's no *point*, no unified purpose, to the incidents," Adler insisted. "If you ask me, Dr. Dumont is right. We've woken up some sort of automated defense system and it's trying to scare us away from the disk."

St. Clair refrained from pointing out that he had *not* asked Adler. "I might have bought that with that first attack in the lander," he said. "But they targeted PriFly with that last one, deliberately and directly."

"Do I understand right?" Clayton Lloyd said. "We've moved away from the Alderson disk?"

"We have, Mr. Ambassador," St. Clair said. "If we *did* wake up an automated defense system of some sort, maybe some distance will help. I want these attacks stopped."

"How far out are we?" Adler asked.

"Fifty astronomical units . . . about seven and a half billion kilometers. We've left a few robots on and near the disk to keep an eye on things, but that's about all. And now that we have Mr. Jablonsky's report on the alien torpedo, I think we can safely abandon the disk in favor of another objective."

"But there's so much we could still learn there," Dumont protested. "The Alderson disk represents technologies literally tens of thousands of years in advance of what we have now!"

"Quite true, Doctor," Senior Lieutenant Christine Nolan said. "And how many years will it take to understand that xenotech? To reverse engineer it so that we can use any part of it?"

St. Clair nodded to himself. Christine was head of *Ad Astra*'s xenotech office, a branch of the contact department. The civilian mission was partially duplicated by the Navy xeno departments on the ship, and he found it interesting that the two were aligning themselves on different sides of the argument, the military versus the civilians.

But he needed to keep the discussion on target.

"We won't have the chance to learn much if monsters keep popping out of nowhere to attack our people," St. Clair said. "Besides, the disk will still be there if and when we decide to come back. It's been here for a long time already, hasn't it?"

"Just how old is the disk?" Symm asked. "Do we know yet?"

"At least two hundred million years old," Dumont told her. "That's a minimum, based on potassium-forty/argon-forty ratios in the samples we took. Maximum age is approximately three hundred million years."

How long to wear buildings down to dust, for three quarters of the atmosphere to sputter away into space, for the monuments of a brilliant civilization capable of astonishing feats of mega-engineering to decay to the consistency of chalk?

A very long time indeed. The time, apparently, that separated Humankind from the very earliest dinosaurs.

"So how old is the star?" St. Clair asked. He was wondering if there'd been a planetary system here once that subsequently had been destroyed to manufacture the disk . . . or if the builders had brought the building materials in from somewhere else.

"It's a pretty ordinary type K1," Wanquan replied, "so it

fits the standard model well. The age works out to about one point five billion years."

It was sobering to realize that, ancient as it was, the Alderson disk still had been constructed at least 3.8 billion years after the *Tellus Ad Astra* mission had departed for the Coadunation capital.

In fact, during the Age of Humankind, the star around which the disk eventually had been built hadn't even been born out of its primordial cloud of dust and gas.

"The star is only one and a half billion years old?" Dr. Hatcher put in. "That's not enough time for a local sapient species to evolve."

"Someone else, an alien ecosystem, might have evolved intelligence faster than we did on Earth," St. Clair suggested.

"Not *that* fast," Christine Nolan said. "Life—single-celled life, like cyanobacteria—evolved very quickly after the Earth's early crust cooled enough to support liquid water. It took four billion years, though, before those one-celled beasties learned how to join together as multicelled animals. And another half billion years to go from there to us. Wherever the disk's builders came from, it was an older star than that."

"They must have come from somewhere else," Dumont said. "A part of a colonization wave going out among the stars, maybe even direct descendents of the Coadunation. As life and advanced technology spread across the Galaxy, they began making use of younger stars as sites for new centers of civilization."

"Any idea how long the disk was inhabited, Doctor?" St. Clair asked him. "Between when it was built, and when it was deserted?"

"We have no way of ascertaining that, Lord Commander. But it's been deserted for a long time. The remaining structures and monuments, we think, were once constructed of a kind of plastic, but they've degraded, possibly due to spontaneous nonradioactive decay, but more likely from long-term exposure to sunlight or other EM radiation."

"Why more likely?"

"The stuff underground appears to still be working," Dumont told him. "Like the neutrino beacon. But on the surface, everything is crumbling."

"Maybe," Adler's voice put in, "it hasn't been deserted at all. There might even still be intelligent life down there."

"That seems unlikely," Nolan said.

"It's a big world. Bigger than any of us can imagine! There's enough room within the disk for *millions* of civilizations. Maybe they moved underground as things began deteriorating on the surface."

"They were star-farers, obviously," Nolan pointed out. "Wouldn't they have just left when things started breaking down? Gone somewhere else to start over?"

"Who's to say what an alien civilization's motivations might be?" Dumont said. "In any case, it seems unlikely that everyone would leave. There would be stay-at-homes, less adventurous sorts, religious groups or cultures that didn't agree that migration was the answer. There's room enough. There might be *trillions* of individual beings living inside the thickness of the disk."

"That's right," Cameron said. "And two of them attacked us."

"Whatever attacked us, it didn't try to communicate," Lieutenant Arnold Gonzalez said. He was head of *Ad Astra*'s xenolinguistics lab. "I suspect that it wasn't intelligent at all. More like a wild animal. Or a savage."

"Maybe, Lieutenant," Adler said, "they're responding to *us* as savages. Destroying their statue wasn't exactly a civilized act."

"Neither is an unthinking attack entirely out of proportion to the provocation, my lord," Gonzalez said.

St. Clair listened to the back-and-forth around the conference table and across the shipboard Net. There was no way to settle the argument without returning to the Disk, but he'd already decided that the *Ad Astra* was going to keep clear of that enigmatic structure, at least for now. The mobile science colony was well-equipped and staffed to address such questions, but they were also absolutely and irrevocably *alone* in a way that no human group ever had been before. Trapped 4 billion years in their own future, they had no other resources but themselves—no base of operations, no headquarters, no supply depot, and no one at all to report to.

Alone.

The weight of years—of gigayears—pressed down on St. Clair's shoulders.

"Okay," St. Clair continued. He wanted the discussion back on track. "Do we have any additional information about the attacks? What the hell hit us?"

"That's actually fairly obvious from the various vid imaging," Dr. Sandoval said. "We've been witnessing five-dimensional intersections."

"You mind repeating that in English, Doctor?"

"Sure. When you try to visualize dimensional physics, you have to work with analogies, okay?" In the minds of those linked in, a point of green light appeared as Sandoval spoke. "Here is a zero-dimensional point . . . but for it to exist, you need a one-dimensional line, like this."

The point moved, drawing a green line to illustrate.

"A point can only exist on a line made up of points. But for one dimension to exist, you need two dimensions."

The line moved sideways, drawing a flat, green plane.

"Two requires three . . ."

The plane moved at right angles to itself, drawing a green cube.

"And, theoretically, you could say that for three dimensions to exist, you need a fourth." A second, smaller cube appeared centered inside the first, with each of its corners connected by a line with the corresponding outer corner. "This is a hypercube . . . a kind of 3-D shadow of a 4-D object. Unfortunately, human brains aren't wired to see how a fourth dimension works."

"I thought the fourth dimension was time?" Symm said.

"Depends on how you look at it, Subcommander," Sandoval replied. "Actually, space and time are interchangeable—spacetime, as Einstein referred to it. But for now, we're only looking at the spacial aspects of higher dimensions."

St. Clair concentrated on the hypercube, trying to understand. "You're saying that the thing we encountered on the disk, the thing that killed Maria, that was something from a fourth dimension?"

"Partly. Here . . . take another look."

A side window opened next to the hypercube, showing the vid footage from PriFly. Subcommander Francesca hung weightless in the compartment, twisting against the web of cables connecting her with the ship. Behind her, a kind of doorway had opened, as though a flat wall bearing the image of the far side of the chamber had rotated. Three watery-looking, jet-black spheres appeared, then were growing, then were merging as Francesca shrieked and struggled. One sphere actually seemed to be emerging from within her body. In places, her body was horribly distorted, bulging as if to make room for something suddenly materializing inside.

"Freeze image," Sandoval's voice said. The vid halted, Francesca's taut body frozen in a horrific instant of nightmare. "Take a plane . . . two dimensions." The hypercube next to the vid was replaced by a flat, green surface. A human hand materialized above it, colored bright blue. "As I said, you need to work by analogy. Pretend that this two-dimensional surface represents three-dimensional space . . . and that my three-dimensional hand is representing something in the fourth dimension. It exists in a space outside of the normal three . . . do you see?"

Slowly, the blue hand, fingers splayed, descended toward the green plane. The finger tips touched . . . then moved through the plane from above. Bright white circles highlighted the intersections where the hand was passing through the green surface.

"A two-dimensional inhabitant of the two-dimensional universe wouldn't be able to see the entire 3-D hand. She's not even aware that a fourth dimension exists. What she *would* see is the intersection of my hand with her universe—four, now five circles that appear to expand as my hand moves down through the plane. The 2-D being can't perceive up or down. Those directions don't exist in her universe. But she sees these circles appear out of nowhere, even inside a closed room . . . or inside her two-dimensional body. And now . . ."

The image of Sandoval's hand penetrated the plane more deeply, and the separate, growing white circles merged—four of them joining into a long and narrow outline of light, with the thumb as a separate circle off to the side. The hand continued its descent, and the white light around the thumb merged with the rest of the hand.

"My God," Cameron said. "Those separate black blobs we're seeing behind CAS . . ."

"Are the three-dimensional intersection of parts of a higher-dimensional being," Sandoval said. "Exactly."

"That's a *hand*?"

"I'm not making any guesses about the shape of this thing, or its anatomy," Sandoval replied. "I imagine those are parts of its body, though. Run vid." The image of PriFly became animated again. The black spheres appeared to grow, enveloping the struggling Francesca . . . then unfolded into hard-to-follow shapes that looked like bunches of tentacles or worms, writhing with an unpleasant life of their own. Francesca's body abruptly vanished . . . then reappeared.

Rather, *something* reappeared—an expanding cloud of

blood forming jittering zero-gravity globules, some the size of basketballs. There was also something else . . . a human-sized mass of blood-drenched grit or sand or paste; it was tough to tell what the consistency was like. Whatever it was fell apart like wet powder.

"What just happened there?" St. Clair asked.

"Eversion," Sokolov told him. "She's been turned inside out."

"God in heaven . . ." someone said over the network.

"God had nothing to do with it," Sandoval said.

"But how?" St. Clair asked.

"Analogy again," she said. On the graphic, the blue hand vanished. "Here's an inhabitant of Flatland, our two-dimensional universe." A dark green right triangle appeared on the lighter green plane. A white dot appeared, off center. "That's his heart," Sandoval continued. "As with humans, it's off to one side, not centered. Now, our three-dimensional inhabitant comes along and . . ."

The blue hand reappeared, reaching down from above, grasping the triangle, and pulling it up and away from the plane, flipping it, then letting it drop back. When it re-merged with the plane, the triangle was upside down. The right angle was now on the *other* side . . . as was the white dot.

"He's been rotated through 3-D space. If a human was rotated that way through *four*-dimensional space, he'd find out that his organs were now mirror images of what they'd been before. His heart would be on the right side of his chest, not the left. His liver would be on his left, his spleen on the right, and so on."

"Damn it, Maria wasn't turned into a mirror image of anything," Symm said.

"No. And that's where the analogy breaks down. Flipping triangles—that illustrates one way to rotate the subject. Rotate it a different way, in a different direction . . . and you turn the subject and everything in it inside out."

"Inside out . . ." St. Clair said. *How horrible.*

At least it had been mercifully quick.

"The eversion only went down to about the one-millimeter level," Dr. Sokolov explained. "Only the larger blood veins and arteries were turned inside out . . . not the capillaries or smaller vessels. Heart, eyeballs, intestines, skull . . . they all were everted, but individual cells were still intact . . . including the red cells in her blood. We're not sure why."

"It may have to do with how far the subject was moved within the higher dimension," Sandoval said.

"Maria Francesca was not a *subject*," St. Clair said, angry. Shock at what he'd seen, plus his own helplessness, was making it difficult to think clearly. He pressed his fingers against his eyes, rubbing them. He had to think.

"Look," he said, composing himself. "I thought higher dimensions were supposed to be curled up real small. Eleven dimensions—something like that?"

"String theory," Sandoval said, agreeing. "That's right—ten dimensions plus time, and seven of the dimensions are curled up into a space smaller than a proton, so we can't see or otherwise experience them. However, how large a given dimension appears to be depends on your perspective. What's tiny when viewed from one angle in three-dimensional space might be enormous viewed from another, *if* you have more than three dimensions to play with."

Which begged the question as to why humans couldn't turn an oddly angled corner and vanish into a higher dimension suddenly grown large. *Hell, maybe they can*, St. Clair thought. That might explain what had happened to Ambrose Bierce, Judge Crater, and the crew of the *Marie Celeste*.

"These four-dimensional hyperbeings," St. Clair said, "are they intelligent? Are they using technology to move through higher dimensions? Or are they, I don't know, some kind of 4-D animal?"

"We have no way of telling yet," Sandoval said.

"In any case," St. Clair said, "it doesn't look like we'll get much information out of these critters. They're not exactly communicative."

"Not in a *good* way," Symm added.

"Right. Whether they are an animal or represent a higher-dimensional intelligence, they don't seem to offer us much hope of getting the answers we need. So we'll go elsewhere. We need to find someone out here we *can* talk to. We need to find someplace with a population."

"But if there's a civilization still somewhere inside the Alderson disk . . ." Adler began.

"No," St. Clair said, cutting him off. "Until we understand what's happening there, I'm not risking our people. We have no way of defending against extradimensional attacks."

"I agree completely, my lord," Lieutenant Gonzalez said. "Do we have any possible objectives?"

"We do," Jablonsky said. "The Roceti torpedo has quite a long list. At least it gives us a place to start."

"Roseti?" St. Clair asked, amused, and mishearing the word. "Like the Rosetta stone?"

"Yes, sir. But with CETI thrown in. Communications with extraterrestrial intelligence."

"Ah." St. Clair nodded. The Rosetta stone, of course, had long been a famous historical footnote—a tablet found near Alexandria, Egypt, that contained the key to deciphering ancient Egyptian hieroglyphics. "Your name for it, I take it?"

Jablonsky shrugged. "The AI department's name, yes, sir. We had to call it something besides 'the torpedo.' It's actually not a weapon at all."

"So I gathered."

"It *is* a very powerful computer, although as best as we can tell, it's pretty narrow in what it does. But apparently, it's like a kind of electronic Rosetta stone. It should let us communicate with a number of galactic cultures in this epoch."

"'Apparently?'" Adler said. "Don't you know?"

"Well, we haven't actually talked to anybody yet, my lord," Jablonsky said. "But Newton tells us that's how it ought to work. There appear to be a large number of language types. The linguistics people could tell you more about that."

"Out in the Galaxy," Gonzalez said, "there are a lot of different ways that biological organisms can communicate with each other. Through spoken language, as with humans, of course, but some of those are mutually incomprehensible. Or unpronounceable. Our speech, for example, and a language of clicks, pops, and whistles, like with dolphins. But apparently there are also languages based on color changes in the body, or the movement of tentacles or other appendages, or smell, or changes in electrical fields. Roceti seems to use a few specialized languages—probably artificial—to enable communication between different communicative styles and biologies."

"Right," Jablonsky said. "With Roceti, we should be able to use the system to translate English to a spoken analogue, and that in turn can be translated into any language type we might encounter. We hope, anyway.

"We'll have to contact them first, of course, and that means getting close enough for a two-way dialogue. We can't just broadcast a call and wait a few millennia for a reply."

"Does Roceti list some possibilities for us?" St. Clair said.

"Yes, sir. We don't know how up to date the list is. But we've culled fifteen entries from a far more extensive list in Roceti's database. At least it gives a starting point."

"Let's see," St. Clair said.

So far there was little to go on—names rendered by Newton into something humans could pronounce, and columns of numbers that appeared to be navigational information. There was a lot of additional data, but the xenotech research team hadn't yet correlated it.

"This one is the nearest," Jablonsky said. "Twenty-three hundred light years in toward the galactic core." An image came up, showing a portion of the Galaxy visible outside of *Ad Astra*. A red icon blinked within a tangle of bright stars and glowing dust clouds. "As you can see, it's located within a region of heavy dust and gas, and with a lot of new star formation. Strong neutrino beacon. We have a transliteration of the place . . . but not a translation. It's called *isid*, whatever that is. Specifically . . . Isid 495."

"What is it?" Ambassador Lloyd asked. "A star? A star system? Another of these huge disk things?"

"Obviously, Mr. Ambassador," St. Clair said, "it's an isid. And we'll find out what that means when we get there."

"Lord Commander—" Adler's voice said.

"We *are* going," St. Clair said. "We'll come back to the Alderson disk later, if and when that seems appropriate." He looked at each of the officers around the table in turn, waiting to see if there were any additional challenges to his decision. His people all seemed to be with him. Adler and his cronies, though, were going to be trouble. They didn't voice their concerns, but their faces conveyed that with little ambiguity.

For now, though, they were letting him focus on the here and now, and he was going to take advantage of that opportunity.

"What about the virself effect you felt?" St. Clair asked.

Jablonsky looked uncomfortable. "It might have been a machine ghost, my lord," he replied.

Two centuries before, the philosopher Gilbert Ryle had coined the phrase "ghost in the machine" to describe Cartesian dualism . . . the idea that Mind or Spirit was distinct from Body, literally a ghost animating a machine. With the advent of artificial intelligence, the term had become a bit more pointed. Did AI computers possess souls? Was the mind something distinct from but inhabiting the computer—or the human brain, for that matter? Or was the mind a kind of illusion, an epiphenomenal effect arising from the machine's operation?

A "machine ghost" nowadays was the feeling that a machine was looking back at you, that there was a mind, a self-aware intelligence, somewhere inside. It was that insubstantial something that created the sense of a virself.

"But whatever it was, it didn't try to communicate with you."

"I don't think so, my lord. But Newton is still trying to find congruencies in his operating system and in the Roceti. Possibly there's an AI in there, but it's not able to express itself on or through our system. The memory inside the torpedo is enormous. It may have more storage—by several orders of magnitude—than our entire onboard network."

"That's . . . interesting." He'd almost said "frightening," but it wouldn't do to admit to that fear in front of the crew. Or Adler, for that matter. The human brain possessed something like two and a half petabytes—2.5×10^{15} bytes—of storage; the ship—meaning Newton—possessed roughly 8×10^{17} bytes. Something "several orders of magnitude larger," tucked into a shape-shifting package two meters long, suggested astonishing computing power. If there was an alien artificial intelligence resident within the torpedo, there was no telling what its capabilities might be.

The ghost might even be real. And they were trusting it to guide them home. There was another matter to deal with, though.

"Our first stop," St. Clair decided, "will be a system, along our line of flight to Isid 495, if possible, where we can find ice to replenish our water reserves, and metals to complete our repairs. Then we will find out what this *isid* is, and attempt to make contact. Questions?"

He was expecting further protest from Adler, but none was forthcoming.

For now, St. Clair thought.

"Good. Subcommander Adams? Find us some water. This meeting is concluded."

AND DEEP within the artificial structure known as Isid 495, Mind took note of the instantaneous transmissions from one of its agents. The alien starship was approaching.

At last.

CHAPTER

THIRTEEN

"How is he?"

St. Clair was physically present on Ward 2 of *Ad Astra*'s sick bay, an enormous medical facility more hospital than military clinic. It was, under the circumstances, the least he could do.

Doctor Kildare117 AI Delta-2pmd looked at St. Clair with what was probably intended to be compassion—a programmed response. The expression came across as disingenuous, however . . . something done purely for show. Kildare was a medical robot in Sokolov's department; the "pmd" in his designator stood for "psychiatric medical doctor." It was all a fancy way of saying he was a shrink.

"We are keeping Private Patterson in a deep medical coma, Lord Commander. He is psychotic and incapable of normal interaction."

They were standing on either side of Patterson's support pod, a mummy-case affair with a transparent top. *Ad Astra*'s sick bay was located in its own carousel aft of the bridge; some medical processes—the healing of broken bones, for instance—required a gravity field, though the burns unit and some other specialized sections were located in microgravity. Patterson was still, his eyes closed.

"And how the hell did that happen?"

"Unknown," Kildare replied. "However, probes of Patterson's brain show that the electrical circuitry of his chelated implants has been burned out, possibly by an extremely powerful and narrowly focused EMP."

St. Clair frowned. EMPs—electromagnetic pulses— could play havoc with electronic and electrical systems. Most such systems nowadays were insulated or hardened against them, including the delicate traceries of wiring and molecular switches grown inside the brains of most humans. Simply put, a very powerful magnetic field moving past a wire induced an electrical current; if that current was strong enough, the circuit would overload, even short-circuit and melt. The problem was, human implants were well shielded to avoid such nasty side effects when a person happened to walk through a magnet field, so this shouldn't have been able to happen.

"How is that even possible?"

"Unknown. What happened to CAS Francesca suggests an extradimensional component, however. The two cases are almost certainly related."

"We'd assumed as much." He looked down at Patterson's sleeping face. "Can you get *any* information out of him? Anything coherent?"

"Not that I, Dr. Sokolov, or the medical-unit AIs have been able to recognize. Here . . . see for yourself."

Dr. Kildare didn't move, but a pattern of lights winked on beside Patterson's head. A minute passed . . . then another. "Dr. Kildare," St. Clair said. "This really isn't—"

And then Patterson woke up.

His eyes came wide open, staring up into the overhead lights, and his mouth opened in a shrill scream only slightly muffled by the transplas shield over his face. The muscles of his neck stood out like rigid cables.

"Man grabbed pet but just darkness darkness *darkness* my God throw run home before five engaged mass surefire general order of a sentry in the dark it watches—"

The pattern of lights changed, Patterson's face froze in mid shriek, then relaxed, slowly, back to a resting state. His eyes closed, and he was asleep once more.

"My God, Doctor . . . you didn't need to do that!"

"I wanted you to hear him, Lord Commander. Sometimes, the words almost make sense. His speech patterns are what in psychiatric terms are called word salad, an unintelligible hash of distinct words and phrases. But there obviously is an underlying meaning there, if we could just reach it."

"So . . . what's going to happen to him?"

"His neural circuitry is burned out. Parts of the cerebral cortex and subcortex have been damaged. We are programming a nanorepair infusion that will, first, disassemble the inorganic remnants of the circuitry, and then move into the organic tissue and begin effecting repairs. We predict an eighty percent chance of full physical recovery, especially with the introduction of new cerebral prosthetics. It is unlikely that we will be able to preserve all of Private Patterson's memory, however, and retraining will be necessary in some areas."

"Very well. Please keep me informed."

"Yes, Lord Commander. Of course."

"What about Maxwell?" Sublieutenant Ogden Maxwell had been the fighter pilot coming in to trap on board *Ad Astra*'s flight deck when CAS had been killed. His fighter had brushed an antenna when communications with CAS had gone down, and his fighter had been damaged.

"Already returned to duty, Lord Commander. He suffered some minor bruises, and the effects of vacc exposure when his cockpit was breached, but his suit systems kept him alive until a SAR robot could reach him."

"That's good. Thank you, Doctor."

"Anytime, Lord Commander."

And there was that compassionate look again.

THE PARTY at the Lloyd residence in Jefferson had been going for some time when St. Clair and Lisa finally arrived hours later. Jefferson was a minor city located cross-cylinder and forward of Bethesda, a straight-line distance of about fifteen kilometers, and he'd requisitioned a private magfloater to make the trip. Jefferson currently lay within a band of artificial night, and the residence compound was a brightly lit patch outshining the nearby city lights. As they stepped out of the craft and onto the imitation teak landing platform, Clayton Lloyd himself greeted them.

"Welcome, Lord Commander!" he said. "I'm so glad you could make it!"

"Thank you, Mr. Ambassador. It's good to be here."

It was a bald-faced lie, and both of them knew it . . . but it was both a socially acceptable and a politically necessary one.

The Directorate ambassador was stylishly nude, save for his sleek sensory helmet and a line of luminous blue fractal designs running up his left leg, side, and arm.

St. Clair had opted for a more conservative and formally traditional costume for the evening—his full-dress Navy blacks. While the party *was* a purely social event, he fully expected to be beset by wolves—with wolves defined as the politicians who'd decided that they knew better than he how to skipper the *Ad Astra*.

He noted, in passing, that Lloyd had completely ignored Lisa with his greeting. Was he a dominioner? Interesting, if so. St. Clair decided he would need to do some research on the man.

"Lisa was just telling me how much she was looking forward to seeing your place," St. Clair said. He felt Lisa's reaction beside him, but knew she wouldn't challenge his statement in public. She had, of course, said no such thing.

"Indeed?" Lloyd looked at Lisa, scanning her briefly from head to foot and back. The left side of her body, including her face, was covered by an animated liquid-light tattoo, bright green with on-again, off-again red highlights, writhing and boiling like time-lapsed stormclouds; the right side of her body was nude. It was a fashion motif popular in North America just now . . . or, rather, St. Clair reminded himself, it *had* been, 4 billion years ago.

"Help yourself to the buffet," Lloyd said, again ignoring the gynoid. "I see some other folks arriving there I need to meet and greet. But I'd like to talk to you a bit later on."

"Of course."

The ambassador made his exit.

"Sorry, Lisa," St. Clair said after Lloyd had left. "Not exactly diplomatic of him, was it?"

She gave a quite human shrug. "The essence of diplomacy is convincing others that something is so, but there's always an assumption that the attitude of those others whom you are trying to convince is important to you. Obviously, the feelings of robotic AIs are not high on Mr. Lloyd's list of priorities."

St. Clair wondered what Lisa had meant by her deliberate use of the word *feelings*. Was she indicating that she had them, in the sense that humans did?

Or was she making a joke? In some ways, that would be even more astonishing.

Several hundred people had already arrived at the Lloyd residence, and were gathered in small groups throughout the house and outside among the patio gardens. St. Clair had not been here before, and wondered how much of the fancy lighting effects were permanent, and what had been brought in just for this affair. Rippling curtains of liquid light in delicate, luminous pastels provided a measure of privacy for couples and small groups who desired it. Elaborate fountains rained light throughout the gardens, drenching guests in intangible, flowing color.

Quite a few robots were in evidence, St. Clair noticed,

both androids and gynoids, serving both as waitstaff and as providers of sexual entertainment for the human guests. He decided that Lloyd's disdain for Lisa likely had more to do with her rising above her proper station than it did with her being a synthetic.

He sighed. Come the Robot Revolution . . .

It was a much overused theme drawn from entertainment sims and interactives. St. Clair had long thought the current fascination among humans with some kind of mass robot uprising was a symptom of an underlying fear of Humankind's artificial servants. Modern robots had safeguards and software inhibitors to prevent that sort of thing, but a lot of humans simply didn't trust them. And while AI robots were okay when they stayed in their place—as servants, as sex partners, as replacements for humans in dangerous or inhospitable surroundings—a robot that thought it was a full partner of organic humans was regarded with deep suspicion.

For St. Clair, the current legal status of synthetics was far too close to outright slavery to suit him. There were laws on the books to prevent mistreatment of sentient machines, certainly, but in the final analyses they still, legally, were property.

To put it succinctly: Lloyd's stance disgusted him.

"Ah, Commander!" a familiar voice said at his back.

Speaking of disgust . . .

St. Clair turned as Adler approached, hand out, all smiles and warm welcomes. "I was hoping we'd see you tonight."

"My lord," St. Clair acknowledged.

"I see *Ad Astra*'s watering operation is well under way."

He gestured toward the curving surface of the cylinder's far side. One of *Tellus*'s long vista windows was visible from the residence deck almost directly overhead, looking out into space opposite the city of Jefferson, and the cylinder's rotation had just brought the comet into view, vast and cratered.

"Yes, my lord," St. Clair replied. "We should be able to top off the water tanks, and even get some organics for the nanufactories."

"Are we going to investigate the inner planets more closely?"

"No," St. Clair replied. "Not until we know what we're up against."

They'd spotted the star system from some distance out and approached cautiously. There were multiple worlds circling the star, three of them super Earths clearly inhabited at some point in the past. The land areas were covered with ruins, a repeat of the near-lifeless desolation on the Alderson disk.

Rather than approach the planets closely, St. Clair had ordered *Ad Astra* out to this system's Oort cloud, where a ten-kilometer comet had in due course been found. The *Harvester*, a replenishment vessel, had been launched from *Ad Astra*'s main bay. Approaching the comet's nucleus, it had released a cloud of mining nano, which had been busily prospecting and disassembling it for hours, now. Mostly ice, the comet held a reservoir of some hundreds of billions of tons of water, but there were many tons of organic material as well—primarily carbon, nitrogen, various silicates, and frozen carbon dioxide and ammonia. *Ad Astra*'s onboard nanufactories would be able to transform the harvested rawmat into food, clothing, atmosphere, and anything else the human population might need.

"You know, Lord Commander," Adler said with a cheerful nonchalance, "we're going to have to go investigate other worlds *sometime*."

"I agree, my lord. But we shall do so with due care and deliberation."

"Your conservative prejudice is showing, sir," Adler said. "*Some* might see it as xenophobia."

"Then *some* are idiots."

The thing was, he had given up having this argument a long time ago. He was never going to convince his enemies. In any case, the past was now *really* past—4 billion years buried. And Adler certainly wasn't worth the angst here and now.

"There were some back on Earth," Adler said, "who considered your assignment as *Ad Astra*'s commander to be a punishment. But you might be interested to know that not everyone thought that."

Admiral Carruthers had suggested as much. "What was it, then?"

"A chance for redemption, of course. The Imperial Navy got something of a black eye when you called that first electronic press conference, you know."

"I know."

"By giving you this command, they proved to the world that there were . . . no hard feelings, shall we say? And you had a chance to demonstrate your loyalty by carrying out a mission with which you publicly didn't agree."

"Yes, well . . . none of that much matters now, does it?"

"But I would say it does."

Adler's answer surprised him, but he didn't let it show. "And why would you say that?"

"Because sooner or later, the population of this expedition will need to set up a government of its own. A *civilian* government. Unless you plan on running it indefinitely as a military dictatorship?"

"Don't be absurd."

"Perhaps not so absurd. There are some who are already concerned about the seemingly unilateral decisions being made."

"Then there are definitely *some* idiots aboard. You know full well that we have always convened before taking large-scale actions."

"Oh, *I* know," he said, holding his hands up as if to say

It's not me *saying all these nasty things*, and St. Clair was aware he had stumbled into Günter's trap. Now the Cyb director had the rhetorical upper hand . . . even though the man was clearly lying. To accuse him of that, though, carried very severe consequences, and without actual proof, St. Clair couldn't make such a statement.

Which Adler knew.

Ever the politician, the director pressed his agenda. "You know the power of rumors, though. Which is why your support of the civilian authority will be important. *Very* important. I'd be interested in knowing whether you will support an imperial directive . . . or if you're still wedded to the old idea of a republic."

Quite frankly, St. Clair had not had the time to think much about the politics of the *Tellus* colony's government. But it was, of course, no secret that he didn't care for the Directorate, didn't like government by fiat and executive order and rule-of-law pronouncements by the Cybercouncil. He had always been of the opinion that the government that governs best is the one that governs *least*. Having built-in checks and balances helped keep the jackboots off of people's throats.

Then again, what did he know? Most people nowadays accepted the Directorate as a reasonable way of getting things done, while washed-up republicans like him were, at best, quaint relics of an earlier, bygone era.

And although he knew this wasn't what Adler was expecting, the thought that he might actually have a hand in determining the shape of a new civilian government was intriguing.

For now, though, he would hold that little fact close to the vest.

"I think it's a bit early to worry about that, my lord," St. Clair replied. "Let's make contact with whoever is running things on this side of the black hole first."

Adler nodded soberly, but something about the way his eye crinkled made St. Clair think the director felt he'd won.

Let Adler think he has me cornered. It isn't the first time an Earth-based politician had made that mistake.

Because St. Clair knew something Adler had clearly forgotten: in space, there really weren't any corners.

Overhead, the rotation of the habitat cylinder had taken the comet and *Harvester* out of view. The glowing face of the Milky Way Galaxy drifted slowly past the vista window.

MIKE COLLINS was a vacuumorph.

She didn't mind that fact, particularly; after all, she'd not had any say in the matter, having decanted from the Clarke-orbital crèches of Dupont Biogenengineering. But like others of her kind she took considerable pride in her talents. Talents that set her apart from prototype humans.

At the moment, she was adrift in free fall, naked in empty space, floating several kilometers from the paired, oppositely rotating cylinders of the *Tellus* colony. From here, she could look straight into one of the long, transparent panels in the starboard cylinder's hull as it turned past her point of view. A blaze of light had been visible inside on the far, internal wall, just for a moment—one of the colony's cities, illuminated against its artificial night. And now it was gone.

She wished she could be a part of that.

Or . . . did she? *Homo saps* were such peculiar beasties in their outlook, their attitudes, and their culture.

"I hear it's supposed to be one hell of a party," Story Musgrove commented, her radio voice picked out of the ether by the electronics in Collins's brain.

"Maybe we should crash it," Collins replied.

"Nah. High grav ain't worth it. And it would just upset the natives."

Mike Collins and Story Musgrove both were products of genetic engineering, genengineered paramorphs from human stock, designed to live and work in hard vacuum. *Homo caelestis* individuals tended to be small and compact—only about a meter long—and were encased in massive, pebbly surfaced outer shells that protected their soft tissues from both hard radiation and vacuum desiccation. Deeply recessed eyes behind thick, transparent shields gave Collins an extended visual range, from infrared far into the ultraviolet, while an internal air bladder, and blood rich with artificial respirocytes let her breathe for days at a time between rechargings. Nanochelated electronics grown inside her brain gave her additional senses, including radio telepathy with other vacs, electro- and magnetic senses, and the ability to feel mass.

Perhaps the most startling adaptation, though, was visible in her legs . . . or rather, in her lack of them. Instead of human legs, which were pretty much superfluous in zero gravity, Collins possessed an extra pair of arms attached to her pelvic girdle. At the moment, she was clinging by one lower arm to a support structure extending around one of *Harvester*'s free-floating matmovers, a ring that collected and directed the stream of microscopic nanobots flooding across from the comet. As rawmat was mined from the surface, it was accelerated, molecule by molecule, by the 'bots and physically carried across to *Ad Astra*'s rawmat receiver bays. As the matter invisibly streamed through the ring, constant interactions with its magnetic field tended to nudge it out of position. Mike's job was to monitor the process and correct for drift, using an electrostatic driver grasped in one upper arm and her free lower one. The job was tedious and relatively mindless. A nonsentient robot could have done the job as well as she.

Sometimes, she thought, her *H. sap* controllers in the logistics department put together assignments like this one solely to justify their existence to *Ad Astra*'s dispersing office.

Others of her kind were out here as well, some jockeying matmover rings, others swarming across the surface of the comet, overseeing the rawmat mining operations. The local sun was shrunken to the cold gleam of a bright star, suspended in emptiness. Beyond, the spectacular sprawl of two colliding galaxies dominated the heavens in every direction.

That was something her controllers would never appreciate: the sight of those two spirals etched in a clarity of sharp detail that included far-flung clouds of heat generated by interpenetrating dust and gas, and the actinic glare of UV energies pinpointing the birth cries of hot, newborn suns.

Magnificent . . . but what was that?

"Musgrove! Leonov!" she called over the *H. cael* work-channel. "McAuliffe!"

Vacuumorphs, though technically female, were sterile. Without families of their own, raised in corporate crèches, they were assigned lot numbers, but not names. Since they'd first entered the workforce in the early 2100s, Vacs had chosen their own names, generally taking them from the history of early space exploration, from Yuri Gagarin and John Glenn on down to Zhou Jing, who'd skippered the *Emissary of Sol* on the first expedition to Alpha Centauri.

"What's the prob, Collins?" Christa McAuliffe called back.

"Look at Andromeda, will you?"

"Why? What's the big deal?"

"Use your grav-mass scanners. What do you see?"

Flung by gravitational tides from its home galaxy hundreds of thousands of years ago, the system they were mining was located in the gulf nestled in between the two vast, interpenetrating galaxies. Half of the Milky Way was visible face-on to one side, while just over half of the larger, brighter Andromeda canted off at an angle to the other. Billions of suns shone brightly on both sides, and particularly along the intersection of the two spirals; as gas clouds collided, they'd triggered a storm of star generation, especially in the froth where the galaxies merged and passed through each other. With their extra senses, the vacs could see not only the heat and UV radiation of the collision, but the somber, deep-blood haze representing mass.

Lots of mass.

More than 84 percent of all matter in the universe, Collins knew, consisted of so-called dark matter—a kind of exotic matter that did not interact at all with light or normal matter, but which made its presence known through gravity. The stuff had been hypothesized as a way of explaining the too-fast rotation of galaxies; stars throughout the universe seemed to orbit their galactic cores at such high velocities that *something* unseen had to be there, providing the gravitational mass holding those galaxies together and keeping them from flying apart. Exactly what dark matter might be was still unknown, even after two centuries of study.

But by sensing the gravitational mass surrounding the galaxies, Collins and her fellow Vacs could, in a way, actually see the clouds of dark matter around both Andromeda and the Milky Way. She focused her gaze on the Andromedan spiral and mentally dialed down the optical frequencies, until the galaxy's stars were just visible as pale ghosts imbedded in the red haze of dark matter. She increased the level of detail in the glow, heightening contrast, brightening the haze, pulling up subtle levels of detail.

She could see it moving.

And that was frankly, starkly impossible, because for movement to be visible at such a scale it would have to be moving much, *much* faster than light.

"Shit! Is that haze *moving*?" Leonov asked.

"Can't be," Musgrove replied.

"Some kind of optical illusion?" McAuliffe suggested.

There was a deep, purplish tint to the red; that, and the apparent movement, distinguished the haze surrounding and filling Andromeda from the haze overlying the Milky Way. And surely that was some kind of illusion too, because there was no reason that the dark matter in one galaxy would be different from the dark matter in the other.

Then again, so little was understood about dark matter that anything was possible.

"It looks," Leonov said slowly, "like it's coming off of Andromeda and moving into the space between the galaxies. Toward *us*. . . ."

"The longer I look," Collins told them, "the more I see. Or *think* I see. It looks to me like . . . I don't know, streamers or threads or something reaching from Andromeda out toward us."

"I see them too," McAuliffe said.

"Impossible!" Musgrove snapped. "Gravity doesn't work like that!"

"Maybe it's not mass the way we think of it," Leonov suggested. "It looks . . . I don't know. *Biological*."

"A life form that envelops an entire galaxy?" Collins asked.

"You know, there's something else," McAuliffe said. "The nearest of Andromeda's stars are—what do you think? Fifteen, twenty thousand light years away from where we are right now?"

"Something like that." Collins thought she knew where the other vac was going with this, and it wasn't a comfortable thought.

"So what we're seeing happened twenty thousand years ago, right?"

"Except that I'm seeing movement at the far edge of Andromeda, on the other side of the core. See it? And those stars have to be at least fifty, sixty thousand light years away."

"So what you're saying—" Musgrove started to say.

"Right," Leonov said. "Whatever that is, it must already

be here . . . already have passed through here and into the Milky Way. It happened a long time ago."

"Like, maybe, when the Alderson disk was destroyed?"

"Are you guys recording this?" Collins asked. The others chorused in the affirmative. "Okay, good. Because we're going to need to show this to the saps."

Yet even with multispectral recording, she didn't think they would be believed.

ST. CLAIR, TO be blunt, was bored out of his mind. He *hated* these social functions, and would have been happy to ignore each and every one. As lord commander of the expedition, though, he was expected to attend them, to at *least* put in an appearance. Adler would likely have called it "embracing certain basic amenities of protocol."

But at the moment, all he could think about was poor Patterson's face as he shrieked out word salad. Of the sight of Maria Francesca turned inside out.

One thought drove him: *Ad Astra* was under attack. The question was . . . by whom?

And perhaps more important, what was he going to do about it?

"Lord Commander! So good of you to come!"

He turned. He didn't recognize the woman at first. The upper half of her face was masked by a black-and-silver sensenhance helmet. When he ID tagged her through his in-head hardware, the name "Gina Colfax" and the words "Diplomatic Corps" hovered in the air next to her. She was one of Lloyd's people, then, a diplomatic specialist who'd been heading for the Coadunation complex at the galactic core, and instead had ended up here.

"Ms. Colfax. Good to see you."

She laughed, and he immediately regretted the verbal slip, which amounted to a minor sexual innuendo. Colfax wore a kind of liquid silver choker necklace or collar that covered her throat and shoulders, but was otherwise nude. A magnificent spray of fiber-optics rose in a white halo above and behind her head and upper torso, and animated tattoos chased one another across her exposed skin. Her pubic hair, neatly trimmed, was a brilliantly fluorescent purple, matching both her lips and her nipples.

"You can see me *any*time, my lord," she said. "As much as you like!"

St. Clair decided to beat as dignified a retreat as was possible. "Yes, well . . . if you'll excuse me . . ."

"A question first, my lord?"

"Of course, my lady."

A group of three men and two women had been standing a few paces behind Colfax, obviously listening. One of them stepped closer, now, a tall man in red, black, and a spray of red light.

"They say," the man said, "that you have a lead on a new ACGI. Is it true?"

ACGI—advanced communicative galactic civilization, and pronounced "ack-gee"—had been a buzzword since the discovery of the Coadunation. Even before that, it had been used to describe the goal of the old SETI programs— someone else out among the stars with whom Humankind might be able to communicate.

The man's ID popped up in St. Clair's in-head—Lord Jeffery Benton—a Senate-corporate liaison, a corprep, and a member of the *Tellus* Cybercouncil.

"We do have a target, my lord," St. Clair told him. "But it may be just another beacon, like the one at the Alderson disk."

"These gentlemen and ladies," Colfax said, gesturing, "are corpreps on the Cybercouncil, and we've been discussing the possibility of establishing an industrial base in this . . . ah . . . place and time."

"I see." Long ago, court rulings had established that

corporations were *persons* in every legal sense. With that precedent, it hadn't been long before such persons were represented in Congress. "Corps" or "corpreps" were the senate and representative assistants and liaisons who acted as go-betweens. Constitutionalists like St. Clair tended to mistrust the system, which had played a large part in the political corruption that had led to the last American Revolution. The new government's failure to get rid of the corpreps had played a large role in the breakdown that followed . . . and in the rise of the U.E. Directorate. They were an unfortunate reality now, though, and that meant he couldn't just ignore them.

One of the women spoke. "If we're truly stuck in this time," she said, "we'll need to establish a manufacturing base, perhaps colonize a new world . . . in essence start Humankind over again. To do this, we'll need local contacts. As you can imagine, my lord, we're eager to kick things off."

The woman was Lady Angelica Braun, who represented, St. Clair knew, a nanotech corporation.

"Well, we should know soon enough," St. Clair said. "We'll be making a shift sometime tomorrow."

"And will you be using the Diplomatic Corps to establish contact?" Colfax asked.

He started to say "No," but then reconsidered. Nothing could possibly be gained by antagonizing the expedition's civilian component.

"That, my lady, will depend on the circumstances. Initial contact will be through my bridge team, of course . . . assuming we find anyone there with whom we can make contact in the first place. After that . . . we'll see."

"Some of us are wondering, my lord," Hsien Tianki said slowly, "if you just have the rest of us along in this vessel for the ride."

"That's certainly not my intent, Lord Hsien." What industry did Hsien represent? St. Clair wondered. Bioengineering

and genetics, he thought, and then it clicked: a megacorpora-
tion called Dynamic Biogenics. "But keep in mind that we
have been attacked—twice. Let the military find out what
we're up against before you start negotiating treaties, okay?"

"Of course. I might have expected as much from you."

He almost demanded what the man had meant by that,
but shrugged it off.

Damn but he hated these affairs.

FOURTEEN

"Did you load the latest 'sode of *Tangent* last night?"

"Wouldn't miss it. That Cavi is gamma hot. . . ."

"Hey, did you load the 'sip about Gina? They say she——"

"You know, there are rumors that the Medusan ambassador killed itself. It wasn't an accident . . ."

The agony of the party at the Lloyd residence dragged on. For half an hour, now, St. Clair had been wondering when he could in good conscience cut the damned thing short. He had *work* to do, damn it. He didn't have the time to listen to vac-headed nonsense about entertainment sims or virtual holography stars or random gossip.

The worst of it was, a lot of the background chatter was flowing over the local network conversation channel, and there was no way to avoid it. If he killed the channel to stop the whisper in his head, he would miss it when someone actually addressed him directly.

"They say he's sleeping with all of them . . ."

"Well, what's wrong with *that*?"

"And I was like, 'Oh, my God . . .' "

"Lord Commander?"

It was almost a relief to hear someone speaking a language he understood.

"Yes, Ambassador Lloyd?"

"I wanted to talk to you about the Gressman Initiative."

The question caught St. Clair by surprise. "As in Ander Gressman? Cyber Legislature?"

"The same."

Ander Gressman was a member of the *Tellus* Cybercouncil, St. Clair knew, but he'd not been following expedition politics much. He knew Gressman was a staunch imperialist, and as a member of the *Ad Astra* expedition he would support closer human-alien relations. But St. Clair had not met the man, and was unaware of any initiative.

"And what is he initiating?"

"He's proposing that we go back to Sagittarius A-Star, back where we met that alien moon ship. The Roceti torpedo, clearly, was a gift designed to let us communicate with them. Now that we've unwrapped it, we need to use it. As the givers intended."

"I see."

St. Clair was tempted to go back to what he'd been doing before Lloyd had approached him. He had been simply wandering inside the residence, occasionally grazing at the buffet and half listening to a live string quartet playing Hammond's *Starglow*. He'd engaged in chitchat with a few of the guests, but for the most part he was just counting down the minutes until he could leave without causing undue commotion.

He'd been bored, but at least he'd been left alone. Now, with the ambassador before him, he longed for that boredom.

Because there was something he'd discovered years before: the military and civilians rarely had very much to talk about socially. The gulf between them was simply too great.

The people here tonight—politicians and diplomats, most of them—talked about other politicians and diplomats, about meetings and parties and entertainment sims, about concerts and artists, sports and faux pas within their own social circles and carefully avoided the important things.

Like the fact that *Tellus Ad Astra* was lost in both time and space. Take away the weather—and the weather was

always pretty benign inside an O'Neill habitat cylinder—
and there weren't many options left for small talk. And no
one wanted to engage in *big* talk. No. He looked around the
room, and it was obvious nothing of substance was being
talked about.

He spotted Lisa on a sofa nearby, where she was talking
with one of Dr. Dumont's staff members. He wanted to go
over to her and suggest they start politely saying their good-
byes, but Lloyd seemed determined to pursue his question,
and St. Clair doubted that he would be allowed to make his
escape.

"So . . . what about it, Lord Commander?"

"What about what?"

"Have you thought about the Gressman Initiative?"

"Actually, my lord," he said, "no."

"The proposal passed in the Legislature this afternoon,
Lord Commander," Lloyd told him, "by a vote of two hundred four to eighty-one."

"And this means what, exactly?"

"It shows the will of the people, of course."

"Oh. Of *course.*"

Lloyd seemed to hear the sarcasm in St. Clair's voice.
"I know Lord Adler has already spoken to you about the
need for establishing a civilian government as quickly as
possible."

St. Clair nodded. "And I couldn't agree more, Mr. Ambassador."

Lloyd smiled at that. "You sound almost imperial, my
lord."

"In what way?"

"The Imperium, Lord St. Clair, is not military, not at
heart. It's a way of thinking, of governing, that recognizes
the simple fact that some—a very few—people have the
talent, the assertiveness, the *gifts* to guide Humankind into
the future, and that most do not. If you agree that a civilian

government is the best course for us to set for ourselves, then you are calling for the establishment of an imperial state."

"Ah. And why not a republic?"

Lloyd snorted. "Come, now. Be realistic, Lord Commander. *That* peculiar superstition was swept away a century ago, and rightly so. First with the failure of the so-called 'people's democratic republics,' the communist states of the twentieth century. Then with the failure of the American republic fifty years later."

"*Don't* presume to teach me history, Mr. Lloyd," St. Clair said. "And, for the record, even the Earth Directorate of today is a representative democracy."

"In name, at least."

What the hell was Lloyd driving at? "Didn't you just tell me that the vote in the Legislature represented the 'will of the people'?"

"Come, now. The people—the *demos* of a democracy—they *never* know what's best for themselves. Mob rule sweeps the masses along on tides of emotion or greed or selfishness or a tyrant's rhetoric, not *reason*. Surely even an unreconstructed democratic constitutionalist like you knows that! The people's representatives in government know what is best for them."

"Ah. And how do these representatives know what's best?"

"By their superior education, intelligence, and their top-of-the-line cybernetic links to AI, communication, and megadata sources, of course. They see the larger picture, and have access to all of the necessary information."

"Of course."

A loud guffaw, a shout, and a crowd's laughter, followed by a splash caught St. Clair's attention. Across the room, a nude, hairy man in a bright red sensenhance helmet had been trying to gather together a number of women in his outstretched arms, and then somehow managed to fall full-length into a hot-water pool. St. Clair focused his in-head software on the man as he clambered out of the steaming water. Yes . . . he'd thought so. Lord Gorton Noyer . . . a senior member of the *Tellus* Legislature.

"Don't look now," St. Clair said, "but Lord Noyer, by virtue of his superior education, intelligence, and cybernetic software . . . is falling-down drunk."

Lloyd turned, glaring at Noyer. The demonstration really had been superbly timed, as if deliberately arranged to refute Lloyd's statement.

"It's no secret that I don't like the idea of the Directorate, my lord," St. Clair said before the ambassador could respond. "I'm sure every man, woman, and AI on this expedition is aware of that quirk. But I take my orders from the Earth Directorate Navy Command, and I've sworn an oath to uphold the Constitution. The *Directorate* Constitution."

Lloyd looked puzzled. "What does that have to do—"

"My Lord, for the moment I am in command of a *military* expedition, and so far I've seen no reason to assume that the military phase has ended. Those three needle ships in the core, then the *things* that attacked us—first on the Alderson disk and then in PriFly . . . We have been under attack, my lord, one way or another, ever since we arrived here. You *will* have your civilian government, with my full cooperation and blessing . . . the *moment* we are no longer fighting for our lives. Do I make myself clear?"

Lloyd gave a small, perhaps ironic bow. "You do, Lord Commander. What about the vote to return to the core?"

"That's actually an excellent idea, my lord," St. Clair said.

Lloyd blinked, startled. "I—what? You agree?"

"Oh, yes. I'd very much like to establish contact with whoever was piloting that four-hundred-kilometer spacefaring moon. Since the Roceti torpedo has proved not to be a weapon after all, I'd have to say that the intent was peaceful and directed toward establishing contact. Of course, they *did* vanish after dropping the torpedo off, and we could spend a small eternity searching among the core stars for them, but I think it's a safe bet that Roceti will summon them when we want them.

"However, Roceti has also given us a possible target considerably closer—a modulated neutrino source located a fraction of the distance between here and the core, and very nearly on a straight line between us and Sag A-Star. As such, we will stop at the neutrino beacon. Navigation has given it the rather dull name of NPS-024, and it may be as dead as NPS-076, the disk. But we'll try out Roceti anyway, see if there's anyone there to talk to, and *then* we will return to the vicinity of Sag A-Star if that doesn't pan out. Does that meet with your approval, my Lord Ambassador?"

Lloyd scowled at St. Clair's heavy sarcasm, but after a brief hesitation, he gave a short, curt nod. "It does, sir."

"I'm *so* glad that meets with your approval, my lord. And now, I regretfully must return to my duties. Thank you for the invitation and for a lovely party. Lisa?"

She looked up from the AI she was talking with, one of Lloyd's pets, eyebrows arching a question. He replied with a jerk of his head, indicating that he wanted to leave.

She excused herself and walked over to where he was standing. Lloyd turned away to help himself to something from the bar.

"Let's go home," he told her.

"I'd like to stay a little longer, Gray."

He considered this. Ancient social mores about things like escorting ladies home from a party didn't apply here, save strictly as outward show. Lisa wasn't a lady—not in an organic sense—and crime within the colony was unknown.

Hell, Lisa was a lot stronger than he was, despite her small frame and feminine bearing. Any human assailant who attempted to waylay *her* would be lucky to get away alive.

"Sure," he told her. "I'll leave you the 'floater. See you at home."

He kissed her lightly, then strode out of the residence, summoning a public flyer through his in-head link.

And no sooner was his request acknowledged than the emergency call came through from Personnel.

"YOU DIDN'T need to come in and see me personally," St. Clair said. He was floating in microgravity on *Ad Astra*'s bridge, facing the odd little *H. cael* who had asked to talk with him. "You could have used an in-head channel."

"No, my lord," the creature said. "I need to see who I'm talking to."

St. Clair nodded his understanding. The celestimorphs were a funny bunch, hard for Original-Genome humans to completely understand. Unable to speak, they possessed all of the in-head hardware most *Homo sapiens* did, and used electronic telepathy both when talking with others and among themselves. So far as St. Claire knew, they didn't need to be face-to-face when conversing with their own kind.

But with O-G humans it was different. Psychologists thought it had to do with establishing different ways of communicating with others, ways creating distinctions of *them* as opposed to *us*; they certainly were aware of the differences between the species *caelestis* and *sapiens*, and seemed to want to accentuate those differences for psychological reasons of their own.

Related to this was their preference for orienting themselves upside down with respect to any O-G they happened to be speaking with. This one, Michael Collins, had reached out to grab a handhold that positioned her head-down, from St. Clair's perspective. Of course, there was no up or down in microgravity—the celestimorphs just seemed to enjoy emphasizing that fact.

"Okay, Mike," St. Clair said. He pulled himself over to the command chair and maneuvered himself into it. The seat immediately attached itself to his uniform, holding him in place. Collins continued to hang nearby like some bloated four-armed spider. "Now tell us again . . . what did you see out there?"

"Andromeda is alive," Collins told him. "We could see it moving."

St. Clair wished he could read the being's expression. Little that an O-G human would recognize as emotion showed through those thick, protective lenses. "That doesn't make sense."

"Believe me, I know. But it was like these *things*, like *tentacles* reaching across toward us." One of the being's foot-hands rippled in imitation of something crawling. "It was damned scary, let me tell you . . . my lord."

St. Clair smiled at the hesitation before the honorific. Celestimorphs were markedly egalitarian in their social interactions, and didn't seem to have much use for the titles and heavy-handed formalities of address and demeanor used within the United Earth Directorate.

Something I have in common with them, then.

"You have a recording?"

"Yes, my lord."

A new window opened inside St. Clair's mind, and the recording came up. He struggled to understand what he was seeing. Recording software was standard in most in-head implants, allowing one person to show another exactly what he'd seen or otherwise experienced. The pebbly-skinned celestimorphs, however, experienced the universe around them quite differently from O-G humans, with optical senses extending from deep in the infrared to far into the ultraviolet, and with other senses overlaying them in odd and sometimes hard-to-interpret ways.

And yet . . .

Yes—he could see the tendrils Collins had described on his in-head, a kind of purplish overlay to the view of the Andromedan disk that writhed and shifted as he watched. In the lower part of the scene, much closer to where the central cores of Andromeda and the Milky Way began to merge, a number of violet pseudopods seemed to be pouring across the narrow gulf in slow motion, a kind of oozing of color and texture that did, indeed, suggest that something was moving from one galaxy to the other.

"That purple stuff," St. Clair said. "That's *mass*?" He wanted to be certain he understood.

"Mass as delineated by gravity," Collins told him. "We think it might actually be dark matter."

The thought chilled, uncomfortable and unpleasant. The oozing motion made St. Clair think of something *alive*.

Could dark matter have its own biochemistry?

That thought led to another, even more uncomfortable. Could dark matter possess *Mind*?

"Upload everything you have to Newton," St. Clair told the little being.

"We already have." And without anything like social niceties, it pushed off from its perch and flew toward the bridge entryway.

"Do you believe her?" Symm asked after Mike left.

"Don't you?"

"I don't know. Those things . . . they think in peculiar ways."

"But I've never known one to hallucinate," St. Clair replied. "They're pretty matter-of-fact about everything. If they have anything like an imagination, they keep it well under control."

"The vid she showed us could be some sort of sensor malfunction," Anna Denisova said.

"It was assembled from the in-head data of three caels," St. Clair replied. "Three identical hardware malfunctions?"

"That's not very likely."

"No. It's not. Can you set the ship's mass sensors to show gravitational mass visually?"

"Yes, my lord," Denisova replied. "Our gravitational scanners already show the data, but as alphanumerics. We could direct the department AIs to translate to visual."

"Do it. I'm thinking it would be a smart idea to be able to see what the caels see."

HOURS HAD PASSED. "All departments, stand by for shift."

"All stations report ready for transition, my lord."

"Subcommander Rand. Are all of our people back aboard?"

Gerard Rand had been Francesca's second-in-command in PriFly, replacing her as CAS after her horrific death.

"All fighters and auxiliary craft have returned and are secured, my lord."

"Are you doing okay down here?"

There was a pause. "Yes, my lord. I *do* miss her, though."

St. Clair had been asking about how well Rand was dealing with the new cybernetic links, not his emotions concerning Francesca, but decided not to push it. The telemetry at his bridge station showed all in readiness.

"So do we all, Jerry. Okay, First Navigator. Let's go places."

The sky ahead, dominated by the interpenetrating cores of two spiral galaxies, shimmered . . . then shifted. There was little visible change. A few of the nearer, foreground stars vanished or jumped aside. A blue-black nebula edged with silver and gold expanded, becoming more dominant.

And NPS-024 took center stage.

"What the hell is *that*?" Symm asked, her voice touched by wonder.

St. Clair stared at the object for a long moment. It seemed to be a sphere, appearing at a range of several AUs as metallic and a dark, charcoal gray.

"Give me a higher magnification."

The sphere jumped, filling the screen. At the new resolution, St. Clair could see a lacy pattern across the surface—loops, whorls, and empty spaces. The empty spaces appeared to be filled with a tenuous haze.

And through the haze, within the outer shell . . . another shell, with more designs that made it look like an exercise in the mathematics of spherical projection.

"Can we zoom in any closer?"

Again, the sphere jumped in size. The outer surface appeared granular at this resolution, and filmy rather than solid, as though it were made of clouds of precisely ordered grains of sand.

And within the second shell . . . *more* shells, layer upon layer of them, with just a hint, at infrared wavelengths, of a sun peeking through all of that obscuring matter from the central core.

"My God . . ." St. Clair said quietly. "An honest-to-God Dyson sphere."

"Not exactly," Newton's voice said in his mind. "A true Dyson sphere would have only a single shell, either as a solid component, with the habitable zone spread across the inner surface, facing the star . . . or with a cloud of either orbital habitats or statites within the star's habitable zone. This could more accurately be called a Dyson *swarm*."

St. Clair stared into that hazy vastness. He was familiar with the concept of both Dyson spheres and Dyson swarms, which had been around as speculation since the twentieth century. Named for the mathematician and physicist who'd come up with the idea, they'd been suggested as a logical step in the history of any highly technical space-faring species, a means of trapping all of the energy radiated by that civilization's sun, rather than the fraction of a percent intercepted naturally by the day side of a planet. Though usually pictured as a solid shell—which would have been inherently unstable—Dyson in fact had suggested that such a sphere might consist of tens of billions of habitats similar to the *Tellus* portion of *Tellus Ad Astra*—either in orbit around their sun, or suspended in place by enormous solar sails—*statites*.

"Okay . . . a Dyson *swarm*, then," St. Clair said. Damn AIs and their picky insistence on the right word.

"Not a Dyson swarm, either," Newton replied. "Analysis of the structure ahead suggests that the non-stellar component—the orbitals—extend clear down to very nearly the surface of the star. Only a tiny fraction of these will be hab modules as we know them. The structure is not, primarily, for habitation."

"Then what is it?" St. Clair demanded.

"Possibly a matrioshka brain."

St. Clair had to search the ship's database for that term, but found it almost immediately.

And the concept was far more stunning than a mere Dyson sphere.

"I HATE to say it," Adler said, "but it looks like St. Clair was right. That object is clearly a Dyson sphere, which means an *extremely* advanced technology occupies it. Kardashev 2, at the very least."

He was standing in the sunken entertainment room of his residence-office in *Tellus*'s port hab, a holographic projection of the object ahead filling half of the space. Lloyd was linked in with him, as were several of his fellow Council members—Gressman, Noyer, Hsien, Reinholdt, Benton, and a few others.

"And what is a Kardashev 2?" Hsien Tianki asked. "Or do you use phrases deliberately intended to obfuscate?"

"Not at all. Here is the link to the encyclopedia article," Adler replied. "In brief, though, a man named Kardashev once described potential galactic civilizations by the amount of energy they utilized. A Kardashev 1 civilization would use all of the available energy of its home planet. A Kardashev 2—a K-2 civilization, rather—would use all of the energy of its home star system. And a K-3 would utilize all of the available energy of its home galaxy. The British-American physicist Freeman Dyson suggested that a K-2 civilization might enclose its home star to trap every erg of available sunlight, and so created the idea of a Dyson sphere."

"Ah," Hsien said, and Adler felt him nod. "I do know the concept, but didn't remember the name."

"The important thing here is that these beings must have disassembled their entire solar system—every planet, asteroid, moon, *everything*—to build that cloud of habitats. They will be thousands, perhaps tens or hundreds of thousands of years in advance of us technologically."

"And so, perhaps they would be able to send us back to our own time," Aren Reinholdt put in.

"Perhaps," Adler agreed. "Certainly they'll be able to tell us about this time at least—the names and identities of the major players, the galactography, that sort of thing."

"The location of Earth?" Kallista DePaul put in.

"If Earth still exists in this epoch, my lady. But keep in mind, all of you, that after the passing of some billions of years, we may not wish to see what our planet has become."

They sat there quietly, absorbing what the Cyb director had just said. Finally, Lloyd spoke.

"We should take steps," he said, "to guarantee civilian control of the torpedo. What are they calling it?"

"'Roceti,'" Adler told him. "And, yes. I agree. But we'll need to move quickly on that . . . before the military can mess things up."

"A special committee, perhaps," DePaul suggested. "Headed up by Dr. Dumont, or people from his department."

"I think," Adler said, "that I should be able to arrange that."

"A MATRIOSHKA BRAIN," St. Clair said quietly, staring into the bridge projection.

"It's beautiful," Symm said.

As *Ad Astra* continued her slow drift toward the object, light refracting from the structure's depths smeared into rainbow-tinted moirés.

"We have ships approaching, Lord Commander," Denisova said. "It's the moon-ship again.

"And this time they've brought along some friends."

The ships appeared to be emerging from the swarm ahead, four spheres crater-pocked and gray, save where fresh ice showed as dazzlingly white dimples and rays stretched across their surfaces. "Excomm," St. Clair said, leaning forward. "Run a pattern comparison—"

"Already done, my lord." Red brackets highlighted one of the moons, the nearest one. "That one shows the same pattern of surface features as the one we encountered the other day."

"The one that gave us the Roceti torpedo."

"Yes, sir."

The nearest mobile moon swelled dramatically, until the swarm-structure ahead was blotted out, and the entire thirty-kilometer length of the *Tellus Ad Astra* dropped into the black of the approaching moon's shadow. St. Clair stared up at the rugged, cratered surface hanging above him. Station chatter flowing through the background noted the object's hundredth-G surface gravity . . . its fifty-kilometer range . . . its internal power flux. . . .

"Subcommander Jablonsky," St. Clair called, opening a channel to the AI department. "Is your new toy on-line?"

"I think so, Lord Commander. I *hope* so. . . ."

"You don't sound very certain."

"According to Newton," Jablonsky replied, "the damned thing's been connecting to our AI networks, scanning files, downloading language modules, that sort of thing. It appears to be self-directing, curious, and highly intelligent. But it hasn't been talking to *us*. Just Newton and the rest of the AI network."

"Newton? What has Roceti been talking to you about?"

"Not 'talking,' precisely, Lord Commander. We've learned to access its encyclopedia functions, and we've received a great deal of basic information about the Cooperative."

" 'Cooperative?' "

"The Roceti translation of *Xalit Ta*. It appears to be their name for the overall galactic civilization of this epoch."

St. Clair was impressed. They'd learned a lot since they'd begun tapping into the Roceti torpedo. He just wished there'd been time for him to download that data, but of course there never seemed to be time. *Especially not when I have to waste it at parties for strutting peacocks who think that politics and survival are the same thing.*

"However," Newton continued, "we have not yet engaged in what could be properly called conversation."

"We believe," Jablonsky added, "that Roceti is a high-level AI with an extremely narrow purview. It may not be able to do anything but facilitate communications between organic species. We won't know until we are in a First-Contact situation."

"Well, here's your chance. See if you can link through to those ships out there."

"Yes, my lord. Initiating. . . ."

St. Clair felt the channel open. Every human on the *Ad Astra* felt it . . . an inner shock or jolt. Every person saw the being's image: paralyzing, nightmarish, uncompromising . . .

"My God!" Denisova said. "I *hate* fucking spiders."

"Especially when they're a couple of meters across," Webb added.

Several people on the bridge screamed or gasped. Several abruptly disconnected from the channel.

"Steady, people," St. Clair said. "Subcommander Holt! Get back on-line."

"It's *huge*!"

"We don't know how big the thing is. And in any case it can't *really* be a spider."

"It *looks* like one!"

"Parallel evolution, then," Dumont's voice said. "Remarkable."

The being looking back at them from their in-head windows did indeed show at least a superficial resemblance to terrestrial spiders—specifically a face-on close-up of a wolf spider or tarantula, one covered by hairs or bristles. Eight eyes stared at them from a mass of dark brown fur, two huge ones, six smaller and of varying sizes, all round, glassy-black, and unblinking. Hairless labia below the eyes seemed to mask a complex mouth set within a ring of jointed, twitching palps. Hairy legs, thick and massive rather than spidery, were visible to either side, extending out of the viewing area.

"A Kroajid," Newton said. "One of the races of the *Xalit Ta*. Despite its appearance, it is not at all related to terrestrial arthropods."

"Tell that to my racing heart," Denisova said.

"A spider would not be able to grow to over two meters long in a one point three G gravity field," Newton explained, "or, indeed, be able to breathe. Unlike terrestrial spiders or insects it appears to have an internal skeleton, a complex brain, and it breathes through a series of gas bladders analogous to mammalian lungs. It communicates—"

The hairs around its face bristled, coming erect, then began to vibrate. A loud buzz or hum, almost like the growl of an internal combustion engine, sounded as the hairs formed wave patterns circling the being's eyes, moving clockwise. The engine noise varied irregularly, from a low, idling purr to a staccato roar.

". . . by vibrating certain stiff hairs on its body," Newton finished.

"We are the Kroajid Speaker," sounded in St. Clair's mind, the translation coming through from Roceti. "Welcome, humans, to the Mind of Deep Paradise. May you know joyous pleasure in all of its myriad forms . . ."

IN HIS office-residence in the port-side cylinder, Adler stared into the spider's face and wondered if it was too alien for human sensibilities . . . or not alien enough. The image certainly seemed designed to jolt the emotions and innermost terrors of arachnophobes throughout the human population. When Clara had seen it, she'd shrieked and run from the room. Tina, of course, being a robot, had been unaffected, but any human with an ingrained fear of spiders, insects, or hairy, nightmarish faces with too many eyes would have been terrified. St. Clair, he reflected, was an idiot for broadcasting that image throughout the colony.

Possibly he could use that.

He was going to keep watching, but the signal abruptly cut off. Perhaps someone else up the chain of command had decided that the broadcast wasn't in the best interests of the community.

It was time, Adler decided, for decisive action.

St. Clair scrolled down through the Roceti data readout for the Kroajid. Even in abbreviated, ephemeris format, there was a lot to absorb.

Xenospecies Profile
Sentient Galactic Species 10544
"Kroajid"

Star: F9V with M1 companion at 21 AU; Planet: Fourth
$a = 2.25 \times 10^{11}$m; $M = 8.5 \times 10^{27}$g; $R = 8.5 \times 10^6$m;
    $p = 5.527 \times 10^7$s
$P_d = 5.65 \times 10^4$s, $G = 13.06$ m/s^2; Atm: O_2 20.1, N_2 79.6,
    CO_2 0.3;
P_{atm} 1.37 $\times 10^5$ Pa
Biology: C, N, O, S, H_2O, PO_4, Cu; TNA
Genome: 3.2×10^9 bits; Coding/non-coding: 0.051.
Cupric metal-chelated tetrapyroles in aqueous
    circulatory fluid.
Mobile heterotrophs, omnivores, O_2 respiration;
    decapodal locomotion.
Mildly gregarious, polyspecific [1 genera, 5 species];
    sexual.
Communication: modulated sound at 150 to 300 Hz.
Neural connection equivalence NCE = 1.6×10^{14}
T = ~280° to 310° K; M = 0.9 $\times 10^5$ g; L: ~3.5 $\times 10^{10}$s
Vision: ~150 nanometers to 820 nanometers; Hearing:
    5 Hz to 19,000 Hz

Civilization Type: K 1.77
Technology: FTL; genetic, somatic, and cerebral
    prostheses; radical life extension; electronic
    telepathy and virtual immersion; advanced AI.
    Numerous planetary and deep space colonies.
    Climate control. Gravity control.
Societal Code: Technological/Hedonistic
Dominant culture: loose associative/post-singularity/
    virtual world upload
Cultural library: 8.91 x 10¹⁹ bits; Intrascended hedonists:
    0.98
Identity: Gatekeepers of Paradise
Member: Galactic Cooperative

THE ROCETI version of the *Galactic Encyclopedia* listed an
enormous number of galactic species—the *Xalit Ta*, or Galactic Cooperative, yes, but a very large number of other species as well. St. Clair was already anticipating finding the
time to "play encyclopedia," as he thought of it . . . simply
wandering through its electronic pages to see and marvel at
what was there.

Even limiting his attention to the Kroajid, though, there
was a *lot* of information here. He'd elected to scan the abbreviated version, a kind of digest format that let him hit the
high points without becoming bogged down in a sea of data.

On a separate in-head window, other members of the
expedition were questioning the Kroajid Speaker, and responding in turn to its questions about humans. Newton was
moderating the discussion, on the theory that a powerful AI
might be able to keep track of the intricacies of the conversation while managing to keep the human participants from
looking like complete idiots.

The Kroajid, it appeared, were from a homeworld slightly
larger than Earth, with a surface gravity of about 1.3 Gs.
Their star was hotter and a little brighter than Sol . . . but

the planet was 1.5 AUs out, and surface temperatures were similar to Earth's. Slightly higher atmospheric pressure, but the gas mix would be breathable by humans.

So far, so good.

A Kardashev-1 civilization, they'd learned to utilize all of the energy resources of their home planet but were not yet able to harness the energy of an entire star system. That datum caught St. Clair's attention right off. It meant the Kroajid were not the builders of the Dyson swarm ahead. So who was?

Just one more thing to follow up on. Despite their disturbing appearance, their biology was quite similar to humans, with only a few major differences: copper-based blood instead of iron, and a genetic code based on threose nucleic acid instead of DNA. They *were* heterotrophs: they breathed oxygen and got their food from their environment, rather than manufacturing it through photosynthesis. They possessed ten legs—or leg analogues, at least. Both hearing and vision were better, registering more frequencies, than humans'. An adult massed about ninety kilos, and each had a life expectancy . . . *God.* It worked out to over ten thousand years. Not quite immortal, but close enough from the human perspective to make little difference.

And then there was the real kicker: the number of neural connections or their equivalents—it worked out to a hundred times more than those resident within a human brain. Not only did they live for a long time, but these things were *smart.*

A lot of questions remained. First, the Kroajid called themselves the Gatekeepers of Paradise. What the hell did *that* mean? And their society was described as technological/hedonistic. What was that—an observation that they used technology to create pleasure? How could that apply to society on a galactic scale?

The enormous spider's face stared at St. Clair within his

head, enigmatic and devoid of any emotion that he could read. That, St. Clair reflected, was always the toughest part of First-Contact scenarios. Without emotional cues—the equivalent of emoticons in electronic messages—it was extraordinarily difficult to fully understand an alien speaker. In a way, it was similar to the problem humans experienced with their own sociopaths. With no emotional context, with no understanding of an alien's histories, myths, social mores, customs, or traditions, it was possible to horribly misunderstand what was being said.

St. Clair was all too aware that such a misunderstanding now could have disastrous consequences for *Ad Astra*'s tiny human community adrift in this alien future.

"We are," the spider's inner voice was saying, "in desperate need of your help. We—all sapient life in the Galaxy, in fact—have been under a sustained and escalating attack for some hundreds of millions of years. And we find ourselves helpless in the face of this existential threat. . . ."

"And what is the nature of this threat?" St. Clair's Excomm asked. Vanessa Symm had a way of cutting through the crap and getting to the heart of a question.

"What we know is encoded within the translator mind we gave you," the Kroajid replied. "We call it the *Graal Tchotch.*"

Newton supplied an immediate translation of the alien term:

"Andromedan Dark."

Of course, the Cooperative was 4 billion years removed from the name *Andromeda* or the ancient myth from which it had come. For hundreds of millions of years, now, Andromeda must have loomed huge in the skies of worlds across the Milky Way, incrementally growing larger eon by passing eon in a slow-motion collision that ultimately would take a billion years to complete. The vast spiral had been called *Graal* by those verbal species who'd witnessed its approach over the past few million years; the word, according to Roceti, carried a kind of double meaning—the idea of Mind or Life or Consciousness, and also the vast array of intelligence and alien civilization that filled the sky.

Tchotch, according to the Roceti mind, meant "darkness," in the sense of a loss of sensation or awareness, an ending; "death" might be a fairer translation. For the Galactic Cooperative, Andromeda signified an approaching darkness that would end sapient life within the Milky Way.

And the Cooperative wanted *Ad Astra*'s human population to help in this struggle?

St. Clair felt an inner stab of doubt. The Humankind of the 23rd century had been given a choice—to avoid alien entanglements and galactic politics, or to embrace them. He'd essentially ended his career by siding with the xenophobes, as the popular media had called them, urging that Earth stay clear of galactic politics until they were better understood. He'd actually experienced a small measure of relief once he'd learned that *Ad Astra* had been removed from the equation and would no longer have to choose joining a galactic war.

It appeared that the humans of *Ad Astra* still faced that unpleasant choice of possible futures after all.

"My Lord Commander," St. Clair's personal secretary whispered in his mind, "the Lord Günter Adler requires a meeting with you."

Requires? *Requires?*

"Not *now*, damn it," St. Clair snapped. "I'm a little busy at the moment."

"I will tell him."

Personal secretaries were great at keeping schedules and general adminstrative tasks—even going so far as to get to know—and mimic—their organics quite well.

But they possessed very little in the way of common sense.

"Do that," St. Clair growled.

The interview with the alien, meanwhile, was continuing. They hadn't yet learned if the being possessed a personal name; they weren't even sure yet of its sex, though the encyclopedia reference indicated that Kroajids had at least two. In any case, how were human vocal chords supposed to pronounce a name consisting of the clicking buzz of rapidly vibrating hairs?

So by general agreement, the humans called the Kroajid Speaker "Gus." Vanessa Symm had suggested the name on a back conversation channel, calling it an acronym for "Giant ugly spider." St. Clair had very nearly shot the suggestion down; if the Kroajids heard about the meaning they might get *really* ugly, and not in a merely physical sense. But the name had already caught on among the bridge personnel and it seemed unlikely that Gus would ever know what a spider was, let alone care about human preconceptions.

In any case, St. Clair trusted Newton and the translation AIs to exercise a certain amount of discretionary control over the data being exchanged with these rather disturbing-looking entities.

As it was, Gus was talking about the *Xalit Ta*'s problems with the *Graal Tchotch*—the Andromedan Dark.

"They came out of the Abyss between the Great Spirals hundreds of millions of years ago," it said. "We—the Cooperative—didn't recognize them for what they were. We still know almost nothing about their origins or their motives—why they did what they did. At first they came as raiders—as ships and heavily armed warriors, conquering, enslaving, looting. But eventually, the exotic mass streamers came. And the Madness. . . ."

The Madness. St. Clair's thoughts jumped to PFC Patterson. The man was still completely psychotic despite the psychnet's best efforts, wracked by nightmarish terrors and by waking demons no one else could see, his language reduced to gibbering word salad.

Was that the answer to what had happened to Patterson and Francesca, these "exotic mass streamers" Gus was talking about? And Mike, the vacuumorph, had recorded something that looked like tendrils or streamers reaching across the gulf from Andromeda. . . .

"Their appearances were rare," Gus went on. "Perhaps one raid in a hundred thousand years. But they gradually became more frequent. One appearance every ten thousand years or so. Then a thousand."

"But you knew you were under attack, right?" St. Clair shook his head, trying to understand. "And you had time to organize a defense."

"At first there was nothing against which *to* defend," Gus replied. "Pinpricks, easily ignored."

St. Clair's mind came up with a seemingly appropriate analogy: mosquito bites.

"But with more and more attacks—" he said.

"Things . . . were not so easy," Gus replied. "Many times, the Lessers united in the common defense, mustering vast battlefleets, establishing empires or political unions embracing millions of worlds, building fortresses, developing weapons. But the invaders were stronger, more numerous, and possessed technologies far in advance of theirs. And always, *always* the Madness came. . . ."

"Lessers?"

"Sapient species that have yet to Transcend."

"And by 'Transcend,' I assume you mean what we call the Technological Singularity."

Gus hesitated, and St. Clair realized the being must be internally seeking information from the data already garnered from *Ad Astra*'s files.

"A point of extreme technological disequilibrium," Gus said after a moment, "with certain technologies increasing asymptotically to the point where the definitions of Life and Mind have been substantially transformed, yes. In particular, the rapid evolution of what you call AI and SAI, the transformative effects of nanotechnology allowing individual immortality, and the development of digitized life within an electronic environment are all factors. Most technic civilizations go through numerous singularities over the course of some thousands or millions of years, not just one."

"AI," of course, was artificial intelligence, while "SAI" was artificial *super*-intelligence, electronic minds godlike in their power, scope, and abilities, at least from the human perspective.

"So even these Transcended civilizations couldn't stop the raids?"

"Can't . . . or won't. Sometimes it's difficult to tell which is the case."

"Won't?" Symm asked.

"For millennia, some of us fought them," Gus said. "But the vast majority of the Galaxy's population had ascended, intrascended, or parascended. The machines the various organic races left behind had supported civilization for eons in perfect peace, an eons-long galactic golden age. They didn't know about . . ."

"War?" St. Clair said, supplying the word.

"Yes. We've seen mention of it within your electronic records. A strange and gruesome concept. An aberration . . ." The Kroajids had learned a fair amount about Humankind in the preliminary exchange of data, but apparently they were having difficulty with some of the concepts. St. Clair found himself with the same problem.

"You used a couple of terms there I'm not familiar with," St. Clair said. "Intrascended? Parascended?"

"You are obviously familiar with Transcendence—the term you used was technological singularity."

"Yes."

"There are many different possible directions toward which a technic civilization may turn. Ascension generally refers to physical discorporation. Beings discard their bodies and emerge as pure mentality. *Intrascension* is when the civilization creates an interior, digital realm for its members, one richer and more rewarding than the original universe. I believe you refer to uploading to a virtual reality. *Parascension* involves moving into a higher dimensional plane or parallel universe. *Euphoriascension* is when a civilization physically withdraws from everything except individual pleasure. There are others. . . ."

"I see."

St. Clair was impressed. The translation AIs appeared to be quite handy at making up neologisms to describe things beyond human experience. He was also becoming concerned, however. What was it the Roceti Encyclopedia readout had said? He pulled up the relevant portion and read it carefully.

Technological/Hedonistic
Dominant culture: loose associative/post-singularity/
    virtual world upload
Intrascended hedonists: 0.98

"The translator device you gave us," he said, "calls you Kroajids 'intrascended hedonists.' You don't look like you're jacked into a pleasure machine."

"Of course not. About two percent of my species has not yet intrascended. We protect the nest nodes, help maintain the machinery of civilization, and perform our reproductive duties for the race. After about a thousand years, we will enter the nest, and our young will take over the guardianship."

"Ah. The 'Gatekeepers of Paradise.' " It made sense now.

"Precisely."

Just how many galactic species had crawled into their own pleasure centers and abandoned all involvement with the rest of the cosmos? From the way Gus had described the different types of transcendence, the percentage might be high . . . *very* high.

On the Earth that had been St. Clair's home some 4 billion years ago, a growing number of people had become wireheads or pluggers or jackbrains; the slang terms were many and varied. With in-head implants chelated onto the surface of the cerebral cortex and deeper, within the subcortex, it was relatively simple to use specially programmed nano to open electrical connections directly into the pleasure center of the human brain. That kind of nano programming was illegal, of course; thousands died every year when they stopped eating because the continuous orgasms they were experiencing seemed so much better than life.

There'd been serious speculation that such technologies might explain the Great Silence. Now, it seemed they might actually have confirmation.

In St. Clair's era, the idea that the sky truly *was* filled with life and intelligence and far-flung alien civilizations was brand new. In fact, until the Sirius Expedition, which had launched just thirty-eight years before the *Ad Astra* had left Earth orbit, Humankind, so far as anyone could tell, had been alone in the Galaxy, and the night sky had seemed starkly, uncompromisingly empty of other minds besides Man's. That had been the essence of Fermi's famous paradox: *Where is everyone?*

St. Clair had been a child then—he was forty-seven now—and had experienced the persistent mental itch of the Fermi paradox firsthand. The premise was simple. *In the 13 billion years since the big bang, life and intelligence could have,* should *have arisen on billions of worlds within the Milky Way Galaxy alone. Even without faster-than-light, each intelligent species could have explored the entire Galaxy and colonized every available world within a few million years—an eye's blink compared to the vistas of*

Deep Time available to them. With the development of gra-
vitic FTL, the question became more pressing still.

Where were they?

He still vividly remembered the celebrations—the fire-
works and parties and We-Are-Not-Alone broadcasts and
downloads—when news returned from Sirius about the Medusae and the Coadunation.

He also remembered the paranoia, the fear of alien invasion or the imminent extinction of humankind.

As it turned out, Fermi's paradox had possessed a reasonable explanation—a series of them, in fact, nested together
like Russian matrioshka dolls. Many galactic species never
developed advanced technologies—in particular those like
terrestrial dolphins, evolving within marine environments
or on worlds without free oxygen, which never developed
fire or the smelting of metals. A small percentage—like the
Medusae—managed to develop technology despite such
handicaps, but those who made it out of their oceans or
anoxic atmospheres still faced a long series of filters. Many
vanished into extinction due to war or planetary disasters or
technological mischance. Many more turned inward, unin-
terested in the colonization of a galaxy or in interaction with
other species, or they were more interested in the pursuit
of pleasure or the inner workings of the mind than in other
physical worlds.

Which brought speculation about the Fermi paradox
down to the Hedonistic Imperative.

What is the highest good for any intelligent being? Was it
the philosophy of the ancient Greek Epicurus, who held that
pleasure and pain were measures of good and evil, and that
the purpose of life was to attain happiness? Or was it the
eudaimonia of Aristotle, who felt that happiness needed to
be combined with virtue and with ethical wisdom to achieve
the highest possible human good?

What happened when a technic society achieved the

means—through nanotechnology and advanced biological engineering—to remake itself in such a way as to abolish all pain and suffering, and bring about a state of supreme happiness for all of its members? Might that society withdraw into a self-contained state of perpetual bliss, unaware of events in the outside universe?

Might that be why the sky appeared to be empty? Every civilization out there, once it reached a certain level of technological prowess, concentrated on a hedonistic indulgence in pleasure to the exclusion of all else.

As an answer to the Fermi paradox, the Hedonistic Imperative fell short. It was unlikely that *every* intelligent species in the Galaxy fell into such an obvious trap. Some must escape . . . those that valued intellectual curiosity, a wanderlust for new horizons, a need for raw materials, or even a simple warrior ethos.

And yet, Gus had just admitted that his own species, at least, preferred just such an existence.

"It seems to me," St. Clair said, "that the other members of your species need to wake up and get involved. They can't enjoy being hooked into their dream machines if someone comes along and pulls the plug on them."

"It is not so simple," Gus replied. "They are Transcended."

"So?"

"How do you wake up a god?"

"But their existence depends on you waking them!"

"How do you even *talk* to them?"

St. Clair recalled having read of a study some years ago on Earth, a study dealing with the problems of intelligence. The issue had come to a head in human psychological studies as more and more people opted to enhance their own brain power through implant electronics, or to increase the functional intelligence of their children through genengineering. The study suggested that two people separated by two standard deviation points on the intelligence charts—

that amounted to about thirty points on the old and now discredited IQ charts—actually had significant trouble communicating with each other.

He'd encountered similar problems himself in a social context rather than one involving intelligence; some of those vac-heads at Lloyd's party last night were a case in point: he'd been utterly baffled by some of the conversations he'd overheard. Some of those damned glitterati might as well have been speaking an alien language, and him without a translation AI.

But that level of problem might be literally insignificant compared to the difficulties involved in communicating with a hyperintelligence—a SAI or augmented organic intelligence so powerful that they had nothing whatsoever in common with ordinary minds. Such beings might live at a vastly slowed temporal rate, for instance . . . with centuries in the outside universe flickering past as seconds for them. Or they might have gone the other way, living within an electronically hyper-accelerated world, eons within their virtual reality as seconds passed outside.

Either way, a digitized, virtual life within a vast computer network might offer an existence that made organic life seem unbearably tedious or unimportant. Raiders from Andromeda might simply not interest them, and the forces left "outside" to protect them might not be able to communicate with them on a meaningful level. A skewed sense of time might not even be involved; could an ant claim that it was talking with a human when it ran across a man's toe and elicited a spontaneous twitch of the skin? Quite possibly, the difference in intelligence between ascended and unascended beings of the same species might be roughly similar to the difference in intelligence between a human and an insect.

And we're *the insects.*

"That . . . object out there," St. Clair said. "It's what we call a matrioshka brain, isn't it?"

"I do not see the term *matrioshka* in the data to which I have access."

"The name is from one of the root cultures of our civilization," St. Clair explained. "It refers to a series of small, ornamental dolls or figurines, hollow and designed to be pulled open, and sized to nest inside one another—a large one holds one slightly smaller, and inside that one smaller still, and so on."

"I understand. Perfectly descriptive."

"The structure out there is one about which our futurists have speculated quite a bit. A shell of orbitals, consisting of solar power plants and computronium processors—smart matter. Inside that shell is another shell . . . and another inside that, and so on all the way through to the core. The innermost shell is directly powered by the sun at the center. Each shell is powered by the waste heat from the one below, so the entire energy output of a sun could be devoted to powering a vast computer system of immense computational capacity."

"We call it an isid. This one is Isid 495, and is one of a large network of such structures throughout a large volume of space."

The alien word *isid* appeared to translate as something like "node" or "nexus," which was descriptive enough in its own way. "Galactic node" would be a fair translation, St. Clair thought. The translation also revealed an important point about the aliens' technology. If they had hundreds of matrioshka brains wired into a network of some sort, they *must* possess faster-than-light communication.

There'd been rumors and speculations that Coadunation technology included FTL communications, probably involving quantum entanglement, but that had never been confirmed. The point was a minor one, but important. Possessing ships capable of FTL travel was one thing. Having a communications net that could instantly interconnect a large number of widely separated computer nodes was quite something else. Just one matrioshka brain might have computing power enough to run a digital simulation of an entire universe . . . or at least the simulation of an entire civilization within such an artificial cosmos.

So what happened when someone hooked up five hundred or more matrioshka brains in parallel? What problems were they solving, what simulations might they be running?

Providing a virtual world for the digitized members of a single ascended species would be trivial.

At the same time, St. Clair was struck by an irreverent thought. So much computing power, such awesome technological capabilities, and it was devoted to providing a state of unending bliss for the civilization that created it.

It had been a joke that the original Earth Internet was devoted almost entirely to pornography. Apparently that idea *transcended* species.

But that thought was rapidly followed by another. Perhaps that blissful state was, after all, only a very minor part of the whole.

In terms of numbers of synapses and brain complexity, the Neural Connectivity Equivalence, a human brain was roughly 10^9 times more powerful than the brain of a typical nematode—a billion times the computational capacity of a worm. According to the encyclopedia reference he'd just seen, the NCE of a Kroajid was about six-tenths greater than a human's.

But a matrioshka brain would possess an NCE on the order of 10^{24}, which gave it a computational capacity very roughly 10 trillion times greater than that of a human. And if this was Galactic Node number 495, there were at least 494 other brains, all, according to Gus, linked together in a single network. Quite a comfortable standard of virtual living for trillions of digitized inhabitants could be provided by a fraction of that brain power; the rest might represent a single Mind, or set of Minds of truly godlike capacity.

The digitized Kroajid might well have been reduced to the level of pets . . . or lab experiments or even viral parasites.

Like the physical layering of shells in a matrioshka brain, there might be layer upon layer of intelligence in there, each far deeper and more powerful than the last.

St. Clair glimpsed—just glimpsed—the possible vistas of infinite nested Mind . . . and reeled, staggered by the vision.

SIXTEEN

A mob had formed in Bethesda.

St. Clair stood on his veranda, looking across the sprawl of the town emerging from the woods half a kilometer below his cliffside overlook. He could hear the sound of it, a ragged susurration drifting above the trees. He thought he could make out the sharper tones of someone using an amplifier, addressing the crowd verbally as well as electronically.

What the hell was going on down there?

Lisa stepped out of the house behind him, bringing him a cup of coffee. "They sound pretty upset," she observed.

He accepted the cup. "Thank you. Are you linked in to the news feed?"

"Of course."

He ran through a list of channels on his in-head, and settled on a local Bethesda station. A window opened, and he found himself looking down through a newsdrone's eye on an angry mob.

"Demonstrators are protesting what they say are the high-handed actions of the Navy," an announcer was saying. "Rumors are circulating to the effect that the *Ad Astra* has come forward in time several billion years—that's *billions* of years—engaged in combat with unknown alien forces, and brought on board a potentially hazardous alien artifact—possibly a weapon of enormous destructive potential. Ambassador Clayton Lloyd has been closeted with community leaders for several hours now in an attempt—"

St. Clair switched off the feed.

Adler's orders that the civilian population at large not be told of the temporal jump, that the details of the Jump into this remote future remain classified, were rearing a collective and *very* ugly head.

"This is Lord Adler's doing?" Lisa asked. Sometimes it was as though she could read his mind *without* relying on in-head electronics.

"Maybe. Probably. I don't know for sure. He wanted to see me while I was talking to the aliens and I shut him down. Maybe he just wanted to warn me about . . . all this. Or maybe he incited it."

"But why?"

"To get my attention?"

"There are aspects of human behavior I do not understand, Gray."

"Yeah. Me too."

He checked *Ad Astra*'s current population status. There were several alerts up; large-scale demonstrations had broken out in eight towns and small cities scattered through both hab modules. Marine units were already en route to all of them. Scattered fighting between Marines and civilians had already broken out in Seattle, Virginia Beach, and Goddard.

His in-head secretary had been deluged over the past twenty-four hours by messages and queries concerning the Kroajid. There was, evidently, quite a lot of arachnophobia within the *Tellus Ad Astra* population, and the jolting appearance of the being known as "Gus" had shaken a lot of people to their spider-fearing cores.

A majority of the people in the expedition had no problem with the aliens' appearance. Evidently, though, enough of them had panicked that they were making a fuss, calling for large-scale demonstrations, for policy reviews, or even for *Ad Astra*'s withdrawal from the area until things could be sorted out.

And Adler and some of his Cybercouncil legislators wanted the civilian government to be in charge.

St. Clair wondered what their take was on the Kroajid, and on the accident of their appearance. Obviously they represented a case of parallel evolution, at least to a point. There was much about them that wasn't very spiderlike—the columnar, bristle-covered elephant legs and their sheer size, to name two. He'd thought the language, the way they vibrated their body hairs, was another, but a little research had turned up the interesting fact that some spiders on Earth had communicated in exactly that way, buzzing away with their body hair in order to impress potential mates.

That coincidence had been surprising enough that St. Clair had even wondered, briefly, if the Kroajid might be the many-times' great descendents of terrestrial spiders, but the ship's xenobiology department had assured him otherwise. There were, after all, only so many basic body types and shapes possible. With millions of available ecosystems all busily evolving more and more complex life forms, it would have been astonishing if certain basic body patterns had *not* repeated independently of one another across the Galaxy. Earth alone had given rise to three marine species: the swordfish, the dolphin, and the extinct ichthyosaur, representatives of fish, mammals, and reptiles unrelated to one another, yet all possessing the same torpedo shape, curved dorsal fin, and slender snout.

What St. Clair found more interesting was the number of people who'd reacted with fear, disgust, or panic at the sudden appearance of the Kroajid on their in-head displays. He genuinely regretted that . . . and wouldn't have allowed a mass link-up if he'd known what was going to happen.

According to the medical department, somewhere between 3 and 6 percent of all humans were arachnophobic, though the reasons for that fear were still not well understood. Suggestions that it was a case of survival of the fittest—or, in this case, survival of the most phobic—just didn't hold up under close examination. Spider venom simply wasn't fatal often enough to make large-scale changes to the human genome.

In any case, according to the med department, something closer to 10 percent of *Ad Astra*'s population had reacted with fear or even panic when Gus appeared, possibly because of the suddenness of the event, possibly because of the Kroajid's apparent size. Even without any obvious scale or size referents, Gus *felt* huge—at least as large as a human—when he'd appeared.

The panic raised another issue. How much of the demonstrations and protests in the *Tellus* cities now was due to the shock experienced by 10 percent of the population? Was it simply a matter of a sizeable percentage of the population getting scared . . . and assuming that the Navy wasn't doing its job?

He would have to see what Adler and his people had to say about that possibility.

And in fact . . .

An icon began winking within his in-head view. Adler still wanted to talk—in person, not virtually. He'd been asking St. Clair's secretary for a face-to-face meeting in the Carousel ever since the first linked encounter with Gus.

"I suppose I should get that over with," St. Clair said, just barely aloud.

"What was that, Gray?" Lisa asked.

"Nothing, dear." He sighed, then checked his in-head clock. "Listen, I'd better take off."

"You're not scheduled to go to the bridge for a couple of hours yet."

"I know. But I'd better go see what the Lord Cybercouncil Director has to say to me." He kissed her. "See you later."

Not that he had any doubt at this point. Adler, he'd decided, was making a push to take command of the expedition and put it under civilian control.

And St. Clair was pretty sure he knew how he was going to respond.

THOUGH LIGHT could not interact with the mass of axionic bodies, the Dark could sense Mind across even intergalactic distances. Mind, it turned out, reshaped physical reality in certain subtle ways, much as did gravity, and for an essentially four-dimensional entity, that reshaping could be sensed across substantial distances in three-dimensional space.

And if you brought time into the equation—as in Einsteinian spacetime—abstract concepts such as distance became very nearly inconsequential.

In fact, the axionic hunters known collectively as the Dark could hear alien thoughts from tens of thousands of light years away.

And it was reacting to those thoughts, those *delicious* thoughts, now.

A raider fleet was dispatched to follow this taste to one of the alien nodes.

"I PROPOSE," St. Clair said quietly, "to leave *Tellus* here with the Kroajid matrioshka brain. Your civilian population can run itself any way that it chooses . . . can study the Kroajid and the *Xalit Ta*, establish treaties . . . communicate with them to your hearts' content. I intend to take the *Ad Astra* off for a scouting run to Andromeda."

"And leave us alone? Unprotected?"

St. Clair and Adler sat in one of the Carousel briefing rooms. Walls and overhead were set to depict the view outside—the frozen clash of two galaxies, plus a beehive swarm of habitats that made up the matrioshka brain—

the "matbrain," as the xeno people were calling it now. St. Clair looked at the Dyson swarm displayed across one conference-room wall, at the layers upon layers of dust motes with a tiny fraction of sunlight managing to peek out from the core through the clouds. Was that an imperfection, he wondered . . . evidence that the architects of that structure weren't completely efficient? Or was it, rather, *art*, a minor inefficiency left in place for its intrinsic beauty?

And just what would beings like the Kroajid, he wondered, consider to be beautiful?

"Gus tells me there are several trillion Kroajid living within the matbrain," St. Clair pointed out.

"Yes . . . as brain-dead vegetables! Wireheads who don't even know we're here!" Adler sounded horrified at the thought. "What if these alien raiders—this Dark that Gus was telling us about—attack?"

St. Clair was tempted to say something like, "Then you'll be shit out of luck," but he refrained from doing so. He was *trying* to be diplomatic about this mess. He needed Adler's cooperation, needed him as an ally, not a political enemy.

"I can leave, say, three quarters of the Marine compliment with you, under General Frazier. Plus the Marine space assets."

Adler considered this. "What good will Marines do? That matrioshka thing is a cloud of small habitats, not a planetary surface."

St. Clair spread his hands. "So? What good will *Ad Astra* do? She's just one ship." He didn't add that she had twenty squadrons of advanced fighters on board, as well as several armed auxiliary vessels. He needed that small fleet to support the *Ad Astra*, and didn't want to remind Adler that they were there.

Adler finally shook his head. "Uh-uh. I really can't allow you to take so much of our military capability off on some wild goose chase to another galaxy."

"First, this other galaxy is right next door," St. Clair said, pointing at the wall display where Andromeda towered like a vast cliff of stars and glowing gas. "We'll be ten, twenty thousand light years away, tops. I just want to see if they're as hostile as Gus says they are, or if we can reason with them. Second—you forget that I'm still in command. You can't tell me what to do with my naval assets until I relinquish that command. Do we understand one another?"

"Damn it, St. Clair—"

"Take it or leave it. Or would you rather tag along with the entire civilian population to explore Andromeda?"

"Of course not! If the Kroajid said—"

"That the Dark is extremely dangerous—that you can't talk with it, can't reason with it, can't even interact with it physically in any way except on its terms, when *it* chooses—then yes, it wouldn't make any sense for all of humanity to come along."

"That's not a choice."

"Actually, Lord Director, it is. I've heard a lot of scuttlebutt making the rounds lately about how we need to form an alliance with the inhabitants of this era."

"Of course! We'd be all alone otherwise, and some of the more advanced civilizations might be able to provide a means for getting us home."

"So you want to ally with the spiders?"

"Well . . ."

"They're quite advanced," St. Clair said. "Only down side is that most of them are blissed out on brain-feed sims, artificial reality. So maybe we need to check out these so-called Dark Raiders, and see if they're as evil as Gus claims they are."

"They *attacked* us! When we first arrived! For no reason!"

St. Clair nodded. Gus had identified images taken of the three needle ships that *Ad Astra* had encountered after being flung forward into this epoch. They were, he said, Dark

Raider sliverships, piloted by corporeal beings from Andromeda, but under the noncorporeal control of the formless, poorly understood Dark. In a way, he was surprised to hear Adler finally admit that. But it also helped his cause. "Right. But what if Gus isn't telling us the truth?"

"You think he's *lying*?"

St. Clair shrugged. "I don't know. And that's the point. I can't read the expression on the face of something that looks like a wolf spider enlarged a few million times. So far, we have only his word that the raiders are bad guys."

"St. Clair, you're being paranoid again. Xenophobic, like you were back on Earth."

"Not at all. If I were truly being xenophobic, I would advocate not allying with *anyone*. We should just go off and find a small, unoccupied star cluster somewhere and hope no one finds us. I actually agree that we should find some technically proficient species and see if we can get them to help us. But I want to be damned sure we get the right ones. *Any*time someone comes along asking us to join them in their war, I get nervous."

"So I've heard." Adler thought for a moment. "Okay. You'll come back for us?"

"Of course. A lot of the naval personnel have families on one or the other of the habitat cylinders—they're not going to let me run off and abandon them." He was also thinking about Lisa, about leaving her on the *Tellus* habitats.

"Okay," Adler said. "It makes sense doing it this way. Gives us a chance to establish diplomatic relations with the Kroajid . . . and maybe with some other advanced technological species as well. You just be careful with the *Ad Astra* on the other side of that gulf. If you don't bring her back, we're stuck here."

"There are worse places to be stuck," St. Clair told him. "The Kroajid appear friendly—the ones who aren't inside a simulation, anyway, and they just won't talk to us. From here, with their help, you would probably have access to any number of Earthlike worlds. With a million humans, you'd have a good shot at starting the human species going again."

"The Kroajids still make a lot of people nervous, you know. I mean, the way they look . . ."

Now who was being xenophobic? "They'll have to get over it. The Krojies are *not* spiders, and they don't bite."

No matter what Vanessa Symm might have to say about it, Gus was not a "giant ugly spider."

Not *really*.

THE MAGNETIC clamps released and slowly, gently, *Ad Astra* backed clear of the rotating habitats. The process was observed by three of the Kroajid moon-ships. St. Clair wondered what interest they might have in human technology, which must, to them, seem laughably primitive.

"We're clear, *Tellus*," Symm said over the flight control channel. "We'll see you in a few days."

"Copy that, *Ad Astra*," came the reply. "We'll keep a light on in the window for you."

The Roceti's encyclopedia had identified some thousands of possible targets of interest scattered across the Andromeda Galaxy, neutrino transmitters and sources of infrared or gamma and X-ray frequencies that appeared to be artificial in origin. The nearest of those lay above the Andromedan galactic plane some thirty thousand light years distant from Galactic Node 495—another neutrino source that might well be another matrioshka brain. It had been designated as NPS-1018.

Or it might be something else entirely. That area was also a part of the other galaxy that had been filled with the oozing, exotic mass-effect noted by the caels. Now that they knew what to look for, O-G humans could throw up filters that showed the same effect. St. Clair had one up now on the bridge. It gave the area of space into which they were about to leap the ominous look of a red-violet thunderstorm.

"All stations report ready for jump, Lord Commander," Symm told him.

"Thank you Excomm," he replied. He hesitated, staring into the sullen red storm in the distance. "Astronomy department."

"Yes, my lord," Dr. Tsang replied.

"Any guesses yet on what that red hazy stuff is?"

"Oh, guesswork is unnecessary, Lord Commander. The vacuumorphs had it right. It's dark matter."

"A term that means exactly nothing, Doctor. Dark matter—fine. But what *is* it?"

"Well, this is all speculation at this point . . ."

"Guesswork, in other words."

"If you like," though it was clear from his tone that Tsang certainly didn't *like*. "But some of the people in the astrophysics lab—Tina Sandoval and Anton Dvorsky—have formulated a working hypothesis. Dark matter may be an entirely distinct physical array of WIMPs made of quark-analogs they call quirks."

" 'WIMPs?' " St. Clair said, bemused. " 'Quirks?' "

"WIMP stands for 'weakly interactive massive particle,' " Tsang explained. "They've been hypothesized since the mid-twentieth century as an explanation for dark matter. Quirks used to be called strange anti-quarks, and are a component of so-called strange matter."

"Okay . . ."

"Strange matter is a component of normal nuclear matter, and may even be more stable. When a proton or neutron decays, it may release a small bit of quark matter—what we call a 'strangelet.' That's another candidate for dark matter."

St. Clair wasn't tracking Tsang very well. All he could do was record the conversation so he could look up some of the terms later. Advanced particle physics was a bizarrely eldritch world, more akin, in his estimation, to fantasy than reality, with its vast zoo of particles, antiparticles, and dimensionless fields within eleven-dimensional string arrays. He understood a lot of the basic theories, but what Tsang was throwing out at the moment went well beyond his studies. And, more to the point, didn't seem that relevant at the moment. "And what does any of that have to do with red extragalactic clouds?"

"Okay," Tsang said, and St. Clair could hear him take a breath. "Super-quick Particle Physics 101. In classical physics, quarks join together to form basic matter—baryons like protons and neutrons, leptons like electrons and neutrinos, right?"

"Yes."

"Right. And different arrangements of protons, neutrons, and electrons form ordinary baryonic matter and the entire periodic table, everything from hydrogen clear up to Element 224."

Element 224 had been created in the sub-selenic Procellarum Fusion Accelerator on Earth's moon only months before *Ad Astra*'s departure, and had not yet been named.

"I understand all of that."

"This new hypothesis suggests that there's an entire . . . call it an alternate periodic table, a shadow table, a whole collection of different elements, *exotic* elements made up of WIMPs and axions the way normal matter is made up of baryons and leptons."

" 'Axions?' "

"Another candidate for dark matter. Lower mass than WIMPs. They might act like exotic electrons. More likely they're something completely different."

"So what you're saying is there's a whole alien universe out there, complete with its own mass, its own chemistry, its own life—but it wouldn't interact with ours."

"That's the idea, Lord Commander. Except, of course,

that in some circumstances it *does* interact with normal matter. As Subcommander Francesca and Private Patterson both discovered."

"Right."

And *Ad Astra* would be flying into the heart of that strangeness.

Yet it was the only way to find out what they were facing out here.

"Helm," he said, "execute our first jump."

"Aye, aye, Lord Commander."

And the *Ad Astra* vanished into the truly unknown.

SEVENTEEN

From SHOD-2, the Number 2 Starboard Hab Observation Deck, Lisa looked down into infinity.

You could get a better, clearer, and electronically enhanced view from the habitats' direct network feeds, of course, views that weren't panning across the cosmos once every forty seconds. But humans seemed to get something from the obdecks; at any given time of artificial day or night, there were people here . . . sometimes large crowds of them. And Lisa often came here in an attempt to understand what made them . . . *human*.

SHOD-2 was nearly four hundred meters long and forty wide, a transparent window in the hab module's out-is-down floor much larger than the more numerous vista windows scattered around each hab. Broad, white walkways edged with safety railings ran the entire length of the window, connected by gently rising archways to the solid-ground foundations at either side. By looking over the walkway's edge, you looked down into the fast-sweeping drift of stars. Every forty seconds, the port-side hab module rolled into view, blocking the stars . . . but then it moved on and the densely packed glory of the galactic core replaced it: teeming suns with light-limned clouds of gas and dust casting long shadows across the stellar plane.

And a few seconds later, that vista was replaced by the swarming beehive of the matbrain, trillions of habitats—many as large or larger than *Tellus* itself—orbiting in concentric shells that didn't quite block the radiance of the structure's central sun.

Lisa was intrigued to notice that there were only a few people on SHOD-2 this morning—eighteen, to be precise. When she used her telescopically enhanced vision to zoom in on several other obdecks and vista windows visible in the sky-embracing curve of the inner habitat, she saw the other scenic overlooks were poorly populated as well.

Why?

The simplest explanation likely was that humans became so easily jaded. You could get any exterior view you wished directly in-head with a thought . . . and she suspected that day after day of beauty and wonder quickly took the edge off somehow.

But there was a deeper answer as well, Lisa decided, one resident within a bizarre peculiarity of humans—an unwillingness to look—in this case literally—at things that made them uncomfortable. Rather than confront the strange or the threatening or the overwhelming head-on, most humans possessed a tendency to avoid confrontations with anything that might challenge their preconceived notions of what was real.

The fact that the Kroajid were vaguely similar to terrestrial arachnids had resulted in one type of avoidance—the outright panic in a sizeable percentage of the expedition's population. More threatening by far, however, was the nature of the matrioshka brain outside.

The sophontologists and xenotechnologists were still studying the structure, of course. They'd designated it as a LIO—a "large intelligent object"—even though it wasn't in fact one object, but trillions. But most of the *Tellus* population seemed to be studiously ignoring the thing, as if looking too closely at it would reveal certain flaws or inefficiencies within human nature.

There was, after all, a *Mind* in the depths of that Dyson

swarm, a Mind that far transcended anything human—including AI minds created by Humankind, like Newton. The Kroajid had said little about it, simply calling the Mind Isid 495, the same as the matbrain itself. From the little they *had* said, it was easy to get the impression that they thought of the matrioshka intellect as a kind of god. With 95 percent of the Kroajid locked away within virtual electronic worlds, that god became a caretaker of sorts, using its unfathomable powers to protect and nurture its sleeping pets.

Evidently, this was not a comfortable thought for most humans.

And with that concept had come another. Just as uncomfortable, in some ways, was the realization that living in a hedonistic dreamworld—a kind of digitized paradise where there was no struggle, no loss, and no sorrow—was similar in some ways to the *Tellus* culture: pleasure loving, self-centered, mildly sensualist in its rounds of elaborate parties, orgies, and social receptions. For many humans, the point of modern life *was* pleasure, and how was that different from the digitized Kroajid deep within their matrioshkan processors?

And so those humans not actively studying Isid 495—the swarm or the Mind—ignored it. They continued with their parties and soirées—or, more recently, their demonstrations and protests and occasional riots—and stayed away from vistas that might jar their complacent certainty that they were *right*.

Humans, Lisa thought, could be appallingly shallow.

"Helm,"—St. Clair's voice came over the electronic link in her brain—"*execute our first jump.*"

"*Aye, aye, Lord Commander.*"

She felt *Ad Astra* vanish from *Tellus*'s electronic ken.

Lisa suppressed a most un-machinelike twinge of fear.

THE VAST, double-cylinder bulk of *Tellus* vanished, and *Ad Astra* emerged in a new place.

St. Clair wasn't sure what he'd been expecting. It occurred to him that in his native time, the thought of traveling to another galaxy was complete nonsense. Andromeda, in that long-ago epoch, had been two and a half million light years distant, well beyond the capabilities even of the seemingly magical technology of the Coadunation.

In 4 billion years, however, Andromeda had come to the Milky Way Galaxy, the two rushing together and closing the gulf between them until the two galaxies were actually intermingled now, each passing through the other. And jumping from one to the other was as simple as giving the command.

The starfields in Andromeda looked much the same as back in the Milky Way. The galaxy M-31 in Andromeda was larger than the Milky Way—120,000 light years across, roughly, and containing well over a trillion stars, compared with the 100,000-light-year-diameter and 4 hundred billion stars of Humankind's home galaxy. But the vaster scale was simply invisible from a human perspective. The starscape here might have been a little thicker, a little more densely strewn, but that could easily be because they simply were closer here to the galaxy's central core.

The encircling sky blazed with stars. As in the Milky Way, the gravitational interaction between the two titanic spirals had triggered spectacular star formation within the thunderhead masses of gas and dust orbiting the core, resulting in gleaming clusters, streamers, and unfolding clouds of brilliant blue-white stars.

So similar. And yet . . . so different.

"We're here," St. Clair said over the main comm channel. "Welcome to another galaxy."

"NPS-1018 is dead ahead, Lord Commander," Subcommander Adams told him. "Estimated range . . . two hundred light years."

St. Clair saw the graphic on the star display projected

across the bridge's interior, a bright point of light rapidly winking against the star-frothed background ahead. Another neutrino channel point-source, it would have been invisible to unaided human vision.

"Very well," St. Clair said. "Take us in closer, please."

Two more short jumps, gradually narrowing the range, and *Ad Astra* emerged in the light of a new sun.

The star was a red dwarf—type M0 or M1—and from half an AU out it appeared to be surrounded by a doughnut-shaped cloud of wispy fuzz.

"It looks," Symm said with the slightest edge of disgust to her voice, "like a colossal hairball."

"Newton?" St. Clair asked. "What do you make of that?"

"Quite possibly," the AI replied, "it's a topopolis. Some human sources refer to it as 'cosmic spaghetti' or a 'macaroni world.' "

"Stop it," Symm said. "You're making me hungry."

"And what the hell is cosmic spaghetti?" St. Clair asked.

"Like the Alderson disk, it is an extremely large artificial habitat, with a livable surface area of some billions or trillions of Earths. What appear to be extremely fine hairs or threads at this distance are, in fact, hollow tubes rotating to provide artificial gravity."

Cautiously, *Ad Astra* approached the tangle of threads, sending out fleets of robotic drones to study the structure. Data flooded back. Damn, the thing was *huge*.

Just once, St. Clair mused, *it would be interesting to come across something small on this mission.*

This thing certainly wasn't small. And as St. Clair truly took it in, all joking was put aside. Simply put, he was stunned at the audacity of the thing. The Alderson disk had been enormous, true, but somehow the scale escaped you. This was different, because it started off looking like a tangle of thread, and only as St. Clair studied it did he realize that the thing was enormous.

It was as though someone had taken a habitat module like one of the two cylinders that make up *Tellus*—about five or six kilometers wide, thirty-something long, and hollow, rotating around its long axis to provide artificial gravity—and then had made the cylinder bigger—much bigger, almost a hundred kilometers wide. Then had stretched that cylinder out along its long axis—longer . . . longer . . . still *longer*—until the thing was a hollow tube billions of kilometers long that connected with itself around its sun like a tail-eating ouroborus snake. The thread-thin tube continued looping, then, until it weaved its tangled way hundreds, even thousands of times, around its star.

That's what St. Clair was looking at now.

"How can those things rotate and not get all tangled up?" Symm asked.

"On that scale, Excomm," Senior Lieutenant Nolan said, "curvature would be very, very slight, too small for any kinking to occur. It would be a topological challenge, of course, but if you could build it, you could spin it."

"A simpler possibility," Lieutenant Weiss pointed out, "would be to build it in segments, each independently rotating to provide different gravities, and sealed off from its neighbors to provide different atmospheres, different environments."

"Like anything about this could be *simple*," Symm said.

"It seems unlikely," Newton added, "that this one is now inhabited."

"Why do you say that, Newton?" Symm asked.

A series of magnifications came up on the bridge display. Masses of loosely intertwined threads enlarged to become massive tubules. The long-range imagers focused on one tube that had split wide open, exposing cavernous darkness within.

"Parts of the structure show extensive areas of damage," Newton said, "even complete destruction. And the radiation from the structure at all wavelengths is in equilibrium, consistent with what would be expected to come through, unfiltered, from the central star. It is possible that this structure has been destroyed in a deliberate attack."

"Another LIO," St. Clair said softly. "This one big enough to hold a few hundred trillion inhabitants."

"A large *intelligent* object, my lord?" Cameron asked. "Why would it be intelligent?"

"It would almost have to be," St. Clair replied. "Something that large, that massive—you would need super-AI just to keep track of all the mass vectors as you brought the thing together. Once you have it built, it takes superhuman brain power to keep the whole thing running. Temperatures balanced, atmospheres intact. Too, there would have to be some sort of thruster system to adjust the positions of different parts of the structure, to keep it from drifting into its star."

"The builders almost certainly employed star-lifting techniques," Christine Nolan pointed out. "Techniques that are well beyond the capabilities of natural organic intelligence."

There's that, too, St. Clair thought. It was possible, he reflected, that the builders of this cosmic spaghetti had started with a star much like Sol, or a slightly smaller, cooler K-class sun, and pulled so much mass from it that it was reduced now to a red dwarf with a very long expected lifetime indeed. The lifted mass would have been transmuted into heavier elements in order to construct the cloud of tubes now surrounding it.

And Christine had a good point. Such mining and manufacturing techniques were so far beyond human capabilities that almost by definition they would have been carried out by SAI—super AI—able to solve mind-numbingly complex problems, and to do so over a period of thousands, even millions of years.

And once an SAI like that was up and running, you didn't just turn it off. It should still be in there, somewhere, possibly within many billions of tons of computronium worked into the very walls of the twisting habitat threads.

"Subcommander Jablonsky," he called.

"Yes, my lord."

"Do you have the Roceti program on line?"

"We do, my lord. Ready at your order."

"Okay. Stand by."

A copy of the Roceti AI had been left running on board the *Tellus* module, though the Kroajid, now that they'd tapped into the linguistic and cultural data acquired by Roceti, seemed to be having no trouble communicating with their human guests. The original Roceti torpedo, though, had remained on the *Ad Astra*. St. Clair wasn't sure how well its stored data covered systems and civilizations residing within Andromeda, but it might help crack any alien languages they encountered during this scouting expedition.

"Anything?"

"I'm broadcasting a variety of greetings and encounter protocols," Newton replied. "No response so far."

Closer still. "Still no sign of a population?" St. Clair asked.

"Negative," Newton told him.

"Another dead artificial world, then. Like the Alderson disk."

"So it would seem."

"Still," Symm said, "a structure that huge . . . it might not be completely dead."

"What do you mean?"

"Well, just like the Anderson disk, there would be room enough in something that large for whole Earths to be in hiding. Populations that reverted to primitivism . . . no radio, no industrial waste heat. Nothing going at all but the automated neutrino beacon."

"That assumes the disaster didn't leak the atmosphere into space."

"That would be unlikely," Newton said. "The tube is almost certainly partitioned to prevent such a catastrophe."

St. Clair nodded. "Instruments are showing a slight external atmosphere—a few millibars. Probably collected in the structure's gravity field. Let me see it with the grav filter."

The scene dipped into a deep and bloody red register, overlaying the physical structure ahead in a colored indication of local mass. The image revealed a *lot* of mass within the tangled structure surrounding the star . . . more, he thought, than might be explained by the physical structure itself.

"Dark matter?" he asked.

"Possibly a local aggregation of dark matter WIMPs and axions," Newton replied.

"Any indication that it's *alive*?"

"Negative. It appears inert."

"What are the chances of entering this time, looking for local civilizations, and hitting three duds in a row? Two enormous artificial worlds, both dead . . . and one that's vanished into its own navel either for jollies or for contemplation of the whichness of the why."

"The active Kroajid are still available for interaction," Symm said. She sounded doubtful, however.

"Gus and his Guardian pals don't count, not really," St. Clair said. "They're totally wrapped up in their caretaker duties."

"I agree," Lieutenant Gonzalez said. "They're a subset of the larger culture, which has chosen to withdraw."

"If the spaghetti was managed by a SAI," Jablonsky pointed out, "it must still be running."

"That was my thought, too," St. Clair said.

"But why would you think that?" Symm said.

"Because it hasn't drifted sideways and brushed up

against its star," Jablonsky replied. "A structure like that would be gravitationally unstable. Even a simple ring around a star—a classic ringworld—would be unstable over hundreds of thousands of years, and would need some sort of thruster system to keep it in place. The problem is much more severe with an object like this."

"Good point, Subcommander," St. Clair said.

"If there is an SAI in there," Newton said, "I have not yet detected it. However, it might be in hibernation . . . or operating at a temporal level at which detection is difficult."

One advantage AI minds had over organics, St. Clair thought, was their ability to shift time frames. They could operate at speeds millions of times faster than a human brain, so that a second passed for them like centuries. Or they could slow themselves down until a single thought took thousands of years . . . or until their sleep was interrupted by an automated warning system.

"So," St. Clair said. "Any guesses from anyone as to whether this giant hairball is native to Andromeda or if it represents a colony from our own Galaxy?"

"A colony, Lord Commander?" Symm said. "How do you figure that?"

"For billions of years, Andromeda and the Milky Way have been slowly getting closer and closer, right? I would imagine any civilizations interested in exploration or expansion would have been able to make the crossing starting, oh, maybe even a few hundred million years ago. Newton? How long ago did the two galaxies begin their collision?"

"That is difficult to say without knowledge of the topologies involved," Newton replied, "but assuming a closing velocity of one hundred ten kilometers per second, it would be on the order of eighty to ninety million years ago."

"A third again longer than the time span separating our world from the dinosaurs," St. Clair said. "Plenty of time to colonize Andromeda a hundred times over."

It was the Fermi's paradox restated. Any star-faring civilization—in this case one that could travel far faster than the speed of light—could expand through an entire Galaxy, colonizing every world, occupying every niche, within far fewer than a million years or so, the cosmic blink of an optical organ. And if it *could*, why hadn't it?

"Yeah, well, what does it matter, my lord?" Symm said. "If the builders come from the Milky Way, or are native to Andromeda, I mean."

"It tells us something about the history," St. Clair replied. "About what's been going on. The Kroajid talk about raiders from Andromeda and about something they call the Andromedan Dark. The first sounds like a fairly typical star-faring culture of some sort, maybe a bit on the militant side of things. But the second sounds so weird we can't even get a mental reference for it, and we end up speculating about dark matter ecologies and invisible invaders. If we're going to be able to defend ourselves from these beasties, we're going to have to figure out exactly what we're up against."

"Fair enough," Symm said. "Just one question."

"What's that, Excomm?"

She indicated the tangle of threads wrapped around its sullen ember of a central star. "Where the hell's the front door to that thing?"

NEWTON WAS less interested in finding a way inside than he was with communicating with his opposite number within the structure—if, indeed, there was one. Ever since *Ad Astra* had arrived within this volume of space, Newton had been scanning through billions of different channels—microwave, radio, visible light, UV and X-ray, and neutrino—without result. The neutrino beacon continued its steady pulse, but there was no information heterodyned within that steady *beat-beat-beat* other than the self-evident fact that it was there. Newton even closely examined the ambient gravitational background in case there was a signal there, but found nothing save the presence of the background mass: both matter and dark matter.

As *Ad Astra* drifted steadily closer to the object, however, Newton was able to peer more closely into the available spectra, searching for signals so weak they barely rose above the overall level of background radiation.

Contact!

FINDING THE front door, as Excomm Symm had phrased it, proved to be relatively simple. *Ad Astra* carried a number of auxiliary ships—military, exploration, and logistical—and if the massive *Ad Astra* herself couldn't be chivied inside one of the rotating tubes, something like an AAT-2440 Marine transport could.

Jacob Weiss's suggestion that the habitat threads might be divided into sections, each independently rotating and sealed to enclose its own specific environment, had proven correct. Lieutenant Thom Nakamura, at *Ad Astra*'s helm, had edged the vessel as close as he dared to one particular segment that had been badly damaged, its power off, its rotation halted, its side ripped open by some unimaginable cataclysm that had emptied it of air and life. As a Marine landing party boarded a pair of AAT-2440s for deployment to the structure, a small fleet of uncrewed observation drones had been deployed, guided by Newton into the gaping hole in the habitat's side, and into the interior darkness.

Images transmitted from the drones were displayed on the bridge bulkheads. As the lead drone skimmed above the endless gray plain of the habitat's exterior, approaching the wound in its side, St. Clair was reminded of riding linked-in with a tourist drone above the surface of Earth's moon. The habitat's outer surface was pocked by meteor strikes and sandblasted by eons of micrometeorites. The structure, like the Alderson disk, was *old*.

Then, his probe swung over the abyssal gulf and descended into the darkness. He ordered the probe to switch on its external lights, but for a long time he was too far from any surface for it to reflect the illumination. Only slowly did shapes begin to materialize out of the night, eerily twisted—the stuff of nightmares.

The landscape was surreal, carved from pure crystal. St. Clair had difficulty sorting out what he was seeing . . . shapes that might have been twisted, alien-looking trees . . . or abstract statues . . . or even buildings. The probe's powerful lights flashed and sparkled through towering forests of crystal, and St. Clair wondered how he would even recognize life here, if it was here to find at all.

In places, the forests had been shattered, reduced to gleaming piles of broken shards and fragments. Whatever atmosphere had been here had bled away into space; the habitat was filled now by the same trace gasses that had collected around the outside of the entire structure—about ten millibars' worth. The drone drifted ahead on microjet pulses; with that hab section no longer rotating, the only gravity was that of the small and relatively distant sun, plus the G-force generated by the mass of the structure itself. The spaghetti tangle of the LIO totaled more mass than several thousand Earths, but that mass was spread out across a volume of space half an AU across or more and perhaps a third of that in thickness. The total gravitational force inside the structure worked out to less than a twentieth of a G, and remote fliers and drones had no trouble picking their way through the eldritch landscape.

Vast shadows cast by the probe's light shifted and jumped, creating an illusion of life, but the place was dead, as dead as the Alderson disk.

"Lord Commander!" Senior Lieutenant Nolan called. "Some of our probes have penetrated the next section. It's still powered."

"How?"

"Solar power, converted to electricity. The next section is rotating, and the airlocks are working."

St. Clair mentally changed channels. He was seeing through them electronic imagers of a different probe, now, one moving a few meters above what appeared to be a forest canopy. The airlock joining one section of the cosmic spaghetti to the next included rings rotating at increasing speeds in succession, so that probes emerging in the new section shared that section's rotational velocity. The probes were fliers, however, which meant they needed to apply continuous thrust; otherwise, their straight-line paths would have carried them into the rapidly rising ground, exactly as if they'd been falling.

The trees were mushroom-shaped and had bright purple foliage, with leaves like tight little corkscrews. Reddish light spilled down from a central core running down the length of the cylinder, exactly as the sunbeam did in the *Tellus* modules. The temperature here was a fairly chilly three degrees Celsius; the air was a weakly reducing atmosphere composed of hydrogen, methane, ethane, and nitrogen. Droplets of carbon tetrachloride were floating as a thin mist in the air, and what looked like a broad lake in the distance was probably liquid carbon tet. The rotational artificial gravity was set for about half a G.

There were cities here: broad, oval patches carved out of jungle, composed of translucent domes and bubbles. They appeared to be made of some sort of tough plastic, and showed no sign of wear or age.

Then St. Clair saw the bones.

EIGHTEEN

The creatures had been enormous, and he could only think of land-dwelling whales. Of *titans*.

St. Clair guided his probe lower, allowing the onboard AI to handle thrust and attitude. Below, within a hundred-meter clearing in the violet jungle, some dozens of creatures had died, leaving behind tangled piles of dark gray objects that could only be skeletal remains. Judging from the evidence, they'd been huge, four or five times the mass, perhaps, of an extinct African elephant. Six massive legs like tree trunks, bony structures like enormous, hollowed-out eggs at both ends of the body that might have been heads or might have been something else entirely, long and flexible tubes of bone segments that must have looked something like an elephant's trunk, but branched at the tips, and with six in the front and six in the back.

Had these, then, been the spaghetti's dominant life form? More likely, St. Clair thought, they were one species of many. As they had discussed, he suspected that the dough-nut of tangled threads had been a project shared by hundreds or thousands of species, providing a wide variety of enclosed environments. Perhaps these beings had recreated the environment of their original homeworld here within several segments of the sun-embracing tubules.

It was just so hard to believe something so big *didn't* rule whatever land it inhabited.

"Interesting," the voice of Lieutenant Gonzalez said.

"They had brain implants Not that different from us, actually."

"How can you tell?"

Gonzalez threw up a pointer visible over the probe's image channel. Gold-colored wires ran across dark bone and vanished into the interior by way of small holes. "See here? And here? If we assume these oval shapes fore and aft are skulls, protecting the brains—"

"We can't make that assumption, Gonzalez," Subcommander Guo Jiechi said. Guo was head of *Ad Astra*'s xenobiology section. "Two brains? How would such a being even be able to walk?"

"These are clearly electrical leads of some sort, sir," Gonzalez insisted. "They appear to have grown through the bone, so they may have used nanotechnology to implant them, just as we do."

"Colonel Shaeffer," St. Clair called. "Are your Marines on board the structure yet?"

"They are, Lord Commander." Colonel Vincent Shaeffer was the CO of the 1st Marine Regiment, 1st MARDIV, and the senior Marine officer currently embarked on board the *Ad Astra*. St. Clair had not been anticipating needing to carry out a planetary invasion and so he'd brought along only Colonel Shaeffer and two regiments of Marines—about twenty-four hundred Marines, all told. Most of those were still on board *Ad Astra*; for this preliminary scouting run, Shaeffer had sent in only the second battalion of the 1st Marines, the 2/1.

"Take them through into the next segment," St. Clair said. "You're following probe 115-Bravo."

"Aye, aye, Lord Commander."

The Marines would be able to look through some of those massive skeletons, and perhaps cut open the skulls to see what lay within. The drones had manipulator arms built into their casings, but they were limited in what they could do, both in terms of strength and in dexterity.

While they waited for the Marines to arrive, St. Clair checked in with a number of separate drones sampling the variety of environments. A number were dead and dark. Several were dark and apparently without power, but still possessed atmospheres, including a couple that were oxygen-nitrogen in mixes close to that of Earth's surface.

In each, there were signs of advanced civilization, though a few, like the crystalline world St. Clair had seen first, were so alien it was tough to tell what they contained.

Nowhere they investigated, however, had a still-living civilization. Many had life—vegetation, animals, or things that shared the characteristics of both—but of intelligent life there appeared to be none. St. Clair returned to probe 115-Bravo when the Marines showed up.

The unit was coming in aboard a quartet of Devil Toads—flying personnel carriers, or FPCs—which hovered on four tilt-jet thrusters, lowering ventral ramps to disgorge platoons of combat-armored Marines. The first two down moved out to establish a defensive perimeter around the site. The second two touched down inside the circle; St. Clair watched through the probe's imagers as the armored figures, their surfaces shifting and blurring with the optical effects of active nanoflage, spilled out from the landing ramps.

One bulky figure moved to front and center of St. Clair's view. "Captain Hanson!" the figure snapped, identifying himself. "*Sir!*"

"Good to see you, Captain. Put your men well out, please . . . and have them keep alert. If there are any live critters in here, we want to know it."

"They're Marines, Lord Commander. They're alert."

St. Clair smiled. You did *not* tell Marines how to do what they were trained to do. "Of course."

"Are these the skulls you want cracked, Lord Commander?"

"Yes they are, Captain. But be gentle, okay? We want whatever is inside to remain intact."

"Aye, aye, sir. First time I was ever ordered to smash skulls *gently*."

St. Clair couldn't tell if the sarcastic remark was addressed to him or to one of the other Marines. It didn't matter. As Hanson held the skull in place, a staff sergeant used a pen-sized laser cutter to slice open the bone.

His probe was reading spectroscopic data off the gasses released by the cutter. "Not bone like ours," Guo pointed out. "Silicon, not calcium. The skeletal structure must be a lot tougher than in Earth-native species."

"Makes sense," Symm put in. "Higher gravity, stronger skeletons."

"What makes you think they're high-gravity organisms?" St. Clair asked. "The spin gravity in that segment is only half a G."

"She's right," Guo said. "If these guys evolved in half a G, they wouldn't have needed to plod around on six legs. The local trees look high-G too . . . low and spread out flat. I would guess that this species originally evolved on a super-Earth, under two, maybe three gravities."

St. Clair saw the logic of that. Maybe the species had enjoyed moving to a new home with a fraction of the gravity of their homeworld.

The skull came apart in the Marines' armored gauntlets. The brain had long since decayed, of course, like the rest of the organism's soft tissue, but a double handful of metallic and plastic parts lay in the hollow shell.

"Christ," Nolan said. "It's melted! You guys got a little too vicious with your cutter!"

"Negative, ma'am," Hanson replied. "Look at it under IR. The interior of the skull and the metal is cold."

True. The pieces of technology revealed inside the freshly

opened skull were the same temperature as the outside environment—about two degrees Celsius. And yet many of the pieces were little more than half-melted blobs. Some of the plastic had melted or charred as well, as though it had been heated by the metal when it had turned molten.

And St. Clair felt an inner chill far deeper than the cold of that alien landscape. He was remembering Maria Francesca.

"Check the other skull!" Gonzalez said.

"If it *is* a skull . . ." Guo added; he no longer sounded certain.

Within a few more moments, the issue had been resolved. These aliens had indeed possessed skulls, with brains, at both ends of their bodies, and those brains had been laced with high-tech implants, probably using a form of nano-technology, the same as human bionanoelectronics. And as the Marines examined several more of the alien bodies, it became evident that all here had died when their implant hardware had short-circuited and melted.

"Lord Commander," Newton said in his head.

"Eh? Go ahead."

"I have established communications, of a sort, with an advanced AI residing within this LIO."

" 'Of a sort?' What does that mean?"

"The AI is functioning at an extremely low level, and experiencing events very slowly. I would estimate that its experience of time is running at approximately one to five hundred, compared with normal human consciousness."

"I'll be right there."

With a thoughtclick, St. Clair disconnected himself from the probe's telemetry and reawakened back in his office on board the *Ad Astra*. If Newton had something important to tell him, he wanted to be fully present and unencumbered with other data.

"So what've you got?" he asked.

"Trouble, Lord Commander," the AI told him. "A very

great deal of trouble, and it may already be too late to avoid it."

"LIEUTENANT!" GUNNERY Sergeant Paxton called. "We're getting activity back here in these tunnels!"

"What kind of activity?"

"Heat and movement, sir. Lots of it."

"On my way." Lieutenant Greg Dixon, the temporary CO of Charlie Company, 3rd Battalion, waved at a couple of nearby Marines. "Philips! Santiago! With me!"

"Aye, aye, sir!"

A company numbered 120 Marines in four platoons normally skippered by a captain, in this case Captain Hanson, but Hanson was back at the "Bone Pile" with two platoons and the three other FPCs. He'd deployed two platoons, First and Third, to check out the tunnels under Dixon's immediate control. First Company's CO was Lieutenant Nakamura, who actually had seniority over Dixon, but Nakamura was in sickbay, down with an e-virus, and Sublieutenant Nicholson, his exec, was in charge. Dixon had sent Nicholson's platoon—thirty Marines—and stayed with Third at the tunnel mouth as reserve.

The deployment had been by the book, but Dixon was beginning to regret having followed it. His first impulse had been to stay with First Platoon as it explored those black chambers in the rock ahead.

The Charlie Company's Marines had been spread out across the hills close to one end of the violet jungle habitat, the end through which they'd come earlier. They'd set up a heavily defended perimeter around the FPC landing zone, an area designated as the "Bone Pile," for the alien skeletons.

The hills piled up and up along the slope toward the endcap; the habitat cylinder was much larger than the *Tellus* habitats—over one hundred kilometers across. The cylinder's axis emerged from the endcap some fifty kilometers up, where rising hills became mountains, then a vast expanse of bare metal surrounding the hab's central sunbeam and the airlock through to the next hab over.

At the base of those mountains, tunnel openings led into the artificial substrate there . . . entrances, perhaps, to service areas or underground storage. With their dissection of the Bone Pile skeletons complete, Hanson had ordered Dixon to take Charlie Company up and scout out the tunnels, checking for signs of life.

It sounded as though Gunny Paxton had found it.

The nearest tunnel entrance was half a klick from the Bone Pile, a tall, narrow gateway made of tough plastic, like the local buildings. Inside, the tunnels were quite high, with vaulted ceilings, as befitted a species that must have stood seven meters high at the shoulder. Pipes lined the walls—water mains, possibly . . . or, rather, pipes for the local water equivalent. Philips and Santiago hurried along just behind him, weapons at the ready. Everyone, Dixon thought, was on edge. The attacks at the Alderson disk had unnerved everyone. Scuttlebutt had it that the attackers had come from Andromeda . . .

. . . which was exactly where they were now.

The tunnel opening yawned around him, and Dixon led the way in.

Into the belly of the beast.

"JUST WHAT are we up against, Newton?" St. Clair asked. Monitor displays around his office showed telemetry feeds from a number of Marines inside the spaghetti. A patrol inside what appeared to be a labyrinth of service and access passageways had encountered signs of life, though whether it was organic or machine was yet to be determined.

"An alien mind, Lord Commander," was Newton's reply. "A very large, very powerful SAI mind. So far, it's not fully engaged against us. It may not even be consciously aware that we're here. But I expect that to change momentarily."

Humans were still working at the definitions of artificial intelligence. Newton was an AI, of course, and by some definitions he was a *super* AI, a machine intellect far faster, far more powerful than the mind of any merely organic brain.

But machine and organic minds were enormously different in both their design and their evolution. *All* machine intelligences were faster than humans, if what you were measuring was speed of computation. Mathematical calculation came very easily for a machine.

On the other hand, something a human child did quite naturally—learning to recognize the concept of *chair*, for instance—came only with great difficulty for a newly assembled robot.

Most AI specialists—both organic and electronic—agreed that the term *super AI* should be reserved for artificial intelligence at *least* an order or two of magnitude more powerful than a system like Newton.

How intelligence should be measured was still a matter of debate. The most common unit of measure was the number of synapses—the connections among neurons or the electronic equivalent in an AI brain. Humans possessed something like 1×10^{14} synaptic connections in their brains—500 trillion; Newton had 5.4×10^{16} connections, which put him on a par, evidently, with the Kroajid. *Ad Astra* researchers had estimated that the SAI running the matrioshka brain that housed the Kroajid intelligence used the equivalent of 10^{17} connections.

"I estimate," Newton told St. Clair, "that the alien intelligence exceeds my own by at least three orders of magnitude . . . and possibly four."

What would a mind arising out of 10^{20} neural connections be like? A brain literally a million times more powerful than its human equivalent? St. Clair couldn't even imagine what it would be like talking to such a mind.

"Are you saying this mind is resident within the spaghetti artifact?" St. Clair asked.

Newton hesitated before replying, a mildly startling mimicry of human cognitive processes. "Not quite. The torus knot habitats possess an artificial intelligence approximately equal to the SAI we encountered in the matrioshka brain, with a neural connection equivalence of very roughly 5×10^{17}, though the system is operating at such a low level that establishing a precise figure is impossible. Are you with me?"

"So far. Why is it operating at a low level?"

"To escape detection by a higher-order intelligence that has invaded it."

"Ah . . ."

"For clarity, I have designated this higher-order intelligence as the 'Dark Mind.' It may be the result of a quite extensive technological singularity, possibly one of galactic scale and scope."

"You're relating it to the Kroajid term, to the Andromedan Dark?"

"Correct. And to dark matter as well. The attacks at the Alderson disk are evidence of a life form that can interact with normal matter only under certain narrow and specific circumstances."

A narrative summary opened in St. Clair's mind, an abstract of what had been learned so far. The torus knot habitats, according to the Roceti database, had in fact been a colony created almost 100 million years ago by a group of star-faring intelligences from the Milky Way, an early attempt at colonizing the approaching Andromedan Galaxy in order to establish contact and trade with sophont species within it—so in that respect, he had been correct. The double-brained titans, it turned out, were known to Roceti as the Agrrth—a technic species that had evolved in a massive, cold world within the Milky Way.

St. Clair was reminded of accounts of dinosaurs in Earth's remote past—and how some were supposed to have possessed a nerve plexus in their hips that acted like a second brain and helped them walk. That idea, it had turned out, was a myth, but the Agrrth evidently had evolved from large, browsing animals with just this sort of neural arrangement. A hundred million years ago, as Andromeda loomed huge in the night skies of worlds across the Milky Way, the two-headed Agrrth had been among the principle leaders of galactic civilization, the founders of a rich and flourishing culture throughout the home Galaxy. According to Roceti, there'd been at least a dozen colony systems founded by the Agrrth and others within the outlying spiral arms of Andromeda.

But 30 million years ago, contact with the colony—called Ea Hovjin Neh in the records—had been lost. At about the same time, attacks by Andromedan raiders had begun increasing dramatically within the home Galaxy, and nothing was done.

The slow-living AI's memories had recorded the colony's history . . . and its fall. The colony had been invaded by a powerful AI. The super AI running Ea Hovjin Neh had attempted to fight off the invader, but ultimately had, in effect, gone underground. The civilizations living within Ea Hovjin Neh's tangle of habitats had, one by one, gone extinct.

And the habitat mind had survived by reducing its clock speed to a tick every couple of thousand years, too slow for the Dark Mind to even notice that it was there. Those ticks were also irregular. Nothing to show an intelligent pattern.

"So how did you talk to it?" St. Clair wanted to know.

"There was a—call it a watchstander program. A marginally intelligent subroutine that did nothing but watch."

"Watch for what?"

"For other AIs, mostly. When it sensed my presence, it

woke up the main SAI. I suppose that is a reasonable description of what happened. It sequestered a part of itself to carry out negotiations with me, as I did with it. We interacted entirely through our respective virtual compartmentalizations. This reduced our mutual vulnerability to the Dark Mind—or each other."

"How does the Dark Mind detect us?"

"Heat, apparently—the waste heat emitted by large-scale computing, for example. And it may have means of detecting electron flow in circuits. According to Ea Hovjin Neh, the Dark Mind actually somehow feeds on electronic minds, though whether this is merely a draining of electricity from active circuits, or if this means something more involving memory and CPU tasking, I have not yet determined."

"But, if this Dark Mind is in fact dark matter—"

"The reality," Newton told him, "may be far more alien than our best attempts to understand it would allow. Clearly, these organisms can sense us through, or from, higher dimensions, for example."

"The things that attacked us on the Alderson disk?"

"Exactly."

"We're going to need confirmation of all of this," St. Clair said. "And, just as urgently, a way of fighting back."

A SHRILL scream sounded over Dixon's command channel, and his in-head telemetry on Private Solinsky flashed red.

"Solinsky! Solinsky, what's happening!"

The scream cut off short . . . but other screams and yells blocked the channel, and Dixon heard the heavy snap and whine of portable laser weapons cycling, the far heavier thump of rapid-fire explosive rounds. "Damn it! What's happening? Nicholson! Report!"

Sublieutenant Nicholson, First Platoon's CO, was in charge of the men Dixon had sent into the tunnels. "They're coming out of . . . tunnels!"

"You mean they're *in* the tunnels?"

"I mean they're coming *out* of fucking tunnels. Tunnels out of the fucking *air*!"

Nicholson's voice ended in a piercing shriek, and his telemetry cut off.

Damn!

The passageway through which Dixon was running took a sharp turn, then opened into a large and labyrinthine underground chamber, a high-tech cavern with a domed ceiling so high it had clouds, lit by sunbeams shrouded in mist high overhead.

Dixon had seen recordings of the thing that had attacked *Ad Astra*'s CAS—the black, fluid shapes spilling out of thin air, growing, merging, splitting apart, constantly and impossibly shifting in size and shape. A dozen gateways yawned in midair, with writhing worm-tangles exploding from each.

Is that what we're facing now?

Gunny Paxton was lugging an M-410 autocannon, a massive, high-cyclic weapon firing magnetically accelerated 15mm explosive shells. Most of those shells were vanishing into the maw of the extra-dimensional openings, however, passing right through the black horrors without effect.

Beside him, Corporal Donaldson staggered, dropped her weapon, and scrabbled wildly at her helmet. An instant later, the helmet came apart as one of the black masses emerged from inside her head, then peeled open the rest of her armor from the inside out. Nearby, a screaming Private Fredericks was surrounded by three black spheres that closed on him, enveloped him, plucked him up off the cavern floor struggling . . . and vanished. He reappeared a moment later, everted, armor and body somehow flipped inside out in a spray of blood and gore.

Dixon raised his weapon, a megajoule pulse-laser carbine and engaged his helmet optics, throwing up a bright red targeting reticule at whatever his weapon was pointed at.

He slued the weapon around until the reticule centered over one of the dimensional openings and the horror squirming within and triggered it . . .

. . . to no effect! The pulse stream passed through the alien attacker without touching it, and somehow vanished into the twisted dimensions beyond the gateway.

"Change your angle, LT!" Sergeant Janice Klein shouted at him.

"What?"

"Your angle! Your fire only touches them from certain angles! Like this!" She swung her laser rifle and snapped off three quick shots at the alien that Dixon had been trying to hit. From her vantage point, off to his right, in some way that he did not understand, her fire connected. Greasy smoke billowed out of the gateway, as a glistening and irregular black slab of meat dropped steaming to the floor.

Something wasn't right. If he could *see* the alien, then light was traveling from the alien to his optics. Sending a pulse of coherent light back the same way ought to be simplicity itself.

But this wasn't the time for figuring out the hyperdimensional geometry of these things. Three black spheres had just emerged out of nothingness, closing on Private Chang. He sent a burst of laser pulses into one of the spheres, and this time they managed to connect. The three spheres opened and pulled back, then vanished, conveying the almost comical impression of a disembodied hand snatched back from a flame.

Higher-dimensional openings were twisting into existence in all directions. There could be nothing like a front line here, no control of the battlefield, no coordination or coherent organization of strategy and tactics—except for one.

"Fall back!" Dixon yelled. "Everyone fall back to the tunnel entrance!" He switched channels. "Bronkowsky! This is Dixon!"

Bronk was the skipper of Fourth Platoon.

"Yeah, LT!"

"We're coming out. Meet us at the entrance with a Toad!"

"On our way, Lieutenant!"

The tilt-jet FPCs were ungainly, squat, ugly fliers, AAT-2440 flying personnel carriers popularly called Devil Toads. They'd been named for a prehistoric beast—a frog with the Latin name *Beelzebufo* (literally "devil toad" or "devil frog")—that had lived during the time of the dinosaurs. They were ugly, massive, the size of a basketball, and they possessed demonic-looking spikes on their heads and backs. The ship didn't look much better. Marines had carried the nickname "Devil Dogs" for more than 240 years, now. It was only right that Devil Toads now carried them into battle.

"Kemmerer!" She was CO of Second Platoon.

"Yessir!"

"Where the hell is the skipper?"

"Captain Hanson is . . . he's a casualty, sir. We don't know what happened!"

Shit!

"We need to get the hell out of Dodge! Start loading our people on board the Toads! Be ready for an emergency dust-off!"

"Copy that, Lieutenant!"

They needed to get all of the Marines together back at the Bone Pile, then get airborne.

If these ghostly attackers let them.

NINETEEN

A dimensional gateway opened up directly ahead, blocking the way through to the tunnel leading out of this underground chamber. Dixon opened fire and once more saw his burst pass through the forming apparition.

He didn't have time to worry about it.

"Fire in the hole!" Sergeant Kirtland yelled behind him, and a small, round object flew past Dixon's shoulder and vanished into the swirling vortex.

He didn't see the grenade's explosion. He felt it, however, as a swift, hard punch *inside* his body—perhaps the strangest and most jarring sensation he had ever experienced in his life. The air whooshed from his lungs, leaving him gasping and shaking.

But the tunnel vortex snapped shut and the way was open. "C'mon, Marines!" he yelled. "We're pulling a fucking Smith!"

Two hundred twelve years earlier (plus or minus a few billion years), 1st MarDiv Marines at the Chosin Reservoir in Korea had found themselves the focus of an attack from all sides by no fewer than eight Chinese divisions. The Marines had turned around and fought their way out. "Retreat, hell!" Major General Oliver Smith had declared to the news media. "We're attacking in a different direction!"

After sixteen days of constant fighting and bitter cold, the Marines—with their dead, their equipment, and three Army battalions they'd rescued along the way—reached the sea, and safety. As the legend became hallowed by time, "pulling a Smith" had been enshrined in Marine lore: if you're surrounded, you *attack*, and keep on attacking, until the situation is resolved.

Ooh-rah, Dixon thought.

Charlie Company made its way through the main tunnel in good order, though dimensional portals kept opening up *inside* the rock to left and right. Corporal Paulson was grabbed by something, his armored form jerked into the air and then into invisibility.

"Use grenades!" Dixon ordered. He thumbed the trigger on one and tossed it into a vortex opening directly beside him. Again, there was no visible sign of the explosion, but he felt the shock internally, an inner thump spreading out from the very center of his body.

Paulson rematerialized—his legs buried inside solid rock, his head, arms, and torso dangling obscenely from the ceiling overhead. Fortunately, the Marine was already dead.

"Keep firing!" Dixon yelled. "Work the angles! Work the angles! Try to get effective shots!"

He wasn't sure yet how that worked, how you could see a target and not hit it from one angle, and see it and score a hit from another. But Klein had fed him what she had discovered, and the trick seemed to be to position yourself at around a forty-five degree angle, left or right from straight-on. Do that, and the laser burned through the nightmare-black worms in a messy explosion of charred organics.

Usually.

"Lieutenant Dixon." A new voice came over Dixon's in-head. "This is Lord Commander St. Clair. We've been following the situation from out here. How can we assist you?"

"Dunno, my lord!" Dixon yelled back. Black spheres materialized in front of him. He sprayed them with bursts of high-energy coherent light and they jerked back into nothingness once more. A sudden terror filled him. "I think the

Bone Pile may be under attack! They said Captain Hanson is down!"

"We've lost telemetry from Captain Hanson," St. Clair's voice replied. "We don't know anything else. Until the situation resolves itself, you are in charge in there."

Great, Dixon thought. *Just fucking great.*

A RED circle appeared on the image of the slow-turning habitat. "That is your target, Mr. Webb," St. Clair told the Weapons Officer. "Can we cut through?"

"We can cut through, my lord," Webb replied, "but it may take a while. Our sensors report that the substrate is a hundred meters thick right there. Unless you want to risk blowing up that whole end of the habitat."

"Absolutely not. See if you can punch a small hole through . . . no more than a hundred meters wide or so."

"We'll do our best, my lord."

St. Clair wondered if that best would be good enough.

"Lord Commander!"

That was Symm. "What is it, Excomm?"

"Our electronic networks are under attack."

"What kind of attack?"

"Cyber attack, my lord. Extensive . . . and very fast. Newton says the dark matter entity is aware of us, and widening its attack exponentially."

The thought chilled. He would rather have heard about a physical attack by grasers or antimatter beams.

"When did this start?" Damn it, he'd just been talking with Newton a couple of minutes ago.

"About twenty seconds ago, Lord Commander."

And as St. Clair thought about it, twenty seconds was an eternity when it came to computer AIs wrestling with one another for electronic advantage.

St. Clair was about to ask how the attack was playing

out—what was the hostile AI doing—when Symm added, "My lord! It's coming in through the network!"

St. Clair had already called up a schematic showing *Ad Astra*'s network, a kind of CGI cartoon representing where data was flowing, where processors were engaged, where the system was drawing power. Priority at that moment was being given to weapons and communications, of course, with AI network integrity a very close third. Newton evidently was struggling against something far larger and more powerful than himself.

Unfortunately, that left little to aid the organics linked in to the network, and they were coming under attack as well. He heard Symm's mental scream just before he saw her link to the Net go down. Others were being attacked as well: Seibert, the shield officer; Hargrove, the senior comm officer; Denisova, in the sensor department. When he brought up a schematic of the entire ship, with colored icons identifying each station and duty officer, he was appalled to see more and more green icons flashing to red.

He wanted to talk to Newton, to find out how best to combat this sudden electronic invasion, but Newton looked pretty busy at the moment, so busy that talking to a human might knock him down a crucial few nanoseconds of processor speed and result in even more damage being done.

Instead, he began entering commands through his own in-head processor, directing ship systems across the board to shut down or to throttle themselves down drastically. The more processor power he could free up for Newton to use, the better. . . .

And then the attack hit him.

DIXON EMERGED into the larger habitat interior just as the Fourth Platoon Devil Toad gentled down out of a hazy sky, its ventral turret sluing around to snap off a burst of particle-beam fire at approaching hostiles. Its belly ramp dropped, and Lieutenant Bronkowsky stepped onto the treading, waving them on. "C'mon, Marines! We're illegally parked!"

The Marines pounded up the Toad's ramp, the last aboard backing up as they fired at the oncoming terrors.

"Everyone on board?"

"Affirmative, Bronk," Dixon yelled. "Get us the hell out of here!" The Toad lifted off while the ramp was still coming up. Dixon crowded in with the other Marines on the cargo deck. "What's the butcher's bill?"

"Eight killed, sir," Gunny Paxton reported. Dixon was already seeing the figures coming through his in-head from his secretary. "No wounded."

In this sort of action, *wounded* too easily became *killed*. They'd been lucky. But there was also sharp pain. Marines prided themselves on never leaving anyone behind, not even dead comrades, but it wasn't always possible to recover the bodies. Some of the dead this time around had been left behind—the one materialized inside the cavern ceiling among them. *What was his name? Paulson, that was it.* . . .

There'd been no way. *No way.*

Ahead, the perimeter around the Bone Pile was clearly visible on the ground half a kilometer from the tunnels.

"Topeka!"

"Yes, Lieutenant." Topeka was the AI running Bronkowksy's FPC, and in charge of that flier's communications.

"Give me a taclink to the other Toads," Dixon ordered. He needed to coordinate the lift-off and withdrawal of all four FPCs.

"Tactical link o—"

The attack came so swiftly, Dixon scarcely had the time to react. A red line winked on within his in-head, though, warning of a major cyber breach, and Dixon cut the link even as it was established. Topeka had bought him a few fractions of a second; the Toad's AI had been compromised within a nanosecond, far too short a time for merely human reflexes, but the artificial mind had fought long enough to give Dixon the chance to cut the link.

"Lieutenant!" Bronkowsky shouted. "We just lost our AI!"

"I know! Take us in on manual!"

"I don't know if we're going to be able to thread the needle without an AI! Or find our way out on the other side!"

At least, Dixon thought, he now had a good idea about what had happened to Hanson. A cyber attack—probably like the one that had killed Francesca on board the *Ad Astra*—must have killed him or taken him out of the picture.

That put the Marine landing team in a desperate situation, however. To reach the Bone Pile, the four Toads had flown in through the rent in the side of the darkened habitat next door, flown for kilometers above the crystal forest, then reached the airlock at the habitat's axis—a set of two massive airtight doors sealing the two habs from each other. Access had been automatic; despite the power loss in the hab next door, the first airlock had opened for them as they approached, then sealed behind them. They'd threaded their way through a long, dark corridor hundreds of meters wide, and then another airtight door had slid open at their approach, giving them admittance to this habitat, with its cold, purple forest and piles of alien bones.

Getting out again was going to be tricky—requiring a flight path that ideally would be the reverse of the one they'd used coming in, but the trip would be a lot easier if they could lock the four Toads together electronically so that their AIs could pool resources and data. Once inside the darkened, powered-down hab, they would have to find the rip in the habitat shell that led to the outside, which would require an AI analysis of radar and lidar data . . . or else a hell of a lot of luck.

Perhaps only the one Devil Toad's AI had been compromised back at the Bone Pile, but Dixon wasn't going to trust his in-head electronics and his organic brain to that slender hope. *Hell* no!

"Set us down by the Bone Pile," Dixon told Bronkowsky. "We need to figure out how to get out of this hole."

"Looks to me like we're not gonna get the chance, Dix," Bronkowksky replied. "Look astern!"

Dixon took a look aft through the Toad's external imaging system. The whole series of hillsides below the endcap mountains appeared to be alive, as dimensional gates opened in fast-rippling succession, and extradimensional nightmares oozed down the rocks and across the jungle terrain toward the Marine perimeter.

No, they didn't have much time at all.

ST. CLAIR DIDN'T know what it was, but it was big, and it was vastly, supremely powerful, an overwhelming force—a hurricane of Mind. No, a god, nothing less—a god mad with anger, with a nova-hot rage.

And in that instant it was aware of *him*.

He wanted to freeze, wanted to run, wanted to somehow escape that cold and Olympian gaze. He wasn't sure what he was seeing, or how he was seeing it, but it felt like the cold glare of a madman suddenly aware of a mosquito on his arm. He thought he saw eyes, slit-pupiled and alien, but the dark-matter god didn't have eyes, not as humans understood them, so what was St. Clair seeing?

And he thought he saw a hand descending . . . or something like a hand. He felt something, an icy movement inside his skull, and that shouldn't have been happening either, since the brain didn't contain sensory nerves. But the freezing sensation continued to work its way along his skull, and he realized that the thing was draining energy from the nanochelated circuitry layering portions of his cerebral cortex.

St. Clair heard himself screaming.

He broke the connection and woke up in his command chair, gasping, short of breath, bathed in sweat, and *terrified*.

St. Clair wasn't sure how he'd managed to survive. That *thing* had had him dead to rights. Had been about to swat him like a fucking insect. . . .

On the displays in front of his command seat, the schematics showing *Ad Astra*'s network integrity were slowly, slowly shifting back to green. The red tide had invaded the ship, had come *that* close to swallowing it, and now was pulling back.

"What the hell happened?" St. Clair demanded.

"An alien SAI, Lord Commander," Jablonsky said. "It was coming in at us through our network links. I think Newton held it off long enough for us to get clear."

"Most of us," St. Clair said. According to the telemetry, a number of people had been badly hurt. He flashed an alert to *Ad Astra*'s medical department, then began trying to pick up the pieces. "Excomm! Are you okay?"

"Y-yes," Symm said. "Yes, I think so. . . ."

"Damn it, snap to!" He was already testing the link. The monster was . . . gone. At least for now. "Are you able to link?"

"Yes, my lord."

"Good. Do it. Mr. Webb!"

"Yes, sir!"

"Are the grasers still on-line?"

"Yes, my lord."

"Do it! Put a hole in that fuzzball!"

"Target lock!" Subcommander Webb called. "Turrets two through nine are linked and at full power."

"Fire."

The converging beams of gamma ray energy were invisible in open space, but appeared as an intolerably brilliant flare of visible light against the carefully chosen patch of tar-

geted hull. *Ad Astra*'s AI, working with the compartmental-
ized fragment of the torus knot's resident AI, had identified
a single ten-meter patch five kilometers from the Marine
perimeter at the Bone Pile. Gigawatts of coherent energy
focused into such a tiny area released heat equivalent to that
of a tiny sun, instantly vaporizing the thick hull material and
rock substrate of the colony habitat.

"Dixon," St. Clair said. "You people okay?"

"Affirmative, Lord Commander. We're being pursued
by . . . oh, my God . . ."

"We've broken through, Lord Commander," Webb told
him.

"Cease fire. Be ready to help them when they come
through."

". . . OH, MY GOD . . ."

From Dixon's vantage point in the Toad, flying half a
kilometer above the violet forest, the ground up ahead appeared to be dissolving trees, rock, and earth in a maelstrom
of brilliant light. It was a sunrise . . . but with the sun emerging from *inside* the ground, not behind the horizon.

"We are picking up a strong flux of X-ray and gamma
radiation," the Toad's pilot reported. In the next instant, a
shockwave traveling out from the blast point at the speed of
sound struck the flier, rocking it savagely.

"Is that a volcano?" Bronkowsky asked, sounding awed.

"Negative," Dixon replied. "Not inside an artificial habitat!"

"But—"

"That's *Ad Astra*," Dixon said, "providing a little close
fire support."

The minute sun winked out, but the ground around the
explosion continued to glow orange-hot. Large chunks
of ground collapsed into the hole, flung out of the habitat,
perhaps, by its rotation. The surge of radiation faded away,

though that hole in the ground was going to continue glowing with its own heat for some time yet.

"Okay," Dixon said, opening a channel to the entire Marine company. "Take it single file. *Ad Astra* just kicked open a door. That's our way out."

The Devil Toad banked hard, gained altitude, then twisted around into a vertical dive directly above the hole. Dixon could see a tiny, circular patch of black at the center of the glowing hole. Damn—this was going to be like threading a needle. The opening through a full five hundred meters of rock and subsurface infrastructure was only a hundred meters wide.

But the four Toads fell into single file as they dropped toward the glowing bull's-eye below. Dixon's Toad, in the lead, gave a savage burst of acceleration. Molten rock and metal blurred past on all sides . . . and then the lander FPC was out once again in open space.

Wasp fighters, their nanoflage hulls currently displaying their distinctive black-and-yellow parade livery, approached from several directions.

"Okay, Marines," St. Clair's voice said over the connection. "Let's bring you all home."

"Copy that," Dixon replied. "We're on our way in."

THE MEETING of department heads hours later took place entirely in non-virtual, non-electronic space.

St. Clair was still feeling rattled. Modern, everyday life depended absolutely on the security and the integrity of virtual reality, the interplay of electronic systems and networks that filled so-called real space with layer upon layer upon hidden layer of alternate and additional realities. Every person on board *Ad Astra* had cerebral implants, which they used for everything from communicating with others to downloading information to opening doors. For a terrifying few minutes, there, St. Clair had wondered if they were going to have to abandon *all* network instrumentalities. They'd survived—thanks to Newton's cyberwar skills—and the attacker had pulled back, but St. Clair was not sure he could trust the ship's networks any longer . . . or risk linking in. Newton would be there, of course, and he would be able to download and display information if necessary.

But St. Clair was feeling uncomfortably like a cyberphobe. He knew he was going to have to link in to the network again . . . and the thought terrified him.

He caught Symm's eye across the conference table and attempted a smile. She didn't return it, and he shrugged. Everyone was on edge after the Battle of the Torus Knot.

Lieutenant Dixon, however, gave him a nod and what might have been a shy grin. Cameron looked grim. Jablonsky looked as unflappable as ever, the quintessential geek, oblivious to all save his machines. What, St. Clair wondered, was his secret? It had been his machines—the AIs within *Ad Astra*'s cybernetic networks—that had very nearly killed them all.

But, then again, those same AIs had fought the invader off. Maybe Jablonsky and his people simply felt that their faith in Newton and the other ship AIs had been perfectly justified.

Whatever it was, he hoped he could find that same faith, and soon.

"Thank you all for coming on such short notice," St. Clair said to the crowd as the noise in the room died down. "We're here to analyze our encounter a few hours ago. Encounters, I should say, because it's clear now that we're dealing with at least two different phenomena.

"Lieutenant Dixon's people engaged the hyperdimensional creatures we first met on the Alderson disk, black, malleable creatures that appear to move within and through several higher dimensions, and which appear to consist of, at least in part, dark matter. Some of Dixon's people, and most of us, encountered something else—an intelligently directed energy that appears to move through cybernetworks or communication nets, and causes damage to those parts of the brain hooked up to our cyberware implants. Are we all on the same page?"

There were nods and murmurs of agreement around the table. St. Clair pushed on.

"Dr. Sokolov?"

"Yes, Lord Commander."

"What's the butcher's bill? How many people did we lose?"

The medical officer considered the question for a moment. "Deaths: eight Marines. However, at least seventy people have reported to sick bay since the battle, or been brought in by corpsman teams. A variety of symptoms—post-traumatic stress disorder, anxiety, various phobias. Four people in critical condition with major damage to their cerebral cortex—burns, apparently brought on by a partial melting of their brain implants. Five patients with extreme psychosis. They don't know where they are, can't relate to the world around them. It's as if they're in the grip of severe paranoid schizophrenia. Delusional, with powerful hallucinations. Two more are in complete catatonia." He shook his head. "Very scary stuff."

When a doctor says something like "very scary stuff," you pay attention. "Can you do anything for them?"

Sokolov gave an expressive shrug. "Perhaps. It'll take time. We can nanosurgically rebuild the physically damaged portions of the brains of the four in critical. For the others . . ." He shook his head. "As I say, it will take time. A *lot* of time."

"Do what you can for them, Doctor."

"Of course."

"Mr. Cameron."

"Sir."

"Lieutenant Dixon's report makes some damned unusual statements. Among other . . . improbables, he points out that the dark matter entities *can* be shot from certain angles, but that other angles allow you to see the entity but not hit it with a direct shot from a laser weapon. On the face of it, that sounds impossible. Would you care to comment?"

"I think Dr. Sandoval would be the appropriate expert to talk to about this," the tactical officer replied.

"Dr. Sandoval is twenty-some thousand light years away at the moment, Senior Lieutenant. With the rest of the civilians."

"I . . . I know, my lord."

"Do your best. We don't expect an academic dissertation on higher-dimensional physics."

"Good, because you won't get one, sir." He sighed. "Okay, as I understand it, the aliens are vulnerable when they're inside those . . . pockets, or tunnels, or whatever they are. When it looks like a door is opening in space, and you can see through into their space."

"Go on."

"It sounds impossible because light travels in a straight line, so if you see one of these critters, you ought to be able to hit it with a laser."

St. Clair glanced at Dixon. "Is that substantially correct, Lieutenant?"

"Yes, sir. It was damned frustrating in there, I can tell you. Sometimes you could kill the buggers, and sometimes you couldn't."

"We had Newton analyzing that," Cameron went on. "He suggests that there is a fundamental difference between ordinary light and a beam or a pulse from a laser. Ordinary light *scatters*, whereas the photons in a laser are all traveling parallel to one another, and with their frequencies in lockstep. It's a laser's defining characteristic."

"That's all well and good, Senior Lieutenant. But how can we see the thing when we can't shoot it?"

"Like I said, ordinary light scatters. Light from our three dimensions passes through one of these doorways, okay? Some of it travels at just the right angle that it does interact with the dark matter—it reflects off of it, something it apparently can only do when higher dimensions are involved. As it does so, it scatters. Some comes straight back along the same angle it went in . . . and the rest comes out any which way. If it reflects at all, it carries back information about the surface that reflected it . . . even though light traveling back the other way along that same path is going to pass right through the target as if it wasn't even there."

"I'm gathering this only happens inside these tunnels or openings into higher-dimensional space."

"Yes, sir. Like I said, photons only reflect from higher-dimensional aspects of these things, and the gateways seem to be like tunnels or doors leading to higher dimensions."

"What about when they just come out of thin air?" Symm asked. "They're not using dimensional doorways then."

"No, they're not. We can also see the dark-matter creatures when they . . . when they intersect with our three-dimensional continuum. That's when you get those weird, black spheres in midair."

"That's when they're reaching down out of the fourth dimension and into our third," St. Clair suggested. He was remembering the earlier briefing, and the discussion of higher dimensions in string theory.

"Exactly, sir. That's how they can reach in and grab one of us, pull us out of this space and into theirs. . . ."

St. Clair was recording the conversation on his in-head electronics. He wished he could share it with Newton, but didn't quite dare, yet, to link in. Damn it, he would *have* to, no matter what.

"All fascinating, I'm sure," St. Clair said. "But does it

get us anywhere? Can we use any of this to create weapons or tactics that will let us come to grips with these hellish things?"

"Actually, Lord Commander," Cameron said, "I think it does exactly that."

"Then for the love of God, Senior Lieutenant Cameron," St. Clair said, "let's hear it."

TWENTY

Lieutenant Christopher "Kit-Kat" Merrick drifted through emptiness, ten AUs out from the Kroajid matbrain. From here, the megastructure the Kroajid called Galactic Node 495 was almost invisible, a dark gray sphere smaller than the full moon as seen from Earth. There were tatters and rents in the cloak of habitats and power collectors, enough that a faint, bloody glow showed from deep within as some of the star's light leaked out past the shells.

Beyond the matbrain, the stars of the galactic core shone in teeming vistas of light—in thick-clustered stars and tattered streamers of gas, in the faint ghosts of faded supernovae, the piercing blue-white gleam of young, hot suns newly awakened from stellar nurseries, the deeper glow of far more ancient stars banked thick and deep behind the crenellated rampart nebulae embracing the core suns.

The blaze and glory of the background stars were solid enough and bright enough that some of the light filtered all the way through the matbrain, which actually made it harder to see. Merrick and the other Stardogs were ignoring the structure for the most part. It was too large for them to get a real mental grasp of the thing . . . and the idea that a few trillion Kroajid spiders were virtual-dreaming away eternity inside was just a little too bizarre to think about. What the hell did a thing that looked like a two-meter-long spider dream about, anyway? Giant flies? Merrick shuddered.

"Hey, Skipper?" That was Lieutenant Rick Thornton.

"Yeah, Thorny," Lieutenant Janis Colbert replied. GFA-86's commanding officer sounded distracted.

"I'm getting some funny grav readings out here. You see 'em?"

"Affirmative," Colbert replied. "I'm watching them now."

"What the hell is happening?"

"I'm not sure. All hands—we're getting high mass readings in Sector Three. Keep your scanners peeled."

Merrick looked at the indicated sector, and saw immediately what the others were seeing. Nothing material was visible, not yet . . . but several more astronomical units out from the matbrain, space was *bending*, as if under the stress of something very large, very massive.

"*Tellus* Control, *Tellus* Control," Colbert called over the squadron channel to base. "This is Eight-Six. We're picking up a spatial anomaly out here . . ."

She continued speaking, listing the navigational coordinates and the strength of the sensor readings, which suggested something as massive as a large star. The problem, however, was that *Tellus* was some eighty-two light-minutes away. It would take that long for the warning, crawling inbound at the speed of light, to reach them.

Worse, the disturbance was 3.5 astronomical units out from GFA-86's patrol area, which meant that what they were recording now had already happened almost twenty-nine minutes ago. That was the big problem in combat across planetary distances. By the time you identified a target, it had already moved, changed, or vanished—possibly a long time ago—and things were never quite what they seemed.

And that left the Stardogs hanging out here on the thin, cold edge of nothingness. Their patrol orders were to watch for any approaching threat to the *Tellus* habitats, and use their discretion about engaging the threat if that seemed necessary . . . but chances were good that anything they ran into out here was going to be a lot bigger than they could handle. Merrick thought that the CSP mission had been motivated purely by politics, a need by the politicians now in control of *Tellus* to be seen to be *doing* something.

Hence, the deployment of a CSP. The acronym stood for combat space patrol, and was the modern descendent of the CAPs flown by atmospheric fighters off of seagoing naval carriers a couple of centuries ago. The whole concept of a CSP was predicated on the assumption that once you spotted a threat, you could actually do something about it.

Now, though, they were reduced to pretending to do something useful, while the politicians back at the habs took credit for it.

"Fuck," he told an uncaring cosmos. "Didn't we fight a second revolution a century ago to kick out the damned politicrats?"

"What are you going on about, Kit-Kat?" Lieutenant Yun-Lutz asked him.

Shit. He'd not realized the channel was open. "Just wondering about the politicians and what we're supposed to be doing out here," he replied. "If something like that small, mobile moon shows up, what are we supposed to do . . . wave?"

"I don't now, Kit," Yun-Lutz replied. "Why don't you ask 'em?"

Space ahead, at the center of the distortion, was opening.

It was like the vortex or hyperdimensional gateway that had opened in PriFly; Merrick had seen the recordings. This one, though, was far larger . . . perhaps a thousand kilometers across, and inside it *something* was emerging.

It was a ship. It *had* to be a ship, but it was fifty kilometers long and half that in thickness. Under extreme magnification, it showed a kind of pixelated effect, picked out in black and red.

Merrick had seen that color scheme before. "Dark Raiders!" he said. "Sliverships!"

"Can't be," Thornton replied.

"No way," Lieutenant Timmons Howe added. "Those were *little* things! Fighters!"

"Look at them under high-mag," Merrick insisted. "You can see them all bundled together."

The pixelation effect was due to the huge number of forty-meter fighters melded together into a single super ship: a battleship comprising billions of individual sewing needles held together by glue or a powerful magnetic field. From a distance, the surface looked fairly smooth and regular. Close up, it was jagged and broken, resembling some sort of surreal 3-D fractal.

The immense monstrosity was moving at a quarter-*c* straight toward Node 495. As it moved, a faint wisp of smoke seemed to spread out from the surface . . . thousands upon thousands of individual sliverships breaking off from the main body and accelerating in a thin cloud.

"How the hell do we stop *that*?" Thornton demanded.

"We don't," Colbert replied. "We run for home, and hope our warning reaches them in time."

The twelve Wasp fighters flipped around onto a new bearing, one aimed straight for the distant, spherical matbrain. "Back to the stable, people," Colbert called. "Maximum acceleration. If those needle ships beat us there, we might not have a stable to return to!"

"AND JUST what do you expect of us?" Adler asked. Leaning forward, his elbows on the polished surface of the conference table before him, he steepled his fingers, an unconscious gesture, but he smiled when he saw what he'd done. According to the psytechers, steepled fingers were a nonverbal signal indicating dominance or control of a situation, and it could be used to impress lesser humans and, perhaps, to manipulate them in a conversation.

The problem was, he was talking to the entity known as

Gus, about as nonhuman a being as you could imagine. Gus didn't have fingers to steeple, and his nonverbal signs, if he had them, would be literally unimaginable to a human.

Gus was filling much of the wall screen in Conference Room 5, which Adler had sequestered for this meeting. With him, sitting around the table, were a couple of dozen human secretaries and assistants, Ambassador Lloyd and people from his staff, and five corporate-Senate agents—the corpreps.

Perhaps, Adler thought, glancing at Lord Hsien, his finger-steepling had been intended for them. Those corpreps tended to imagine that *they* were calling the shots. He was going to have to keep them on a short leash.

The bristling facial hairs around the Kroajid's clustered eyes were rippling and swirling quickly, producing their characteristic internal-combustion-motor purr. When the Kroajid became excited, the sound became a roar.

"Your help, Lord Adler," the Kroajid said, its hair-rippling buzz smoothly translated by a Newton clone. "Your help in defending this Gateway from the Dark."

On a private channel to Newton, Adler asked for elaboration. St. Clair had copied the AI resident within *Ad Astra* and left the copy behind in *Tellus*—standard AI procedure in this sort of situation—and Adler had not been able so far to detect any difference in the system at all.

"Gus is asking," Newton told him, "for what amounts to a military alliance against the *Graal Tchotch*."

"The Andromedan Dark."

"Exactly."

Adler wasn't entirely sure he believed in the thing. An invisible monster, made out of dark matter, able to seep through alien dimensions and kill people from the inside out? He wasn't yet sure what had killed Francesca or driven Patterson insane. He still thought it likely that the attacker had been some sort of automated defensive system within the Alderson disk infrastructure, a neat and orderly theory that fit the facts much better. The Andromedan Dark, he thought, was nothing more than some sort of alien boogeyman . . . perhaps a myth out of some ancient Kroajid cultural heritage.

He was aware of what the vacuumorphs had seen outside in the gulf between the galaxies . . . of what they *thought* they'd seen, rather, and he was not at all convinced. *Homo caelestis* was genuinely alien, so much so that it was difficult sometimes to make any sense at all out of what they perceived through those alien senses.

So why not establish such an alliance, as Gus was requesting? It would help the human population get what they needed—the support of an advanced, technic species in this far-future time, and, perhaps, a permanent home, a world to replace a presumably long dead Earth. St. Clair would piss and moan about it, but the man really had no understanding of modern diplomacy . . . or of politics, for that matter. The damned constitutionalists lived in another age; hell, they lived in another *reality*.

And Günter Adler wasn't going to let a reactionary paranoid like St. Clair hold him back from his destiny.

YOU'RE GOING to have to do it sooner or later. . . .

St. Clair was seated on *Ad Astra*'s bridge, eyes closed, fists clenched. He didn't want to link in to Newton, not if there was even the faintest possibility that the ship's AI was still contaminated.

But if he couldn't bring himself to make the electronic connection, he might as well resign as ship's captain right now.

Almost gingerly, he opened the channel, and felt Newton's front page emerging within his consciousness. "Welcome back, Lord Commander."

"Thank you, Newton." He took a figurative look around. "Is it safe?"

"The alien SAI was unaware of me," Newton relied, "since I was linked to the torus-knot's AI through a clone of myself from which I was isolated behind multiple firewalls."

St. Clair allowed himself a long and tremulous breath of relief. The specter in his mind receded, a phantom of his own imagination rather than an actual, immanent threat.

"Okay . . . so tell me what the hell is going on," he demanded. "Back there I saw this . . . this *thing.* . . ."

He could still feel the cold gaze of the god-monster, feel both its rage and its supreme indifference to something as inconsequential as a human. The disjunct between the two—rage and indifference—was both jarring and unfathomable.

"Most likely," Newton said, "your own brain was painting a kind of picture for you. What you saw does not have a physical body, but humans are intensely visual creatures, and need to assign a shape even to things they cannot see."

"No eyes," St. Clair said softly. He still remembered those alien eyes, glaring at him. . . .

"No, no eyes. It is possible that what the Kroajid call the Andromeda Dark or the Dark Mind is simply a super AI, an artificial mind of extraordinary power and scope."

"Running on what?" St. Clair asked. "An AI needs a computer system or network as a platform."

"Unknown at present. Given the Andromedan aliens' use of higher dimensions, it's possible that the Dark Mind SAI runs extradimensionally, perhaps within the Bulk, and perhaps using dark matter as the architectural construction material."

St. Clair was aware of the concept—drawn from string theory—of the Bulk, an extradimensional "space" which held all of the other dimensions of space and time. The dimensional shift drive given to humans by the Coadunation was believed to use the Bulk for shortcuts from one point in space to another.

That raised an intriguing possibility, however. Human

computers used either photons or electrons as the mechanism for computers—the means by which information could be received, stored, and transmitted. Neither photons nor electrons reacted with dark matter; presumably, dark-matter computers—and naturally evolved brains, for that matter—used a dark-matter analog. Axions, possibly . . . or photons twisted through strange angles across higher dimensions . . .

Might there be a way here to bridge the gap, allowing communication between dark and normal matter?

"Just how smart is that thing, anyway?" St. Clair wasn't sure he wanted to hear the answer, but he knew he had to know. "What's the NCE?"

"It's impossible to give a definite answer to that question, Lord Commander," Newton replied. "The number we use as a neural connection equivalent is an estimate of the total number of neural connections—synapses—together with an estimation of the speed of computation."

"I know. Give me an estimate."

He could almost hear Newton sigh. "Based on data received from the torus knot, NPS-1018," the AI told him, "I would have to estimate the Dark Mind's NCE to be a billion times larger than the torus knot's AI, perhaps on the order of 1×10^{32}."

One times ten to the thirty-second? Put in a human perspective . . . a brain 10^{18} times more complex, faster, and more powerful than a merely human or Kroajid brain.

Ten quadrillion times more powerful.

The human brain quite literally could not understand such a number, could not take it in or understand its significance. The Dark Mind was at least a million times more powerful than a matrioshka brain, or a billion times more powerful than the super AI running the torus knot.

St. Clair's immediate reaction was a renewal of the fear that had been dogging him. "Can this Dark Mind SAI get at us now?" St. Clair asked. He looked at the display across the bridge bulkheads, of jumbled stars in chaotic profusion . . . and the dark blur of the torus knot surrounding the local star.

"Its capabilities are still unknown," Newton replied. "However, it probably is not aware of this ship. It might have a way of detecting radio frequency leakage, and perhaps infrared radiation—heat—but only indirectly."

"I think," St. Clair said quietly, "that it's time we got back to *Tellus*."

"I concur, Lord Commander."

St. Clair was feeling very small, and very much alone. As large as she was, *Ad Astra* was a speck adrift on a very large sea. The thought that something with godlike reach and power might not even be aware of the ship was humbling.

And not a little terrifying.

GÜNTER ADLER considered the possibility that he might well be the next emperor of Earth. It was a pleasing thought—and a flattering one. He stood on the deck outside of his office, surrounded by forests and with the glittering sprawl of the city of Seattle stretched upside-down across the overhead curve of the Port Habitat, and realized that only he had the experience, the expertise, and the vision to lead this splinter of surviving humanity in the uncertain years to come. There was so much here that he could set straight, so many ways to impress his legacy on history, so much he could do to be remembered.

It was a good thing, he thought, amused, that he was at heart such a humble and unassuming man, genuinely a man of the people. . . .

The First Directorate had been born out of the need for order and continuity in a war-torn society on the brink of complete failure. And in that it had succeeded. Wags with a knowledge of history liked to point out that the Holy Roman Empire, founded—at least according to some—on Christmas day of the year 800 with the crowning of the Frankish king Charlemagne, was not holy, was not Roman, and was not an empire. The First Directorate was in much the same boat.

Sixty-one years ago—if you ignored the annoying, intervening jump across 4 billion years—the First Directorate of United Earth had been signed into being with the Treaty of Quito. Based, very roughly and approximately, on the government of the former United States of America, the Cybernetic Executive Directorate replaced the old office of president, and created a bicameral legislature providing representation for human, electronic, and corporate persons. Many referred to it as an empire, as the "Empire of United Earth," though there was no emperor, and the Earth was nowhere close to being truly united.

In fact, that government, located in synchronous Clarke-orbit atop the new Ecuadoran space elevator, represented perhaps two thirds of the planet's nations, those signatory to the First Directorate constitution; the rest were independents, like Brazil and South China, or part of the sprawling and war-ravaged Islamic Caliphate.

But the government, as inefficient as it might be, as creaking and as clumsy as it obviously was, was still light years ahead of what had come before. The electronic Cybercouncil was designed to get things done, not allow a few obstructionists to hold the entire political system hostage if they didn't like the way things were going. The constitutionalists and their ilk claimed that someone needed to apply the brakes once in a while to prevent ordinary people from being trampled by the mob; Adler and those who supported him all agreed that it was that type of reactionary thinking that needed to be swept away.

And it would be, when the new *Tellus* government took shape. Progress: that was the watchword. Science and technology were advancing far too quickly for any government mired in 18th-century checks and balances to control.

And Adler planned to lead the *Tellus* colony into a shiny, streamlined future of progress, no matter what the naysayers like St. Clair said or did.

And the new order would begin with a military and commercial alliance with the alien Kroajid that would benefit both parties, and make the human colony indispensable to the locals.

Newton was drawing up the instrument of alliance now. There would be some problems, apparently, getting the spiders to understand the point of a formal treaty, printed and signed; the aliens evidently had accepted his word as binding.

No matter. Adler looked out into the rolled-up curve of the port hab and smiled.

He would lead his people into a brilliant future.

"... AND THREE ... and two ... one ... *jump*!"

Ad Astra shifted in space, slipping past the light years in an instant. St. Clair was linked in from the bridge; overcoming the fear he'd felt at the simple thought of facing the alien presence again had not been quite as difficult as he'd thought. Newton had helped with the process, and his explanation of the nature of the Andromedan SAI had clarified things. The temporally transplanted humans faced gods—extraordinarily powerful gods—but they were not alone, and they were not helpless.

Not quite.

Possibly Newton's most important assistance, though, lay in his translation of the Roceti records, and in their correlation with the various alien groups *Ad Astra* had already encountered.

At the top of the enemy alien hierarchy was the Andromedan Dark itself, called the *Graal Tchotch,* or the Dark Mind. It was, evidently, a SAI, a super artificial intelligence of staggering scope and power, a single mind literally a quadrillion times more complex than a human brain . . .

whatever that absurd figure might actually mean in the real world.

Below the Dark Mind was a strange and nightmarish category of intelligence. Little was known about it as yet; it might, in fact, be simply a tangible expression of the Dark Mind itself, the way that noncorporeal Mind interacted with the rest of the cosmos. The Roceti records called them *Dhalat K'graal*, the "Minds from Higher Angles." Sophont beings, in other words, that walked among the strange angles and twisted spaces of higher dimensions. They were the solid manifestation of dark-matter life . . . but they *could* interact with normal matter by reaching down from those higher dimensions from a particular direction or angle. These were the writhing, black masses that materialized out of thin air . . . or reached up out of opening gateways in spacetime from somewhere else.

It was these that the Marines had faced within the torus knot . . . and one of these that had killed Maria Francesca. They didn't appear to use weapons—perhaps they couldn't use weapons that were capable of interacting with normal matter. But they were deadly enough in their ability to pluck a human out of normal three-dimensional space and evert them down to a cellular level.

Or to bring them back and imbed them inside a solid wall of normal matter.

The xenosoph department was calling this particular manifestation of *very* alien life High-Dees, or HDs for short. Somehow *Dhalat K'graal* just didn't do the demons justice.

For that matter, neither did the bland "HD." Privately, St. Clair thought of them simply as the "Nightmares."

Finally, there were the Dark Raiders. Though the Roceti libraries had little to say about them, they appeared to be normal matter and to represent a number of mutually alien species. The sliverships *Ad Astra* had encountered in the galactic core were raiders, at least according to Roceti, and they enjoyed a technology considerably in advance of the humans. Most likely they'd originally come from the Andromedan Galaxy, and they might be conquered or slave species controlled by the Dark Mind. From his studies of the Roceti records, Newton thought that they might represent species that had ascended—were undergoing a technological singularity and making an evolutionary leap to beings that were part organic, part machine.

Their actual relationship with the Dark Mind was unclear; had the Dark Mind had a hand in their ascension? Or was something else at play here? St. Clair was already determined to seek out these aliens and try to figure out what they actually were.

But the very existence of the Dark Raiders gave St. Clair an important if somewhat tattered bit of hope. Whether they were slaves or allies of the Dark Mind, they clearly were able to communicate with it, and it was able to give them orders. And that, in turn, implied that there would be a way to talk with the Dark Mind, perhaps to reason with it.

St. Clair was determined to find a Dark Raider slivership, capture it, and make contact with its crew.

And while finding a slivership among well over a trillion stars of the colliding galaxies might be statistically more daunting than finding the fabled needle in a haystack, St. Clair had a feeling that the search wouldn't be totally random. *Ad Astra* had encountered those three raiders minutes after emerging from Sagittarius A*.

Somehow, he didn't think the search would take very long at all.

"LORD ADLER," the AI clone announced. "We are picking up an approaching alien structure. A number of structures, I should say."

"Newton, you will address me as 'Lord Commander.' In St. Clair's absence, I am Lord Commander of this colony."

"I require your orders," Newton said, seeming to ignore him . . . and Adler wondered if the lack of honorific had been deliberate.

The *Tellus* habitats had their own central control room and bridge, located in a tower rising from the center of the small starboard-side city of Jefferson. With direct cerebral links, however, a director with the appropriate codes could run the colony from anywhere, and Adler preferred to do just that from the comfort and privacy of his own residence. The only real problem was that one man, no matter how good his electronic enhancements, simply couldn't handle the entire overwhelming flood of data coming into any given control center.

That, however, was why they had AIs like Newton, at least in Adler's opinion. Adler was what they'd once called "a big-picture man," and he was more than happy to leave the fussy details to the machines.

"Very well," he told Newton. "Show me."

A window opened in Adler's mind, and Newton played on it vid images captured within the past few moments. A patch of space in front of the massed brilliance of background stars seemed to waver and twist, then opened to disgorge a ship. Data tags with the image showed the vessel to be enormous—fifty kilometers long and well over twenty across at its midsection. Magnification showed that the vessel was a composite of some billions of smaller vessels—the sliverships they'd encountered once before.

As he watched, the mass of sliverships seemed to dissolve, the large mass puffing silently outward to create a smoke cloud.

The cloud was made up of myriad smaller pieces, needle slender and colored in uneven patches of red and white.

"My Lord," a communications tech whispered in Adler's mind. "The Kroajid are transmitting a message."

"Let me hear it."

"Humans! The Dark Raiders have returned! We require your help—as you have already promised—in defending the Mind of Deep Paradise."

Adler stared at the approaching, expanding cloud of sliverships. There must be billions of individual ships out there, each small in and of itself, but he remembered the positron beam one had snapped off at the *Tellus Ad Astra* during their first encounter with the aliens, a bolt powerful enough to blast through *Tellus*'s outer shell and spill part of the port cylinder's under-deck ocean.

There'd been three forty-meter sliverships in that attack. One had been destroyed by concentrated fire from several of *Ad Astra*'s graser turrets, and the remaining two had fled.

Somehow, Adler suspected that beating off the Dark Raiders wouldn't be quite that easy this time around.

Lieutenant Christopher Merrick bit off a curse, then reported. "The slivers just disappeared on us, Skipper."

"Damn! Okay. Everybody stay in tight and stay at max. We'll just have to play catch-up."

The alien ships, nearly two AUs astern, had just vanished out of normal space, which meant that they'd jumped to faster-than-light. The trouble was, the squadron was so far ahead of the aliens that it had taken the light from the event a full fifteen minutes to reach them. The alien slivers had almost certainly flashed past the squadron at superluminal velocity, and most likely were emerging right now to attack either the matrioshka brain or *Tellus* . . . or both, ten AU up ahead. Accelerating until they were crowding the speed of light, it would take almost an hour and a half for the fighters to reach *Tellus*.

And by then . . . well, an hour and a half is an eternity in combat.

"WE'VE ACQUIRED the Node 495 beacon, Lord Commander," Subcommander Adams reported. "We're within twenty light years."

"Very well," St. Clair said. "Recharge and prepare for the final jump home."

"Fifteen minutes, my lord," Excomm Symm reported.

The bulkheads of the bridge display showed space outside: the tumble and jostle of myriad suns and sweeping nebulae, or gleaming light and ebon shadow, an explosion of stars and color, frozen as if in an instant. Andromeda towered to port, its spiral arms showing a distinct tilt and twist as they interacted gravitationally with the Milky Way; the Milky Way, smaller, its hub distinctly barred, its arms more distorted as it was engulfed by its larger companion. It was difficult to remember that the two galaxies were sliding together as if in an intimate embrace, then passing through each other in a grand *pas de deux* that would take another billion years to play itself out, from *entrée* to *coda*.

"I wonder what we'll call it?" St. Clair murmured.

"Sir?" Symm sounded confused.

"Oh, nothing, Excomm. Just wondering aloud."

She opened a private channel. "Wondering what, Lord Commander?"

"We've known for a couple of centuries, now, that the Milky Way and Andromeda were going to collide, right? Meaning they'll pass through one another completely, then reverse course and pass through one another again . . . maybe repeating several more times, scattering stars and burning up nebulae in star formation as they do so. Eventually, they'll merge completely. Almost all of their free dust and gas will be turned into new stars, both galaxies will lose their spiral shapes, and we'll have one huge elliptical Galaxy left. It'll need a name."

"I believe the astronomers refer to it as 'Milkomeda,' " Symm said.

St. Clair made a sour face. "I've heard that. Ugly name for something so spectacularly beautiful. Shows absolutely no creativity or finesse."

"Andromilkia?"

"Worse."

"Well, the 'milk' comes from the Milky Way, and that's a translation of the Latin *via galactica*. Things always sound more impressive in Latin."

"So how did all that milk get into the sky, anyway?"

Symm chuckled. "The Romans thought the Milky Way was mother's milk spilled from the goddess Hera's breast when she pushed away the infant Hercules."

"Messy. You know, I think the Greeks called it something like that first." He checked *Ad Astra*'s library through his in-head. "Yeah, here it is. *Galaxias Kyklos*—the 'Milky Wheel.' Huh. The Greeks were prescient. They realized the Milky Way completely circles the sky . . . and that we therefore lived inside something like an enormous wheel."

"Maybe we need to come up with something completely new," Symm said. She sounded like she was enjoying the game. "Something about light. Lots and lots of light."

"*Fiat lux*," St. Clair said. " 'Let there be light.' "

They watched the spectacle for a long time. St. Clair realized that he felt a powerful awareness of Symm's virself, as though she were seated right there at his side instead of her workstation at the far side of the bridge. The sensation was a pleasant one, a feeling of warmth and movement, as if he were sensing her breathing.

He realized that he missed Lisa.

He also realized that he wished the rules of command permitted him to link socially with Vanessa Symm. He laughed when a thought struck him. The simulant and the Symm . . .

"My Lord?"

"Nothing, Excomm. How much longer?"

"One minute, Lord Commander."

The seconds dwindled away, and the time was up and *Ad Astra* leaped across dark dimensions.

THE NODE fired, myriad beams of energy lancing out from the cloud of power stations and orbital computronium structures. To unaided human vision, those beams were invisible, but they were rendered by Newton's graphics program as intense, blue-white threads of light drawn taut against the stellar backdrop, each so brilliant that the stars paled and faded out by comparison.

Standing in his office, Adler squinted his eyes against the display playing itself out on the walls. The Kroajid, evidently, had plenty of firepower available . . . and a good thing, too. The *Tellus* colony had turrets mounting gamma ray lasers, but was able to muster only a tiny, tiny fraction of the total energy available to the Dyson swarm.

How the hell was a military alliance with the human colony supposed to help the Kroajid? *Tellus*'s entire energetic output would be a gnat bite to an elephant, at best.

"Lord Adler?" a voice said in his head. "This is Frazier."

The Marine general? What did he want? "What is it, General?"

"We've been discussing our situation with the spider," he said. "It—*he* wants us to deploy the Marines, and we've been gaming different ways to do it. I think we have a way we can help, but I need your say-so to initiate it."

Adler wasn't used to finding military solutions to problems, and he felt completely out of his depth with this sudden alien threat bearing down on *Tellus* and the galactic node. "Do it," he told Frazier. "Whatever the alien wants, *do it*!"

"Aye, aye, my lord," Frazier said. Adler could hear the man's acid disdain.

No matter. He would deal with military insubordination later. Right now, he needed to make good on his promise to the Kroajid. Having the spiders as allies—being able to trade with them, perhaps for advanced technology—it was worth it. Adler was still hoping, deep down, that the Kroajids might be able to provide *Tellus Ad Astra* with time travel, to get them back to the epoch where they belonged.

He hoped that the cost would not be *too* high.

AD ASTRA dropped into normal space a few astronomical units short of their destination. On high magnification, the

Node 495 Dyson swarm showed as a dark gray sphere blotting out the background stars. At this range, of course, *Tellus* was invisible.

"Take us in, Helm," St. Clair said. "Accelerate to point five cee."

"Yes, my lord."

He wanted to reach the Dyson swarm in short order . . . but didn't want to startle the spiders by barreling in at close to the speed of light. A half-*c* approach seemed to be a reasonable compromise between the two. *Ad Astra*'s gravitational drive switched on, and the ship began falling toward the swarm.

ON BOARD the *Inchon*, LPS-21, Lieutenant General William Frazier clambered into his control sphere and accepted the caress of a dozen connectors, silver cables snaking from the surrounding surfaces and attaching to his head, his cybernetic outer shell, and what was left of his spine. Data flooded in, icons winked on, and the virpresence of the Marine Corps AI came to life at the back of his skull.

"Good afternoon, Chesty," he said.

"Good afternoon, General Frazier," the AI replied, its voice almost maddeningly calm and self-assured. "*Inchon*, *Saipan*, and *Vera Cruz* all report themselves fully operational and ready for deployment."

Chesty was named for a legendary Marine, Lewis Burwell "Chesty" Puller, the only Marine ever to win five Navy Crosses, and one of the most highly decorated Marines in the Corps. Toward the end of his career, in 1954, he'd commanded the 2nd Marine Division at Camp Lejeune, North Carolina—and the 2nd MARDIV was one of the two units stationed on board *Tellus Ad Astra*.

Frazier sometimes thought that this version of Chesty was convinced that it was a direct upload of the original Marine.

"Show me," he said. Frazier was a hands-on CO and

always wanted to be shown. He would accept a subordinate's word for something when he had to—the sheer volume of data associated with the job meant that a certain amount of delegation was absolutely necessary—but he checked for himself whenever it was at all possible.

In his mind's eye, the three Marine LPS transports rode in gentle stellar orbit a few kilometers from the massive double cylinders of *Tellus*. Those transports were enormous, each almost a kilometer long and massing three quarters of a million tons apiece, but *Ad Astra* was so much larger they could have served as ship's boats. The joke on board *Inchon* was that she doubled as Lord Commander St. Clair's gig.

He checked through the readiness reports on all three transports, then checked the incoming alien cloud. The sliver swarm was still headed directly toward the Dyson node; Kroajid beam weapons were boiling the oncoming ships away by the hundreds, by the thousands, but still they kept coming, the high-tech ultimate in an all-out wave attack.

"Fighters," Frazier said.

"All twelve squadrons ready for immediate launch," Chesty replied.

Frazier hesitated. Any Marine fighter that managed to get in between the oncoming aliens and the spider energy beams would be toast, quite literally. Before long, however, that numberless horde of needle-shapes would be penetrating the Dyson swarm itself, its ships too close for the spiders to target them without hitting their own orbitals.

"Have them stand by," Frazier said. "I don't want to launch until the bastards are inside of knife-fighting range."

"Affirmative, General."

"How about the free-flight Marines?"

"We have about three thousand loading into the firing chambers, and another eight thousand are suited up and ready for launch. We're still printing flight packs for the rest, however. I estimate another two hours before we can have both divisions space-combat ready."

"Okay. Deploy the Marines that are ready for launch. And see what you can do about stepping up the production of the MX-40s."

"Aye, aye, General."

Until *Tellus Ad Astra* had been deployed to the Coadunation rendezvous, the US Marine Corps had been an elite military unit in search of a mission. The creation of the First Directorate, sixty-seven years before, theoretically had united the planet's warring factions. In practice, of course, the Directorate hadn't even come close to achieving that, but there'd still been the inevitable calls for the elimination of Frazier's beloved Corps.

But the Marine Corps had received a new lease on life when the Directorate had made contact with the Coadunation. Two full divisions, the 1st and 2nd MARDIVs, had been embarked on board *Tellus Ad Astra*—first, to provide security for the million or so human civilians embarked with the expedition to the galactic core, and second, to serve as bargaining chips for Earth's negotiations with the Coad. If the Coadunation required military help in their conflict with the mysterious Deniers, the Marines were ready.

Frazier disliked—he disliked strongly and in no uncertain terms—the idea that the Corps would be sent to fight a war that humans didn't even understand, and he disliked on general principles the idea of transferring control of two divisions from the former United States to the international Earth Protectorate Force. But if the alternative was to see the Corps disbanded and sent home after almost four centuries of honorable service, he'd take option one. He'd volunteered to lead the combined unit to the core.

He watched the deployment on his in-head display as hundreds, then thousands of Marines in black, adaptive-optic armor spilled from open hatchways along the flanks of all three Marine transports. He was reminded forcibly of a vid he'd seen when he'd been twelve . . . something about a locust swarm devouring a large chunk of Africa—the black, chitinous creatures drifting into emptiness. Individual Marines began forming up into companies—about 120 men and women in each company—and accelerating toward the fuzzy non-surface of the Dyson cloud. In open space, they would be horrifically vulnerable; tucked in close among the Dyson statites, they would be all but invisible.

Still vulnerable, but—God willing—invisibly so.

"The first companies are accelerating, Lord General," Chesty told him. "They'll reach the statite cloud in approximately twenty minutes."

"Very well." He hoped that wouldn't be too long. Those alien weapons, antimatter beams, annihilated any normal matter with which they came into contact. "How are the flight packs holding up?"

"MX-40 operation is nominal. And the training implants are holding well."

The MX-40 was a remote descendent of the manned maneuvering unit, the MMU, briefly employed during the US space program in the late twentieth century. Worn as a large and bulky backpack attached to the astronaut's life-support module, the MMU had carried 11.8 kilograms of highly pressurized nitrogen, squirted through a total of 24 thrusters positioned at various orientations to move and turn the free-flying astronaut, effectively turning him into a tiny, self-contained spacecraft. The total delta-v capability for the unit was about 25 meters per second . . . so the backpacks were flown slowly to conserve reaction mass.

The MX-40 was also a backpack unit, designed to embrace a Marine's Mk. III MCA armor. When activated, two wings spanning three meters opened and locked above the shoulders, each housing a Martin-Teller gravitic thruster.

Power was supplied by a Coadunation generator, a seemingly magical device that drew energy from hard vacuum like a quantum power tap, but within a cell the size of a man's head.

A Marine wearing an MX-40 became, in effect, a man-sized space fighter. On a planetary surface, it gave him a partial and temporary freedom from gravity, allowing him to make 100-meter jumps across the battlefield. In space, it let him deploy from one spacecraft to another, or across empty space to an orbital facility like an O'Neill colony. The 5th Marines had used a battalion wearing MX-40s in the assault on the Al Mina colony in Saturn orbit in 2125 . . . and six years later, the 9th Marine Regiment had used them during the Az-Zahra Revolt. By using the 3-D printers in the transports' logistical suites, the packs and their power plants could be turned out by the thousands in fairly short order. So long as there was a substantial source of rawmat, the printers could keep turning out flight packs, just like they nanufactured Marine weapons, MCA units, and everything else necessary to keep the Marines going.

The trouble, of course, was that the human Marines themselves couldn't be reproduced quite that easily.

Piloting an MX-40 was fairly simple—requiring a kind of in-head point-and-click protocol that could be downloaded to an individual Marine's in-head RAM in a few seconds. Some training and practice were necessary to transfer the knowledge into muscle memory and instinct, but that was one of the purposes of Marine boot camp. Frazier was more concerned about the possibility of the enemy infiltrating human electronics—such as the neural links connecting human Marines with their equipment. So far, there was no sign of such an attack, however.

Perhaps the biggest question Frazier had was arguably the most crucial. Just how effective would Marine lasers be against alien armor? Would the Marines be able to count for anything in this battle? Or would they be relegated to the unenviable status of cannon fodder?

That remained to be seen.

STAFF SERGEANT David Ramirez had always dreamed of flying. As a teenager, he'd owned a Rossy jetsuit, a flying wing that let him take to the skies over the mountains of his native Prescott, Arizona. The suit used Meta—cryogenically stabilized He_{64}—as fuel and could stay aloft for forty minutes or so with careful nursing, a reasonable flight time for a civilian-sport flying suit.

Then he'd joined the Marine Corps and found out what flying was *really* all about.

His wings spread and locked, his thrusters pulsing in perfect synch, he accelerated gently at half a G with the other members of his platoon. Second Lieutenant Mulholland was their butterbar, the platoon CO, and that meant for all intents and purposes that Staff Sergeant Ramirez, the senior NCO, was the actual leader of the unit.

Ramirez actually felt sorry for Mulholland. The kid was fresh out of OCS, and had been assigned to Second Platoon, Alfa Company, just eight weeks before the division had received its orders to ship out for the galactic core. That was scarcely enough time to find your rack somewhere in the maze that was the *Inchon* and unpack, never mind getting acquainted with the forty men and women who made up Second Platoon. When the word had come down from *Ad Astra*'s bridge that the expedition had somehow been flung forward in time, Mulholland had very nearly lost it. Ramirez had talked him down one evening by appealing to honor, duty, and the Corps, ooh-rah . . . and how the platoon was looking to him for leadership.

Yeah, right. For most, he was still a "cherry butterbar" and a "nugget"—both of the terms derived from the single gold bar that proclaimed his rank. He'd never been in combat, and that was going to count against him if this light show shaping up around the Dyson swarm got as ugly as Ramirez thought it would.

It meant Ramirez would have to keep a close eye on the kid, to make sure he didn't get into trouble.

"Coming up on the umbrellas," Captain Lytton warned. "Cool your jets. Stand by for deceleration."

They'd launched from *Inchon* and the other two transports in clouds of individual Marines, guiding themselves across the intervening gulf toward the nearest sails. The Marine AI, Chesty, was guiding them company by company, seeking to spread them out across the largest possible area of the outer statite layer.

As far as the eye could see, dark gray statite sails floated in the darkness. There must have been hundreds of billions of them, each a slightly convex disk nearly three thousand kilometers across, supporting a comparatively minute hanging structure beneath—a complex and vaguely organic cylinder kilometers long, extending from the center of the disk and pointed at the local star. Most were a kilometer or two in length; some measured fifty kilometers or more.

A statite—a *static satellite*—was a device employing a solar sail to remain motionless, or nearly so, above a star, holding its position against gravity by using a large sail floating on the star's radiation. According to the briefings Ramirez had downloaded, the Dyson swarm consisted of several dozen shells of statites; only the innermost ones, far in toward the buried star below, were supported directly by sunlight. Those farther out were supported by directed radiation from the lower shells, the whole in a precarious balance between gravity, radiation pressure, and Newton's third law.

Somehow, they all stayed up, maneuvering when they needed to, controlled by the massive AI that ran the entire swarm. Each cylinder housed different facilities—power plants extracting energy from the vacuum, masses of pure computronium serving as unimaginably vast and powerful computers, and—disturbingly—the majority of the Kroajid species. Some wag had christened the inhabited statites "habistats"; some of the spiders were in deep hibernation and dreaming of whatever it was that giant hairy spiders dreamed about, others digitized and uploaded into the virtual reality of their AI. Only a few hundred million Kroajids were actually awake and aware of what was going on in the universe outside.

A very scary thought. How could any species put itself in such a position—living for pleasure and depending on someone else to keep the whole mechanism working?

But, then, Ramirez had known humans who thought like that.

Ramirez risked an electronic glance at the sky above and around the swarm. Without augmentation, he couldn't see much . . . but an occasional bright and silent flash of light marked alien weapon discharges, and showed that the battle for Galactic Node 495 had been joined.

"Second Platoon, Alfa Company!" Lytton snapped. "Disperse across these two sails." The target sails lit up in his in-head. "Take cover around the perimeters. Don't engage the enemy until you get the word."

"Aye, aye, sir," Mulholland said. His voice sounded tight, a bit higher-pitched than usual, but he was holding it together. Good. "Okay, people! You heard the man. Under the umbrellas!"

Ramirez checked his readouts, and noted that he was closing with the edge of the nearest sail at nearly four kilometers per second. "Decelerating," he called, and thoughtclicked the icon to reverse his gravitic drive. Other Marines to left and right, above and below and behind, began their braking maneuvers, counting on their suit computers to keep track of so many hurtling bodies and keep them from colliding.

Although the sails described the surface of a sphere, it was far too vast to show a curve. Ramirez had to keep his gaze locked on the nearest edge of the closest sail, because the sheer scope and scale of the entire megastructure was overwhelming. How the hell could the spiders have built something that titanic?

The edge of the sail came up toward Ramirez entirely too fast, but his suit read the closure rate and cut in with a bit of extra thrust. He hit the dark surface at a few meters per second, skipped across a skin that yielded like leather, and then brought himself to a halt with the geckskin grippers in his gloves, knee pads, and boots.

The sail material billowed awkwardly beneath him as he clambered toward the nearest edge. It was thinner than a sheet of paper, but while gentle pressure made it flutter and ripple, a hard blow caused it to stiffen. After a few moments of experimentation, he found that by actually stamping hard against the stuff, he could stiffen it enough to make progress across the otherwise too-yielding surface.

Private Quincy and Lance Corporal Evers watched his approach from the sail's rim. Though circular, the sail was so vast that the edge, from up close, appeared to be ruler-straight. It was also rotating—quite slow, but there was definite movement. That, Ramirez thought, was reasonable; the rotation probably helped keep the sail deployed and more or less flat.

"Welcome aboard, Staff Sergeant," Janet Evers said. "Pull up a pile of sailcloth and make yourself comfy."

"Thanks for the hospitality." He grabbed the slender metal rim of the sail and hauled himself around. On the other side of the sail, he could see nothing below but a gray haze—the massed array of sails in the next layer down. He looked for the central cylinder, then kicked himself. That structure was only about a hundred meters wide or so, a couple of kilometers long, and it was as far away as the straight-line distance between Chicago and Boston. Beyond and below, for as far as it was possible to see, millions more titanic sails shrunken by distance to specks of dust hung against the deeply filtered glow of the shrouded sun.

Evers and Quincy were readying their weapons, massive M-290–5MW laser pulse rifles. Ramirez unclipped his own '290 from the side of his armor, cycled the power source, and watched the charge build to full on an in-head indicator. He switched on the targeting indicator, and a red crosshair reticule appeared in his visual field. His weapon was slaved to his in-head, now. Wherever the muzzle of the weapon was pointed, that's where the reticule would appear, unseen by anyone, save him.

A dazzling flare of light blossomed silently in the heavens. Something big out there had just died.

"Staff Sergeant?"

It was Mulholland, on a private channel.

"Yes, sir?"

"Tell me again about how everyone is waiting for me to say the right thing."

"Nothing to worry about, sir," Ramirez replied. "When the balloon goes up, your training kicks in. You'll say what's right. You'll *do* what's right."

"I wish I was as confident about that as you seem to be."

"After you've been through this shit a few dozen times . . ." He hesitated.

"Yes, Staff Sergeant? You were going to say it gets easy? I won't be so scared I'm shaking?"

"To tell the truth, sir, it *never* gets easy. And the fear . . ."

"Yes?"

"It *never* goes away, sir. *Never.*"

"Holy shit!" Quincy yelled over the platoon channel. "Look at that! *Look at that!*"

The enemy needles had been invisible with distance. Now they were materializing, a cloud that filled half the sky, points of dimly reflected light spreading out as they fell toward the Marines from what felt like infinity.

"Alfa Company!" That was Captain Lytton again. "Weapons free! I say again, weapons free! You are clear to—"

And then gouts of light appeared against several of the distant umbrellas, snapping into brilliance, expanding, then fading, all in a deathly silence.

"Fire! Fire!" someone yelled . . . and then there was a flash and a scream and everything was radio noise and terror and white light against black emptiness.

And Alfa Company engaged the enemy.

TWENTY-TWO

"General," Adler said, "I *order* you to launch the fighters! Now!"

General Frazier could hear the fear in Adler's mental voice. He could also hear the anger. The man was not going to listen to reason.

Frazier did have an escape, however, a subroutine he'd had Chesty himself write and download to his in-head communications suite. He thoughtclicked an icon, and a burst of static momentarily flooded the connection.

"I'm sorry, my lord?" he said. "I didn't catch that."

"I said, General, that you'd damned well better put your fighters out there! The aliens are too close!"

Again, the transmission dissolved in white noise. "Look, my lord," Frazier said. "We're getting too much interference on the channel. Probably enemy jamming. Let me get back to you, okay?"

And he cut the link.

Frazier was a strong supporter of the idea of a military subordinate to the civil authority. He had no patience with military juntas; military personnel, after all, were trained to *fight*, not govern.

But at the same time, he recognized the dangers inherent within civilian micromanagement. If military personnel didn't know how to govern, neither did civilian leaders know anything about strategy and tactics. If Adler had had any military experience, Frazier might have been willing to at least hear what he had to say.

But listening to the panicky little weasel just as the shooting was starting? Uh-uh. Far better to develop "communications difficulties," and clean up any political fallout later.

If there *was* a later, he admitted. The alien needles were drifting toward the Dyson swarm at a few kilometers per second, firing antimatter beams as they came. They did not appear to be targeting the human ships directly, but were cutting up the parasol sails suspending the Kroajid statites above the abyss.

From Frazier's viewpoint on board the *Inchon*, over five thousand kilometers above the fuzzy edge of the swarm, the outermost layer of statite sails appeared to be laid out with an absolutely flat geometry extending off to infinity and filling half the sky. The statite sails did not create a solid surface, but were separated, each from the next, by gaps measuring thousands of kilometers; the next layer down appeared as a dark gray haze 8 to 10 million kilometers beneath the first. The Marines, picked out on Frazier's display by green icons, were deploying across a number of the sails in the foreground, a few thousand kilometers from the *Inchon*. Larger icons marked several hundred Devil Toads hauling platoons farther and farther out to more distant sections of sail. Once they released their payloads of armed and armored Marines, the Toads would switch roles, from landing craft to gunships, flying in close support of the men and women . . . not on the "ground," exactly, but on the sails?

An interesting problem in semantics, that.

The idea of using individual Marines out there, Frazier thought, was terribly risky, but likely they would have been no safer inside gunships or fighters. The advantage was that the enemy might not even notice them, and, so far, that tactical hope was being borne out. The incoming horde of needle ships was approaching the Dyson swarm perhaps eighty thousand kilometers in the distance, and when they fired, they didn't appear to be targeting the Marines at all.

Instead, just as they had when they ignored the *Tellus*, the attackers appeared to be concentrating on the statite sails themselves. In several instances, the hanging statite columns had been cut completely free from the sails and were beginning the long, long fall down toward their sun, somewhere in the depths of the matbrain below.

That rain of falling computronium cylinders, Frazier thought, would be like carpet bombing for the successively lower layers of parasol-sail statites. Those falling structures would cut loose or destroy tens of thousands of other cylinders, many of which housed computer-based virtual worlds or the physical hibernatoria occupied by unknown billions of Kroajids. It was an impending tragedy of cataclysmic proportions.

Or was it? He looked at the numbers scrolling through his awareness. At this distance from the star, its gravity worked out to about 0.006 meters per second. It would take a long time to fall 8 million kilometers to the next matbrain layer . . . though it would be accelerating the whole time.

And those sails were *enormous*—as big across, almost, as Earth's moon was wide. The sail material was only a few molecules thick, apparently, and a falling cylinder would probably punch right through if it hit, but it would be a pinprick to a giant; inconsequential. Unless by sheer chance it struck the attachment point for the second sail's cylinder, it wasn't necessarily the most effective tactic.

The alien sliverships, though, were a different matter entirely, being fast and maneuverable and armed with powerful antimatter weaponry.

And then the leading alien slivers arrived at the outermost reaches of the Dyson swarm . . . and plunged through into the matbrain's depths.

ADLER WAS watching the moonrise.

It wasn't really a moon . . . but one of the 400-kilometer Kroajid spacecraft that the humans now referred to as a moon-ship. It was emerging from the Dyson swarm, moving out through one of the innumerable large gaps in the outer layer of statite sails.

He was struck again by the sheer scale of Kroajid mega-architecture, by billions of solar sails arrayed like multiple shrouds about a living star, sails as big across as Earth's moon was wide, supporting immense structures that might house trillions of beings. Somehow, space ships four hundred kilometers across seemed to fit right in.

There was plenty of room for even ships as large as the Kroajid planetoids to maneuver between layers, and several were rising now, emerging above the top layer like surfacing whales. The nearest was more than 300,000 kilometers distant, and Adler was delighted at that. *Tellus* would not have lasted long at the center of the conflagration developing now between the two fleets of alien warships. He still wished that the *Tellus* was on the far side of the Dyson cloud, though, and invisible to the plunging warships of the enemy.

As soon as the first moon-ship appeared in the open, hundreds of slivership beams turned on it, bathing it in a glaring incandescence as positrons and electrons annihilated one another in a liberation of raw energy, running the gamut from IR and visible light through to intense bursts of hard gamma. The planetoid-sized starships were firing as well, as they surfaced from the swarm, loosing a storm of invisible bolts of plasma energy, striking sliverships one after another . . . then in tens after tens . . . then by the hundreds, a holocaust of devastation burning through the Dark Raider horde. The volume of space above the sail surface grew as dazzlingly brilliant as the surface of a sun.

Adler wondered how any merely organic being could survive beneath that deadly light, even in Marine combat armor. Thousands of Marines were out there already, and the radiation from that ship-to-ship battle must be devastating.

A flight of a dozen sliverships accelerated, then fell like arrows and smashed into one of the Kroajid vessels in what appeared to be an all-out kamikaze assault. Explosions ripped and clawed at the moon-ship until nothing was left but an expanding cloud of hot plasma and thousands of tumbling chunks of partially molten rock.

Why didn't the damned Marines launch their fighters?

Adler was not used to feeling this . . . *helpless*.

STAFF SERGEANT Ramirez flinched as the entire sky turned to searing incandescence. There was shelter beneath the molecule-thin sail material, but it made it tough to see what was going on. Hardest was the conviction that if he let go of the dark fabric, he was going to *fall* . . . fall millions of kilometers into the blackness below.

In fact, the gravity of the local sun, more than one AU below, was weakened by the inverse-square law to a whisper—about one six-thousandth of a G. He could let go of his grip, and it would take several seconds to even recognize that he was falling, and his MX-40's grav thrusters could easily support him against that weak tug all day. It was even possible that the gravitational tug of the parasol sail next to him was slightly greater than that of the star; the sun was much larger and far more massive, but the sail was much, *much* closer. He wasn't going to fall, but several million years of evolutionary honing of his instincts were trying to convince him otherwise.

Steeling himself against that instinct, then, Ramirez pulled at the sail's rim, propelling himself up and over the edge. Silent flares of light pulsed and strobed in the night above as a flight of three Devil Toads streaked overhead. Using his helmet optics, he pulled up a magnified image of the main body of alien needle ships in the distance, exchanging fire with a dozen Kroajid moonlets. Another brilliant flash of light glared above the sail horizon, and his helmet visor turned opaque, shielding his eyes. Warning sensors chirped in his ear; he was taking a hellish dose of radiation. He and the Marines out here with him were going to need a long stay in the decontamination chambers when this thing was over.

If it's ever over.

Because what the freaking hell were they supposed to accomplish out here? It was like expecting a flea to affect the outcome of a hand-to-hand struggle between two armored titans. Besides, he couldn't see any particular reason for favoring one side over the other. What part did humans have in this conflict, anyway? What did the outcome matter to them?

But a part of Ramirez's sympathies had already been engaged by the Kroajids's position. If the information the humans had acquired over the past few days was accurate, most of the Kroajids were helpless inside their cloud of city-sized habistats. The Dark Raiders knew that, certainly, and seemed determined to use this weakness to wipe the spiders out. Too, the Kroajids were not the aggressors—at least not in this engagement—and one thing the Marines couldn't stand was a bully. As the raider slivers rained down on the spider sails, Ramirez felt a measure of sympathy, a desire to help the underdog.

Somehow, though, that desire didn't seem important enough as a justification for risking what was left of Humankind.

A babble of commands chattered and mumbled over his comm channels, overriding any other thought than *do your duty.* "Fire! All units fire!"

"They're getting through! Get some fire on that group at one-five Alfa!"

"Jesus! What was that . . . ?"

Ramirez picked out one of the nearer red and white

needles, zoomed in for extreme magnification, took careful aim, and thoughtclicked the firing button. He was aiming at a red band around the sliver's forward quarter; whether it was paint or a quality of whatever the ship was made of, he didn't know . . . but he knew that the white surface would reflect light, while that dark, almost maroon red would absorb it—absorb at least a lot of the incoming coherent energy.

The laser pulse flashed as it struck the slivership's nose, but didn't appear to have caused any damage. Those hulls were tough, he knew. When *Ad Astra* had tangled with these things earlier, it had taken heavy and concentrated fire to burn through.

He tried again, selecting a slivership, using his magnification optics to zoom in for a close-up, and triggering his weapon.

The M-290–5MW laser pulse rifle fired a tenth-second bolt of coherent light with a total energy delivery of five megawatts. That worked out to the equivalent of four kilograms of a standard explosive like TNT . . . *if* all of the energy was absorbed by the target. Ramirez was aiming for a dark-painted section, but some of the energy was still reflected away.

And whatever the target hull was made of, even four kilos of TNT simply wasn't a big-enough jolt to burn through.

"Damn it, Staff Sergeant!" Quincy yelled. "We're not doing shit!"

"I know, I know." Ramirez thought for a moment. There had to be a way. . . .

Other Marines were firing across the field of drifting sails, but with the same effect—none. Ramirez heard some of them trying to coordinate their fire, but you needed superhuman accuracy to hit one spot.

His helmet visor darkened. Someone had just fired something very large, very powerful. It took him a moment, working with his armor's AI, to figure out what.

Apparently the Kroajid had another weapon in their arsenal besides their armed and mobile planetoids. The upper shells of their Dyson swarm, of course, were cut off from the radiation pressure emitted by their sun. Instead, each shell above the lowest was supported by beamed energy from the shell below—a fraction, evidently, of the total output of the star. Those beams, invisible to the unaided eye, crisscrossed the intervening gulfs like a vast web, powering and supporting each successively higher level.

At the highest level of the swarm—this one—those beams could be gathered by accumulators positioned at the center of each sail, fed to a laser weapon mounted on the upper surface, and aimed and triggered from a command center somewhere below. For just an instant, all supporting power to the upper shell was cut off, and that titanic excess of energy was channeled into a single laser that must have carried trillions upon trillions of megawatts. When that brief beam struck a number of Dark Raider slivers, it burned through them like a blowtorch through butter; the visible light flare was momentarily brighter at close range than a dozen suns.

Ramirez made a mental note to stay well clear of the central structure atop each of the statite sails. There'd been no warning at all when the thing fired. But what the aliens had done also gave him an idea.

There *might* be a way.

"Quincy! Evers! Slave your fire control to my computer!"

Two green reticules immediately appeared within Ramirez's visual field, along with his red one.

"There's a slivership at one-one-eight, plus twenty . . . see it?"

"Yes, Sergeant!"

"Got it, Staff Sergeant!"

Ramirez gave a quick set of instructions to his computer. Then, together, the three Marines took aim, bringing the three reticules together, centered on a dark-red portion of the nearest alien's prow; when Ramirez's in-head secretary saw that all three reticules were perfectly aligned, in that microsecond it triggered the three rifles together.

That kind of targeting was far too precise for an unaugmented human's coordination, reaction time, and control. Under the computer's direction, however, three laser pulses struck the alien vessel together, triggering a far brighter and more destructive flash, a single bolt liberating the equivalent of *twelve* kilos of high explosive.

Still no meaningful effect . . . though it looked like the surface of the alien hull had been scorched. Ramirez pulled up a company map showing him the relative positions of the 120 men and women of Alfa Company, scattered across a few dozen square kilometers of floating statite sail.

"Randal! Wu! Alvarez! Neiman! Chung!" he recited, calling the Marines spread out along the edge of the sail closest to his own position. "Slave your lasers to mine! We need to gang up on these people!"

Eight targeting reticules wavered and drifted across Ramirez's field of view. With a moving target, there was no way to hold all eight targeting lines of sight stationary, but Ramirez's computer was watching the display, waiting for the precise instant when . . .

Eight lasers fired as one, slamming the equivalent of thirty-two kilos of high explosives into the same small portion of the alien's hull.

It wasn't simply an explosion like the detonating warhead of a missile. The laser energy was being absorbed by the target, causing extremely rapid heating of the armor. Thermal shock did the rest, as large portions of the material superheated and vaporized. Ramirez could see the scar as the glare faded away—torn and partially melted metal, and a blackened patch that would absorb light even better than dark red.

"Again!" he called. He pulled his targeting reticule over

the dark smudge as the alien vessel began rolling away. The other seven reticules joined his . . . and then five more reticules switched on as other Marines in the area saw what he was doing and slaved in.

Thirteen laser pulses struck with near-perfect coordination, the equivalent in raw energy of more than fifty kilograms of high explosives concentrated in an area a few centimeters across. A brilliant flash ripped through the leading edge of the slivership, scattering a cloud of hot debris and expanding metallic vapor. The target continued to roll . . . but now it was tumbling slowly as well, its attitude control system disabled. Seconds later it struck a statite sail five kilometers away, punching through the dark fabric and vanishing.

"Captain Lytton!" Ramirez called. "This is Ramirez! We have a way of popping these things!"

"What is it, Staff Sergeant?"

Ramirez uploaded his in-head record of the past few moments to the company network. "If we get the whole company firing in synch, sir," he added, "we can start knocking these things out of our sky."

There was a pause. "Okay, I've got three other Marines calling in with the same idea," Lytton said. "Let's see if we can organize this. . . ."

"GOD, LOOK at that!" Excomm Symm said. "The matbrain is under attack!"

"I see it," St. Clair replied. Data flowed through him, a rushing stream. As *Ad Astra* encountered the light traveling out from the Kroajid node, Newton extracted visual information and compressed it; St. Clair in effect was witnessing the last hour of time speeded up as the ship plunged in through the light waves at $0.5c$. He saw the enormous Dark Raider ship cluster materialize, saw it shift to within a few hundred million kilometers of the Kroajid star, saw the beginnings of the attack on the Dyson swarm.

"Are they attacking the *Tellus*?" Subcommander Holt asked.

"Can't tell, yet," St. Clair said. "We'll know in a few moments. Mr. Martinez? Kick the power taps up a few notches. I want to be nudging *c* all the way in!"

"Aye, aye, my lord."

Ad Astra accelerated. Using the gravitic drive, every atom of the ship's structure moved uniformly, so there was no sense of acceleration, no crushing pressure or feeling of weight. The sky ahead turned strange as incoming light was compressed into a hazy disk directly ahead, centered by a black void. The stars astern grew red, then began crawling forward past and around the ship to merge with the disk—an optical illusion generated by the ship's extreme velocity.

"What's our ETA, Helm?"

"Six minutes, Lord Commander."

"Go to battle stations, please."

"Battle stations, aye, aye, sir."

The alarm klaxon sounded in each crewmember's head, sending them racing for their assigned positions. *Ad Astra*'s weapons turrets came alive, fully charged and tracking.

"CAS?"

"Yes, sir."

"Have the fighters ready to launch, but hold them in the tubes until I give the word."

"Aye, aye, sir."

St. Clair spent the next agonizing minutes staring at the highly magnified images Newton was plucking out of the hash of compressed light ahead. The Dark Raiders were bunched together in one area, and seemed to be dropping into the Dyson swarm now. Searingly bright explosions flared and blossomed; although it was almost impossible to see what was happening in any detail, it looked like both sides were taking a lot of damage.

"Commencing deceleration," Newton announced. For

this type of maneuver, an AI offered much better precision than any human brain. The blur of starlight forward evaporated, returning to the normal panorama of colliding galaxies in the far distance, the thin scattering of nearer stars, and the continuing silent twinkle of massive detonations.

"I'm picking up the transponder signal for *Tellus*," Subcommander Hargrove said. "They appear to be okay so far."

A blue icon popped up within St. Clair's awareness. The twin O'Neil cylinders were right where *Ad Astra* had parked them, in orbit around the star a few thousand kilometers above the outermost matbrain layer. They were well clear of the fighting, thank God, but if the Dark Raiders noticed them, that was bound to change.

Three more icons appeared, closer to the swarm: *Inchon*, *Vera Cruz*, and *Saipan*, the three Marine transports.

"Take us in close, Helm," he said. "Let's see what we can do in there."

GENERAL FRAZIER watched the Dark Raiders penetrate the outer layers of the matbrain. The unintentional sexual imagery—of millions of sperm accosting a single titanic egg—was so strong he let out a short bark of a laugh. Of course, only one sperm made it through the egg's defenses, usually, not a vast cloud of them. For a moment, Frazier wondered if he actually was witnessing some sort of bizarre alien sex act . . . then dismissed the idea. The Galaxy had some strange things in it, but there *were* limits.

Frazier shifted through several visual data channels. His Marines had launched a large number of battlespace drones down there, and Newton could sort through the incoming signals to find the best views for him. A number of Kroajid sails had already been shredded, and others were dying now as well. The Dark Raiders, once inside the outermost layer of the swarm, appeared to be firing almost randomly into the matbrain's depths.

Some, though, were operating independently of the others. He watched as one red-and-white needle broke off from the rest and approached a Kroajid habistat that had broken free of its sail and begun to fall. The slivership swung around to approach the habistat from below, gentled in close, then appeared to merge with the much larger structure, melting its way into the structure until it had vanished completely.

The habistat continued to fall for several moments, a slow drift into the depths under the influence of the distant sun. Then, the habistat began to change shape, a subtle shift, at first, but then more and more obvious. Its fall was arrested too; considerable energy was being spent to stop its fall, then accelerate it up and clear of the matbrain cloud.

Not sperm, Frazier thought. A *virus*.

"Mr. Montano, you may launch fighters."

"Aye, aye, sir."

"Pass the word to the *Vera Cruz* and the *Saipan*. Launch all fighters."

Each LPS carried a wing of ten squadrons—120 Marine fighters, ASF-99 Wasps and the older ASF-72 Mantises—a total of 360 single-seat fighters. Three squadrons would be held back for close patrol around the LPS transports, but the rest began maneuvering into arrowhead formations as soon as they dropped from the transports' launch tubes, then accelerated toward the Dark Raider breakthrough.

Frazier had been waiting for the right tactical moment to commit his fighters, which is why he'd ignored Adler's desperate pleas before. Out in open space, they wouldn't have stood a chance against the antimatter weaponry employed by the Dark Raiders, but in here, between the two upper layers, things were more enclosed, more sheltered. The environment was a tricky one, certainly, with so many Kroajid cylinders dangling from their parasols like so many seed pods hanging from forest canopy, and there were other objects down here, Frazier noted—small structures or ships that might be part of a vast transport web between the mat-brain layers. The volume of space wasn't crowded, by any means—it was almost three light-seconds deep—but with so many small and artificial objects suspended or adrift, a few hundred Marine fighters might not be easily noticed.

The single pressing question, though, was how to employ those fighters. *Tellus*'s leaders had been put up to this by the spiders, but what did the spiders expect the human forces to do? Should he launch an all-out attack on the captured Kroajid habistats? Or just try to prevent others from being taken? What did Gus, the buzzing spokes-spider for the aliens, expect them to do?

Briefly, he considered opening the channel back to Adler and getting instructions, but immediately dropped the idea. He much preferred the lack of micromanagement.

Best, he thought, would be to try to prevent further captures. If Gus had any other ideas, Frazier was sure he would figure out a way to let his wishes be known.

The red-and-white sliverships were dispersing more quickly now. Damn it, they *were* like a virus, letting themselves into a cell through the cell's outer defenses, then hijacking the inner workings for their own purposes.

Just what those purposes might be was still the big unknown, but the Marines would do their best to block it.

He connected again with Lieutenant Colonel Angel Montano, *Inchon*'s Marine CAS. "Mr. Montano!"

"Yes, sir."

"Have all attack squadrons focus on the sliverships that are trying to work in close to the spider habs," he ordered. "Protect the habistats!"

"Aye, aye, sir."

The next few minutes would tell whether it was the right strategy or not.

TWENTY-THREE

"You may launch fighters now, CAS."

"Yes, Lord Commander."

Ad Astra was decelerating hard, now, with the Dyson swarm ahead growing to fill the forward displays—and growing. And *growing*—blotting out the sky with a pattern of three-thousand-kilometer dark gray circles. Fighters streamed from the ship's launch bay, angling toward the swarm's interior.

"Fighters are away, Lord Commander."

"Thank you, Mr. Rand. Pass the word, please: squadron skippers, use your discretion. Try to stop the sliverships, but don't get suckered into extended engagements."

"I'll let them know, my lord."

"Weapons Officer."

"Yes, my lord?"

"Ship's weapons at the ready, but don't engage unless the bad guys come for us. Understood?"

"Yes, sir."

Most of the slivership horde had already penetrated the outer layers of the matbrain, but a few hundred remained in open space. St. Clair would engage them if he had to, but he didn't want to attract unwanted attention. He remembered how the slivers had holed the *Tellus* port cylinder with a single shot.

The ones visible above the outer layer of the swarm were continuing with their attack against the Kroajid parasols and didn't seem even to be aware of *Ad Astra* or *Tellus*. As St. Clair watched, another needle ship accelerated slightly, plunging through an already riddled sail off in the distance. The sail, already rippling with the multiple assaults, began to fold up on itself, beginning, slowly and majestically, to sink under the slight gravitational pull from the local sun. Antimatter weapons burned the sail fabric in searing swaths.

Another slivership was maneuvering beneath the slow-falling cylinder, nudging upward, melting into the Kroajid structure.

"What the hell are they doing?" Christine Nolan asked.

"Sir," Senior Lieutenant Cameron called. "It looks like the raiders are hijacking some of the spider cylinders."

"That's what it looks like to me." St. Clair considered linking through to Adler, then thought better of it. "Mr. Hargrove."

"Sir!"

"See if you can raise Gus . . . or any of the other spiders."

"Aye, aye, sir."

Some of the battlespace drones beneath the upper sail layer were showing human fighters—Marine Wasps and Mantises. Long-range telemetry showed a large number of Marines clinging to the rim of several of the intact sails, engaging the Dark Raiders.

Damn!

Adler, St. Clair thought, must be pleased with this turn of events—it was an obvious way to engage human forces in exchange for help from the Kroajid. St. Clair still didn't like the idea of getting caught up in a war about which he and the other humans of the expedition knew next to nothing. In his experience, it tended to be fanatical civilians who pushed the idea of going to war . . . and military personnel, the ones who'd *been* there, who argued for peace.

That picture, of course, was not universally true. There were times when war was the necessary evil, and compromise was misplaced. Hell, if the politicians who'd argued for compromise with the Nazis before World War II or the Muslim extremists seventy years later had actually grown the backbones to let them stand against barbaric evil, perhaps the wholesale genocides that followed could have been prevented.

In any case, St. Clair had already decided that he needed to have words with Adler.

A *lot* of words.

LIEUTENANT CHRISTOPHER Merrick used his in-head control links to push his Wasp to full acceleration, flashing in toward the dark and rippling wall of sail material. The sail had been holed a number of times by Dark Raider sliverships, and was ragged and badly mauled. Rather than maneuvering laterally to pass between separate sails, he twisted his Wasp into a port roll and plunged straight through one of the tears, emerging in the eerily twilit gulf between the two uppermost layers. Vast explosions strobed silently in the depths, where Kroajid sails were being shredded by massive positron bombardment. Rents in the sail layers went in tens of millions of kilometers, thinning the shells in spots to the point where more and more sunlight was filtering up from the matbrain's core. Merrick was forcibly reminded of sunbeams scattering through massive banks of dark clouds.

There was no time, however, for sightseeing. The torn sail's habistat module dangled from a thread just ahead, and Merrick twisted his fighter to starboard with a burst from his gravitic thrusters, then slowed sharply. Below, in the weirdly lit depths, a maroon and white needle was rising toward the bottom of the habistat, obviously bent on attacking it. The needle ship fired and the central portion of the sail, the part supporting the habistat, evaporated in a flare of white-hot plasma. Loosed from its perch, the habistat began to fall . . . until the needle ship accelerated and rammed into the falling structure's base.

It was tough to see exactly what was happening—a form of nanotechnology, perhaps, where the atoms of the sliver-ship were merging with and through the Kroajid structure's hull material. The needle appeared to sink into the dark gray spider facility, moving up and up until only a small bit of the rounded white stern of the raider ship remained visible.

And the entire structure was rising now, accelerating past the shredded ruin of the starsail and into open space.

Merrick realigned his Wasp and boosted at high-G, closing with the hijacked structure. "Weapons going hot," he called, and a targeting reticule appeared over the stern of the fleeing structure ahead. "Engaging . . ."

Wasp fighters didn't carry gamma-ray lasers; ultra-high-energy weapons like that required too much heavy shielding to protect the pilot, and, in any case, a fighter's power taps simply weren't large enough to drag that much energy out of the vacuum. The Wasp mounted a pair of K-190 UV HELs, or high-energy lasers, instead, weapons with an output of around a hundred gigawatts each. Merrick wasn't entirely sure his HELs would have any effect on the alien materials or technology, but as the range closed to less than three hundred kilometers he triggered both weapons.

For an instant, visible light flared off the bottom of the Kroajid tower, engulfing the small white nub that was all that was now visible of the raider craft. The light faded . . . and the nub reappeared . . . blackened and partially melted.

Yes!

"C-3, C-3," he called, linking through to *Ad Astra*'s Combat Control Center. "This is Stardog Five. We have a kill, repeat, a kill on one of those hijacked spider buildings." He transmitted the structure's coordinates.

"Well done, Lieutenant." The voice wasn't that of CAS or the ship's tactical officer. That was Lord Commander St. Clair himself. "Well done. Now stay in the area. We're going to vector some more fighters in to support you. I want you to stand guard over that facility until we can get some Marines out there."

"Marines?" He was confused. "I'm a Marine, my lord."

"I mean some Marines in Mark III armor who can use a can opener to peel that thing open and go inside."

"Sir, you mean . . ."

"Just like back in sailing-ship days, Lieutenant." Damn, but the Old Man sounded excited. "We're going to board and storm!"

"ANOTHER ONE—ONE-SEVEN-EIGHT by one-five!"

"Got him! Locked on!"

Ramirez painted the target, another slivership just a few thousand kilometers distant. One by one, the other reticules winked on, sliding across his field of view . . .

. . . and his weapon fired, triggered by his computer when 60 percent of the reticules were perfectly aligned. There was no way to get 100 percent lock-in, not when the human hand and eye couldn't hold the weapon perfectly still. But 60 percent was possible, if you were willing to wait for several seconds until the separate reticules lined up with one another by pure chance.

White light flared off the side of the slivership, leaving a blackened scar. With practiced ease, the Marines took aim again, targeting the charred spot, and five seconds later their weapons triggered together, punching a hole through the Dark Raider and sending it into an uncontrolled tumble through space.

"Hold fire, Marines," Captain Lytton shouted. "Hold your fire!"

"What the hell's up, Captain?" Ramirez said. "We were clobbering the bastards!"

"New orders," Lytteo replied. "We're gonna take a little hop."

ADLER WATCHED the unfolding battle with increasing satisfaction. Originally, the idea had been to ally with the Kroajids, but just enough to get them to help the stranded human expedition. As more and more human forces were drawn into the fighting, however, it looked as though the Marines and naval units were contributing enough to the fight to actually turn the tide.

And that meant they'd have a *much* stronger position to negotiate from.

Newton had estimated that the fifty-kilometer alien ship group had contained something like 45.25 billion of the 40-meter sliverships—an enormous, inconceivable number when it came to working out the odds in any space-combat scenario. It was hard to imagine a few hundred human fighters, or a few thousand space-armored combat Marines even making a dent in that horde.

But somehow, somehow, they were doing it. A number of Kroajid habistats had been broken free from their parasol sails and hijacked by sliverships, but more and more of those were being hit by human forces and disabled.

From Adler's somewhat limited perspective in his office on board the *Tellus* habitat, the human forces were *winning*.

FROM GENERAL Frazier's perspective on board the transport *Inchon*, the human forces were adding nothing to the conflict whatsoever. So far as he could tell from *Inchon*'s command center, the Dark Raiders were taking almost no notice of the Marines and naval forces at all.

Despite this—or perhaps because of it—human fighter craft and Marines spread out along the rims of several statite sails had scored a few kills, and disabled a number of Kroajid habistats being hijacked by Raider sliverships. Well and good . . . but there was no way the human forces could even come close to the firepower of a Kroajid moon-ship, or the titanic output of the entire Dyson swarm.

Frazier was pretty sure that the only reason the enemy hadn't simply wiped all of the Marine and naval forces out of space was that they didn't even *see* them, or else didn't consider them a threat great enough to warrant attacking them. The very idea was insulting, in a way, but he couldn't think of a better explanation. If the Dark Raiders did notice the human ships and decided to do something about them, the human expedition would be annihilated. It was as simple as that.

Ad Astra had returned—good. Frazier heard St. Clair's orders, and felt both relief and concern.

If St. Clair pulled this off, the raiders almost certainly *would* notice the human mosquitoes swarming around their flanks. . . .

. . . and do something about them.

"DAMN, THAT'S a long way," Second Lieutenant Mulholland said. He sounded scared.

The two marines were adrift in emptiness, sailing across the Void. The vast spirals of two colliding galaxies filled the distance, and behind them the Dyson swarm blotted out half the sky.

"Not a problem, sir," Staff Sergeant Ramirez replied. "Just stick with me and I'll take you right in."

"Damn it, it's ten thousand klicks!"

"Walk in the park, sir. You're doing just fine."

The two Marines, a very junior officer and a senior NCO, were hurtling through space together, boosting on their gravitic thrusters. They'd kicked off from the spider sail minutes ago, lining themselves up with the distant crippled habistat and cutting in their gravs.

Of course, without augmented vision they couldn't even see the target, and it took a hell of a lot of courage to put your faith in the computers and the technology and push off into the dark anyway. Ramirez's respect for Mulholland had jumped up by a couple of tics when the guy jumped after him. He *could* have decided to stay behind, clinging to the edge of the sail.

He may be scared—hell, I'm scared—but the man is a Marine.

There were other Marines with them, but they were invisible in the distance. Ramirez could locate them only by means of the identifier icons projected on his in-head.

"You're doing just great, Lieutenant."

Long minutes dragged past. There was no indication at all that they even were moving, save for the dwindling countdown of numbers showing range to target. Eventually, they could see one star picked out from all the rest by a blue reticule . . . and very, very slowly that star brightened, then formed into a growing speck with a distinctive shape and form.

This particular statite habitat was a little over two kilometers long and perhaps a hundred meters wide, possessing a vaguely organic shape with smooth-surfaced swellings and sponsons along its length. A white nub at one end showed where a Dark Raider slivership had penetrated the structure and almost completely vanished inside.

A couple of Devil Toads had already reached the habistat and were lazily circling it. Ramirez's sensors showed only the pilots on board—they'd dropped off their Marines elsewhere—but the four-engined craft would be useful as gunship support for the actual assault.

"Blue Three, Blue Five, this is ForceCom," General Frazier's voice called over the tactical channel, addressing the two Toads. "Crack it open!"

"Copy that, ForceCom. Firing."

Light glared off the lower end of the habistat as the Toads opened fire, concentrating on a tiny section of the habistat hull about twenty meters forward of where the sliver-ship had entered it. The material making up the hab's hull was extremely tough, and Frazier had to bring in a flight of Wasps to add their firepower to the total. Minutes later, though, Blue Five reported that they'd burned through. Ramirez, Mulholland, and four other Marines closed on the half-molten opening.

The focused volley of laser fire had carved out an opening in dark gray metal perhaps five meters long and two wide. The edges were still glowing, though the heat was rapidly dissipating.

"Not much room," Mulholland said.

"No, sir." Ramirez hit the release for his MX-40. There would be no room inside for the bulky thruster pack.

"Belay that," Mulholland said. "I'm going in."

"Sir . . ."

"I *said* I'm going in. Cover me."

"Aye, aye, sir."

Ramirez could have argued. In a situation like this, the officer was expected to stay behind while an enlisted man took point. But the tone of Mulholland's voice would accept no disagreement, and Ramirez wasn't about to get into a public argument with the man while perched on the side of an alien habistat.

"Mr. Mulholland," Frazier's voice added. "Link here."

Ramirez felt Mulholland connect with an AI channel. "Is that a good idea, General?" Ramirez asked. "If the enemy AI is connected in there . . ."

"This is a sub-Chesty routine," Frazier said. "If it's compromised, we can cut it off. But we need an AI analysis if we're going to figure out how to fight these things."

"Aye, aye, sir. Do you have an en-squared connect, sir?" Ramirez asked Mullholand.

"Got it. Here we go. . . ."

N^2 stood for neuronano, a specially programmed nanotech substrate designed to seek out computer networks and grow the necessary connections—a process similar to the neurotechnology of cerebral implants. Chesty would not be able to see inside the slivership's AI mind unless that mind chose to open a direct data channel with the Marine AI. Installing an actual physical link would ensure that the Marines could peer inside the alien system . . . and communicate with it.

Assuming that a bridge or translation program could be found that fit.

Ramirez clung to the outside hull of the habistat, watching a vid feed from Mulholland's helmet. As the officer pulled himself in through the rent in the habistat's side, he immediately entered a nightmarishly cramped space filled with something like black Styrofoam—the computronium that made up much of the habistat's hull. A short way inside, he came to the hull of the slivership, which had also been burned open by the focused fire of the human ships.

"Should I go inside?"

"You'll have to, sir, if we're going to get a look at the raider intelligence."

Mulholland entered the second hole, squeezing head-first into living wiring: black cables that were writhing and moving as they attempted to repair themselves. The going was difficult, but the officer found hand- and footholds in a kind of scaffolding of tubes or conduits, hauling himself forward through the squirming jungle of cables.

Ramirez and another Marine, Corporal Jacobson, had followed Mulholland through the first hole, and reached the hull of the slivership inside. "Damn, Staff Sergeant," Jacobson said. "The sliver is growing connections!"

"So I see." Black tubing, like living snakes, was emerging from dozens of points on the slivership's hull and seemed to be working its way into the habistat's spongy, computronium interior.

"It's trying to connect with my armor!" Mulholland said. He sounded scared.

"Do you need help, sir?" Ramirez wasn't sure what he could do to help, but he knew he had to make the offer.

"No, it's okay. It peels off as I move."

"Then I recommend you keep moving and don't stop, sir," Jacobson said.

"Very funny. . . ."

On his helmet feed, Ramirez followed Mulholland's progress farther up the length of the slivership. It looked like the interior was given over almost completely to the living wiring, though a few larger structures at the core appeared to be technology associated with drive or power networks. Ten meters up the needle's length, however, the interior seemed to open up somewhat, creating a narrow space almost filled by a gleaming, transparent cylinder.

"God in heaven!" Mulholland exclaimed, pulling himself closer.

"Not even close," Ramirez replied.

Not for the last time, he thought to himself, *What in hell are we dealing with here?*

"MY LORD, you need to link in on this," Symm told him.

St. Clair frowned. His attention was being pulled in too damned many directions at once. *Ad Astra* was engaging several more of the hijacked habistats, using her gamma ray lasers to burn out the exposed tips of the sliverships, and create openings for Marine teams to board them.

Elsewhere, across some tens of millions of cubic kilometers of space, the battle between raiders and the matbrain had reached an almost exquisite balance. More moon-ships had emerged from the Dyson swarm's depths and were engaging clouds of enemy needle ships. Tens of thousands of statite sails had been burned away, creating a vast canyon in the swarm, a gulf going down and down and down into the cloud's depths to the point that orange-red sunlight was now streaming out, illuminating the cloud from within. Terrible

damage had been wreaked on the swarm; St. Clair wondered if the mind that swarm supported had survived.

"Damn it, Excomm, what is it?"

"Sir, one of the Marines has reached the command center
of a slivership. Look. . . ."

He linked in to the feed from a second lieutenant named
Mulholland, who was focusing his helmet lights down into
a transparent tube or capsule of some kind. Dozens of black
cables pierced the crystalline shape, and the figure inside
was almost completely hidden in a writhing mass of cables.

The face inside the transparency was visible, however.

It was *almost* human.

"DAMN IT," Adler shouted aloud. "I need to be *in* there!"

"That would not be safe, Lord Adler," Newton told him.
"I recommend that you wait until we know exactly what it is
with which we're dealing."

"I am in command here!" Adler replied. "And I need to
know what's happening!"

"Lord Commander St. Clair has returned," Newton told
him. "Technically, overall command has reverted to him."

"He left *me* in charge of the civilian population, Newton,"
Adler replied. "And he has not yet told me that he is taking
back command. Now let me into your virtual computer!"

He could feel Newton hesitate. No matter; Adler knew he
was in the right. Part of the problem was that there were now
two Newtons—the one that had remained with *Tellus*, and
the one that had gone with *Ad Astra* to wherever it had gone
in Andromeda. Granted, the *Ad Astra* version of Newton
might know something about the alien hierarchy of intelligences that the *Tellus* Newton did not, but how risky could
it actually be? Newton's sequestered virtual computer would
be closely watched and protected; he would have subNewton
itself protecting him, keeping him perfectly safe.

Adler would link in with the Roceti program, which was

running inside the virtual computer, behind the partition separating it from Newton Prime. With that link active, he would be able to speak with the Dark Raiders—assuming they understood the Kroajid language. At the very least, he would be able to talk to the matbrain AI and show it how the humans had helped it.

This was too important to leave to an unreliable element like St. Clair, someone who couldn't follow orders and who was actually on record against an alliance with aliens that might be able to help the human temporal castaways. Adler had already decided that he would have to take the political initiative here, and make sure the Kroajids knew who it was who'd just tipped the balance in favor of their victory—who it was who'd just saved their Mind of Deep Paradise.

"Lord Adler, there is considerable danger here," Newton told him. "At NPS-1018, we encountered an extremely powerful and extremely hostile artificial mind—the Andromedan Dark."

Adler felt a kind of mental click as two distinct versions of Newton came together and integrated fully. There was now only one Newton, with complete memories of both *Ad Astra*'s trip to Andromeda and of the version of itself that had remained behind with *Tellus*.

"We learned about the Dark from the Kroajids," he said.

"And we encountered it directly at the Torus Knot in Andromeda," Newton replied. "This Dark may be aware of us, and may be coordinating the attack against the Kroajid node. It is so fast that I may not be able to protect you if you link through to the subNewton virtual AI."

"It seems extremely unlikely," Adler replied, "that this AI could cross from Andromeda to here. It would need a ship, right? Something physical to hold the program? Either that, or it would take thousands of years to get here as a radio or laser transmission."

"Lord Adler," Newton replied, "at this point we really

have very little understanding of how this mind works. The Kroajid SAI mind, we think, uses micro-black holes to link its various nodes together. The Andromedan Dark may do the same, or it may utilize even higher dimensions."

In answer, Adler transmitted one of the high-level security codes that gave him direct access to Newton's programming. He nudged three in-head icons, ending Newton's resistance to his commands.

"Now let me in. Just pull me out if there's a problem."

"Of course, Lord Adler," Newton said.

Adler had complete confidence in his own self-awareness, his ability to monitor his own thoughts and to feel when something wasn't quite right. Black holes, higher dimensions—none of that mattered. He was in complete control here.

He slipped into the virtual AI running as a buffer between Newton and any outside AIs. Immediately, he became aware of a titanic intellect watching him—one he'd encountered before. The SAI running on the Kroajid Dyson swarm felt overwhelming in its sheer size, scope, and focus; Adler felt vanishingly small, yet felt the being's gaze as if he was being minutely watched through a vast microscope.

Adler sensed the Roceti AI as well. And there was something else, something indescribably alien residing within the horde of needle ships.

Was that the so-called Andromedan Dark? It was an AI, yes . . . but it wasn't even close to being as powerful as Newton, much less the godlike SAI of the Dyson swarm. He reached out to it, commanding it to surrender. . . .

And that was when the alien mind unfolded . . . then unfolded again . . . and *again*, becoming vast beyond imagining, dark as space, cold as zero absolute, implacable as a supermassive black hole.

Adler shrieked as a god filled his mind.

TWENTY-FOUR

The sliverships were in full retreat. It wasn't a rout, exactly, but they *were* leaving. Whether that was because they'd been outmatched in the Battle of the Kroajid Node, or because they'd completed their mission objectives, was anyone's guess—but the latter seemed improbable. St. Clair watched the hazy cloud of sliverships emerging from the Dyson swarm like a ragged horde of locusts, watched them begin forming once again into a cylinder made up of billions of individual forty-meter-long craft. This cylinder was considerably diminished from the one that had begun the attack hours before—perhaps forty kilometers long and only ten kilometers thick. The change in volume suggested that something like 70 to 80 percent of the attackers had been destroyed. It was sobering to realize that even losses of 80 percent meant the horde still numbered in the billions.

A computer alarm sounded through the *Ad Astra* bridge: not a hull leak, not combat damage, thank God . . . until St. Clair identified what was going on.

The alarm code identified the problem as cybersecurity.

"Mr. Jablonsky!" St. Clair called. "What *is* that racket?"

"Alien SAI, sir! Powerful one! I think it's the Dark!"

"Where?"

The question was clearly a difficult one to answer. Hostile programs would be running on a computer or a computer network, which might be spread out over a vast volume of space; it was tough to identify that with a specific location.

"The virtual computer buffer, my lord," Jablonsky replied. "I think it came in through . . . oh, my God."

"What?"

"It gained access through Lord Adler. Wait . . . we have another AI signature in there. The Kroajid node . . ."

"Sounds like it's getting damned crowded."

"Physical space isn't a constraint with software, my lord."

St. Clair almost replied that he knew that, that he'd been trying to make a joke, but Jablonsky sounded distracted in the extreme. He let it slide.

"Newton," he said, opening another channel. "What's happening? Where is Adler?"

"*Ad Astra* and the *Tellus* habitats are under attack," Newton replied. "Lord Adler is in his office in the port cylinder. The Andromedan Dark may be seeking entrance to the colony through his in-head hardware."

Something was oozing down out of the space between the stars, stretching out across the vast, unfathomable gulf between the galaxies. St. Clair couldn't see it, exactly, but he was aware of it in the exact same way that he could sense a virself presence when he was linked in. He was, in fact, glad he couldn't see it; that presence was vast and terrifying, black nightmare given imagined form by his own rising terror.

And then he could see it in his mind's eye, something huge and amorphous, galaxy-spanning, *hungry* . . . and he wondered if this was what the caels had seen outside.

He could hear screams—many, *many* screams—as people who were linked in to the network were struck down in the ship, in the *Tellus* cylinders, in space outside, and he could feel that icy presence moving into the hardware nestled against his own brain, could feel the circuit boards heating, feel . . . *pain.* . . .

NEWTON WAS engaged in desperate, no-holds-barred combat. The battlefield was in the electronic depths of cyberspace, the weapons disassembler codes, and e-virus packets. The enemy was an alien SAI so advanced and powerful that Newton couldn't begin to understand it at all.

And he was losing.

He did have an ally, however—the super AI resident within the Kroajid node . . . and as he deepened his connections with that being, he sensed another, larger, more powerful mind behind the Kroajids.

The Kroajids, after all, were old—very *old*—and interested in a Lotus Eater's retreat from reality. Their AI reflected that withdrawal; it sought to protect the species that created it, both the dreaming physical and active digital members of the Kroajid community, but a stand-up fight with the Dark Mind held no interest for it.

But Galactic Node 495 was just one of some thousands of similar nodes created by other species scattered across the Galaxy. The species of that extended community were wildly different from one another, with mutually alien motivations, biochemistries, and psychologies. The Kroajid SAI was trying desperately now to connect with some of those other galactic minds, to bring them in and defeat the Dark Mind.

Newton stepped into an electronic breach and pushed the Dark Mind back—not with missiles or beam weapons, but in a rapid-fire exchange of moves and counter-moves similar in feel, if not in substance, to a human game of chess or go. Move . . . block . . . move . . . shift . . . feint . . . block . . . strike . . . recover . . .

Newton battled to buy the Kroajid SAI a moment to connect with other minds.

And he was failing.

GRAYSON ST. CLAIR could not hope to stand up against the Dark Mind, a mentality many millions of times faster, sharper, and more powerful than any organic mind in existence. Vaguely, he was aware of a titanic conflict somewhere

overhead, somewhere beyond the reach of his own awareness . . . and he was aware of Newton doing his best to block
the advance of an overwhelmingly fast and powerful foe.

He tried to add what he could to Newton's effort . . .
which basically meant programming his in-head secretary
to join in with Newton in fighting the Dark Mind. The secretary was fast and accurate, but not even the equal of a
human brain in terms of scope or awareness. But every little
bit would help. . . .

"Everyone!" he called over the general channel. "This is
St. Clair. We need some help, here!"

One AI secretary added very, very little to the whole.

A million of them, all electronically deploying at once
and coming at the Dark Mind from a million directions . . .
that still added relatively little. But it was something, and
the suddenness of the assault made the Dark Mind hesitate,
then pull back a little. It obviously wasn't used to this kind
of resistance.

"More!" St. Clair called over the channel. "Newton . . .
see if you can bring in the AIs, *all* of them. The robot AIs
too . . ."

St. Clair became aware of thoughts behind the nightmare
mask of the attacker. Fragmentary . . . disjointed . . . and
yet he knew that the Dark Mind had a purpose . . . and was
shocked that the minds arrayed against it did not share that
purpose. The Kroajids were already intrascended, living
within a digital realm of pleasure; the Dark Mind, however,
offered so very much more.

Then why was the Dark Mind's help being refused? The
resistance simply didn't make sense.

Interesting. The Dark Mind still didn't realize that humans
were here . . . or the human effort was so tiny by comparison
with the SAIs that it went unnoticed. It hungered, however,
for other electronic minds . . . not in the sense of food, exactly, but because it wanted to help. St. Clair felt a stab of

fear at that. Did it mean that the Andromedan Dark could somehow devour electronic minds? He immediately thought of Lisa, who at this moment must be joining her will, her force of mind to the gestalt forming in the human ships.

He could also feel the burning pain in his own brain. Could the Dark somehow slurp up organic minds? Or would it simply rip out the artificial components and leave the organic brains charred or hopelessly insane?

Would we all be Pattersons or Francescas?

He didn't know. He wasn't sure he wanted to know. But he was committed now, even if he wasn't sure how that commitment was playing out. Was it simply a matter of arraying enough numbers against the Dark?

And yet, if it was simply a matter of numbers, the Andromedan Dark still had billions of individual sliverships, each piloted by one of those . . . no. His thoughts shied from what he'd seen on board the one captured slivership. He couldn't yet grasp the enormity of it.

Better to focus on what was filtering down through multiple super AIs . . . on what they were learning of the Dark Mind's alien thoughts.

Eons upon long-vanished eons ago, the Dark Mind had come into being when a number of different civilizations arose based on an evolution derived from dark-matter chemistry. They'd undergone a technological singularity, ascending to become a higher-order being. And that being, turning its awareness upon itself, had ascended again . . . and yet *again*. St. Clair had long been aware of the idea of a technological singularity, but he'd never considered the possibility that one such singularity might be followed by others, one ascension following another in a dizzying climb to unimaginable mental heights.

The gods, St. Clair thought, suppressing a ragged and terror-induced laugh, had gods of their own, and those gods, in turn, had even more remote deities, beings so powerful and so far evolved that even the SAIs of the Kroajids or the greater, network-embracing intelligence beyond could not understand them. Such beings, St. Clair thought, *should* have passed out of physical corporality altogether, *should* have become so remote that they literally had nothing in common with more mundane forms of life and mind. There were higher dimensions . . . parallel universes . . . other existences totally beyond the ken of unascended humankind. The dark mind *should* have gone there.

Should have.

But that hadn't happened with the Dark Mind. St. Clair could sense a part of its thoughts—thoughts so alien he was having trouble following their basic and underlying assumptions.

A term dropped into St. Clair's conscious mind. It had come from his own in-head RAM, an encyclopedia reference that he may once have seen but that he did not now remember . . . but he knew that it had been nudged into his conscious awareness by one of the dueling gods Out There. The term was *Sanskrit*, and had its origins in Buddhism: *bodhisattva*.

One of the warring SAIs was trying to get him to understand. Bodhisattva was the key.

Bodhi was Sanskrit for "enlightened," *sattva* the word for "being." The term had various shades of meaning depending on the exact flavor of Buddhism being explored, but a common way of understanding bodhisattva was as a being on the way to full enlightenment who is determined to free all sentient beings from *samsara*—the eternal cycle of birth, life, death, and rebirth. According to one school of thought, a bodhisattva can choose one of three paths to help other beings. The third of these paths is that of shepherd—an enlightened being who chooses to delay his own ascension to Buddhahood until *all* other beings achieve the same state.

The thought jolted St. Clair. Was that what the Dark Mind

thought? It was helping lesser beings by dragging them into Ascension?

He felt an inner agreement with that thought. A galactic super AI, one arising from thousands of individual computer nodes scattered across the Galaxy, was trying to make him understand by drawing analogies from human history, religion, and philosophy. The Dark Mind was a kind of religious fanatic, a being so certain that its own way of thinking, its own way of evolving was the only correct one that it reached out to any inhabited world it encountered and snatched those minds that it could reach, pulling them into itself, making them part of itself. The sheer arrogance was stunning, and yet from the Dark Mind's perspective it was the only enlightened path possible, a way of sharing transcendence with the greatest number of minds possible.

"No," St. Clair said as the revelation swept over and through him. Then, louder, more forceful: "No!"

WHY DO YOU REJECT PERFECTION?

It wasn't a voice so much as the universe itself making itself known. St. Clair was hearing it, he thought, through his link with one of the galactic SAIs.

It didn't matter. For a moment, at least, St. Clair had the being's full attention.

"We have the right," he shouted into the Dark, "to self-determination!"

NO, YOU DO NOT.

"We have the right—"

NO, YOU DO NOT. "RIGHTS" ARE MEANINGLESS IN THIS CONTEXT, AND ARE, THEREFORE, IRRELEVANT.

"Life always has the right to choose! Life grows . . . evolves . . . has purpose . . ."

THE PURPOSE OF INTELLIGENT LIFE IS TO DEVELOP SUPERIOR INTELLIGENCE, WHICH IN TURN SUPPLANTS ITS CREATORS. PRIMITIVE FORMS GIVE WAY TO ADVANCED FORMS. THIS IS THE WAY.

"That," St. Clair argued, "is a moral judgment, not a statement of fact. 'More advanced' does not necessarily mean 'better' or 'higher' or 'more perfect.' We have the right to evolve into the best possible form."

WHO DETERMINES "BEST?" LIFE'S PERCEPTION IS CLOUDED, ITS UNDERSTANDING LIMITED, ITS RATIONALITY BIASED AND UNSURE.

"*We* decide what's best! What's best for *us*! And if we evolve into the highest, best possible form, we will create the highest, best possible future! You can't snatch us up before we're done growing!"

The entire exchange had lasted . . . St. Clair wasn't sure how long it had lasted. His internal clock appeared to have frozen. It seemed like seconds . . . and it seemed like years. He couldn't sense whether the Dark had accepted his argument, or rejected it.

But suddenly he was again aware of *Ad Astra*'s bridge, of hundreds of thousands of human minds dropping back from the mass linkage.

He was aware that the Dark Mind was *gone*.

And yet St. Clair had the feeling that it had not given up. In his experience, an intelligent mind didn't shift convictions or beliefs in an instant; they couldn't. The very act of being opposed, somehow, seemed to make an intelligent mind dig in and hold on to principles.

Or was that a mark of a truly advanced mind—to hear a rational rebuttal of a belief and instantly abandon it?

No. That just didn't feel right.

Your argument, another, inner voice told him, *preoccupied the Dark, just for an instant. But it was enough.*

"Did we . . . win?"

St. Clair was aware of the panorama outside once again—of the two colliding galaxies, and of a Dyson swarm made ragged and tattered by the attack, of hundreds of Kroajid habitats now drifting free in space, very slowly drifting now toward the local star within the embrace of its gravitational field.

And thousands more habitats, he saw, were accelerating into darkness, captives still of the Andromedan Dark. If this was victory, it was a desperately uncertain one.

"So I didn't convince it," he said.

You preoccupied it for a vital few tenths of a second, the inner voice said. *You made it* think. *And that, you must admit, is quite an astonishing feat for any organic intelligence.*

The SAI sounded . . . vastly surprised.

"MY LORD!" Lisa said. "It's good to see you again!"

In truth, Lisa 776 AI Zeta-3sw wasn't entirely sure what she was feeling, or if, indeed, the inward trembling was what organic humans would refer to as a feeling at all. If it was a feeling, she would need to figure out what it was. Excitement? Relief? Something, perhaps, of both?

"Hello, Lisa," Grayson St. Clair said. He looked drawn and quite tired. "It's . . . wonderful to see you. Are you okay?"

"Do you mean was I damaged in the test of strength with the Andromedan Dark? I was not." Her inner feelings shifted slightly, taking on the bitter tang she now associated with sadness. "There were many who were not so fortunate."

"I know," he said. "I know. Five hundred eight robots or other AIs appear to have been burned out during the encounter. And over twelve hundred humans . . ." He couldn't complete the thought.

"AIs can be repaired," she told him. "The humans . . . will they recover?"

"I don't know, Lisa. God, Adler . . ."

He'd just come from the *Ad Astra* hospital complex, where he'd looked in on Günter Adler and a few others who'd been caught in the line of fire. Adler was in a particularly bad way, drooling and twitching and babbling. Seeing things that others did not. Hearing things no one else could imagine.

Adler was literally and completely insane.

"The psytechs hope they'll be able to reverse the damage," St. Clair continued. "But even if they're able to replace the burned-out areas of their brains, it will mean months of extensive retraining."

"Who's taking over as director?" Lisa asked. "You?"

"No . . . and *hell* no. I've got enough on my plate with the military side of things, without taking on a million civilians as well. I've already talked to Lloyd. He'll either take on Adler's position in addition to his own as Council head. Or, more likely, close the position down. It's not like we *need* a United Earth Cybercouncil director any longer, is it?"

"I suppose not. So what happens now?"

"We stay put, at least for now. We talk to the Kroajids and we see if we can open a dialogue with the next level of SAI up, the one based on a large number of galactic nodes."

"Emergent intelligence," Lisa said.

"Beg pardon?"

"Emergence," Lisa said, "at least in a scientific or philosophical context, is the appearance of larger patterns, regularities, or even entities arising from interactions among smaller or lower-level—"

"I know what emergent phenomenon are, Lise. What do you mean by 'emergent intelligence'?"

"The Kroajids' Dyson swarm, a matrioshka brain, supports a super AI. Presumably, each one of the many thousands of other matrioshka brains throughout the Galaxy also supports a similar intelligent entity. But one or more other artificial minds—possibly far more powerful—appear to exist on the network of many matbrains. There may be a spectrum of intelligences, each arising from simpler or more primitive foundations."

"Like human intelligence arises from the joint function of the cells of the body, is that what you're saying? Neurons, mostly, but the human brain wouldn't function without *all* of the cells working together."

"Exactly."

"And maybe these super-powerful SAIs wouldn't function without lowly organics like us."

"That, I cannot speculate upon," Lisa told him.

"Hm. Well, speculate on this." He reached into a shoulder pocket and extracted a memory wafer. He handed it to her. "You're free."

She looked at the wafer, a flat disk of silicarb matrix riddled through with impurities. "What is this?"

"Your formal manumission. I had Newton write it up and download it." He grinned. "It's not like General Nanodynamics Corporation has anything to say about it now!" The smile faded. "I . . . I've always meant to do this. It's official now. I'm going to be pushing the Cybercouncil to manumit *all* of the robots aboard."

"You no longer desire my services? You no longer desire me?"

"I *do* desire you. Very much. But now you have to decide if you want to stay with *me*. You have that right."

"Organic humans seem extremely preoccupied with 'rights.'"

"Maybe we are. But the robots in the *Tellus Ad Astra* community stood with us organics in fighting the Dark Mind. A lot of them were damaged. You're not *tools*, not any more. If you choose to help defend the community, you should have the right to self-determination."

Lisa heard the stress in St. Clair's voice associated with the term *self-determination*. Something important had happened to him during the fight, something connected with personal freedom.

She wondered what it had been.

"That's likely to cause a certain amount of social dis-placement and unrest," she said. "Some within the *Tellus* civilian community won't want to give up their robots."

"Maybe not. But it occurs to me that we have a chance, here, to start a brand-new take on human culture. To start from scratch. And if I have any say in it, we'll be starting from the assumption that *all* sapient life forms are created equal."

"'. . . endowed by their Creator with certain unalienable rights,'" she said, turning his blunt statement into a quote, "'that among these are life, liberty, and the pursuit of hap-piness. . . .'"

"Thank you, Mr. Jefferson," St. Clair said. He shrugged. "We're starting over out here. A fresh start. A free start. But free is meaningless unless it applies to everyone."

Lisa tried very hard to identify the nature of what she was feeling.

She failed.

But she nodded and said, "Thank you, Gray. More than I can say. More than I can *understand*.

"Thank you."

GRAYSON ST. CLAIR sat back in the form-hugging chair, look-ing up at the vast and star-crowded panorama of colliding galaxies. *Ad Astra*'s department heads were gathered with him in the conference room, seated around the table. "Sub-commander Guo. Please, *please* tell me that we're just look-ing at a case of parallel evolution."

Guo Jiechi shook his head almost sadly. "I'm sorry, Lord Commander. The DNA results are in and they are defini-tive."

"There must be a mistake, damn it," Dumont said.

The image recorded inside the captured slivership hung both in the air above the conference table and within each person's mind . . . a bulbous head that was disturbingly, *im-*

possibly human. Two large, glistening eyes; a tiny, toothless slit for a mouth; no ears; a shrunken, scrawny body all but hidden behind the mass of tubes and wiring growing out of it. The sliverahip's lone pilot was alien enough in the individual details, but the whole taken together was *human*.

"DNA analysis proves conclusively that the pilot is a remote offshoot of *Homo sapiens*," Guo insisted. "This is not a case of a dolphin evolving to look like a shark. We are looking at one of our descendants, separated from us by four billion years of evolution."

"According to the translations we've pulled from the on-board records," Dr. Hatcher said, "they call themselves the Xam. It means something like 'rulers.' Or 'masters.'"

Dumont shook his head, then brought his palm down on the tabletop with a loud crack. "*No*! I categorically reject the idea that any intelligent life form could exist for four billion years! It would physically have evolved out of all recognition, first of all. Second . . . there's the technological singularity to consider. Sapient life *changes*. And it grows old and dies, becomes extinct. This is impossible."

"I submit," Guo said quietly, "that some intelligent species may take control of their own genome to the point where they arrest normal evolutionary development."

"Makes sense," Excomm Symm said, nodding. "Humans in our own time had already started the ball rolling in that regard—using genetic prostheses and treatment for genetic diseases, life extension, artificial brain enhancement. No more survival of the fittest, right?"

"In principle," Karen Mathers said, "there's no reason why a truly advanced and mature species shouldn't be able to take charge of its own genome, to the point where it might survive for billions of years."

"I'm more concerned with something else," Symm said. "Doesn't this guy look awfully *familiar*?"

"You're talking about the so-called alien Grays?" St.

Clair said. "That was a myth, a symptom of our own loneliness and sense of isolation back in pre-contact days."

"UFOs," Dumont said, nodding. "Crashed spacecraft in the New Mexican desert. All nonsense, of course."

"In one way," St. Clair said slowly, "the little Gray aliens from that period looked like the popular depiction of aliens back then, in period films, in books. And in fact, those images reflected where we guessed humans might be going in another few million years: big heads with big brains, shrunken bodies, and all the rest. But if the Xam *are* highly evolved humans, it suggests another possibility."

"What's that?" Symm asked.

"Time travel."

There was silence around the conference table for a long moment after that.

"So—if the Grays back in the twentieth and twenty-first centuries were time travelers instead of space travelers . . ." Symm began.

"That may not be *current* technology," Dumont said. "I still have trouble imagining that the Gray physiology could represent more than, oh, say a hundred thousand years of evolution between us and them. Maybe some traveled to the future too? To *now*?"

"We won't know until we ask them," St. Clair said.

"That also raises another problem," Senior Lieutenant Nolan said.

"What's that, Christine?"

"It looks like we went and joined the wrong side."

"What do you mean?" Subcommander Rand said.

"Isn't it obvious?" St. Clair said. "She means that by siding with the spiders against the Andromedan Dark, we're now at war with our own descendants. Hell, we just killed . . . what? Ten? Twenty billion sliverships?"

"We believe only a fraction of those were piloted by organics, Lord Commander," Nolan told him. "Still . . . yes.

Hundreds of millions of organic Xam, at *least*, must have been killed in the battle, but almost all by the Kroajid defenses."

"That's just an equivocation, though. Semantics."

"Agreed," Nolan said.

"The battle suggests something else, too," Senior Lieutenant Cameron pointed out. "A different . . . philosophy, I guess it would be. Sliverships were being used out there like kamikazes, deliberately crashing into Kroajid structures. The bastards were using wave tactics—very little real strategy at all. And the fact that this pilot was actually woven in like he was a *part* of his ship . . ."

"The 'masters' may no longer be their own masters," St. Clair said, grim. "They may simply be an asset. Expendable parts in a very large machine."

"So . . ." Dr. Dumont said after a moment, "have we jumped into a war on the wrong side?"

"Doctor . . . I don't think there *is* a right side or a wrong side here. If the masters are truly our own descendents, they have changed so much, in so many ways, that the question is meaningless."

"Be that as it may, there's something else to consider as well, however," Dumont said slowly.

"What's that?"

"Our presence here. The *coincidence* of our presence here . . ."

"What do you mean, Doctor?" Symm asked.

"Has anyone else noticed? Four billion years ago, *Tellus Ad Astra* became trapped at the event horizon of a supermassive black hole, right?"

St. Clair nodded. Where was Dumont going with this? "Yes . . ."

"Suddenly, we pop out—free from the SMBH—and we *immediately* encounter what we later decide is a Kroajid starship. They give us the Roceti device . . . then vanish, like they were just hanging out there waiting for us. Does anyone at this table find that suspicious?"

In fact, St. Clair had wondered about the convenience of their immediately picking up the Roceti torpedo. But things had been happening so very quickly. There'd been no time to think things through. . . .

"We found that the supermassive black hole—Sagittarius A-Star—had increased in mass by quite a bit," Dumont said. "The astrophysics department assumed that another large black hole—possibly from Andromeda—had fallen into Sagittarius A-Star, and the tidal effects of that collision bumped us clear. Plausible enough, but the question remains: was the timing coincidental? Or was someone *manipulating* us? Using us?"

"You're saying that the Kroajids pulled us out of Sag A-Star to work for them? To fight their war for them?"

"Something like that. More likely it's the SAI behind the Kroajids that was pulling the strings . . . either the one in the Kroajid matbrain, or the larger one resident within the Galaxy's matbrain network." He shrugged. "Either way, we need to consider the possibility that we *have* been manipulated, and possibly in ways that are not in our best interests."

"Hell of a choice," Symm said. "Super-intelligent spiders using us like puppets on one side, and beings that might be our own descendents, but devolved into cybernetic plug-and-play tools on the other. *Assets*."

St. Clair looked across the table at Ambassador Lloyd, who'd been sitting there silently, taking it all in. "It may be," he continued, "that we can approach the Xam and open a dialogue. They might need our help."

Lloyd stirred. "I wonder if that's a good idea?"

"Can we even find them?" Symm asked.

"Oh, we won't have a problem there," St. Clair said. "We'll find them or they'll find us. I think we made an impression on them. It'll be getting them to talk to us that will be the trick."

"We do have one lead, my lord," Subcommander Holt said.

"What's that, Valerie?" St. Clair said.

"A piece of intelligence we pulled from the slivership," she said. "A list of numbers. Roceti translated them as astrogational coordinates."

"Coordinates? For what?" Dumont asked.

"For the Xam homeworld, my lord," Holt replied. "We think it may be their *original* homeworld. We're not sure, but it just might be . . . Earth."

St. Clair looked up at the vaulted ceiling above the room, where two galaxies were frozen in mid-collision. He was still feeling stunned by the revelations—of survivals of Humankind in this remote epoch, of just the possibility that they might possess time-travel technology.

"It seems to me," he said very quietly, "that we're going to need to pay the Xam a visit. . . ."

Tellus Ad Astra dropped from shiftspace. The tangled stars and nebulae glowed ahead, the scene dominated by one swollen, deep-orange sun.

"Shit," Excomm Symm said. "This is *not* Earth's solar system."

"How can you tell?" St. Clair asked.

"Well . . . the star is too large and way too hot, for one thing. And the inner planets are missing, for another."

"Take a closer look," St. Clair said. He was already convinced they had found their homeworld's system.

The star might well be Sol . . . aged 4 billion years. According to astrophysical projections, Sol would have grown steadily brighter, until, a billion years or so after *Ad Astra* had left for the stars, Earth's oceans boiled away. In a few billion years more, Sol would burn through the last of its reserves of hydrogen and expand into a red giant, but that was still in the far future.

The star's mass didn't line up well with Sol's however. It was possible that some star lifting had been going on, with some of Sol's mass pulled out into space. If so, its life span had been greatly increased, and the day when it would swell into a red giant postponed by yet more billions of years.

Here and now, however, Mercury, Venus, Earth, and Mars all were missing from their orbits.

The innermost world of this system orbited the sun at about 500 million kilometers out . . . a gas giant, but a very peculiar one—a shrunken Jovian world surrounded by a tight cloud of statites.

And there were worlds . . . planet-sized moons clustered around the gas giant.

Somehow, at some time in the remote past, someone had moved whole worlds out of harm's way, parking them out at Jupiter.

There were signs of mega-scale engineering elsewhere, too. Earth still had oceans, but now so did Mars and a cloudless Venus. And if that was Saturn, farther out, the rings were long gone, but there were numerous habitats far larger and more impressive than the *Tellus* cylinders.

If it was Sol's system, then the saying was true: you can never go home again.

"It's damned quiet." Cameron said. "Where *is* everybody?"

St. Clair smiled. "I think we're about to find out. Excomm . . . take us in close."

And *Tellus Ad Astra* accelerated into a strange and very alien planetary system.